A Destiny Decided . . .

Talli lifted her head so she could see him. Akoma started to speak, but Talli put her finger over his lips to silence him. "Do not make this too hard for me, Akoma. I know what must be and have resigned myself to it. If you object, I will fall apart. If you love me . . ."

Akoma rocked his head back and held her close.

Talli broke away and forced a smile. She feathered a finger over his lips. "The Turtle will have the finest cacique," she said. "You will enable the Jeaga to survive. For generations the People will speak of Akoma, the grand cacique who led the Jeaga against the Ais. I will forever be proud that I am Akoma's woman. Even if no one else knows, I will."

Akoma took her hand in his and pressed his lips to her forehead.

Talli rested her head against his chest and closed her eyes. She wished for Akoma to keep some small hidden place in his heart that would belong only to her. "When you are an old man I hope you will remember this time we had," she said. "Do not ever forget. Do not forget me."

"Never," he answered.

Spirit of the Turtle Woman

Lynn Armistead McKee

AN ONYX BOOK

ONYX
Published by the Penguin Group
Penguin Putnam Inc., 375 Hudson Street,
New York, New York 10014, U.S.A.
Penguin Books Ltd, 27 Wrights Lane,
London W8 5TZ, England
Penguin Books Australia Ltd, Ringwood,
Victoria, Australia
Penguin Books Canada Ltd, 10 Alcorn Avenue,
Toronto, Ontario, Canada M4V 3B2
Penguin Books (N.Z.) Ltd, 182–190 Wairau Road,
Auckland 10, New Zealand

Penguin Books Ltd, Registered Offices:
Harmondsworth, Middlesex, England

First published by Onyx, an imprint of Dutton NAL,
a member of Penguin Putnam Inc.

First Printing, April, 1999
10 9 8 7 6 5 4 3 2 1

 REGISTERED TRADEMARK—MARCA REGISTRADA

Printed in the United States of America

For Madison and Gail. I miss you.

Author's Note

By A.D. 1500, at about the time of European contact, there were approximately 10,000 to 25,000 people living in Florida. Among these tribes were the Jeaga and the Ais. The Jeaga lived in what is now Palm Beach County, Florida, and the Ais north of the Jeaga from St. Lucie Inlet through Cape Canaveral.

These tribes were headed by a cacique, or chief, and were related linguistically. Based on the few words recorded phonetically by early explorers, it is believed these Indians spoke what is called Muskogee, a language also spoken by some Seminole and Creek. Therefore, when selecting character names I chose words structurally sympathetic to the language.

No one is certain what these Native Americans called their villages or towns. The Europeans usually named the areas and the rivers after the Indians who lived there.

Physically, the Ais and the Jeaga were relatively short, but robust. In examination of their remains, we find there is very little evidence of dental caries, but considerable attrition of the teeth. Shovel-shaped incisors are also characteristic. In some individuals great crescents are found in molars, a probable result of years of leather working. A full lifespan was probably about thirty-five to forty years.

Food was abundant in the region, the diet was made up of fish (both freshwater and saltwater), oysters, mussels, snails, deer, turtles, snakes, alligators, small mammals, berries, plants, and bread made from the coontie root.

They made their canoes from cypress trunks, and

some were large enough to carry thirty people out to sea. We know they took their dugouts far out into the Atlantic, as we find the remains of tiger sharks in their middens. It is uncertain just how they caught such large fish.

There is still so much we do not know about the Indians of this region whose ancestors went back as far as 12,000 years ago. As Florida continues its rapid growth, undeveloped land becomes more and more scarce. Unfortunately, the sites where the Ais, Jeaga, Calusa, Tequesta, and other Indians lived are destroyed by bulldozers on almost a daily basis. Though legislation has been passed to protect such sites, "accidents" continue to happen.

When Spain ceded Florida to England, there were but a handful of Native Americans left in Florida. They were never defeated in battle, but lost their valiant fight for survival to common diseases such as influenza and chicken pox, for which they had no immunities. Even on the last of the Spanish maps, south Florida is labeled LAND OF THE INFIDELS.

From the scanty records we have of the aboriginal people of South Florida, I have attempted to re-create the culture and weave it into a good story line. I have taken some author's liberties, but for the most part I have tried to ensure authenticity. It is hoped that this novel will bring about an awareness of the people who once lived here and will encourage protection of all historical sites. They are a nonrenewable resource.

Prologue

Southeast coast of the Florida peninsula,
2500 years ago.

Yurok planted the sacred stick in the sand. The clan sat, legs crossed, waiting for the spirits to speak through the stick and show them which way to go. The Jeaga, the People, depended on the spirits for such things. And now they waited for guidance to find the place where they would settle. The eyes of the Jeaga remained fixed on the stick. The staff swayed in the ocean wind, then leaned, the turtle-head effigy at the top pointing south.

Kaya took advantage of the short delay and rested. If she lagged behind when the clan was moving, she would have to run to catch up, and she knew her legs would not carry her that quickly. She was much too weak. She kept her distance from the others because she was no longer allowed to dwell among them. To the clan, she was dead.

Yurok plucked the stick from the ground and held it overhead. Everyone gathered his belongings and took up the journey again. They traveled south, as the stick pointed, as the spirits directed.

The unusual chill of the wind bit at Kaya. There were only two seasons here, wet and dry. Both were usually warm, and sometimes stifling hot. The Jeagas' way of life was adapted to the heat. They were not prepared well for the cold.

Kaya held her new daughter to her breast. She was so very tired and wished they would stop for the day and set up camp. The brief rest while they had waited on the spirits' voices to enter the stick was not long

enough. Only three nights ago she had pushed the new
baby out of her belly. No one had helped.

The night when the child was born, Kaya had gotten
no sleep, the birthing taking until dawn. Then, when it
was over, she wrapped the afterbirth and buried it.
When the sun rose, the clan continued the trek. Kaya
swaddled the infant in a blanket, put her to suckle, and
trailed the group. For days now she had eaten only the
clan's scraps. At night she huddled behind the dunes.
She shivered in the cold air, keeping the child bundled
close to her. In the dark Kaya felt the baby's cold skin,
listened to her labored breathing. The child's suffering
made her heart ache.

In late afternoon, at the mouth of a river, the clan
watched the stick lean to the west. Yurok led them past
the mangroves, upriver, where the foliage thickened with
great oaks, lush vines, sabal palms, and strangler figs.
There by the rushing water he planted the stick again.
Kaya squinted in the distance, hoping the spirits had
spoken. Relief spread through her like warm tea. This
time the staff did not waver. It stood straight, claiming
the spot as their new home.

Kaya's belly cramped as the baby suckled, and she
was anxious to lie down on the patch of green ferns at
her feet. She reached in the pouch at her side, withdrew
a medicine leaf and put it in her mouth. It gave her a
little relief, though it made the bleeding worse. She felt
weak, her head dizzy.

"The stick speaks clearly," Yurok said. He scooped a
handful of sandy dun earth and held it up, letting it
slowly trickle out and catch in the wind.

Kaya sank to the ground. The infant whimpered. The
child stirred fitfully. Kaya put her knuckle in her baby's
mouth. She didn't have enough milk. They were both
going to die.

The clan set up camp, and under the moon they celebrated. Kaya chewed another medicine leaf and cleared
a space beneath a red maple to sleep. Her head ached,
and the dizziness grew stronger. She lay on the ground
and pulled the baby against her. Her arms trembled with
the effort.

In the moonlight she stared down at her beautiful child. Her throat tightened and her eyes teared. The child's skin had lost its wonderful deep reddish-brown tone—her Jeaga heritage. Instead, Kaya saw a gray pallor, dull eyes, and tiny chapped lips.

"No!" she said aloud. She scolded herself for not fighting back, for the child's sake. She could not let this happen. Perhaps *she* deserved to be dead. She was the one with the affliction. But the baby should not suffer.

She had to stop this before it was too late. Kaya got to her knees and put the baby in the deer-hide sling around her neck. She struggled to her feet. Yurok had to hear her.

Her head swam as she pulled herself upright. For an instant, she thought she would fall. She braced herself against the tree and focused on the small hearth fires. Her eyelids fluttered as she took the first step.

She heard the collective gasp as she stumbled into camp.

"Yurok," she called, seeing him by his fire. "It is Kaya, your wife. And this is your child."

A bulky shadow moved nearby. "He does not hear you," the shaman said, coming before her. "No one does. Only I can hear you because I am a man of the spirits."

"No!" she said, taking another step toward Yurok. Her knees wobbled, and she hesitated before she continued. "I have been banished, but I am not dead."

"You have the affliction," the shaman said. "You must be cast out. It has been decided."

Kaya edged in front of Yurok. "I was your wife. Did you not love me before you discovered I carry a curse?"

Yurok's eyes watered and he bit down on the inside of his cheek.

"Do not speak," the shaman warned. "She is dead."

Kaya swayed with dizziness. Her mouth was dry. The bleeding was worse, and she felt it course down her legs.

"Let her speak," Yurok said. "I can hear her."

Kaya held out the baby. "She suffers, Yurok. She grows too weak to cry."

The shaman stepped in front of her. "Her line carries

the affliction . . . passed through the daughters for generations until the debt is paid. It is the spirits' design. The punishment."

Kaya slumped to her knees, unable to stand any longer. A jagged stone sliced her knee, but she didn't flinch. She was numb to pain now.

"Move aside," Yurok told the shaman.

"Save your daughter," Kaya cried. "Your blood also runs through her. See, it is your eyes that she has, and the straight line of your nose. She is a beautiful reflection of her father. It is only I who brings you shame."

"This child might also bear the affliction," the shaman said.

"And she might not," Yurok answered. "Cheena, come here," he called loudly.

Yurok's sister came to his side, holding her own infant.

"Is your milk plentiful?"

Cheena nodded.

Yurok took the baby from Kaya's arms. He stared into the infant's face for a few moments, then handed her to Cheena.

Yurok gazed at the small group that gathered beside the shaman. "Be gone, all of you," he said. "Kaya," he said softly as he lifted her and carried her nearer his fire.

She felt the comforting warmth of him. He sat with her and rested her head in his lap.

"Keep her secret," she whispered. "Do not let your daughter be without a spirit."

Kaya's strength was quickly leaving, but it didn't matter, she thought. This was the way of the spirits, and the child was safe. She closed her eyes. She prayed that the affliction ended with her and her death. She had suffered. Was the debt not paid?

Yurok stroked Kaya's hair and listened to her ragged breaths mingled with the sound of the breeze rustling through the tall grass. The moon was high above them when she crossed over. The strain in her face transformed to peace.

From somewhere in the darkness the shaman chanted prayers.

Yurok rocked her gently until daylight, and then, alone, he carried her body deep into the woods. He dug a shallow grave and lowered her into it. He knelt over her and brushed her hair from her face. His face tightened with grief. The spirits were difficult to understand.

Yurok said a prayer that the ground in which she rested be sacred. And before he covered her with the earth, he said another prayer and slipped a bird feather in her hand so her spirit could take flight.

1

The Jeaga Turtle village was eerily still, though the women busied themselves with daily chores. The children ceased their romping and rested in the shade. The stillness seemed to have weight, and sagged over the village. The air was dense and stifling, and the mosquitoes were incessant pests.

Talli, the oldest of the three sisters, wiped beads of perspiration from her forehead with the back of her hand, then returned to kneading clay. "Like this," she showed her youngest sister, Nocatee, using the heels of her hands for the task.

"Why do you add sand?" Nocatee asked.

"You ask too many questions," Sassa, the middle sister, said. Sassa was younger than Talli by only one full cycle of seasons.

Talli smiled at Nocatee. "How would you know things if you did not ask? Sassa, were you not the same when Nocatee's age?"

Sassa looked apologetic.

"Sand is the temper," Talli said. "The clay will not stay together without it."

Suddenly Talli felt a chill, like cold rain running down her arms. She looked up and her stomach knotted.

"What is it?" Sassa asked. She stared at Talli's face. "What is wrong?"

Talli stood up. "Stay here," she said, moving away.

Nocatee's face squirmed. Her nose wrinkled, and she

squeezed her eyes tight as if she were about to cry. "Talli," she whimpered, but her sister didn't hear her.

Talli spotted Bunta as soon as he broke through the trees. She ran behind him to the center of the village, her heart drumming in her chest. She tried to see who the man was who hung over Bunta's shoulder. The injured man's arms dangled and flopped about, and a runnel of his blood trailed down Bunta's bare back.

"What has happened?" Talli cried, glancing back. More men burst out of the cover of the forest, carrying wounded warriors into the village.

Winded, Bunta laid the man on the ground, dust puffing up in a brown halo. Talli winced at the sight of the broken lance shaft protruding from the man's chest. "An Ais' attack on our hunt party," Bunta huffed.

Talli's hand flew to her throat. The Ais lived to the north and were a contemptible and murderous tribe. The Jeaga tried to stay clear of them, but this morning the men from the Turtle village and the Panther village had gone together on a hunt, and the Ais had attacked.

"Where is Akoma?" she asked, forcing the question out of her mouth.

Bunta shook his head. Sweat dribbled down his face as he lifted the injured man's eyelids. Bunta put his ear to the man's nose and listened for breathing, while his hand searched the man's chest for the feel of a heartbeat. "He is dead," he said and looked up. Talli was gone.

She ran through the village, squinting to fight the glare of the midday sun. Where was Akoma? Was he hurt . . . dead? Fear ripped through her like a jagged-edged chert knife.

Women wailed. Some stood rooted in their horror. Other women darted about, searching for their husbands, their sons, their brothers. Some had found what they feared and knelt in the dirt, the sun hammering their backs as they hovered over their outstretched men. Bodies littered the earth like carcasses brought back from a hunt, but unlike the animals brought down by a hunter, these were not clean kills. Bewildered children shrieked and clutched at their mothers.

Talli wondered how many were hurt. The stream of bloodied men continued to come through the trees. There would be much for the Bone Cleaner to do.

The Bone Cleaner's job was to strip the soft flesh from the bones of the dead, then bundle the bones and place them on the charnel platform in the mud along the bank of the river. The Bone Cleaner stayed isolated and was considered unclean, but was highly respected.

So many were injured or dead, Talli thought. She prayed Akoma was not one of them. "Please," Talli cried. "Please let Akoma be alive," she begged the spirits. Tears trickled into the corners of her mouth.

Akoma was sure his eyes were open, but something was wrong.

He was being joggled, bumped along in the darkness. He heard someone scream.

"Move out of the way!" a deep voice shouted. "I have Akoma."

"Is he alive?"

The jarring stopped with a thump, and Akoma became aware he was lying on the ground on his back. He could smell the dank odor of the soil. He felt heavy, as if he were sinking, being magically swallowed by mother earth.

Was that singing he heard or a woman's voice?

"His wound is bad," a woman said. "Where is his father?"

"He is coming."

Akoma felt pressure and a stinging on the side of his head.

"Hold this here while I bandage the medicine swatch," the woman said.

What has happened? He thought he asked it aloud. He was confused, and it was so dark. Maybe he had asked only in his head.

He strained to see, but still there was only blackness, not even a star in the sky. There came another voice and he thought it was Bunta's, the War Chief. If there was just some moonlight he would be able to see and know for sure. It was so dark.

A pain shot through his head. Akoma tried to sit up, but felt a hand on his chest restrain him.

"Can you hear me, Akoma?" Bunta asked.

Akoma struggled to get his dry lips and heavy tongue to move. He forced air through his throat and made a gurgling sound.

"I think he does hear," the woman said. "He is trying to speak."

The voices became distant echoes, growing softer and softer. He heard a faint buzzing, almost just a vibration, and then he was aware of nothing.

Yahga-ta knelt by his son. "Akoma?"

"He sleeps deep," the woman said.

Bunta turned Akoma's head so the wound could be viewed. "He has suffered a blow to the head."

Yahga-ta stiffened to speak without emotion. "Today my son became a man. He touched the enemy. It is not right that he die and not know he has entered the world of men. Where is Putiwa? Get the shaman here for my son," Yahga-ta said to the woman. "Find him now!"

The woman obeyed and ran through the village, looking for the shaman. Near the central hearth, Talli caught her by the shoulder. "Have you seen Akoma?"

She nodded. "Over there," she said, pointing. "With his father and Bunta. I go for the shaman."

Talli scanned the distance and spotted Yahga-ta, Akoma's father, the cacique, the leader of the clan. He and Bunta stooped next to a body on the ground. Akoma? Did she dare go near?

Talli's chest tightened with dread as she hurried there. She hesitated before coming next to Yahga-ta. She wiped the tears from her face. When she saw the young warrior lying so still, she gasped and fell to her knees. "Akoma," she whispered, then looked up at Yahga-ta.

"It is bad. He does not hear me," Yahga-ta said.

Talli swallowed and choked back a cry. She brushed Akoma's cheek with her fingertips, then quickly pulled her hand away. She should not have done that. "Will he be all right?" she asked. Yahga-ta did not answer.

She bent close to Akoma's ear making certain she did

not touch him. She whispered his name. Blood matted his hair, and some of it was already caked on his face. "It is Talli. Wake up. Wake up."

"He is in the deep sleep," Bunta said. "He does not hear anything."

She straightened, afraid to be so close or *it* might happen.

"Talli!" It was Sassa. "Come. Mother needs you. Father is hurt."

Talli put her fear aside and lifted Akoma's hand in hers. It was limp and cool. She rubbed her thumb across his knuckles. Her shoulders shuddered subtly. Talli dropped his hand and stood up, but it was too late. *The affliction.* She grabbed her head, and shoved her fingers through her hair.

"Come now!" Sassa said, tugging on Talli's arm.

Talli blinked as she struggled to focus.

"Now!" Sassa said, pulling her away from Akoma.

On the way to the family shelter, Talli kept glancing back until the milling people hid Akoma from view.

Nocatee stood inside the shelter which was about man high and constructed of bent saplings covered with palmetto thatch. Her dark eyes were wide with confusion as she stared out the opening.

Talli knelt next to her mother. Kitchi stared at her daughter a moment, then looked down. Talli's eyes settled on her father's injured arm in her mother's lap. Ufala leaned his head back and grimaced as Kitchi's finger probed one of the wounds in his arm. Talli saw her father's heavy jaw clench, his eyes squeeze shut, and his large hands ball into fists, but he did not make a sound.

"The wounds are clean now," Kitchi said. "There is nothing in them, but I fear the bone is smashed."

Perspiration poured out of Ufala's skin, and his long, sweat-soaked, silver-and-black hair clung to him. He was a big man, full of muscle that seemed suddenly to lose definition.

"Be grateful the Ais warrior was not wielding a shark-tooth club," Kitchi said.

The thought of what her father's arm would have

looked like if he had been attacked with such a club made Talli cringe. That kind of club was edged with shark's teeth set in notches along its length. It would have ripped the flesh off his bone and sawed through his arm. He probably would have bled to death.

"Get me some water," Ufala said to Sassa. The girl took a water pouch and hurried to the river.

"Sort through the baskets and find some pilosa and snakebark," Kitchi told Talli. "I need to prepare medicine. Stir the fire, and when Sassa returns with the water, boil the pilosa and snakebark."

Talli rummaged through the baskets her mother stored beside their shelter in the shade of a large oak. Her father would be all right, but what about Akoma? If she hurried, as soon as Ufala was settled, perhaps she could sneak away.

Sassa returned with the water. Talli splashed a bit into the pouch suspended over the fire, then handed the remaining container of water to her father.

Ufala flinched. "Kitchi," Ufala said, nodding at his wife and gesturing with his head toward the pouch. He refused to take the water from Talli.

Kitchi grasped the otter-stomach from her daughter's hand, then gave it to Ufala.

"Back away, Talli," he said after several swallows. "You should not be so close."

Talli stepped back, her head down in respect.

"Do you brew something for the pain?" Ufala asked Kitchi.

"I make a medicine to put on the wounds," she answered. "It will help."

"Something stronger," he said, palming his bruised ribs with his good hand.

"I will ask Putiwa," Kitchi said, wiping the sweat from her husband's face.

"The shaman is with Yahga-ta and Akoma," Talli said. "Akoma is injured and Yahga-ta has summoned Putiwa to help."

Kitchi's head shot up. "You have not been near Akoma, have you? You did not touch him?"

Talli didn't have to answer because Ufala groaned, and Kitchi focused on her husband.

"Do something, woman," he said. "Forget Putiwa."

"Talli will gather the herbs as soon as she finishes preparing this medicine." Kitchi moved to peer in the pouch over the fire. She tweezed two rocks from the hearth and dropped them inside the pouch. There was an instant sizzling as the hot stones hit the water, then a swirl of steam rose. "It is hot enough," she told Talli. "Put in the medicine plants."

Talli tore the leaves and stems and dropped them in. The solution bubbled. Kitchi scooted closer to Ufala.

Talli heard her parents talking behind her, but she did not follow their conversation. She stared across the village, straining to get a glimpse of something that would tell her how Akoma was. The center of the village, the plaza, was clear and the dirt steamed in the heat. The sunlight danced on the shelters as it splintered through the trees that shaded their homes. But there was nothing she could see that enlightened her about Akoma.

He had to be all right. How would she live if he was not?

"What is wrong with you, daughter?" Ufala asked sharply. "Your mother speaks to you, and you do not respond."

Talli whipped around. "I am sorry," she said. She looked back at the brewing medicine and saw that the water had turned dark. "It is ready."

"Then scoop off the residue from the top and bring it here," Kitchi said. "Pay attention to what you are doing. This is not a medicine to drink unless it is a time for cleansing. It is for dressing wounds. It keeps the bad spirits out of wounds and stops bleeding."

Talli prodded the pouch along the suspending stick until it no longer sat over the hot coals.

Her mother took a small busycon-shell ladle and dipped out some of the elixir. She let it cool for a moment, but the concoction was still hot. She tipped the shell and poured the medicine in Ufala's open wounds. The big man thrust back his head and his mouth opened as if to scream. Then his head came forward, and his

chin pressed against his chest. Ufala let out a pent-up
breath, grabbed Kitchi's arm, and squeezed until the
pain abated.

The color drained from Talli's face.

"Move away, daughter," Kitchi said. "Go and gather
the medicine plants that will ease your father's pain."

Talli stepped farther back. She saw her little sister
hiding her eyes. "Can Nocatee go with me?"

Kitchi nodded at her eldest.

"Come, Nocatee," Talli called.

"Gather some sky-flower and pickerelweed," Kitchi
said. Then, just as Talli turned to leave, her mother said,
"Do not stray. Stay away from the others. You do
understand?"

Talli picked up Nocatee. If she was careful, there
would be no danger. Her mother did not need to worry.
She would keep her distance.

Talli threaded through the thicket along the perimeter
of the village, then at a range where she was sure Kitchi
could not see her, she reentered the village and headed
to the spot where she had last seen Akoma.

Nocatee's eyebrows dipped. "Mother said—"

"I know, little sister. We will only be a moment."

Near enough to see clearly, Talli realized that Akoma
was not where she had seen him earlier. Her heart
jumped in her chest, and she felt weak. Had he died?
Her arms tightened about Nocatee.

She spun around and looked toward the leader's
hearth and his shelter, which stood at the head of the
village in the east so the sun first shone on the place of
the cacique. Yahga-ta's shelter was a lodge much larger
than the shelters of the rest of the clan. The interior was
also different. The inside was bordered with log benches
on which clan members sat during council meetings. At
the end of the lodge, slightly elevated, was the place
where Yahga-ta himself sat during those times.

Talli saw a small group gathered in front of Yahga-
ta's lodge. Did they stare down at Akoma's body?

"We will get the medicine plants in a moment," she
told Nocatee, letting her slide down to stand on the
ground. "Walk this way." She took her young sister's

hand, moved a few steps, then stopped. She felt a tingling along her spine. Talli looked at Nocatee and lifted her chin with her fingers. "It is all right," she said. She stooped to Nocatee's height. "Do not be frightened. Your little heart beats so fast."

Nocatee squeezed Talli's hand.

Between the men and women standing about, Talli saw that someone did indeed lie on the ground. Her heart told her it was Akoma. Afraid of what she would see, she approached slowly.

She stopped outside the circle of people at Yahga-ta's hearth, behind Bunta's woman, Chinasi.

Putiwa chanted. His old weathered face was deeply wrinkled from sun, age, and responsibility. His eyes were filled with worry. Akoma was the spirits' chosen one and Yahga-ta's son. One day Akoma would take his father's place. If the shaman failed to save him, it would not be a good thing.

Chinasi looked back at Talli. "Putiwa does his magic. Only the men stand close."

Fear garroted Talli's voice, and her words came out cracked and strained. "Is he dead?"

"No, I do not think so. But I do not believe he will survive. He drifts in the deep sleep."

An unexpected wind whipped through the trees and a flurry of oak and bay leaves swirled about. Talli shivered.

Putiwa's chant grew louder as he strode around the unconscious Akoma. The shaman took his turtle-shell rattle, the hard seeds inside clattering against the shell to Putiwa's rhythm. The deer hooves which were tied beneath the shell clacked together. The peal of Putiwa's old uninhibited voice and the beat of the rattle made the shaman's music magical, and it saturated the village. The people watched and listened in awe, as they always did when the mystical man spoke to the spirits.

Chinasi rubbed the flesh that prickled on her arms. She spoke in a whisper. "If Akoma is to be saved, Putiwa will do it."

Talli nudged past Chinasi and stopped just outside the band of men.

Akoma's bandaged head inclined to the side. He was so still. Mora, Akoma's mother, wept on her sister's shoulder. Yahga-ta stood erect, donning a stern, determined expression. The colors the leader wore on his face for the hunt had already faded.

Talli took another step. Chinasi grasped her arm. "What are you doing?" she whispered. "Do not interrupt."

Talli shook her head as if confused. She was so close to Akoma, but could not tell if he was breathing. She should feel something, but didn't, and it frightened her. .

Nocatee peeped through the mass of legs. She started to cry again and tugged at her sister's hand. "Talli? Is Akoma dead?"

"I do not know," Talli whispered. "Say a prayer, Nocatee. Say a prayer." She picked up the little one again and rocked from side to side, as she often did to comfort her sister.

Nocatee cried into Talli's shoulder. "Is Father going to die, too?"

"No. No, Nocatee. Father will be all right."

"But Akoma—"

"Shh," Talli said, stroking the back of her sister's head.

Suddenly, the shaman fell silent. The breeze ceased and there was a disturbing hush. Talli pressed Nocatee's cheek firmly against her shoulder.

Putiwa knelt at Akoma's head, drew smoke from his pipe and blew it in the young man's face. He uttered some magic words from the ancient tongue. The shaman stood and called out for two men to carry Akoma into Yahga-ta's lodge. Talli's heart thudded as she watched Putiwa present himself in front of Akoma's mother.

Putiwa put his hands on Mora's upper arms, then drew a sign with his thumb on her forehead, smearing some yellow ochre above her brows. He said something Talli could not hear over Nocatee's whimpering. But she did see and hear Mora gasp.

Talli put Nocatee down and pushed through the crowd. She grabbed the arm of one of the men who lifted Akoma.

"Stop, let me see him!"

Shocked by Talli's boldness, the men paused, and Talli looked into Akoma's still face. Abandoning her fear, she let the tip of one finger touch his arm. She felt empty inside, all black, and barren, and hollow. Like death. "Akoma!" she sobbed. Her head jerked up so she could see the eyes of the man in her grip. "Is he dead?"

2

"Move away," the man Talli had grabbed said, loosing himself from her. His face splotched red with aggravation.

Talli stepped back. The two men carried Akoma toward the shelter, and Talli followed. The brown thatch rattled in the wind. The decorative bands of shells that hung in the opening chimed, and the eyes of the wooden turtle above the entrance seemed to stare gravely.

Yahga-ta's heavy hand came down on Talli's shoulder. "Leave us. You cause a disturbance and intrude on our family at this bad time."

Talli attempted to collect herself. "I did not mean to trespass," she said. Nocatee tugged at her sister's hand. "Please," Talli pleaded, "just tell me if he lives."

"Putiwa has done what he can. Akoma breathes, but the shaman has prepared his mother for his death. He painted a sign on her forehead to give her strength."

Talli backed away, numb, stricken with disbelief. Akoma could not die! He was young and strong, and she had just been with him this morning before he left for the hunt. They had hidden near the river's edge. He had held her hand and then pulled her close. Her cheek had rested on his warm shoulder and she smelled his skin. She could still hear the sound of his heartbeat.

As the crowd dispersed, Talli clutched Nocatee's hand. Nocatee huddled by her sister.

"Oh, Nocatee," Talli muttered, opening her arms and embracing the little one.

"We need the medicine plants for Father," Nocatee said softly.

"I know. Father will be angry if we take too long."

Talli wiped her eyes and sniffed. "Help me find the plants. He must already wonder where we are."

They searched nearby, roaming through the floor of ferns and the flowering, sweet-smelling vines of the hardwood forest. "There," Talli said, pointing to a patch of flat-topped clusters of azure blue flowers.

After gathering all they needed of those plants, Talli led Nocatee to a sunken place near the river where the soil stayed soggy and the pickerelweed grew in abundance beneath the cypress. They put the collection inside Talli's pouch and returned to the village.

Nocatee kept out one spike of the violet pickerelweed flowers and pushed the stem behind her ear. She walked backward so her sister could look at her. "What do I look like, Talli? Am I as beautiful as you?"

Yahga-ta took his seat, an elevated platform inside his lodge. Bunta and Putiwa sat on the benches waiting for the cacique to speak. Akoma lay on a deerskin on the ground.

Yahga-ta nodded at Mora, who lowered her eyes in respect, touched her son's cheek with the back of her hand, and then left the lodge so the men could speak.

The cacique held the fletching of an Ais arrow. "The drought stays long in the Ais' memory."

Bunta drew in a noisy breath. "How are we to respond to this Ais attack? They fear the drought will return and they want to position themselves on the river."

"The Ais do not answer to the same spirits," Putiwa said. "They enjoy bloodletting. It is their way. They will take life after life without hesitation and use the excuse that they have need to increase their territory. The Jeaga should strike back swiftly—show no fear."

"And what does the war chief think?" Yahga-ta asked.

Bunta shook his head. "We are a peaceful people. We cannot become like the Ais," he said, turning to Putiwa.

"We need to defend ourselves," Putiwa said.

"Sometimes using a weapon is not a wise defense," Bunta answered. "This should not be a hurried decision."

Yahga-ta felt the heat of the afternoon sun permeating the thatch at his back. "Keep these things we discussed in your head, but let your mind be open through the night. Putiwa, consult the spirits. Bunta, contemplate each option. There will be strong opposition to whatever is decided, but we cannot permit that to divide us. The clan is too fragile at this moment. We will shatter if there is disagreement now. Let the people tend to their wounds and grief, then we will call the council together."

Yahga-ta dismissed them, then sat beside his son. "And who will lead the Turtle clan if the spirits claim you?" he spoke softly. "Are all the Jeaga near their end?"

"It has taken you a long time," Kitchi said upon their return. "Your father suffers, and you dally somewhere in the woods. Why is it when you are off in the trees you become preoccupied and forget time? This morning it was the same thing." Kitchi dug in the pouch around her daughter's waist and grasped a handful of the plant parts. "Bring the rest," she said.

Kitchi shredded the plants into a small wooden bowl, then pounded them with a pestle made from the hard wood of the lignum-vitae. Ufala had traded a knife for it a long time ago when some of the men took a large canoe to the Big Water and followed the coastline south for days. They came upon another tribe. Tegesta was what they called themselves. The trip was an adventure Ufala loved to speak about.

Kitchi added a few drops of water and stirred the medicine paste. "You should watch," she said. "These are lessons every good woman needs to learn. Now, get me a piece of deerskin. Use my woman's knife to cut a long strip. We will use it to bind Ufala's arm so it will heal and not hurt so when he moves. The rest we will use around his middle."

Talli obeyed her mother, but her mind strayed. She knew she would be taking a chance if she got close to Akoma now, but she yearned to see him again, to be near for even a moment. Her heart ached. They were not even betrothed. By custom, Talli was too young, and it was expected of Akoma, the one chosen to be the next cacique, to take a wife from a noble line. Not long ago Yahga-ta suspected that she and Akoma had deep feelings for each other, and he had gone to Ufala. He instructed Ufala to keep his daughter away from Akoma. She distracted the cacique's son from the sacred path he was to follow.

Talli had listened to Ufala's order forbidding her to see Akoma, and Akoma had heard Yahga-ta tell him to dismiss the girl from his thoughts, but neither had been able to dispose of their feelings. They stole away whenever they could for brief moments of hand holding, passionate embraces, and hungry kisses.

Though Talli was not old enough to be officially courted, only the passing of another season was left before her father would entertain offers for her. As it was now, Akoma would not be allowed to speak for her, but she hoped the ways of the old ones would change.

Much was expected of Akoma, especially that he be the example of the People's principles and codes. He could never break custom. Talli prayed that the archaic conventions would be put aside, that the old ones would see that she and Akoma belonged together.

"Come with me," Kitchi said to Talli, breaking into her thoughts. Inside the shelter the shadows hung like the clumps of airplants that dripped from the cypress branches. Ufala lay on a hide atop a grass-woven mat. The braided hank of hair at his forehead fell loose and snarled to the side. The large-shell gorget he wore about his neck rested against his brown skin. The black markings on his chest were smeared and had lost all definition, looking more like dirt than the honorable painted symbols of a respected hunter.

Talli had never seen her father on his mat in the middle of the day. She had never seen him ill or injured. She felt a tinge of fright.

"His wound is not serious, is it, Mother?"

"More painful than dangerous. If the bad spirits do not get into it, he will recover." Then Kitchi whispered, "He will never hunt or do battle again. The arm is maimed." Her voice returned to normal. "His body is

bruised and sore. It will take a few days before he moves
about again without considerable discomfort."

Talli felt relieved knowing he would be all right. That
knowledge also relieved the guilt she felt for worrying
more about Akoma than her father.

"Perhaps Talli should not linger so close," Ufala said.

"And where will she sleep when the night comes?"
Kitchi asked. She looked around. "Talli, move your
sleeping mat near the wall."

"What has taken so long to prepare this medicine?"
Ufala asked.

"One cannot make effective medicines too quickly,"
Kitchi answered.

"Then get on with it."

Kitchi sat beside him and dipped her fingers into the
medicine paste. She daubed it on Ufala's wounds.

Ufala flinched as Kitchi tied a strip of wet hide around
his arm. "That will keep the medicine from coming off,
and when it dries, it will be stiff and keep your arm still
while it heals."

"Do you have to be so rough?"

"The bandage must fit tightly."

"And what about my ribs? What can you do for
that?"

"There is nothing I know to do other than tie a binder
around you so when you move you do not jostle
yourself."

"Aargh, you have no skills," he complained. "Talli,
do you expect to learn anything from this woman?"

Kitchi ignored him and worked a wide strip of soft
hide under his torso. She lifted both ends as he continued berating her. She knotted the binder, then pulled it
taut with a swift, fierce jerk.

Ufala gasped. "Get out!" he bellowed. "You have the
touch of a bungling dullard."

Talli hung in the opening a moment longer after her
mother had gone out.

"Can I do something for you, Father?"

Ufala did not answer. He adjusted his position on his
mat, groaning as he moved.

"Father is so unkind to you," Talli said to her mother as she joined her.

"Ufala is a good provider."

"What was it like when you were young . . . when he courted you? Was he always so gruff and dissatisfied?"

Kitchi gazed in the distance. "He came to this village often," she said, "impressing my father with the kills he made on hunts, giving a portion to our family."

Talli looked at her mother's face. Prematurely drawn and tired, the lines all pulled down. Had her mother looked at her father the way Talli knew her own eyes looked at Akoma?

"I thought he was the most handsome man I had ever seen," Kitchi said. She smiled and took a long breath, speaking on the outflow. "He was so tall compared to the men of my village. He made my heart flutter with all the attention. The other young women were envious that such a man sought only my attention."

Talli emptied the medicine bowl and wiped it out. "What happened to those feelings?"

"It was so long ago," Kitchi said, her fingers busying themselves with a bone awl, punching small holes along the edge of a rabbit fur she would add to a blanket. She wanted to be ready when the season changed. "The first child I bore him was a boy. I have told you about your brother." Talli nodded as Kitchi continued. "Ufala was very proud. He called the child Climbing Bear. He was sure the boy would grow to be the biggest, strongest, most fearsome warrior of our people. During the baby's second winter, just before your birth, the air turned especially cold. The old ones suffered and so did the very young. Climbing Bear was not as strong as your father wanted him to be. He said I coddled the boy, that Climbing Bear had to be raised more as a man."

Kitchi's eyes filled with tears. She blinked them away, then lifted her chin and shoulders, as if her straightened posture would help her brave the story. "When there was a shimmer of frost on the ground, Ufala carried his son into the cold river at dawn. That is a ritual of older boys, a part of their transition into manhood, not for a small one like Climbing Bear. Every morning Ufala trod to the river with him. Climbing Bear cried when immersed in the frigid water, and Ufala would dip him in the water again and again until he stopped crying. He thought it would make his son the strongest, the one with the most endurance. He did many things like that. He demanded too much of the child. Climbing Bear was just a little boy who sometimes still suckled at his mother's breast, another thing that Ufala disapproved of. That winter Climbing Bear got bad spirits inside, and he became ill. When he crossed over to the Other Side, your father could not accept it. He has always blamed me. He said his son died because I did not know how to mother him." Now the tears streamed down Kitchi's cheeks.

"But it was not your fault."

Kitchi looked at the shelter where Ufala lay. "He never forgave me. He discarded his feelings for me with the bones of his firstborn. And then of course there was you. He keeps the secret out of shame. Over the seasons I have hardened my heart. It is difficult for me to remember the man that offered all he had to my father if I would be his wife."

"Woman!" Ufala's voice boomed from inside the shelter.

"What is it?" Kitchi called back.

"My stomach grumbles with hunger. What have you prepared?"

"I will heat some turtle stew for you."

"Bah," he grumbled. "You would let me starve if I did not ask for food."

"He is hungry," she said, returning to the fire. "I told him I would heat some turtle stew, but in all the commotion of the day, I have prepared none." Kitchi's expression darkened. "He will be angry."

"He is always angry," Talli said. "I will go to Chinasi, or take some from the central hearth."

There was always food at the central hearth. It was a spoked hearth, and as the logs burned, the firekeeper pushed them inward. Each man donated a portion of his provisions. It was cooked and kept there for any member of the village who was less fortunate. It was also

available to visitors. No one in a Jeaga village went
hungry.

Sassa had Nocatee on her hip. "Should I go with
Talli?"

"No," Talli said quickly. "I will go alone. Stay with
Mother and Nocatee."

Kitchi cocked her head at her eldest's abrupt response. Talli strode off, and her mother watched.

At Chinasi and Bunta's hearth, Talli stopped. Chinasi
sat by the fire, but Bunta was not there.

"My mother has no stew, and my father is hungry,"
she said.

Chinasi took a black clay bowl that glittered with the
temper of quartz sand when she moved it. She ladled fish
stew out of her cooking pot with a conch-shell dipper.

"Have you heard more about Akoma?" Talli asked.

"Nothing. Putiwa is still there." Chinasi held out the
bowl to Talli. "You are very concerned about him. Your
outburst earlier has stirred rumors."

"It is difficult to see someone so young struck down
by the enemy."

"Bunta says there were three injured from the Panther
village. They fared better than our men. The Ais have
come too close, intruded on our territory and now have
attacked. My husband is troubled. We may lose more
from their wounds . . . like Akoma."

"Do not say that," Talli said.

"The longer he stays in the deep sleep—"

"He will wake," Talli said. "He is young and strong."

"But injured very badly."

"Thank you for the stew," Talli said. "My mother will
repay you soon."

"Yes, I am sure Kitchi will do that."

Ufala lay on his mat, watching the bright light of the
sun fade to a pale straw glow. He ached, and in the pit
of his belly he felt as if there were a stone. Yahga-ta
would have to call the council together. The Ais could
no longer be ignored. The cacique had probably already
spoken to Putiwa and Bunta. Yahga-ta would have in-
cluded him, listened to his advice also, if he were not

wounded. Ufala hated the Ais. He wished he could cut out the heart of the man who had done this to him and keep the enemy alive just long enough to witness his raw heart being eaten by a Jeaga warrior. For truthfully, that was what the Ais warrior had done to him by taking his good arm. Yes, that was what he wished, to taste Ais blood.

Ufala touched his fingers to his wounded arm, but could not bring himself to look at it. If the arm did not heal, he would never hunt again. He would never be a man again. What would Kitchi want with an old woman-man at her hearth? Who would provide for her?

He coughed, gritting his teeth with the pain. He could stand that kind of pain, he thought . . . but not this other that threatened from behind a dark shadow in his head. He had always provided for his family. He was a man. He had seen to it that his children had always had their bellies filled. And he had kept Talli's secret. But now what? If he lost the use of his arm, he would be a burden to Kitchi, his children, and the clan. He would rather be dead.

Ufala thrashed on the mat, deliberately causing himself pain. If he had the strength, he would rise up off this insect-infested mat, take his lance in his good hand and charge the Ais on his own. Let them kill him quickly, and in so doing he might feel the warmth of some Ais blood before the spirits took him. At least he would die as a man!

Talli strayed from the direct path back to her mother, hesitating near Yahga-ta's hearth. The village was quiet, and most people were tending the wounded or thanking the spirits for being spared. She stared at the thatch that prevented her from seeing Akoma, wishing her eyes were magic so she could see through it. Faintly she heard Putiwa's chanting coming from inside. Akoma was still alive! Her heart tumbled with gratitude to the spirits, and she quickly said a prayer of thanks.

"Talli, why do you linger here?"

Talli turned to see Akoma's mother's sister, Raina.

"I am taking some of Chinasi's fish stew to my father. He is hungry."

"That is a good sign that your father will recover," she said. "But you have taken a peculiar return path."

Talli offered no explanation.

"It is my sister's son, Akoma, that detours you, is it not?" Raina asked. "You are still upset."

Talli hesitated, but then confessed with a nod of her head.

"You have affection for him," Raina said. "That is why you tarry outside Yahga-ta's shelter."

Talli swallowed back her urge to cry.

"Oh, my," Raina said. "You are more than friends. Yahga-ta was right."

Talli realized she had disclosed how she felt about Akoma. Raina had caught her off guard.

The woman stepped closer to Talli. Her voice was a whisper. "Would you do almost anything to save him?"

"Yes," Talli answered before her voice choked.

Raina tilted her head and looked curiously at Talli. "The stew will be cold if you do not go now," she said.

Talli took a last glance at Yahga-ta's shelter before moving on.

When she arrived at her mother's side, she said, "Chinasi had fish stew."

"Then he will have fish stew," Kitchi said. "Let Nocatee give it to him. Help her with it."

Nocatee entered the shelter first. Inside, Talli handed her little sister the bowl of stew.

"Father, I have brought you food," Nocatee said.

Ufala opened his eyes. "Ah, my little Nocatee. You take care of your father. Talli, keep your distance. I suffer too greatly."

Talli stopped where she was.

Nocatee put the bowl in Ufala's hands after he sat up. He sipped the stew. "This is not turtle. It is fish."

"Chinasi has shared with us," Talli said.

Ufala lapped up the stew. "Your mother has cooked nothing for me," he groused. He tousled Nocatee's hair and smiled at her. "You are the only one who cares about me," he said.

Talli watched her father's face, the expression so gentle when he talked to her little sister. It was different when he spoke to the rest of them. She understood why Ufala found it difficult to show her affection, but there was no reason not to show a father's love to Sassa. Perhaps it was the boy's name, Nocatee, that won his affection. When Nocatee was older, Putiwa would give her a spirit name, a totem name that she would be called by for the rest of her life. For now her name was Nocatee, the name Ufala had given her at birth, even over Kitchi's objection.

"Yes, little Nocatee, you care for your father." Nocatee hugged him. "And if it were not for Banabas of the Panther village, your father would not be here to provide for you. Banabas saved my life."

Talli knew Banabas. He was close to her father's age. Whenever he visited here, Banabas loitered about her, dawdling near the river if she had tasks there, gawking at her around her father's hearth. Banabas and Ufala would sit beside the fire, telling stories and laughing. Whenever Talli served Banabas, he set his eyes on parts of her in a way that made her feel uncomfortable. She complained to her mother. When Kitchi brought the matter to Ufala, he clearly became irritated and said Talli was too imaginative.

Ufala put down the bowl and looked at Talli. "Sometimes you are so timid you appear rude to Banabas. He deserves your respect. He saved your father's life. You should behave more favorably toward him the next time he is in our village." Ufala's eyes were harsh, and his voice demanding. "Do you understand?"

"Yes," she answered, afraid that she did.

3

"What does that look mean?" Ufala asked Talli.

Talli realized her expression was one of distaste.

"You think being gracious to the man who saved your father's life is too difficult?"

She supposed Banabas was polite enough. He was not the ugliest man. But, she did not want to be expected to show him extra courtesies.

"Are you terribly uncomfortable, Father?" she asked to redirect Ufala's thoughts.

"You know better than anyone. Is that not so? Perhaps you should see how I suffer, then you could tell your mother, and she would have more sympathy."

"Is that what you wish?" Talli asked, taking a step toward him.

"Stay back." Ufala arched up.

Talli halted. "I am sorry you are in pain."

Nocatee wrapped her arms around his neck. "I am sorry, too."

Ufala grunted from the discomfort he permitted in exchange for the hug from his youngest daughter. "Be careful, little mud turtle," he said, fingering her necklace of shell beads.

Talli wished Ufala would dismiss her. Strange, she thought, how the day had started so wonderfully and ended so horribly. She remembered this morning at dawn, when the grasses were still wet with dew and the fog still hovered, when she had met Akoma in their special place by the river. In the pale sandy light of morning she had laid her head against his chest and heard the beating of his heart, his skin warm against her cheek. Now the shadows were long. The gloom in the shelter was thick. The heaviness in her shoulders made her weary. She felt the fatigue in her chest when she breathed, and in her legs when she stepped. "May I leave?" she asked.

Ufala waved her away with his good hand, and Talli gladly joined her mother and Sassa. Kitchi brewed a stew made from things she took from her baskets. There were roots, tubers, stems, cocoplums, sea grapes, hard palmetto berries, and tasty greens, but no meat, other than dried fish. The hunt would have replenished the stock of meat and fish. If there had been no attack, after night fell, the village would have steamed with cook fires and brimmed with smoking grates of fish and game. There would have been a celebration. The men would have recounted the hunt, dramatizing their prowess as hunters and fishermen. The firelight would have cast illumination on their oiled bodies, the olive-shell ornaments winking in the flickering light, the drums sounding the heartbeat of the earth. The village would have been abundant with vibrant song and lusty laughter. Instead, the musty air was going to be as it was now, suffused with the pungent odors of medicines and suffocating with heat and despair.

Talli sat beside Sassa, who whispered softly to her so their mother could not hear. "Have you seen Akoma?"

Talli did not turn her head to look at her sister. "No," she answered quietly. She watched her mother out of the corner of her eye. "Not since they took him inside his father's lodge." Her stomach turned over as she pictured Akoma's pale face.

Sassa stripped mulberries from stems for a tea and tossed them into a basket.

"Would you go and inquire about him?" Talli asked.

Sassa glanced at her sister. "Where?"

Talli casually took another quick look at Kitchi. She kept her voice restrained. "Walk through the village and ask about him. You know I cannot go."

"What do you talk about so quietly?" Kitchi asked.

Talli clutched a sprig of berries. "Sassa asked about Father."

"Um," Kitchi said. Both sisters detected that the tone

in their mother's voice meant she did not believe them, but neither was she going to challenge what they said.

Talli waited a few moments before whispering to Sassa again. "Please."

"There is not enough for the tea," Sassa said loudly. "We need more berries. The drink will be too weak, and Father will complain."

Talli shoved the last few shoots beneath her to hide them.

"We will make do with what we have," Kitchi said.

Sassa stood up. "There is no reason to aggravate him when I can gather a few berries before dusk. We do not need many more." She brushed off her shins. "I will not be long."

Kitchi glanced at Talli, and then watched Sassa go. "Strange," she said. "I was certain there were plenty. Our reserve is low on almost everything, but I did not think we lacked red mulberries."

How did Kitchi always seem to know when they were less than truthful? Even early this morning when Talli had returned from being alone with Akoma, she was sure her mother knew she had been with him. Or that she at least suspected Talli had done something she should not have.

"I have never seen the two of you so interested in your father's tea," Kitchi said.

"He is wounded and even more irritable than usual. He will be quarrelsome if he is dissatisfied."

"Um," Kitchi said, in that tone again.

When Sassa returned, she carried a small bundle of berries. She perched next to Talli. Talli took some of the clusters from her.

"Tell me what you found out," Talli said, almost too loudly in her eagerness.

Sassa made a face to caution her sister, and then went about stripping berries. Talli waited restlessly, plucking the berries and shifting her position.

Finally Sassa spoke. "The tea will take all the water we have." She looked at her older sister. "Talli, go with me to get more water. We may need more for medicines, and Father may get thirsty in the night."

Kitchi nodded her approval and said, "Hurry. Darkness is coming."

Sassa took one large pouch, and Talli took another.

Sassa did not talk as they walked along the path. The sun was low in the sky, burnishing the trees with a golden glaze.

At the river's edge, fingers of moonvine cascaded over the land and slithered up the trunks of trees. Talli could not wait any longer to hear what Sassa had to tell her. "Tell me about Akoma."

"Do you know the disapproval you will suffer if anyone finds out about the two of you? Akoma cannot ever speak for you."

"He is alive!" Talli cried.

Sassa waded into the river with Talli following. "So they say," Sassa said. "But they also say he may never wake."

"But he is alive!" Talli said, embracing her sister. She let go and clasped her hands at her mouth in a swell of jubilation. "He will be all right! He will."

Sassa filled her pouch with water. "How do you know he is the one . . . that you are in love? Does he say wondrous things secretly in your ear? Is it like all the stories told about lovers?"

Talli smiled and dipped her pouch in the river. "Watch for alligators," she said.

Sassa's eyes scanned the river, then returned to her sister. "Please tell me," she said. "I brought you news about Akoma."

Talli straightened. "It is even more than the stories. When I am near him, I am never near enough. I want his hand to touch me, to brush against me. I want to feel his breath carry his words through my hair."

"What does he say?" Sassa asked, standing up. Talli's face was aglow with the fiery colors of the sunset.

"Things," Talli answered, a blush deepening the color in her cheeks. "You will know what it is like soon enough. I see the way you watch the young Panther men when they visit. You behave so coyly when they are about."

Sassa flicked a fine spray of water from her fingers at Talli. "I am too young. You are too young," she said. "Everyone knows that." Sassa waded toward the bank.

"When the summer sun parches the earth again, I will be eligible for marriage," Talli said. "And I know Akoma will speak for me," she said to Sassa's back.

Sassa shook her head and trekked onto the shore. "You know that cannot be."

Talli caught up with her, spattering a burst of water droplets up behind her heels. "I will know it cannot be when Akoma tells me so."

"You are a dreamer," Sassa said. "Fanciful."

"You will see, sister."

Sassa's expression grew solemn as she looked into her sister's eyes. "I hope so, Talli, or I fear your heart will break."

Talli walked ahead of Sassa on the path that led to the village.

"Wait," Sassa said. "There is something I did not tell you."

Talli turned around, her head dipped with curiosity.

Sassa took in a deep breath. "I saw Raina. She said she spoke with you about Akoma."

Talli tensed.

"She said she was surprised to learn you had such affection for Akoma. She wanted to know if I knew it also."

"What did you tell her?" Talli asked.

"I said I knew nothing. She told me she spoke to Akoma's mother about you."

Talli sighed. "I was so upset. I never should have admitted anything."

"Raina said she must see you."

Talli shook her hair back from her face. "I do not need to meet with Raina to be told again to stay away from Akoma."

"She was very firm about speaking to you. I think you have to go. Maybe she will come to Mother . . . or Father if she is not satisfied."

Talli turned and started up the path again.

"Talli, think of Mother, and you know how Father will respond if Raina approaches him with a tale of his daughter's disobedience. He and everyone else has warned you to keep your distance from Akoma. There will be no peace for you or Mother."

Talli's shoulders dropped and she faced her sister. "Where does Raina want me to meet her? When?"

"Just after nightfall. Behind her shelter."

Talli snapped straight. "She knows it is forbidden for a maiden to wander the village alone in the dark! And how does she think I will just slip away?"

Sassa shrugged. "I almost did not tell you, but then I thought what might happen if Akoma's family came to Mother or Father. Maybe Raina's scolding and advice will be enough and nothing more will come of it."

With a weak nod, Talli acknowledged the truth in what Sassa said.

The sun sank swiftly behind the edge of the world. In the twilight, the sparks from the fire at the central hearth fluttered in the air like a shower of miniature falling stars. But no one gathered around it in festive song. Only Putiwa's chant rang plaintively over the village.

"Kitchi!" Ufala's voice sounded loudly.

Kitchi went to his side, taking a small shell of tallow with a burning wick.

"Go out with your sisters, Nocatee," Ufala said.

The little one moved past her mother, obeying her father.

"Come here, woman," he said.

Kitchi positioned herself next to her husband, who propped himself on one elbow.

"Sit next to me. I am lonely."

She seated herself and placed the light on the ground beside her.

"Better," he said, carefully reclining and twisting to his side. "My back aches."

Kitchi reached out and laid her hands on the small of his back.

"Relieve some of this ache."

"The discomfort in your back is from lying still so long. You are not used to it. Your muscles need to stretch. You should move around," she said, applying pressure with her hands. "It is not a good thing for a man to be so still."

"This arm will be useless," he said, so low that Kitchi almost could not make out his words.

"It is only an arm, Ufala, an appendage, not your life or your soul."

There was silence for a while. Kitchi had been with this man long enough that she knew what he was feeling and thinking much of the time. Ufala brooded over his crippled arm. He feared it stripped him of his manhood.

He grunted as she worked his muscles. "Stay away from this side," he said, indicating the bruised ribs. In a few moments, he squirmed. "Help me turn on my back again."

Kitchi offered support as Ufala groaned and rearranged himself.

"Is that all?" she asked.

When he did not immediately respond, she started to get to her feet. Ufala grabbed her wrist.

"Not yet," he said. He stared at her. "There are other ways you can make me feel better." He drew her hand to his belly.

At her touch, she felt a small flutter beneath her fingertips.

"I am in need," he said.

"I do not think you can maneuver that well . . . not with your arm and ribs," Kitchi said. Again she attempted to rise.

Ufala's large hand wrapped around her knee, and she returned to sitting. "Put your hand back where I laid it," he said. "There is another ache I need remedied."

She slowly extended her hand. Ufala grew impatient and grasped her forearm, guiding her hand to his hard belly. "I am your husband," he said. "What makes you so resistant?"

Kitchi shook her head. "You are injured. We cannot . . ."

He began to rotate her hand in circles on his naked

stomach, up to touch the nubs of his nipples, then sweeping low again. He closed his eyes and edged her hand down over his breechclout. Kitchi felt the hardness beneath.

"Unknot my breechclout," he said.

When the deerskin fell away, Ufala breathed in deeply.

"Take off your wrap and pull your hair to your back," he said. After she complied, Ufala glared and circled her hand over him again.

His grip on her hand tightened as he gazed at her nakedness in the dim candlelight. He pushed her hand deeper into his flesh. A long, almost painful sounding moan came from him.

"I do not believe you will be able to do this," Kitchi said.

"I do not intend to do anything, woman." He slid her hand to the root of his need, forcing her fingers to curl. Slowly he guided her hand so she gently stroked the length of him. He showed her the rhythm, building a little faster once her hand relaxed and molded to his form. "Yes, like that," he said, his voice coming from deep inside. His breath caught, and his neck arched. "Keep on," he said, lifting his hand from hers. He reached up behind her neck and pulled her head down to meet the next stroke.

"They cannot be. He is injured," Sassa said.

"Why do you think he sent Nocatee out to us and kept Mother with him. You know how he is," Talli said. "You have heard him climb on her in the night, waking her from sleep if he wants to join with her."

Sassa still argued, wrinkling her face is distaste. "But how? His arm and his ribs . . ."

"He will find a way."

"I am sleepy," Nocatee whined, sitting in Talli's lap.

"Stay with us until Mother comes out," Talli said.

"But I am tired."

"You cannot go to your mat now, Nocatee. Do not argue." Talli's tone was curt, and immediately she was sorry. "Sit with Sassa, sleep in her lap for a while," Talli said, standing up. She walked Nocatee to her other sister. "I am going to take care of something. Do you understand, Sassa?"

"It is well after nightfall. Do you think Raina still waits? And what will I tell Mother?"

"Think of something," Talli said.

"Talli!" Sassa protested as her sister disappeared in the dark.

Talli stayed in the shadows in the forest that bordered the village. There was a hint of coolness in the air, a briskness that came with approaching thunderstorms. She looked at the sky. It was dark, the stars hidden by gathering clouds. In the distance was a flash of light followed by a dull rumble. It would be good if it rained and the threat of drought ended.

Talli slipped through the brush, wincing at the feel of the grasses swiping her legs. Her imagination overtook her sensibility. How different everything seemed when covered by night. In daylight she wouldn't be afraid that she was about to step on a snake or scorpion. If the sun was shining, she wouldn't feel this apprehensive.

"Raina," she whispered, standing in the trees in the rear of Raina's shelter.

There was no answer. She didn't want to reveal herself in the light of the glowing embers of the hearth. She called Raina's name again and waited. Suddenly she questioned the situation. This could be an arrangement to have her discovered wandering about alone in the night. She'd be dishonored, and that would certainly make it impossible for Akoma to ever take her as a wife.

Talli rubbed her upper arms and moved a short distance through the brush to see better. She spied vague silhouettes near the fire. Two people. It could be Raina and her husband, Ishi. She dared not call to the woman or Ishi would also hear. Or it could be someone hoping to catch her out in the night, a snare set for her.

Talli took measured steps, creeping closer. She flattened herself into the shadows and peered around the shelter. The forms were much clearer and no longer just silhouettes.

Bunta squatted across the fire from Ishi. Their voices

were so low she could not make out the words. Talli
drew back. Raina was not here. She feared she had been
deceived and had nearly walked into a trap. She was
thankful she'd kept herself well hidden and had come
so late. Ishi and Bunta had probably waited for her just
after dusk, then finally given up on her. Now they sat
by the fire. She had to hurry home.

Talli crept back toward the safety of the thicket, holding the small medicine bag around her neck. Inside were
totems of good fortune, protective charms and talismans,
totems that explained who she was. Her fingers felt the
fetish that Putiwa had put there when he gave her her
name. "Talli," he had said. "Shadow Heart." She often
wondered if he had given her such a name because he
knew her secret, knew about the affliction. He was, after
all, a man of the spirits.

Her ear caught a sudden breath of something, and the
weight of a hand landed on her shoulder.

4

Sassa swallowed and cracked a knuckle in nervousness.

Kitchi looked around. "Where is Talli?"

Nocatee sat up in her sister's arms as if she wanted to speak, but Sassa pulled her back and said, "She has gone to relieve herself."

"We have a vessel for that to use during the night."

"She thought it better not to retrieve the vessel," Sassa said.

"Oh," Kitchi said. What Ufala had just had her do to him, Kitchi did not think was for anyone to see or hear, and she was thankful Talli was so perceptive.

Nocatee curled in Sassa's lap and yawned.

"Nocatee, go to your mat, but be quiet. Your father sleeps."

"Did you sing him songs to make him rest, like you sing for me when I am sick?"

"Yes," Kitchi answered, petting the back of Nocatee's head as the little one passed her. "Good night, Nocatee."

Kitchi caught Sassa's scowl. "You are older than Nocatee," Kitchi said. "What would you have me tell her? Let her think I was singing to him. There is no harm."

Sassa hung her head. She had not spoken words out of turn, but she had done the same with her expression.

Talli whipped around.

"You are late," Raina said.

"It is not as easy for me as it is for you to be out in the night. I am unmarried."

"Indeed you are. How long has it been now since you became a woman? Last summer, was it not?"

"Yes," Talli answered. "One full cycle of seasons has

nearly passed. And when the next summer comes I will be eligible for marriage."

"You wish for Akoma to speak for you now, even though you know it is forbidden."

"I do not want to discuss my feelings for Akoma."

"You must speak about you and Akoma, Talli. It is important. Does he have the same feelings for you as I suspect you have for him?"

"You will have to ask Akoma."

Raina put both hands on Talli's shoulders. "Mora and Yahga-ta fear their son will die if he stays in the deep sleep. We have seen this kind of thing before. The longer Akoma drifts there, the less chance he has of recovering. He will lose touch with this world and finally slip away to the Other Side."

Talli bit into her bottom lip.

"I told Mora about my suspicions," Raina said. "I told her I believed you and Akoma ignored the customs and that you still had deep feelings for one another. I did not tell Yahga-ta what I thought about you and his son."

"They are only suspicions."

"You are too defensive for it to be only suspicions. Just listen to what I have to say. Akoma may be dying. His mother weeps and there is no consoling her. He is her only child. She had many babies born too early. She cannot face losing her only living son. And if Akoma is lost, who will become the next leader? Putiwa says the spirits have chosen him. It is not only important to Mora that Akoma survives, but also to the People. And I think it is most important to you."

Talli pulled her wrap higher on her neck to keep off the breeze. Thunder cracked nearby and the trees blew in the wind. She was not ready to admit anything to Raina. She had already made one mistake.

"My sister wants you to visit her son. If I have been right about you and Akoma, your voice may bring him out of the deep sleep. Mora says prayers for the spirits to move you to help and for your voice to awaken him."

"Mora wants me to go to Akoma's side?"

"No one needs to know except the three of us. She will send for you when Yahga-ta and Putiwa are away."

"If I go on Mora's request, why should it be so secretive?" Talli asked.

"Yahga-ta has addressed his concerns with your family before. He fears you lure his son. The cacique does not want you tempting him."

"But still they want me to go to Akoma's side, and they want no one to know."

"His mother wishes it, not Yahga-ta."

"Do you really think he is going to die?" Talli asked.

"If you love him, you will come. You will be willing to do anything to save him."

Talli stood silently, staring hard at Raina, thoughts spinning in her head. Mora wanted her to help, but would not recognize that she and Akoma loved each other.

The breeze died and the clouds passed over, leaving the air thick with heat and moisture, but no rain. That was what life would be like without Akoma: empty, dark, choking, and bleak. Perhaps the spirits had just spoken to her. "Tell Mora to send for me," she said.

Talli turned and ran into the brush. She would do anything to save Akoma, she thought. She sped through the black forest, spiderwebs tacking themselves to her face and brittle, dry leaves crunching beneath her feet. If he died, she was certain she would also.

Breathless, she stopped short of coming into the light of the low fire that burned in front of her shelter. She told Raina she would help, but she hadn't considered the danger. She might not have enough control, and her dark and hideous secret would be revealed. But then she pictured Akoma, so still and so pale, and the risk no longer mattered.

The morning sunlight sprinkled through the leaves of the trees, dappling the village with ivory floating motes and slivers of light. The villagers stirred with the twitter of the birds. Some had slept well, and some had slept poorly.

Ufala slept deeply at first, but that was short-lived. When the speckles of daylight seeped through the thatch and doorway, he stared through the opening of his shelter. All the lodges opened toward the place of the rising sun, the place where every day began. Nothing should come between a man and the rising of the sun.

The early light shone on the hard lines of Ufala's forehead and the narrow but deep creases at the corners of his eyes.

He took in a breath, the morning air sharp in his nostrils. Ufala wiped his hand over his face. He gazed down at his mangled arm. He would never really be a man again. That arm would never properly hold a weapon or a woman. What use would it be in battle? What use was he?

"Get up, woman," he said. "I need to welcome the new day."

Kitchi's eyes fluttered open. "What is it, Ufala?"

"Help me up. I am unsteady. I want to greet the day."

Kitchi sluggishly got to her feet and went to him.

"Brace me," he said. "Put your hand on my back for support."

Ufala got to his feet with less trouble than he had expected. His tangled mat of hair hung to his muscled shoulders. "Stay inside and leave me alone," he said. "I will do this privately."

Kitchi obeyed her husband, but sat where she could see him. She watched Ufala weave as he lowered himself to the ground. He seated himself as he always did, with legs crossed. He laid his good arm across his lap, stared for a moment at his bandaged arm, which was swollen to twice its size, then lifted his head.

Her husband at least pretended to remain proud. Kitchi crossed her arms over her chest as she filled with compassion. If only Climbing Bear had lived, things might have been different.

She watched a few moments longer, then returned to her sleeping mat, turned her back to her children and wept without making a sound.

There was a hint of coolness riding the air, intimating the season change. That meant the hot, and what should be wet season would be ending . . . without significant rain.

All the able men of the village gathered in council. Because Akoma lay near death inside the leader's lodge, the men gathered about the central hearth. They each surveyed the small assembly, taking note of those who were missing, the wounded and the dead. Ufala held his breath with the effort to hide his limp and discomfort as he took his place among the others.

They sat quietly for a moment, allowing each to collect his thoughts before beginning. Yahga-ta was the first to speak.

"The Ais will keep coming. They have shown us that by the attack," the cacique said, opening his wrap to the warm fire of the central hearth.

Ufala awkwardly pitched a stick into the blaze. "I do not think they came expecting to do battle or there would have been more of them. They were surprised by so many of us. It is fortunate we chose to join with the Panther village for the hunt."

"I agree," Bunta said. "The Ais fear another drought. And I am certain they were reminded again last night when the storm threatened, but did not come. They have not forgotten what an empty belly feels like. They move toward the river. The Ais stretch the boundaries and flagrantly come into our territory. This time they came only to hunt. They did not battle with us long before they retreated."

"Of course not," Yahga-ta said. "They were a small hunting party, and we were larger."

Putiwa, who was sitting on his haunches, rocked back on his heels. "They will come again."

"Do the spirits show this to you?" Yahga-ta asked.

"Yes," Putiwa answered. "There are many Ais, and their memory of the drought is strong. Hunger motivates any man."

"But the rains returned last summer. Their land was replenished, just as ours was," Wabashaw, a tall, thin young man said.

Ufala shook his head. "But this season has been dry, suggesting perhaps another drought comes. We are fortunate to live along the river. When the water is low, the animals come this way, to the river, to us. During the long arid spell, we did not suffer like our brothers to the west, nor did we suffer like the Ais, where the earth baked dry and the water of salt seeped into their freshwater. They desire territory that will always provide."

Yahga-ta leaned back his head and looked up at the morning sun. "A hungry and thirsty man is a dangerous man."

"We should meet with members of the Panther village," Bunta said. "The Ais are a threat to us both."

"Yes," Yahga-ta said. "I will send a messenger to their chief. Ramo must also have questions about the Ais."

"If the Ais come down the coast to the river, they will reach us first, but they will not stop here. They will work up the river. The Panther village will be next," Putiwa said. "Perhaps they will even want the whole river."

Yahga-ta stood up. "Not if we stand together."

"Do not trust Ramo," Putiwa warned.

"He is one of the People," Yahga-ta said. "He is Jeaga. He will stand against the Ais."

Putiwa stabbed a stick in the ground. "He is hungry like the Ais, but not for game. He is hungry for power."

The corners of Yahga-ta's mouth pulled down into a snarl. "The Jeaga stand together or they perish."

"Keep your mind open, Cacique," Putiwa said. "All men are not just."

Yahga-ta looked behind him toward his shelter where his son lay. "The Jeaga are all the same blood. When one man's blood spills, all Jeaga blood soaks into the earth." Yahga-ta's eyes sought Ufala. "One man's pain belongs to all the People," he said, putting his fist to his chest.

Ufala nodded.

Putiwa drew a bird and a bear in the dirt. "We cannot be like Little Dove," he said.

"What do you mean?" another man asked.

"There is a legend," he said. "Once there was a young maiden, Little Dove, and she liked to walk in the woods by the river. She was the daughter of a great cacique. The chief loved his daughter, and she loved her father.

Little Dove had never known unhappiness, or war, or killing. She had never been afraid. One day she walked the path by the river. She bent to pick a flower, and when she looked up, a bear stood in her path. The bear charged at her, but Little Dove just looked at him, then suddenly the bear fell dead at her feet.

"A warrior had pierced the bear's heart with his lance. The shaft sticking out of the bear bore an unfamiliar painted black-and-white design. As Little Dove looked at the bear, a young warrior came out of the woods and told her the bear would have killed her if he had not speared him. Little Dove invited him into her village.

"Many days later she walked the path by the river again. When she returned, she found her village in flames. She ran to find her beloved father, the cacique. She found him with a lance through his heart. She had seen a lance shaft with a black-and-white crest like that before."

The men shifted and mumbled after hearing Putiwa's story.

"Ramo has fought beside us against the bear, the Ais, but we must always keep watch on him," Putiwa said.

"I understand your story, Putiwa," Yahga-ta said. "It is good you have told it."

The men who were able to hunt and fish gathered their weapons. They would not tread far, but they would restore some of the food supply. The excitement and ritual that accompanied a hunt were discarded. Only the prayers were said. The mood was somber.

Ufala stood at his hearth, watching the warriors of his village gather. His nostrils flared as though he thought he could smell the flesh of a freshly fallen deer. Something spiritual happened to a man when he hunted.

When a man hunted, he was no longer just a man, he was another creation of the Great Spirit as the animals were. When he hunted, every part of his body was in harmony with the earth. A man's muscles drew taut and ready to spring, his hearing sharpened so he could detect a leaf falling through the air, or the water pumping through the gills of a fish beneath his canoe. His eyes became so keen he could see a single thready blade of grass being pulled down by the paw of a rabbit. He could smell the coat of a buck, and taste the prey on the wind. A man became part of the cycle between man and animal, not a separate entity. And when a man made his kill, it was swift and clean so the animal did not suffer. That was man's debt to the animal that gave its flesh so the man might live.

Yes, there was more to hunting than procuring food. It was a sacred rite, a covenant between man and the Great Spirit.

Ufala cursed his arm and the Ais.

5

Bunta took up the paddle. It was the war chief's responsibility to take Yahga-ta's message to Ramo. While the other men of his village hunted, Bunta paddled a dugout up the river to the Panther village to ask Ramo to sit in council with the men of the Turtle village.

There was smoke in the air. In the distance, far to the west, a fire burned. The dried-out muck crumbled in black clots. The grass and sedge turned brown and became easy tinder. It was a bad sign.

Bunta glanced at the sun, noting its position. Before midday he would be in the Panther village. After listening to Putiwa, he was anxious to assess Ramo for himself.

The river flowed swiftly against his dugout, rushing to the Big Water in shallow rapids and falls. Returning with the current would be easier.

Bunta gripped a strip of dried fish with his teeth and cut through it with his macrocallisa shell knife. His mouth watered thinking of the succulent meat that would be cooking over his fire when he returned home.

The sun continued to climb in the sky, and in spots the river churned furiously. Bunta sheared off another piece of fish to eat and dipped the paddle in the water. His estimation of when he would arrive was accurate. The sun was not quite straight overhead when he reached the village.

Bunta guided the canoe toward the landing and stood in the dugout, waiting to be seen. Someone finally appeared on the bank and examined the visitor. The style of the canoe, the dress, the ornaments, and the stature of the man disclosed his tribe.

Banabas, an ordinary-sized man with robust features, signaled for Bunta to come ashore. Bunta banked the canoe and greeted the man of the Panther village.

Banabas wore his hair pulled into a knot at the back of his head, held there by long, highly polished bone pins that gleamed in the sun. A few unruly strands of silver-streaked hair hung at the sides of his face. He wore round shark vertebrae cuffed about the lobes of his ears. His neck dripped with strands of olive shells and his legs were tattooed, markings of high rank.

"Welcome," Banabas said. "It is good to see a brother from the Turtle village."

"I have come to speak with Ramo for Yahga-ta. I bring an invitation."

Banabas led Bunta into the center of the village. "My friend, Ufala, suffered a bad wound to his arm, and I was sure the bone was broken. How is he?" Banabas asked.

"Ufala's flesh wounds heal. He moves about and complains little. My fear is he does not heal inside his mind."

"Ufala is a proud man. A good hunter. A good warrior."

"That is what makes this so difficult for him. He says nothing, but I have seen his arm," Bunta said. "He will not hunt again. The arm is useless. He says you are the one who spared him from the enemy, that you risked your life to help him."

"He would have done the same." Banabas pointed to the lodge that was built on the top of a man-made knoll. Ramo's shelter sat higher than the rest. The thatch dripped with shells, antler, and carved wooden effigies that were half-panther, half-human. Placards carved with animals, real and fantastical, hung near the opening. "That is the place of Ramo."

As they approached, Bunta saw the cacique sitting on the ground in front of his lodge.

Ramo put down his hammer stone and the valuable nodule of chert he held. An incredibly sharp, almost indestructible point could be flaked from such a stone.

Ramo nodded with respect. Bunta responded in kind. The Panther cacique extended his hands, congenially giving Bunta and Banabas permission to sit. There was the customary moment of silence before a discussion began, and it afforded Ramo an opportunity to flaunt his piece of chert.

"So," Ramo began, "do the warriors of the Turtle village recover with speed?"

"Most do. Akoma is in the deep sleep."

"That is unfortunate," Ramo said. "Yahga-ta has said he grows tired and in a short time wants his son to take his place. If Akoma does not recover, your people will be in need of a cacique."

"The Turtle village has many men."

The corners of Ramo's mouth twitched into a faint smile. "Yes, but not all men should be chief."

"And how do the men of the Panther village recover?"

"We are all healthy. The shaman has great power. His medicine is good."

"Yahga-ta will be pleased to hear. He has respect for the Panther. He invites you to sit at our council. Yahga-ta believes the Ais are a joint concern."

"If the Ais push this way, your village will certainly be in danger."

Bunta snapped a twig and arched a brow in irritation. "If the Turtle village should be in danger, the Panther village would soon follow."

"That is not necessarily so," Ramo said. "If we made peace with the Ais, they could become our amicable neighbors. There is benefit in making allies of your enemies."

Bunta felt harsh words scrambling in his mouth, but he held them back. Ramo was a man of limited, self-seeking vision. "Yahga-ta understands that the strength of our tribe is unity. If an enemy threatens one Jeaga, every Jeaga draws his weapon."

Bunta's words fell on inhospitable ground.

A young woman sauntered up behind Ramo. He cast his head in her direction and said, "Liakka."

Bunta nodded at the woman Ramo introduced. She was attractive, he thought, shapely legs, flat belly.

"Your woman?" Bunta asked.

"I have no woman," he answered. Liakka kneaded his shoulders.

"Perhaps you *should* have one," Bunta said. "A family puts different perspectives on things."

"Are you challenging my perspectives?"

"Not at all, Ramo. Only an observation from experience."

Ramo's eyes were hard as he refused to move his gaze from Bunta. Finally Ramo said, "Banabas, you will accompany me to Yahga-ta's village. We will talk with our Jeaga brothers of the Turtle clan."

Talli helped Sassa search the baskets for food to cook.

"Did you see Raina last night? What did she want?"

Talli looked up at her sister. "You must not tell," she whispered. "Mora is going to send for me."

Sassa's eyes blinked with surprise. "Why?"

"They hope my voice will bring Akoma out of the deep sleep."

Sassa dropped the coontie root she had lifted from a basket. "Oh, Talli, you cannot go . . . cannot be close to Akoma. *It* will happen!"

Talli's teeth scored her bottom lip. "I have thought of that."

"Please, Talli. It is too dangerous for you, for all of us."

Talli's eyes filled with tears and she put her face in her hands. "I wish I had never been born," she cried. "I did not even know our ancestor who provoked the spirits so that they put a curse on the women of our line." She sobbed, "I do not understand. I never will. It is not fair."

"The debt is not paid yet, Talli. Mother's grandmother's grandmother was trusted by the Jeaga. She was the wife of a powerful cacique, and even so she betrayed her people! The wound she inflicted in the People ran deep. It will take a long time for our line to be forgiven."

"Why me, Sassa? Why was the affliction not visited upon mother, or you, or Nocatee. Why have the spirits chosen to punish me?"

Sassa felt tears in her own eyes. "Perhaps because you are the strongest, the only one who could bear it. Maybe you were chosen not to be punished, but favored because you are the one to end it."

"I want it ended, now," Talli said, wiping the streams of tears from her cheeks. She tugged at her hair. "I have my own pain. Why do I have to feel others'? Why if someone has cut his hand, my hand pains? If someone has eaten spoiled food and I am close, my stomach also becomes ill? Is my own suffering over Akoma not enough?"

Sassa leaned forward and put her arms around her sister. "I am sorry, Talli. The affliction must be a terrible burden to live with, to keep secret. But that is the curse . . . until the spirits feel the debt is paid. You cannot change that."

There was a pause and then Sassa continued. "If you sit at Akoma's side, you will be overtaken by his pain. It is frightening to see what happens to you. You cannot hide it, and if others see, then there will be questions, and eventually the secret will be revealed. Now, with the trouble with the Ais, the clan will show no mercy. We will all be cast out."

Talli pushed away and tilted her head back so she stared at the sky. She let out a heavy breath. Sassa did not speak, but let her sister calm down. Finally, Talli spoke.

"I will be careful, Sassa. But my heart is Akoma's, and I will do whatever I must to help him heal."

Sassa touched her sister's hand. "Do you think this favor will change things and you and Akoma will be permitted to see each other?"

"Yahga-ta is not part of this. Mora does it on her own."

"Did you already agree?"

"Yes."

"I do not believe you and Akoma will ever be allowed to be together. You are giving so much of yourself away for nothing."

Talli looked at her sister and faintly inclined her head. "I would do anything for him, Sassa. Anything."

Sassa picked up the coontie root again and shook her head. "Forget him, Talli. You are not old enough to have true feelings of love. You are not even eligible for marriage yet."

"I cannot help what my heart has done. Tell my heart there is another season before I should feel love."

"And you think Akoma feels the same for you?"

"I know he does. He will hear my voice."

Sassa rubbed the bridge of her nose and closed her eyes. "I see tragedy for you, sister. You are inviting a wound in your heart that will never heal." Sassa paused, looked at the basket in her lap, then rummaged through it. "You are convinced you are strong enough to be that close to him and still hide the affliction?"

"I will not touch him," Talli said. "Only talk to him."

"Is that precaution enough?"

"The spirits will be with me. I have said the prayers all night. What is meant to be, will be."

"I am afraid, Talli."

Talli embraced Sassa and was awash with her sister's dread.

Sassa pushed Talli back and held her by the shoulders while she stared into her eyes. "One of us feeling this trepidation is enough. Put it out of your head and do what you must." The color suddenly drained from Sassa's face. "Raina is here," she said, looking past Talli.

Talli turned around. Raina stood a short distance away, not near enough to be considered at their hearth, but close enough to communicate to Talli with gestures.

"Be careful," Sassa said as her sister left.

Raina spoke softly. "He has not awakened. Mora wants you to come now."

Talli followed her.

In the middle of the village, Raina said, "Wait here." She proceeded on, then disappeared inside Yahga-ta's shelter.

Talli felt conspicuous just standing about. Finally, Raina appeared and waved Talli forward.

Closer to the lodge, she hesitated and looked to see if anyone was watching.

"Hurry," Raina said pulling her into the shadows of the lodge.

When Talli's eyes adjusted to the darkness inside, she

saw Mora sitting next to Akoma. She appeared unkempt. Her eyes were puffy, and her hair hung in ragged tangles.

Akoma's face was chalky. Talli's throat tightened, and her hand went to her mouth to muffle her cry. The sudden chill convinced her death hovered nearby.

"Come closer to him," Mora said, her voice hoarse from crying.

Talli dared another several steps until she stood at Akoma's side, near his head. Immediately she felt weak and dizzy. She fought the feeling. She had anticipated the difficulty of being near him and hoped she was prepared.

"Sit by him," Mora said, stroking her son's arm.

Talli stared down at Akoma, tears rolling down her cheeks.

"Talk to him, Talli. Let him hear your voice."

"Akoma," she whispered. "It is Talli. I am here." Again dark fingers seeped into her head, coaxing her to slip away. She had to remain in control. She had to be stronger than the affliction.

"Speak louder," Mora said.

Talli attempted to speak again, and her voice cracked.

"Do you hear her?" Mora asked her son, her hand squeezing Akoma's. "Talli has come." She looked up at the young woman. "Say something else."

"I do not know what to say," Talli said, struggling to keep her concentration.

"Anything. Talk to him like you would any time if you thought he could hear you. I know he can hear. He is locked inside and cannot speak. Take his hand, let him feel the warmth of yours."

Talli winced. She could not touch Akoma. *The affliction!* It was difficult enough being this close to him.

Raina said, "I think we should leave, Mora. We may make Talli feel uncomfortable."

"I cannot leave!" Mora shot back. "I will not leave my son's side until he recovers."

Raina stooped beside Mora. "Look at me. Come into the fresh air. We will not be long. Give Talli a chance to be alone with him. It is too awkward for her while we watch. If you want her to talk to Akoma, let her feel relaxed. The sunlight will be good for you. Eat something I have prepared. Then you can come back."

Mora reluctantly rose to her feet. Even as she left, she looked back over her shoulder at her son.

"Akoma," Talli said softly. "Please hear me. I know you are there."

He lay motionless except for the shallow rise and fall of his chest as he breathed. His arms lay limply at his sides. She wished she could feel them around her. Delicately, she edged her hand toward his arm. She lightly touched him with her fingertips. She felt the tingle, the surge of dizziness, and her eyes closed. She pulled back her hand.

"You are in my heart, Akoma. There will never be another. You cannot leave me or I will die."

He had to hear her—he just could not respond. "You are lost in the darkness. Can you hear me? Listen to the true words I speak. I will always be yours, and I need you so to come back to me. I cannot live this life alone, without you. Hear my voice, Akoma, follow it through the darkness. Let me lead you out of this silent place where you sleep. Come to me."

As Talli talked to him, watching his unmoving body, his expressionless face, tears choked her words. "Akoma, Akoma." If he could not come to her, she would go to him. Talli touched his face with the back of her hand, then slowly laid her head on his chest.

The blackness was sudden and absolute, engulfing her, making her tremble and take a gasp of air. She was there with him, feeling what he felt. The utter barrenness was like a living thing that wrapped around her as she knew it must enshroud Akoma. Talli felt herself drowning, losing touch, being pulled under the darkness.

Then, in the distance, there was an echo coming to her through a long black tunnel. She did not want to hear. The voice was garbled, but it was swiftly pulling her out of the blackness, up through the darkness to the surface.

Talli felt the air swirl around her. She heard it being

sucked away, clearing, until there was only a gray mist, and then that, too, was gone.

"Talli, what is wrong?"

She opened her eyes and lifted her head. Raina and Mora huddled together on the other side of Akoma. Their mouths were open, their eyes wide. "Are you all right?" Raina asked.

Talli lifted her head and lurched up straight. They had seen!

6

"Talli, what is the matter with you?" Mora asked. The deep shadows in the platform loitered in the corners. Mora's eyes were wide with alarm. "Is something wrong with Akoma?" Frantically, her hand rushed to her son's chest. His heart still beat.

Talli stood. Her legs quivered. Tiny jewels of perspiration collected on the back of her neck, and a fine moist sheen dampened her body.

"Did he say anything?" Raina asked. "Did he hear you?"

Talli backed away. Their faces were distorted, wavering in the frail light like a mirage. Their echoing, warped voices rode the air, and Talli was not sure she even saw their mouths move when they spoke. Her mind whirled as she struggled to recover.

"Talli?" Raina said, taking a guarded step toward the young girl.

Talli put her fingers to her temples, trying to clear her muddled head. "I have to go," she said.

"Wait. What happened? Talli!" Raina called as the young girl bolted from the lodge.

Talli ran across the center of the village. Kitchi saw her coming. Talli's image sent a chill through her mother's bones.

Kitchi stood up to meet her daughter. "You have been about the village! What have you done? Whom did you touch?"

Talli's voice came out in a sob. "Akoma."

Kitchi's eyes closed, and her hand trembled at her mouth. "Who saw? Who knows?"

Talli rested against a tree and leaned her head back.

Her eyes fixed on the blazing blue sky. "I do not know what they saw."

"Have I not warned you? What made you do this? You knew the danger!"

"Mora wanted Akoma to hear my voice. She hoped it would wake him."

"And you went to Akoma's side? Talli!"

"Yes." She wiped the tears from her face. "I had to try to help. Akoma is in my heart."

Kitchi buffed her forehead with her hand as if she could make the truth go away. "How could you take this risk? You say it is because Akoma is in your heart, but we have already discussed this with you. You have been told he can never have an interest in you. You were to stay away from him. Talli, you are only a child!"

"No, Mother, I am a woman, and my heart does not keep track of the moon and the seasons. How is my heart supposed to know there is an ancient custom that forbids it to love until another season passes? My body has become a woman's and so has my heart. Tell it that it should wait on some old one's traditions."

"The customs are the proper ways."

"They are old and meaningless."

"It does not matter what you think about the practices and traditions. That has nothing to do with the secret. What you did risks us all! Did Mora see?"

"No," Talli answered. "She and Raina left me alone with him. They did not see *it* happen. When Mora and Raina came back inside, they called my name. I was slow to answer, that is all."

"You cannot hide it when the affliction happens. I am certain they thought you acted strangely."

"If someone asks, I will say I was very upset."

"What if they had not left you alone, Talli? Did you think of that? They would have seen your body tremble, your eyelids flutter like you were crazed."

"But they did not," Talli said.

"You paid no mind to the danger you put us in. You were very selfish—because you think you are in love. Ufala is not going to be understanding. He is going to be furious. He has lost the use of his arm and now you may have risked even more loss."

Talli swayed, and she felt the blood drain from her face. "Please, do not tell Father. He does not have to know. Mora and Raina will never tell that they invited me to Akoma's side. Yahga-ta does not know. Father does not have to know."

"And what if Mora and Raina did notice your strange behavior? What if they decide they made a mistake and come to discuss your odd behavior with me or your father? They may think that you are a witch!"

Talli dug her fingers into her scalp. "Why was this curse visited on me?" she cried. Her voice grew loud, and Kitchi looked to the shelter, expecting to see Ufala emerge to investigate.

Kitchi spoke lowly. "And the affliction will show up in one of your girl children, or children's children, until the spirits feel the debt is paid."

"But I have done nothing wrong. Your grandmother's grandmother is the one who made the People suffer. It was generations ago. She deserved the punishment. It was right that she was cursed to feel other's pain. She is the one who betrayed the People. She is the one who caused so much pain that the shaman felt her just punishment would be to feel the pain of others. She was the one. Not me!"

"If anyone in this village finds out we are cursed, we will be exiled. It is a secret the women of our blood must keep. Until the debt is paid, Talli, the affliction will continue. There is nothing you can do. If someone sees this happen, it will be found out that we are descendants of a traitor. No clan will want us. Not any of us."

Talli slumped to a squat. She buried her face in her hands.

"I do not know how you will ever have a man, Talli. The secret would be too hard to keep from a husband."

"Father knows, and he has stayed with you."

"I do not have the affliction. The last of our line to bear this horrible burden was my grandmother, Kaya. The secret was easy for me to keep until after it was evident that you carried the curse. Then, I had to explain to Ufala. Your father does love you . . . in his way. He keeps the secret for that reason, and also because he would be shamed to have me as his wife and you as his child. He would lose the respect of the People. We would all be cast out."

Kitchi knelt and embraced her. "You are marked, Talli. I would spare you if I could. I wish it were me instead of you."

Talli felt her mother's sadness and knew she was sincere.

Kitchi held Talli's face in her hands. "You can feel the terrible grief inside me, the deep regret. I am sorry."

Kitchi let go and stepped back. Talli opened her eyes. "I know you are sorry, Mother. I know."

Talli had lived with the affliction all her life. Her mother explained it to her as soon as she was old enough to understand, but Talli had never truly realized the far-reaching restrictions. She and her mother never discussed that. She hadn't thought of never having a man, a husband, children. There was more to this curse than feeling other people's pain, it also imparted its own anguish and suffering.

"What am I to do?" Talli asked, looking up. "What is to become of me?"

Ufala turned the long piece of greenwood. He had carved the barbed tip several days before, but had not finished the process of making it a useable tool. The tip was buried in the hot dirt beneath the coals of his small fire. The wood no longer hissed and steamed. He turned it again, making sure the heat was evenly distributed. The sap swelled inside, hardening the point so it would resist splintering and splitting.

Satisfied the task was complete, Ufala withdrew the end of the stick and waited for it to cool. As soon as he could, he tested it by attempting to push his thumbnail into the wood.

"Hah!" he said, pleased with his product. He stood and hoisted it over his shoulder, assessing the balance. It was a good fishing spear.

Ufala stumbled over a root as he made his way along

the bank of the river. He mumbled his frustration. He
had to get away from the village where there would be
no witnesses.

The big man gripped the long fishing spear in his good
hand. The binding around the injured arm had drawn
tight and rigid. It held his arm firmly in place. The pain
had abated to a tolerable level. It was time he began to
recover, he thought. No more self-pity.

Ufala found a good spot along the river where the
water was clear and shallow enough that he could see
the bottom. Carefully he hopped from stone to stone on
the rock outcropping that jutted into the river. He
perched like a heron on the last rock and made giant
loops in the cord that was tied to the spear. He put
the gathered loops into his otherwise useless fingers and
gripped the spear with his good hand. Ufala planted his
feet and readied himself. Carefully, he lowered the tip
of the spear into the water. He reached as far back on
the spear as he could.

He waited, squinting from the glare on the water. He
was going to bring home fresh fish. He did not need the
provisions of other men, as if he were a woman or an
old man. Next he would go to the Big Water, where he
would fish and gather oysters.

At last a flurry of silver shiners streaked the water,
flashing back the bright sunlight into Ufala's eyes. His
hand squeezed the shaft. His grip felt awkward, and he
knew he did not have good control. He had never before
done any significant tasks with this arm.

The stout body of a bass stole through the water.
Ufala took aim. His ineptness at handling a spear with
this hand made him lose his balance when he jabbed at
the fish. His feet slipped on the rock, and Ufala plunged
into the water.

He cursed and clambered back onto the rocks. It was
a good thing he had taken the extra precaution of binding the spear with the cord. Slowly, he wound the loops,
retrieving his spear. That was only his first try, he ration-
alized. He knew learning to use this hand was going to
take a lot of practice. Why couldn't the injury have been
to this arm?

He waited on the rock for another fish to come his way.

When the glinting body moved toward him, Ufala flexed his knees, ready to strike. When he thought the time was right, he thrust the spear. The shaft wobbled and slipped from his grip. The point skirted just beneath the surface, curving in an upward arc, then floated to the top.

The sky clouded, hiding the warmth of the sun. The wind whipped. Perhaps it would storm, he thought, looking up. Deep inside he realized he didn't want it to rain. He hoped the drought would come, wanting the Ais to suffer, wanting the Ais to challenge the Jeaga, and this time he would spill their filthy blood.

Without the sun, the breeze chilled his wet body.

After several more tries at spearing fish, Ufala shook so from cold that his efforts got worse instead of improving. Defeated, he returned to the bank, welcoming the shelter of the trees that blocked the wind. While thinking he watched the clouds. He had underestimated how long this training to use his other arm was going to take, and even wondered if he would ever be successful. He was not a patient man. This feeling of being stripped of his manhood because of one brief instant with an Ais warrior ate at him. How suddenly things could change. A man's whole life could be interrupted, and his path altered in the single beat of a bird's wing.

Ufala picked up a pebble and pitched it at a log. The stone fell short. Perhaps that was where he had to start, throwing stones, a simple skill. Maybe he also needed to lift heavy things with his good arm, over and over, to strengthen it.

Wandering the area, he collected stones and put them in a pile. Convinced he had amassed more than he could possibly throw in the short time he intended to spend, he chose the first one and rolled it between his fingers. One by one he threw the rocks at the log. After throwing many stones, the muscles in his shoulder ached, but Ufala refused to give up. He raised a stone over his head, then launched it with as much power as he could muster.

The dull thud of the rock hitting his target made Ufala thrust his arm in the air and whoop. The jar to the rest of his sore body made him collapse to his knees in pain. Ufala rolled back onto the ground and laughed, gingerly holding his ribs. He was going to get through this.

Bunta camped by the central hearth in the Panther village. He unrolled his sleeping skin and stretched out beneath the stars. He liked sleeping in the open, but found he was so distracted by the glittering stars and the drifting of ghostly clouds past the moon that he didn't want to close his eyes. It was good for a man's soul to sleep beneath the burning hearth fires of the spirits. The heavens kept a man humble, reminding him of just how truly small he was in the great design.

Long after the last straggler had vanished into his lodge and found rest upon his mat, Bunta finally slept.

In the morning, Bunta, Banabas, and Ramo left for the Turtle village. As was the appropriate etiquette, Bunta led the way.

Upon arrival, Banabas greeted some of his old friends. Ramo walked silently in long strides. His shoulders were pulled back and his arms swung too casually at his side. His general carriage was drawn into a posture of self-importance. At the central hearth he stopped.

"I will wait for Yahga-ta here," Ramo said.

Banabas and Ramo lowered themselves to the ground, and Bunta went for Yahga-ta.

Talli spied the arrival of the two men from the Panther village, immediately recognizing Banabas. She watched as the men gathered around the central hearth.

"Mother," she said, "does Father know Banabas is in the village?"

Kitchi had a hard time seeing in the distance. She squinted and searched the bodies around the central hearth.

"He is with Ramo," Talli said.

"Ufala said nothing to me," Kitchi said. "Where is your father?"

"He left early this morning."

"Find him. He will want to know about Banabas. But, Talli, keep to yourself."

Talli wandered the village in search of Ufala, but she was unable to find him. Near Yahga-ta's shelter she paused, scanning to see if anyone watched her.

She glanced at the central hearth and the council. They appeared occupied with their discussions . . . all except Banabas, whose eyes were clearly on her. Finally, he turned away.

"Mora," Talli called softly.

In a moment, Akoma's mother appeared.

"Is there any change?" she asked.

"No," Mora said, then disappeared inside.

"Wait," Talli called. "Please, let me see him. I will not stay long."

Mora did not come into view again, and Talli moved on before it became apparent that she hesitated there.

At the riverbank, she shrugged. There was no sign of Ufala. She started to return to the village, but stopped and changed her direction. She ached inside to be near Akoma, and the best she could do was go to their secret meeting place. In the tangle of the forest there was a small plot where the knots of vines, the curtain of tall grass, and the shield of cypress trees parted to form a secret hollow. This was their place, where the walls that hid them were lush and green, and the only ones to hear their whisperings and confessions were the birds.

Talli drew her arms to her chest, wishing for the warmth of Akoma. Even the air here reminded her of him, the stillness of it, the scent of crushed ferns as she stepped. She stood there breathing in, her eyes closed, her imagination finding him.

Thump.

Talli opened her eyes and strained to hear. Perhaps it was only the fall of a dead limb. She waited before she closed her eyes again. In another moment the sound recurred.

She turned in the direction the noise came from. She wound through the trees and brush, working her way toward the noise. She moved as silently as she could, exploring the ground beneath her foot before each step.

Thump.

She was close. Talli sidestepped and peered from behind the trees as she moved. As she hugged close to the trunk of a hackberry, she caught a glimpse of a figure on the riverbank. She eased herself into a better viewing spot.

It was Ufala. He raised his arm and threw a stone. The rock thumped against a log.

Talli mindfully revealed herself and moved closer. "Father," she said softly, not wanting to startle him.

Ufala spun around. His face reddened. "What are you doing here? Can a man have no peace?"

Talli recoiled. "I am sorry to disturb you," she said. "Mother wanted me to find you."

"Go away!" he shouted. "Leave me be. Your mother hovers just like she did with Climbing Bear!"

Talli backed up as she spoke. "The men gather in council. Banabas has come to our village with Ramo. Kitchi wanted me to tell you."

Ufala turned his back. Talli stood staring at him. He went on throwing stones. She would never understand her father. What had turned so rancid inside that it spilled out of him? Other men's sons had died. Ufala was perplexing and filled with rancor. Perhaps it was not Kitchi that he really held responsible for Climbing Bear's death. Maybe he was filled with hate for himself.

Talli reentered the hub of the village, coming from behind Chinasi and Bunta's shelter. She took one glance at Yahga-ta's hearth, then kept on.

Her hurried steps suddenly diminished to cautious ones, and the fist of foreboding squeezed in her chest. Raina stood at Kitchi's hearth.

7

Talli's stomach lurched. Raina and Mora must have seen more than she thought. Maybe they had been inside the shelter with Akoma and her a longer time than she realized. Now Raina came to confront her, and Kitchi, and Ufala.

Panic surged inside her, rushing in stinging ribbons down her arms, through her wrists and fingers. She forced herself to draw closer, but her legs were heavy, her steps gauged and slow.

Raina's face told nothing. Kitchi's expression was just as baffling.

"Talli," Raina said in greeting, her voice plain, disclosing nothing about the topic of her conversation with Kitchi.

Talli's eyes darted between Raina and Kitchi, searching for a clue.

Raina said, "I was passing by and your mother inquired about Akoma. I have told her there is no change. Everyone worries."

The tension inside Talli streamed out. She stopped herself from letting out a sigh of relief.

"We all say prayers for Akoma," Talli said. "Surely the spirits see him. They chose him to be the next leader, the chief. They will not abandon him. I know he will wake. The spirits are with him."

"Who can predict the spirits?" Kitchi remarked. "No one understands their ways."

"It is good to talk to you, Raina," Talli said.

Raina nodded and walked away.

Kitchi kept her eyes on Talli's face, even though she called after Raina. "Yes, it is good," she said.

Kitchi waited for the woman to be out of hearing distance before she spoke again. "When I saw Raina walk this way, I feared she came for unpleasant reasons. I wanted to seem unsuspecting, and so I called out to her and asked about Akoma."

"I have caused you so much apprehension." Talli sighed.

The men sat late at the central hearth. The sun was low, and the golden light shone on their backs. Council had disbanded, but some men still sat and talked, their conversation jolting from moments of riotous laughter to solemn predictions concerning the Ais. They told personal stories, and detailed descriptions of great hunts, tales of youthful escapades, and exaggerated accounts of their sexual prowess. Whenever the laughing and teasing ceased, they always returned to the sobering threat of the Ais.

When they finally broke up, Ufala put his good arm around Banabas's shoulder. The stretch hurt his side, but he didn't show it. "You will not sleep without benefit of shelter. Share my lodge. That is the least I can do for the man responsible for saving my life."

To allow Banabas to share his shelter was more than an obligatory gesture. Ufala owed him more than he could repay, and he wanted Banabas to know he understood that.

Talli lay on her mat as the two men entered the shelter.

"My friend will enjoy our hospitality," Ufala announced, searching the perimeter of the floor for a sleeping mat or skin he could offer Banabas. "Ah," he said picking up a large deerskin roll. "This will keep the dirt from your back." He tossed Banabas the hide.

The moon was full, and the light filtered inside. Banabas listened to Ufala, but he watched Talli.

"Over here," Ufala said, indicating a spot for the sleeping skin.

Kitchi told Sassa and Nocatee to scoot closer together to allow more room for their guest. Nocatee pressed her back against her sister, and Sassa's arm flopped over Nocatee's shoulder.

Talli turned to her side and faced away from Banabas, but she could still feel his eyes on her.

The crickets chirped in the darkness, and the thatch rustled in the breeze. Usually the breeze dwindled once the sun went down, but tonight it soughed through the trees and across the river.

Talli was sure it was morning, that she had slept through the night.

She bolted upright and forced her eyes to open wider. It was still dark, not dark like the night, but a gray so deep nothing could take form. She held her hand close to her face and saw nothing. Her heart thumped swiftly in her chest.

"I am blind," she cried. Talli reached out with both hands, searching the space around her. "Mother, help me," she sobbed. She jumped at the surprise of Kitchi's arm going around her.

"What is wrong, Talli?"

Then came Ufala's voice, gravelly from sleep. "What is it, Kitchi?"

Talli felt Kitchi's hands on her face and could feel her breath, but she couldn't see her mother. There was nothing in front of her but a dull, flat, overwhelming gray. Her hands flew to her eyes. She rubbed them, then fluttered her eyelids. "I cannot see! I am blind!" Talli cried. Again, she raised her arms and groped the air.

Kitchi took her frightened daughter's hands and lowered them.

Talli heard Nocatee whimper and Sassa quickly shush her.

Another set of arms came around her. Hard arms. A man's arms.

"Lie back," Banabas said, guiding her down. "Relax. You are trembling. Take some slow deep breaths."

There was something commanding about his voice. Talli complied and lay back. She felt him tuck her soft sleeping hide around her.

"I cannot see," she said.

"I understand," he said. "And I know you are scared. Close your eyes and do not try to force yourself to see.

Settle yourself for a moment." He brushed the hair back from her face. "Let your breathing slow." Talli felt him stroke her cheek. His hand was big and rough.

"That is better," Banabas said.

She heard faint whispering and the mention of Putiwa.

"No!" Ufala said. "Not yet."

"Why?" Banabas asked. "She needs the shaman."

"No," Ufala said.

"What is wrong with you?" Banabas's voice was tinged with restrained anger and bewilderment.

"You are a guest. I know what is best for my family."

"But, Ufala, your daughter has gone blind!"

"Father," Sassa said, "look. Something has happened in the village." Sassa's voice came from the direction of the opening.

Talli felt cool air replace the warmth of her mother. Banabas also moved away. What was happening? What did Sassa see?

"I will go investigate," Ufala said.

"I will accompany you," Banabas said.

There was a moment of silence, then Talli heard her father's voice. "Say nothing about my daughter. Do you understand?"

She heard them leave. The sound of their footfalls faded. "Mother? I am so afraid," Talli whispered.

Talli felt little Nocatee's hand creep under the hide and pat hers. "Oh, Talli, Talli," Nocatee cried.

Over the empty gray came a swirl of distant voices, a dull drone and hum. What was going on in the village?

"Do you think something has happened to Akoma?" Sassa asked Kitchi.

"Is that what you think?" Talli asked. "Why? Tell me what you see?"

"I am not sure," Sassa answered. "People are roaming, stopping and talking to each other."

Talli let go of Nocatee's hand. There was a dull ache in her head that was refining itself into something more intense. She massaged her temples. A searing pain ripped through her head. She sat up.

"Mother!" she cried out. "Something is wrong!" She held her head and rocked.

8

Kitchi rushed to Talli's side. "What?"

Nocatee sobbed.

"Talli!" Sassa said. "What is it?"

Then just as strangely as the pain had come, it was suddenly gone. Talli sat benumbed, her arms outstretched in front of her. Something was happening. "Give me your hand, Nocatee."

Nocatee rested her palm on her sister's, her cries growing softer.

Talli lifted the little one's hand by the wrist and waved it in front of her face.

"Shadows," Talli said. "Light."

Sassa crouched in front of Talli, weaving back and forth in the beam of sunshine that poured in through the opening of the lodge. She watched the alternate light and shadow fall on her eldest sister's face.

"There," Talli said, pointing at Sassa. "Someone is moving."

"Yes!" Sassa said. "It is me. You see me!"

The gray mist in Talli's head lost its density. At first, Sassa appeared as a hazy outline.

"Move again, Sassa," Talli said.

Sassa swayed on her knees. "Can you see me?"

Talli was slow to answer. "Yes," she whispered. Little by little the blinding gray disappeared, and Talli's sight sharpened.

Kitchi stared. "What happened, Talli? Why could you not see?"

"I do not know," she answered, still feeling weak. "I woke up and was blind."

"Are you all right now?" Nocatee asked.

Talli hugged her, and Nocatee's arms wrapped tightly around Talli's neck.

The sound of footsteps made all of them look to the opening. Banabas and Ufala returned.

"Father!" Nocatee squealed. "Talli can see! She is not blind!"

Ufala did not say anything—he only stared at Banabas.

"Did you not hear Nocatee?" Kitchi asked. "Talli's sight is returned."

"Yes, I heard, woman."

"Ufala, be grateful," Kitchi said. "Your daughter awakened blind, and she has gotten her sight back!"

"Sit down, Kitchi, and secure your tongue. All of you sit and listen to my words. No one must mention what happened to Talli. You must not whisper about it among yourselves because someone may overhear. Be thankful her sight has returned for many reasons. I fear what would happen to us if someone knew."

"What are you talking about?" Kitchi asked.

"Banabas," Ufala said, "leave us. I cannot speak in front of you."

Ufala's eyes stabbed Talli. He paced the floor, then switched his glare to Kitchi as Banabas left the lodge. "Your daughter has disobeyed," he said. He took another three steps back toward Talli. "Is that not so?" The corner of his upper lip twitched and his right eye squinted with a shot of pain that ran through his arm as he twisted to stare squarely at his oldest daughter.

Talli shrunk back, drawing the hide closer to her like a shield.

Ufala grimaced and paced, his jaw muscles tensing and relaxing. His nostrils flared, and his long shadow floated all the way across the lodge.

Talli knew her father and recognized his stance and his expression. He fought to restrain his anger. At any moment she expected to hear the boom of his voice and see his thick finger jabbing the air in front of her face. She felt herself shrinking, huddling into a smaller mass to make less of a target.

"Ufala!" Kitchi stood and stepped between her hus-

band and daughter. "Talli is a victim. She has done nothing to deserve your anger. Talk calmly to us."

Ufala glared at his wife, holding his breath for a moment before speaking. "Do you know what she has
done, woman?"

Kitchi looked at the ground.

"She has been with that boy. She has risked the well-
being of every member of her family."

Nocatee hugged her father's leg. "Talli was sick. She
has not been with Akoma." Her voice was soft with the
effort to soothe him.

Ufala stroked the back of Nocatee's head, succumbing
to her attempt to calm him. "Talli has been near Akoma,
even though I have forbidden it. Akoma's awakening
from the deep sleep caused the stir in the village this
morning."

"That is a good thing," Kitchi said.

One of Ufala's eyebrows arched, his mouth turned
angry, and beneath the deep brown of his eyes was the
fire of rage. "He is blind."

Ufala's words hung in the air, trapped there by the
shock of them.

Talli covered her face with her hands to hide her tears.

Kitchi sank to the floor. "Banabas," she murmured.
"He knows."

"He is curious," Ufala said. "He does not understand,
but expects there is a mystery in Talli. He questioned
me with a look, an expression on his face that did not
require words."

"What did you say?" Kitchi asked.

Ramo snapped a green twig from the strangler fig and
chewed on the end. "I am glad your son has come out
of the deep sleep, Yahga-ta."

"Are you?" Yahga-ta answered, sitting on the bank
of the river. "Then perhaps you will join me in thanking
the spirits."

Ramo leaned against the tree and watched the sun
glancing off the ripples in the water. "I have already
spoken to them this day."

"I suppose you asked them for guidance in council as

I will. It is important the Jeaga remain united or the Ais will have the advantage."

"That is an issue I will discuss with your council. I think the Jeaga need to see the current in the stream more clearly."

Yahga-ta looked up at Ramo. "I wonder if you were injured if you would bleed Jeaga blood. Why is it I feel that way? What do I see?"

"I think you have your son's blind eyes." He took the jagged, hard end of the twig and gouged a shallow cut in his forearm. "My blood is Jeaga," he said, extending his arm as the incision filled with beads of blood. Ramo swiped his index finger over the cut, then wiped a deep red streak down his forehead. "You see, it is the same as yours. You need more trust, Cacique."

Ramo turned his back, tossed the stick on the ground, and walked back to the village. Yahga-ta studied the young cacique's gait, different from proud, more insolent. Defiant. Yahga-ta thought again of Putiwa's Little Dove, the warrior, and the bear. He only wished he knew what Ramo was thinking and wanting. Perhaps he would know more after the council meeting.

"Yahga-ta." It was Bunta. He had come to the river. "I see that Ramo has been to speak with you already," he said, looking behind him on the path. "Do you find any wisdom in his words, or does he speak no sense?"

Yahga-ta waded in the river and splashed water over his body. "I listen with an open ear. We will hear more of his words at council."

"Do you feel the breath of the spirits on the air this morning?" Bunta asked, tilting back his head and sniffing the air with widened nostrils. "The season changes and there has been no rain. Ramo's eyes do not grieve when the possibility of drought is mentioned."

Yahga-ta swirled a handful of water in his mouth, then spat it out. He stooped in the river so the water climbed to his neck. "What do you see in his eyes, War Chief?"

"Flashes of light. Excitement."

Sheets of water spilled down Yahga-ta's chest as he rose. "Perhaps it is the anticipation of the thrill of the hunt or battle, the kind of thoughts that dazzle a young man's imagination."

"No," Bunta answered. "He is Jeaga, but I do not trust him."

Akoma refused to open his mouth when his mother requested. If he had an appetite, he would eat. But the spirits were speaking to him. He would starve.

"You must eat," she said. "The alligator is powerful and his flesh will impart his strength to you. And the gar is difficult to kill. He will give you his persistence."

"I will not live this way," Akoma said, "blind and fed by my mother. A creature to pity, not a man."

"Be patient, my son. The spirits have awakened you. when it is time they will restore your sight."

Akoma felt the pinch of alligator meat and fish touch his lips. The strong smell of the oily garfish turned his belly sour. He pushed his mother's hand away. "The spirits did not choose that I be brought back from the blackness."

Mora put the fish back in the bowl. "Of course it was the spirits. Putiwa has attended to you every day, given you medicines, said prayers, showed you to the spirits. They respect him and find honor in you and have awakened you."

Akoma wondered if his eyes were closed or open. His arm trembled with weakness as he lifted it to touch his lids with his fingers. His eyes were closed.

"They abandoned me," he said, "left me adrift in a world not here or on the Other Side." There was still pain in Akoma's head, sometimes dull and sometimes sharp. He felt his heart beat deep inside his skull and wanted to sleep again.

"Akoma," Mora said, shaking his shoulder. "Open your eyes even though you cannot see."

He heard a tremor of fear rattle her words.

"The spirits forgot me in a world of darkness . . . closed my ears, my eyes, took my sense of touch, and taste, and smell. I was only a soul in a gray cloud, aimlessly wandering."

"But they brought you out of that mist."

Akoma shook his head, then held his temples with both hands. "Talli," he said. "She is the one who came and found me there. Her voice, not the spirits, led me out of the emptiness."

Mora put her hand over her son's mouth. "Shh. Speak of that no more."

Akoma moved her hand away. "It is the truth."

"Yes," she whispered. "Talli was here . . . at my request, but Yahga-ta does not know. He would have objected."

Akoma was silent for a moment. His arms felt heavy and there was a distant droning in his ears. He wanted to slip away, just sink into his body and let the droning grow louder. But he wanted to know about Talli. If she could be his, he would fight to stay in this world.

"In return for her favor, did you promise I would be permitted to speak for her?" he asked.

"No, Akoma. That cannot be."

"I will tell Yahga-ta that Talli is the one who brought me out of the deep sleep. He will be grateful."

"No, Akoma," Mora said, sponging his head wound with a concoction of Putiwa's medicine. "It will only do damage. No good will come of that. Yahga-ta would never forgive Talli or me. Do you understand? The consequences would be grave."

Akoma turned his head to listen as if he heard something or someone else in the lodge.

Mora looked behind her. "Husband!"

9

Mora scrambled to her feet, her mouth screwed into a fearful knot. "Yahga-ta, you startled me. I did not hear you."

"I see that," he said.

"Akoma does not want to eat. Help me persuade your son to accept the food Putiwa and I have prepared."

Yahga-ta lowered himself with crossed legs next to his son. "Your mother and Putiwa are wise. Your body needs nourishment to heal." He looked at the bowl of food. "Putiwa has chosen well. Strength and perseverance. Do as your mother says."

Akoma turned his head away.

"I have called the council. Ramo is here. And Banabas."

Akoma flinched. "Banabas?"

"Yes. Ramo listens to his advice. Why does his presence disturb you?"

Akoma shook his head.

Yahga-ta stared at his son. "Banabas stays with Ufala. He saved Ufala's life. I think he has an interest in Talli."

Mora bit into her cheek. She watched for Akoma's reaction and knew her husband was testing him.

Akoma held his expression still, but his stomach churned and its contents rose in his throat. He needed more time to sort through things. He needed to think clearly. If he remained blind, then it was best if Talli forgot him.

"Cacique." It was Bunta outside the lodge. "The council has gathered."

Yahga-ta looked at his son. "Do not forget your destiny, Akoma, you are to lead our people. Take the food and regain your strength. Fight as you fought the Ais."

Mora stroked her son's face and Yahga-ta left the lodge, following Bunta to the central hearth.

Ramo was slow to rise in respect for the cacique. His subtle statement drew attention, and the air thickened with tension.

Yahga-ta waved his hand, and the men of council sat. The fire was low and snapped with greenwood. Yahga-ta held the talking stick, a polished wooden staff garnished with a crest of white snowy egret feathers and a band of tinkling shells.

"I believe today we should use the talking stick as we have many opinions. The stick will maintain order."

Everyone nodded his agreement.

"It is good of Ramo and Banabas to come to our council. The Ais are a threat to the Panther and the Turtle clans. But our unity gives us great strength. We invite Ramo to tell us how the Panther clan thinks."

Yahga-ta passed the talking stick. Ramo plunged the end of the stick into the dirt and held it upright.

"You speak of unity and strength, Yahga-ta, but only in the most limited way. At this time we are bound only because Jeaga blood runs in our veins. To be strong enough to resist the Ais, there must be more than common blood."

A chill tingled down Yahga-ta's spine.

Ramo let his words settle over the men like a caul before he continued.

Bunta shifted his weight and folded his arms. The fire crackled beneath the shadows of the tall oaks.

"We are too divided," Ramo said.

"I wish to ask a question," Ufala said.

Ramo acknowledged him.

"The blood has given the Jeaga strength through generations. Why do you feel we are divided now?"

"We are many small groups that do not harmonize plans except in crises. Our other brothers are even unaware that we have come in conflict with the Ais. We are too disjointed."

Ufala's face twitched with the pain in his ribs as he breathed deep. "Do you have a proposal?" he asked.

"I wish to speak," Bunta said.

Ramo paused before passing the stick.

"This conversation is not addressing our immediate need. How do we respond to the Ais attack?" Bunta asked. "Should we assume this was a chance encounter? What are the elements that guide the decision? Ramo, you have misled the discussion."

Mumbling and whispering filled the circle of men.

When Ramo held the stick again, he said, "Let my words rest inside your head. We cannot resist the Ais as many separate people. They will come again and again. We are greater if we are one. Consolidate. The Panther and Turtle should merge, giving us more power."

The stillness that followed Ramo's words surged across the hearth in a wave of incredulity. Ramo was suggesting there be only one cacique for the Turtle and Panther clans. It was clear what Ramo intended—that the Turtle clan be taken over by the Panther clan.

Ufala spoke. "Banabas, you are my friend, but I am not certain I like what I hear."

Yahga-ta held up his hand, palm out to silence Ufala. "We will use the stick," he said.

Bunta crossed the circle and snatched the stick from Ramo. He held it up. "You are in favor of attacking the Ais, but only if the Panther and Turtle clans become one. Is that what I hear?"

He moved next to the fire, threw his head back and laughed. "Of course that is what I hear. And certainly, Ramo will lead this group . . . this mixed clan. I see what happens to the Panther. They become the strong, and the Turtle, weak. Ramo, perhaps your idea of unity is a good one, there is strength and power in that, but I will not agree to allow the Turtle to dissolve under your hand. We can communicate more closely, form tighter bonds, and build strength. I disagree that there should be one leader, that we should lose our identity. And besides, your youth and nature need to be tempered with age and experience."

Ramo smiled, flashing a blade of white teeth. "May I have the stick?"

Bunta passed it to him.

"I see I have stirred some passion. That is a good thing. I see the Turtle clan as still, fallow, without zest. I will bring those things to you."

Ramo traveled the inside of the circle, looking at each man's eyes as he passed. "How long has it been since you felt heat in your gut? It is the essence of youth that whips up ardor. Old men give advice and young men meet the challenges of changing times. Blend the two. Zeal and patience, fervor and prudence."

Bunta's jaw clenched and he spoke through his teeth. "Akoma will lead the Turtle clan. You speak of youth, we have it. Yahga-ta trains his son. The spirits have selected him. You have nothing to offer that we do not already have."

"If he recovers."

Yahga-ta stood. "The council is ended," he said.

Putiwa got to his feet and rested his hand on Yahga-ta's shoulder. "He is as dangerous as the Ais," he said in Yahga-ta's ear.

The left side of Ramo's mouth curled into a faint cynical smile.

10

Ufala left the village and went to the place where he practiced throwing stones. His cache rested in an abandoned gopher tortoise hole. He squatted next to it, then sat on the ground and loosened the binding Kitchi had put around his arm. He squinted with the discomfort as he unwrapped it.

The arm was ugly. The bruises were still dark and had not yet faded into a mottling of yellow. The swelling appeared a little less, he thought. Even though the arm remained folded across his chest, it rested at an odd angle. Maybe he should not be thankful to Banabas. Perhaps Banabas had done him no favor in saving his life.

"Ufala." Yahga-ta stood behind him.

"Cacique," he said.

"I wish to speak with you," Yahga-ta said, coming in front of the large man. He glanced at Ufala's injured arm.

"It heals," Ufala said.

Yahga-ta looked at the stone-filled gopher hole.

"I exercise the other arm," Ufala explained. "Small things at first."

Yahga-ta nodded, sympathy flowing through the lines in his face. "Tell me more about Banabas, your friend."

"What do you want to know about him?"

"I understand Ramo listens to him—if Ramo listens to anyone other than himself."

"I think that is true," Ufala said.

"It is clear that Ramo wants to take advantage of our skirmish with the Ais. He wants to merge our two clans, and he wants to be the cacique. I fear for our people if that happens. Ramo is a renegade and will do great damage to the Jeaga. How does Banabas feel? What does he think?"

Ufala shrugged, then grabbed his shoulder. He retrieved the binding and began to wrap the arm. Yahga-ta helped him wind the bandage around his body to immobilize the limb.

"I have not spoken to Banabas about Ramo."

Yahga-ta reached for one of the stones. "What is your target, Ufala?"

"The fallen log."

Yahga-ta pitched the stone, thumping the log and knocking off a chunk of rotten bark. "Putiwa does not trust Ramo. Neither does Bunta."

"They are wise," Ufala said, getting to his feet.

"Ufala," Yahga-ta said, "I have noticed the way Banabas looks at your eldest. It might be insightful to encourage Talli to respond to him, especially if Banabas influences Ramo."

Ufala threw his stone, knocking more bark away.

"She must give up the notion of my son taking her as his woman," Yahga-ta said. "When Akoma is recovered, he will seek a wife from the Panther clan. Someone of a noble line. We must keep peace amongst our own people. These unions, Banabas and Talli, Akoma and a Panther woman, can be two knots in the rope that will hold us together. Ramo will find it more difficult to cut through knots than plain rope. Do you understand?" Yahga-ta asked.

"I will speak to Talli," Ufala said. Yes, he thought, Talli should show more interest in Banabas. If Banabas had figured out her mystery, it would be best if Talli was his woman. He would not tell the secret if Talli was his wife. Ufala stared in the distance. This idea of Yahga-ta's could work for them both. If Talli became the wife of Banabas, it would be good for the clan and good for Ufala and all his family.

Talli stood outside Yahga-ta's lodge. She wanted to see Akoma, speak to him. She'd seen the council break up and Yahga-ta walk to the river, so she knew he was not with Akoma.

"Mora," she called, nervously glancing about to see if anyone noticed her there.

In a moment Mora appeared in the opening. "Talli. What are you doing here?"

"I wish to see Akoma. He has awakened."

"You cannot see him. Yahga-ta forbids it."

"But Yahga-ta is not here. He does not need to know."

"Be gone," Mora said.

From behind Mora, Talli heard Akoma's voice. "Bring her to me," he said.

Mora spun on her heel. "Your father will return any moment."

"Bring her to me," he said.

Mora stepped outside. "I will watch for Yahga-ta's return." She motioned for Talli to pass inside.

"It was you, Talli. Your voice led me out of the sleep."

"I wish I could restore your sight," she said. "I would do that if I could. But it does not matter to me if you can see or not. I will take care of you."

Akoma's grip on Talli's hand loosened. "I will be a burden to no one," he said.

"Akoma, I love you. You could never be a burden." She was quiet for a moment. "But you do not need to worry about such a thing. Just as you awakened, the spirits will let you see again."

"I am not so sure," Akoma said. "Perhaps I was to die by an Ais hand, but was rescued. Or I should have slipped away in the deep sleep, but your voice led me out. Do you understand what I am saying? Maybe it was my destiny to perish, but there were interventions . . . and not from the spirits."

"Do not think that way," she said. Talli brushed his hand across her cheek, then kissed his palm. She laid his hand at his side and stroked his face with her fingertips. "Think of what has happened this way, Akoma. This terrible injury to you has allowed a chance for me to earn grace with your family. Maybe Yahga-ta will permit you to speak for me because he is grateful that I brought you out of the deep sleep."

Akoma reached up and held her hand still against his cheek.

"I will never love another," she said. "You will always be the one."

A stir made Talli turn.

"Yahga-ta comes," Mora said. "Hurry, Talli."

Talli quickly got to her feet and left the lodge.

Yahga-ta's long stride crossed the central plaza. His gray-streaked hair blew behind his shoulders, the single feather that was entwined in a shock of hair floated to the rhythm of his gait.

"Husband," Mora said, "I see trouble in your eyes."

"You know me well," he said, rubbing a thumb across her bottom lip. "How is it that you see inside me?"

"Will you share your concern with me? Tell me what it is that puts the shadows deep in your eyes."

"It is a man's worry."

Mora held his face in her hands. "When you are ready, I will listen," she said.

Yahga-ta held one of her wrists and nodded. "How is our son?" he asked.

"Restless," she answered. "The Ais could not kill him, but I fear the blindness will."

"No," Yahga-ta said. "He is chosen. His destiny is to lead his people."

"What does Putiwa say? Does he believe he will see again?"

Yahga-ta shook his head. "He cannot say. He has no answer from the spirits."

Mora put her hands on her husband's chest. "When the moon is high and the village quiet, I will take all these worries from you. Even if only for a while."

Yahga-ta smiled. "Now," he said, "I must speak with Akoma."

As Yahga-ta passed, Mora's hand stroked down his spine, then she followed him inside.

"Who is there?" Akoma asked.

"Yahga-ta."

"And your mother," Mora said.

Yahga-ta sat and crossed his legs. "The blindness will leave you. I feel certain of that."

"How can you be so sure?" Akoma asked, sitting up and turning to face the direction of his father's voice.

"The spirits have a plan for you. That is why I have only one child, one son. All their strength and trust is in you. They would not leave you blind."

"I have seen no help from the spirits."

"Be patient. We do not always understand their ways. We must believe and have faith."

There was a moment of silence and their breathing could be heard when the thatch did not rattle in the breeze.

Yahga-ta cleared his throat, then spoke. "Ramo thinks he finds a weakness in us because of your injury. He tries to take advantage of it and the Ais' attack."

"What do you mean?" Akoma asked. "He is Jeaga, one of the People."

"I understand the Ais better than I understand Ramo. The Ais fight to survive. They want the river. We fight to keep it. That is easy to understand. But Ramo wants the Turtle clan. Ramo wants power, whatever the cost to the Jeaga."

"What has he proposed?" Akoma asked.

Mora wrapped her arms around herself.

"Ramo spoke in council. He wants the Panther and Turtle to merge."

"How can that be?" Akoma asked.

"One cacique. One clan."

Akoma rubbed his hand down his face.

"I have thought of some ways to mellow his plan. When the blindness leaves you, you must visit the Panther and look over their women. Choose a wife from them . . . one, of course, of a noble line. This will bond the two clans. I will step down just before the marriage, and you will become the Turtle cacique. The leader of the clan will take a Panther woman as his—"

"No," Akoma said.

Mora held herself tightly, watching her son's hardened expression.

Yahga-ta drew back with the surprise of his son's response.

"I cannot do that," Akoma said.

"You must," Yahga-ta said. "It is one of the ways to arrest Ramo's plan."

"Father," Akoma said, "I must tell you something."

Mora clutched at her upper arms. "Akoma, listen to your father. Think about what he has said before you answer. You speak now without thought. Do you hear me?"

Akoma's teeth ground as his jaw slid forward and back again.

The air inside the lodge was still and the rattling of the thatch ceased. Mora's fingernails dug into her flesh. Yaha-ta looked at her, then back at his son.

Finally, Akoma spoke. "Let us first see if my sight does return," he said. "Then we will discuss these options."

Mora's breath spun out in relief.

"Your sight will return," Yahga-ta said, rising. "And when it does, we will implement this plan immediately. There is no time to waste."

Akoma's mouth opened to speak, but Mora spoke first. "Akoma. It is better to let your father's words seep into your head than to speak now."

Banabas gathered his things. "It has been good of you, Ufala, to allow me to stay in your lodge."

Ufala nodded. "I honor you. You saved my life."

The conversation was strained and exceedingly polite. Kitchi and her daughters sat outside. Sassa wove rushes, making a basket; Nocatee twirled a stick between her palms, pretending to start a fire; and Talli pressed an incised checkered wooden paddle into the sides of a wet clay bowl for decoration. She handed the stamped bowl to her mother, who buried it in a pit to be fired.

Talli leaned toward the lodge to better hear her father and Banabas's conversation. She could only catch pieces of what they said. She heard her name mentioned and flinched. Was Banabas probing Ufala about the curious coincidence of the blindness, or worse, were they discussing Banabas's interest in her?

How she wished she could excuse herself from the chores and wander away to meet Akoma in their secret place. She ached to hear him whisper her name as they touched each other. She did not care if he was blind. There was even a part of her that she tried to deny. In a far corner of her mind was a dark part that in a very small way wished the blindness was permanent. If that were true, Akoma could not become cacique. She would care for him for the rest of their lives. She would make baskets, pots, sew skins into blankets and capes to trade for food.

Talli shuddered. What a horrible thought, she scolded herself. What kind of person was she to even have that kind of thought cross her mind? She felt ashamed and confused by the emotions that swam inside her.

"Say good-bye to our guest," Ufala said, emerging from the lodge. "Banabas and Ramo are ready to return to their village."

Kitchi got to her feet, and Nocatee wrapped her arms about her mother's thigh.

"Banabas," Kitchi said.

"Talli, wish him well," Ufala said.

Talli's mouth grew dry as she spoke. "May your journey be a safe one," she said.

Banabas's smile deepened. "I am delighted with your recovery, Talli. Your eyes are much too lovely to suffer any misfortune."

Talli looked down.

"There is no need to be so shy, daughter," Ufala said. "Banabas pays you a compliment."

"Thank you," Talli said. "It is kind of you to say such a thing."

"I speak the truth," Banabas said, lifting her chin with the crook of his forefinger. "Let me see your eyes one more time before I leave."

"Smile, Talli," Ufala said.

Talli made an effort to do as her father requested, but the smile was limited to her lips and did not flow through her face or into her eyes.

"She will be more genial, my friend. She is young yet. Have patience."

Banabas continued to stare at Talli while Ufala spoke.

His finger stayed beneath her chin, keeping her head tilted up, but Talli looked to the side.

"I will walk you to the river," Ufala said.

Banabas nodded a good-bye and walked alongside Ufala.

"You like my daughter, do you not?"Ufala asked.

"She is quite beautiful," Banabas answered.

"I think she will make a good wife."

"She is much younger than I am."

"Yes, but that will not matter. How long have you been without a woman?"

"For a long time. Not since Tawba crossed over."

"That is a long time since your wife was called by the spirits. Not good for a man. A man has needs."

"I will take a wife again."

Ufala put his fist on Banabas's shoulder. "Perhaps my daughter is the one."

Banabas turned to look at Ufala. "Do you offer her?"

Ufala laughed. "Just a thought for you to ponder. She is still too young. But customs are changing. Keep her in mind."

"I will do that," Banabas said.

"She does cause a stir in you, does she not?" Ufala asked.

"Ufala, she is your daughter. How can you speak that way?"

"We are men. I understand what a pretty young woman can do to a man. I only want to understand that you have a real interest in her before I seek to have a custom broken."

"You mean permission for her to marry before next summer?"

"If that is what must be. I am obligated to you. I have my life because of you. It is only reasonable that I give something in return. I can make no promises that Putiwa and Yahga-ta will give permission for her to be eligible before her time, but it is something for you to think about. So tell me, does Talli appeal to you?"

"She does."

"Good," Ufala said, slapping Banabas gently on the back. "I would be proud to offer my daughter to the man who saved my life. She would bring you many sons."

"And Talli? What if she does not agree?"

"Oh, I think she can be encouraged."

Banabas shifted himself inside his breechclout, suddenly feeling too confined and uncomfortable.

Ufala grinned. Banabas was more than interested in Talli. This was going to be a good thing for everyone. Talli's secret would be kept, Ramo would be undermined, and Ufala would gain status with both clans.

Ramo was already in the dugout. Yahga-ta stood on shore with Putiwa, Bunta, and several other men. Most had refused to see off the visitors.

Banabas climbed in the canoe.

"I will talk with Talli today," Ufala called out.

The Panther canoe moved through the water. Banabas held up his hand one last time to bid good-bye before the canoe disappeared around the bend in the river.

"Yahga-ta," Ufala said, "I think the time has come to break customs."

11

Kitchi unwrapped Ufala's injured arm. "Stop your protesting," she said. "The arm must be washed with Putiwa's medicine. Do you want the bad spirits to get inside it?"

Ufala grumbled. "Do what you will."

Kitchi dipped a swatch of chamois into the bowl of medicine, then wrung out the excess. "The wounds are healing nicely," she said, sponging the arm. "You are a fortunate man."

Ufala jerked his head to the side to look at her. "Fortunate? You have strange perceptions, woman."

Kitchi kept on nursing his arm. "Ufala, you need to look at things differently. You dwell upon the worst."

"And what is good about this? Nothing. Nothing."

"There," she said, finishing. "Putiwa has strong medicine."

As Kitchi bound his arm, Ufala grunted with the discomfort. She tied the binding tight. "Soon you will not need this," she said.

"Yahga-ta and I have come up with a plan," he said.

"What kind of plan? For what?"

"To keep Ramo in his place. He is a dangerous one. He will swallow the Turtle if we allow it."

Kitchi sat back on her heels, holding the medicine cloth in her lap. Her eyes darkened. "Why do you share this with me? I am afraid to hear the plan you have devised."

Ufala pulled at his chin. "Yahga-ta and I will speak with Putiwa and, of course, the council about changing custom under these extraordinary circumstances."

Kitchi twisted the hide in her hands. "Break which custom?"

"Times are changing. Our customs must also change to permit us to survive."

"Which customs, Ufala? You seem to be preparing me for something. Get to it."

"Talli," he said. "She is a woman and should be eligible for marriage when the time is right for her, not according to some ancient custom designed by ancestors. Do you not agree?"

"Yes," she said. "When it is right for her."

"My friend Banabas would be most pleased if I offered Talli."

Kitchi stood up. "Banabas? No. Talli has no interest in that man. What is wrong with you, Ufala?"

"Sit down, woman, and listen. Sit!"

Kitchi slowly lowered herself to the ground. "Tell me all of it. Play no games with me about our daughter."

"All right, wife. Do not say anything until I am finished. Will you agree?"

Kitchi nodded.

"Ramo has indicated he wants the two clans to merge, and he will become the cacique. He says that is the only way to be strong against the Ais. Bunta said Ramo even suggested to him that the Panther could befriend the Ais. That would leave us very vulnerable. He planted that idea with Bunta to force us into accepting his plan out of fear that the Turtle would have to stand alone against the Ais."

"What has that—"

"I told you not to speak. Let me finish." Ufala shifted his weight. "Ramo respects Banabas. He listens to his advice. And we are lucky that Banabas expresses an interest in our daughter. If Banabas takes Talli as his woman, he will discourage Ramo from measures that could damage the Turtle clan."

Ufala looked about to see if anyone was close, before he continued. "And you must realize Banabas is curious about Talli's strange blindness. I am certain he has made a connection, but does not understand it. You see, if Talli is his woman, even if he figures out the affliction, he will be bound to keep her secret. So perhaps you are right, Kitchi. I am a fortunate man."

"You are finished?" Kitchi asked.

"Yes," Ufala answered.

"Then the custom breaking is so Banabas can ask for Talli." Kitchi's stomach roiled. "You have given no thought to Talli and how she feels."

"Talli must be sacrificed for the good of us all. She will understand that. Ramo will devour us if we do nothing to stop him. Then it will not matter how Talli or anyone else feels. We will fall at the hands of the Ais or Ramo. It makes no difference to which."

"Is there no one else Banabas would consider? What about Leesee? Her husband was killed by the Ais. She will need a husband and will also want to stop Ramo and the Ais. Why not her?"

"Banabas does not want Leesee. He has an eye for Talli. A strong eye."

"You have spoken to him?"

"Yes, today before he left."

Kitchi rubbed her forehead, pinching at the bridge of her nose. "Do not say anything to Talli yet. Wait until after it is decided if the custom can be broken. Do not upset her before she needs to be. And, Ufala, let me talk to her first."

Ufala held his bound arm as he got to his feet. "I am nothing without this arm. If I can offer Talli to Banabas, it will bring me status. I need to feel like a man."

"You are a man, Ufala. You only suffer a maimed arm."

Ufala stared at his wife. His lips opened as if he were going to speak, but then quickly stilled.

There was a heavy silence, one that grew more intense as each moment passed. Kitchi folded the medicine swatch and stood up.

"I will consult with Yahga-ta and Putiwa about the custom," Ufala said. "This should be done soon."

Kitchi looked in the distance. Talli carried Nocatee. Sassa walked beside them. How was she going to tell Talli?

* * *

Mora spread the clay on the flat rock, working it out into a thin sheet. She sprinkled the sand temper over it, then folded the clay. She could hear Putiwa chanting inside the lodge. His medicine was not as strong as Talli's. Talli's medicine was love, but there was even more. The girl had appeared so strange when she and Raina went back into the lodge that day. Mora thought there was something peculiar about Talli, but even so she would always be beholden to her for bringing Akoma out of the deep sleep. If Yahga-ta ever found out she had conspired with Talli, she was sure she would suffer his wrath. A woman did not disobey her husband or go against his will. Yahga-ta might even be done with her, throw her out, especially if anyone else found out she had disobeyed. That would shame him, and the cacique could not suffer such irreverence by his wife.

Mora shuddered and spread the clay out again and applied the temper before folding and kneading it, working in as much temper as the clay would hold.

She felt her eyes tear and wiped at them with the back of her hand. No, a wife did not go against her husband's will, but a mother would do anything for her son. How could she separate the two—wife, mother? She was not used to keeping secrets from her husband.

"Akoma," she whispered. "My son." Images of him as a little one fluttered in her head, and her eyes teared again. She feared for him. She feared that the pain he endured from his injury would pale next to the pain he would soon feel in his heart.

"Mora!" Putiwa called to her from the lodge. "Come quickly!"

Mora scrambled to her feet. She paused in the opening of the lodge, her hands clenched in nervous fists.

"I see her in shadow," Akoma said. "Mother stands there," he said, pointing at her.

Mora's throat tightened with the want to cry. Akoma was going to see again. How happy she was for that, but she also knew that when his vision returned, he would be instructed to seek a Panther woman as his wife. There was going to be discord between her son and her husband.

"Your medicine is powerful," she said to Putiwa.

The shaman lifted his head toward the thatch roof and called out in a tremulous voice. His song spun through the thatch and filled the lodge. He thanked the spirits and praised his medicine.

The skins from the recent hunt stretched across the village. Some were pulled tightly between trees and others were laced across frames with heavy thongs. The flesh from the kills dried on racks and grates over smoking fires as did whole gar and bass.

Kitchi tightened the lacing thongs, drawing the skin of the deer even more taut. There was little stretch left. The hide only had to dry out in the shade. This one she planned to cut into strips, fold and sew into parfleches. Bunta had given Ufala the kill. Ufala's family shared the meat, and Kitchi would give back handiwork made from the hide. On the outside of the parfleches she and her oldest daughters would paint designs.

Suddenly the sound of the conch horn sounded, calling the men to council. The women looked up, and the men left their tasks to gather about the central hearth.

Ufala grumbled, laying down the fish trap he worked on. It consisted of small branches bound into a funnel shape. When he finished it, Ufala could submerge it in the river and tie it to a nearby tree. After a day he would retrieve the trap and the fish caught inside. He was anxious to finish the trap to prove he could properly provide for his family while recovering from his wounds. Working with only one hand impeded and frustrated him. Now there was another interruption. He mumbled his exasperation as he walked to the central hearth.

As Ufala took his seat in the circle of men, Putiwa appeared in the center. The dry earth puffed up in small clouds about Putiwa's feet as he stomped, starting his dance. A veil of gray clay covered his face and black charcoal coated his lips. Three red lines striped each cheek, from cheekbone to jawbone. He wore a fox-skin cap with the animal's head dipping over his own forehead.

"*Ay yaaa yaaa,*" he sang, his voice vibrating. Knees

flexed, head wobbling to his rhythm, toe to the ground first, then heel, Putiwa danced about the circle. A large shell gorget thumped against his oiled chest.

Good news, Ufala thought. The shaman was thanking the spirits for giving him such good medicine. He was the link to the spirits and expressed the appreciation of the whole clan.

The women gathered at a distance to see what all the excitement was. They stayed back so as not to intrude, but they lingered close enough to hear.

Talli slipped through the crowd of women, working her way around the circle of men, catching glimpses of Putiwa as he sang and danced. Mora's face flickered into sight, then disappeared behind another woman. Talli edged forward, moving in the direction she had seen Mora.

Finally the shaman was quiet. There was a moment of whispering among the men, then silence. Yahga-ta moved to the center of the circle.

Talli leaned to the side to see better. Yahga-ta was smiling.

There was Mora, standing behind the men across the circle. She only caught a quick glimpse of her. Mora did not appear to be donning the same smile as the cacique.

"Akoma's vision is returning!" Yahga-ta announced. "Again the spirits have chosen to favor and succor him. He is the one who will lead us against the Ais. He is endowed with the spirits' blessing."

The men commented to one another. Finally there was something good amidst all this other, but still there was concern for Akoma's youth and inexperience.

"I hear what you say," Yahga-ta said. "I understand your apprehension. The Ais are strong, but so are the Jeaga. Akoma will bind the Panther and Turtle clans to make the Jeaga even stronger. He will take a Panther woman. Ramo must respect that."

Again the men commented to one another, and there was a muffled noise about the circle.

"Come forward, Ufala," Yahga-ta said. "Come so that all may see you."

Ufala stepped next to Yahga-ta.

"This man suffered at the hands of the Ais, as did many of us. He will carry the proof with him every day. Banabas saved his life, and Ufala wishes to repay him. In doing so, he will also assist in the bonding of the Turtle and Panther so we can stand against the enemy. If Ramo is the strange warrior in the Little Dove story, and the Ais the bear, then Ramo needs watching. He must have a tether of loyalty to the Jeaga. Ufala offers his eldest daughter to Banabas as a seal between the Turtle and Panther."

Talli felt the blood rushing from her head. She reeled backward.

". . . *break custom . . . new beginning* . . ." She heard pieces of what Yahga-ta was saying, but she could not comprehend it. What she did understand was that she had been offered to Banabas.

"No, no," she mumbled. And Akoma was to take a Panther woman. Custom was going to be broken, but not in the way she had prayed to the spirits. How could this be?

Talli backed away, then turned and ran. "Akoma. Akoma," she panted. She burst into the lodge where he lay.

"Akoma, did you know? Did you say yes to this plan?" she cried.

Akoma bolted upright. "What is it, Talli? What is wrong?"

"Your vision has returned, has it not?"

"Come closer, you are still a blur."

"Yahga-ta announced that you will take a Panther woman now that you are recovered. And I have been promised to Banabas!"

Talli's knees wobbled with weakness. Akoma stood and put his arms around her. "How have you heard this?"

"The men gather. Yahga-ta speaks."

Talli buried her head in his shoulder. The scent of his skin sent warm waves through her. She could never love another. This was the man . . . the only man.

"You will never be the woman of Banabas. Never!"

Talli sobbed. "I am afraid. I do not want to live if

these things Yahga-ta speaks of come to pass. My heart is yours, Akoma."

Akoma pulled her more tightly against him. His hand brushed down her back, smoothing her long dark hair against her skin.

Suddenly, Talli looked up at him. "You knew! You are not surprised." Her voice grew tinged with panic. "Did you agree, Akoma? Did you?"

12

"Come with me," Kitchi said.

Talli spun around. Her mother was in the doorway.

"You must leave at once before anyone else sees you here."

Talli reached for Akoma's hand and squeezed it. "How can all these promises be made?" she asked, her voice shaking.

"Come, now, Talli. We will talk, but first you must leave."

"I will go with you," Akoma said.

Kitchi was quick to respond. "Stay put. Let me speak with my daughter."

"I want to be with her," he said, running his hands down her upper arms.

"No," Kitchi said. "You will make things worse if you do that. It will be harder on Talli." Her voice softened. "Please, Akoma. If you love her, let her go quietly with me." She took her daughter's hand in hers. "Come."

Talli looked over her shoulder at Akoma. "I am yours," she whispered as her mother led her out of the lodge.

Kitchi took Talli behind the village, circling out of sight until they reached their shelter.

"Sit down, Talli. Let me talk," Kitchi began. "You are a special one, you know that. Our line has many obligations to the spirits. I cry that you suffer."

Talli looked at her mother, at the sadness in her eyes. A feeling of hopelessness swept over her. It was not going to matter what or how she felt, her future had been destined by the spirits even before she was conceived. She saw that clearly in her mother's face. Her stomach knotted. She stared at her mother, but Kitchi's eyes refused to meet her daughter's.

"Mother?" she said, her voice trembling. "There is no way to stop the promises Yahga-ta and father have made, is there?"

Kitchi's eyes pooled. She did not want to look. She knew what she would see. There was so much of herself in Talli . . . when she was young. They shared the same black eyes, the long fingers, the slender figure, the spirit that shone through. But all that had been worn out of Kitchi. After so long a time, her eyes had become dull, her fingers knobby and callused, her spirit broken.

"The Jeaga are a proud people," Kitchi said. "We are good people. The Ais will finish us, wash us from Mother Earth, and nothing will be left but our old bones. Ramo will aid the Ais. The pounding of his heart is not the drum of the Jeaga. Yahga-ta sees this. You are the hope of your people. And for all the girl children yet to come from our line, you may also be the hope. The spirits test us again."

Talli turned away. How she hated the affliction. How she resented it. If she became the woman of Banabas, sacrificed herself for her people, the spirits might end the affliction. She thought of Sassa and Nocatee. Even if she never had children, her sisters would, and somewhere down the line, another would suffer as she did.

"Your father comes," Kitchi said.

Talli watched the dust rise behind his heels. Why did the rains not come and quell the Ais and Ramo? But then she knew why. The drought, the Ais, Ramo, were all a part of the design to test her, to see if the debt incurred by her ancestor could be paid. No matter what she did or said, her destiny had been decided generations ago.

Suddenly Talli felt a sense of reconciliation.

Ufala broke a stick with the fingers of his good hand. He pitched a small piece away and poked the ground with the other as he squatted in front of Talli. "Do you hear Putiwa?" he asked.

In the distance she heard the shaman's song. She

looked in the direction of the quavering voice, seeing a narrow stream of reddish smoke curl into the air.

"He prays for the Turtle and all the Jeaga," Ufala said. "He prays for rain."

Talli nodded.

"He thanks the spirits for keeping their promises to the Jeaga."

Talli's stomach burned. "And you and Yahga-ta have made promises," she said. "Does he thank the spirits for that also?"

Ufala rocked back on his haunches. "I am honored to offer my daughter for such a worthy—"

Talli stood up. "The Jeaga cut my heart from my chest," she said. "My own clan butchers me."

Ufala spoke. "The promise has been made. I am a man of my word. You will not sully my honor." Ufala rose to his feet. "And you, woman," he said to his wife, "do not shame me. You will make our daughter's wedding garment with pride."

Talli tasted sourness in the back of her throat. Banabas was too old. He made her skin creep. How could her father have promised her to him?

Ufala lumbered away from the small hearth. Kitchi wiped her nose and sniffled.

"I will never let Banabas be my husband," Talli said. "They will call us husband and wife, but he will not lie with me. I will never allow the joining." Talli shuddered at her thoughts. No, she would never permit Banabas to crawl on her. She imagined she could hear him grunting, gasping, groaning, the way she heard her father in the night when he joined with her mother.

"Banabas will be sorry he asked for me. I will make him a miserable wife, and I will bear him no children. He will not have a wife that receives his manpart."

Kitchi could not believe her daughter's boldness. "That is a woman's duty to her husband. He provides for her and expects certain favors in return. He will throw you out."

"I would rather have no one. I hope he does throw me out. I will have fulfilled my obligation to the Jeaga and to the spirits by being his wife."

"You do not have to like it, Talli. He will beat you if you turn him from your bed. You must lie with him if you are his wife."

Again, Talli cringed, thinking about Banabas all sweaty and groping her. The thought disgusted her.

"Letting your husband have his way is not so intolerable. It does not take them long. It keeps the peace."

Talli shook her head, part in admiration for her mother and part in pity. She could never be like Kitchi. "No!" Talli blurted out. "I will not do it, and I will tell Banabas so."

Kitchi watched her daughter walk away. Even as an infant Talli had been strong willed. She feared for her. Ufala would not tolerate being embarrassed by her stubbornness.

Sassa came and sat next to her mother.

"You heard?" Kitchi asked.

"Some," Sassa answered. "Where is Talli?"

"She has gone off. Your sister does not think. There is so much at risk."

The moonlight danced between the thatch, needles of it like pinpricks inside the lodge.

Talli brushed her shoulder and turned on her mat. She was sweaty and glad she awakened from her bad dream.

"Talli."

It was a soft whisper accompanied by a light tapping on her shoulder. Talli opened her eyes.

"Nocatee, what is it? Come," she said, making room for the little one on her mat.

"Talli, Sassa is gone."

Talli sat up and looked around. Sassa's mat was empty. Kitchi slept soundly and Ufala snored. "Where did she go?" she asked.

Nocatee shrugged. "There," she said, pointing outside. "I woke up and saw her leaving."

Talli gathered a skin around her shoulders. The night air was chilly. The season had quickly turned. "Wait here," she said. "Do not awaken Mother or Father."

Talli ducked through the lodge opening and went out into the night. What could Sassa be doing? She knew the customs. "Sassa," she called softly, not wanting to wake anyone.

There was no answer. Talli slipped through the shadows, her eyes searching for the silhouette of her sister. Any other time, Talli would have been concerned about wandering the village in the night. She obeyed the customs. Now, suddenly, it did not seem to matter . . . except for Sassa. She did not want any unpleasant consequences for her sister.

Talli weaved through the village, inspecting every shadow that could be Sassa. Putiwa sat alone by his fire, his chanting nearly a whisper.

Talli backed against the rough trunk of a cypress. Across the village she caught a glimpse of a silhouette moving toward the path to the river. Sassa.

Talli moved behind the village shelters and trekked through the brush, the cool ferns swiping her legs, the lacy leaves of the cypress brushing her hair. The blackness seemed to thicken as she left the shimmer of the central hearth behind.

Near the river's edge, Talli called again. "Sassa, are you there?"

"Go back, Talli."

Talli moved toward her sister's voice until she could finally make her out. Her younger sister sat huddled, splashing water on herself. "You should not be about, Sassa. And there is danger this close to the river when you cannot see. What are you doing? What is wrong?"

"Stay back. Do not come close!" Sassa's voice trembled with what sounded like both fear and crying.

13

"Sassa, what is it?"

"Please, Talli, go away."

Sassa vigorously splashed water on her legs, then backed away.

"Talk to me, sister. Tell me what is wrong."

"No. I cannot. I cannot."

Talli shook her head and walked closer. "Sassa, what makes you afraid of me?"

"It is not you, Talli. I am not afraid of you," she sobbed.

"Be still," Talli said, coming closer.

"Oh, Talli," Sassa cried, wrapping her arms around herself.

Talli came in front of Sassa, reached out and embraced her. "You are so cold."

Sassa whimpered into Talli's shoulder.

Suddenly, Talli's eyes fluttered, and she felt her sister's fear run like frigid water down her spine. Then came the heaviness in her belly, the dull ache, the cramping.

"Sassa, you have your moon cycle. Is that it? You have your first moon cycle?"

Sassa cried out loud, and Talli stroked her back.

"Do not tell Mother. Tell no one!"

"But you are a woman! That is something to be proud of. Why does this upset you?"

Sassa pulled back. "I do not want to be a woman. I heard Father has promised you to Banabas. He will promise me to someone also. Someone old and ugly."

"Oh, Sassa," Talli said, brushing her sister's hair back from her face. "That will not happen."

Sassa rubbed her nose. "What about your dreams,

Talli? A woman can have no dreams, that is what I see. A woman carries the responsibility of the clan, doing whatever is best for the husband or the clan, never for herself. I see how unhappy Mother is . . . and you. I do not want to be a woman. I am not ready."

"Come back from the river's edge and we will sit and talk," Talli said.

They sat on the fern-covered ground. Sassa lay back, one hand beneath her head, staring at the night sky. "The fires of our ancestors burn so brightly tonight."

"They have much to think about," Talli said.

Sassa turned to her side and propped up on one elbow. "Will you forget Akoma? Do you think with time he will fade from your heart?"

"I cannot imagine how that would happen. He is a part of me."

"I am sorry you will never be his woman, sister. If I were a spirit, I would see that you were together."

Talli stared into the darkness. Her eyes did not blink.

"What are you thinking, Talli?"

Talli turned to her sister and her face lifted into a smile. "Maybe I will be Akoma's . . . in a special way."

"Akoma's woman? Maybe you will be his? How? That cannot be. You will belong to Banabas."

Talli again seemed in deep thought, far away. She was silent and still for a moment.

Sassa smiled empathetically. "You truly are fanciful, sister."

Talli finally gathered herself and focused on Sassa. "Did you bring your strap?"

Just after the birth of a daughter, the new mother made a strap that would catch the daughter's moon blood when the girl came of age. Every girl had a pouch that contained special articles, including the moon-cycle leather strap. Kitchi had made one for each of her daughters.

"No," Sassa said. "I do not have it with me. I did not want anyone to know."

"Well, it is easier hidden with the strap than having the moon blood trickle down your legs."

Sassa laughed weakly.

"You do have to tell, Sassa. This is not something you should hide. Have you not heard the story of how once a girl did not tell of her moon and her family was struck by lightning?"

Sassa gestured that she had heard. "But I do not want to be alone . . . secluded."

"It is the way."

"Here," Sassa said, touching her lower abdomen. "There is pain. Is something wrong with me?"

"No, dear sister. It is the Grandmother spirits preparing you for womanhood. Childbirth. I will brew you a tea made from maidenhair. The medicine will relieve some of the discomfort. Now, look at the moon. When the moon appears in the same shape again, your cycle will come with it. Women are a part of the moon. The moon is the female Great Spirit. Before we came to Mother Earth, we dwelt with the moon and the stars."

"It would be nice if we could remember those days among the hearth fires of our ancestors," Sassa said.

"That is why we have the stories. Without the stories told from one generation to the next we would not know many things."

"I feel more like a woman already. My eyes have opened. I thought I knew all. I have heard the women talk. And you and Mother. But now I know I am just discovering—"

"And you will keep on discovering and learning all your life." Talli touched her sister's cheek. "Let us return. I will prepare the maidenhair tea and find some packing for your strap."

"Can we wait and tell Mother in the morning?"

"It will wait until dawn," Talli answered.

Bunta slapped Ufala on the back. "Two daughters nearly eligible for marriage!"

Ufala laughed heartily.

"Your daughter is prepared," Kitchi said, coming out of the lodge. "Tell Putiwa."

Ufala and Bunta wandered off as Sassa emerged from the lodge, wearing about her head a narrow hide band edged with fringe. Talli followed with Nocatee.

Young girls gathered close, hearing the news early that morning that Sassa was on her first moon. It was an exciting event.

"Can I run with her?" Nocatee asked.

"Yes," Kitchi answered. "But do not overtake Sassa or you will grow old before she does."

Sassa looked to the east, the direction she would run this morning and each of the next four mornings while in seclusion. A place marked by the grandmothers indicated the spot she should stop and return to the village. The young girls who had not yet entered their moon were permitted to run with the new menstruant. The men would watch from a distance and congratulate Ufala.

Putiwa came from behind them. "I have chosen Nanta to tend to you Sassa."

Nanta, one of the oldest grandmothers of the village, hobbled behind Putiwa. She listed to one side, the weight of the basket in her hand keeping her off balance.

"It is a good choice," Kitchi agreed. She liked Nanta and respected her wisdom. Nanta had lived a long time and would provide good instruction for her daughter.

Putiwa planted his medicine stick in the ground. The shells that dripped from the stick's crest tinkled with the movement.

"Mother Moon has given her daughter. Sassa is a woman. Father Sun wishes to welcome her. Go and present yourself to him."

For the next four days, Sassa stayed in the isolation lodge. It was a special shelter, west of the village, reserved for those who experienced their first moon cycle.

Sassa was given a hollow, bird leg bone through which she drank the unique teas Nanta brewed. As Sassa sipped each new tea, Nanta told her the stories, the legends and tales passed from one generation of women to the next.

On the second day, after the morning run to the east to present herself to Father Sun, Sassa went to the river where Nanta waited for her.

"There is a chill in the air this morning," Nanta said.

"Each morning the air is cooler. Winter is coming." There was a grimace on her face.

"Do you dislike the winter, Nanta?"

"Mmm," she answered, wading into the water with Sassa. "The cold season is not a good one for the old ones or the very young. But that is the spirits' way."

Sassa shivered as she sank into the water, then leaned her head back, spilling a wealth of luxurious black hair into the water.

Between her palms, Nanta lathered the sweet smelling paste she'd made to wash Sassa's hair. Every morning while Sassa was in isolation, the washing of her hair with this special emulsion was a ritual.

It was prepared from sweet flowers of the deep lilac lobelia, and blue day-flower, fruit of the tallowood, then mixed with fat, ash, and lime slaked from shells. The blending of the recipe's ingredients was as much a part of the custom as the deed. Nanta had said the grandmothers' prayers while she made it. She'd leaned her head over the bowl and thought the saddest of thoughts to bring about tears, one of the most important elements of the solution. She watched her tears drip into the concoction. And then she'd made herself think of the happiest times, while she held her hands above the bowl. And finally, she said the prayers.

"I wonder why the spirits choose their ways sometimes," Nanta said, laying her hands on Sassa's crown. "Now that I have the wisdom of age, I am too old to do anything with it. I have spent a lifetime learning, understanding, and now my body does not allow me to do the things I want. Nor do I have the burning passion for things I once did. The spirits prepare me to pass on. Mysteries. So many mysteries."

Nanta rubbed the paste through Sassa's hair as she sang the traditional cleansing song. Sassa kept her eyes closed, breathing in the aroma, listening to Nanta's scratchy voice.

"I told my sister I did not want to be a woman," Sassa said. "Men boast of all their responsibilities. They are proud and speak so boldly, but I believe it is the women who carry the burden of the welfare of the People."

"You speak like the youth," Nanta said, smiling and running her fingers deep to Sassa's scalp. "Always questioning tradition."

Sassa laughed. "You are the one who just told me you wondered about the spirits' ways."

Nanta bound Sassa's hair into a thick cord and wrung out the water. "No respect for their elders, either," she said.

Sassa turned to look at the old woman, worrying that she had offended her, but Nanta was grinning.

"Come," Nanta said. "Putiwa probably awaits you already. Remember to walk with your head down," Nanta reminded her.

Nanta was right. Putiwa sat in the opening of the isolation lodge, a basket next to him. In his hand he held a bundle of slow-burning green pine needles.

Inside, Nanta dried Sassa's hair with a soft, hairless deerskin.

"Coontie for you to grind," Putiwa said, handing her a basket of the root. "For fertility," he said. "You will give forth many children."

Sassa took the basket filled with the coontie root and sat it next to her.

"Today I speak of the power of a woman," Putiwa said. He sat cross-legged, back straight. When he moved his arms, the shell bracelets tinkled. Putiwa waved the smoldering pine bundle, swirling the smoke around his head. It was pungent, and when the wisps of gray wafted her way, Sassa's eyes teared.

"To purify you," he said, taking the pine bundle and moving it about Sassa, beginning above her head and slowly working his way to the floor. The smoke swirled with each wave of his hand. He chanted with his eyes closed. Sassa did not understand the words, if indeed they were words. Putiwa's chants and songs were often of the old tongue, a language spoken to the spirits by medicine men for generations. There was an eerie lilt to his voice, a voice that seemed to come not from his throat, but from deeper inside, and definitely inspired by a mystical force.

Putiwa opened his eyes and withdrew a nodule of red

ochre from his pouch. He pressed the ochre to Sassa's forehead, then drew a line down the center of her face, over her nose and lips, to the jaw line of her chin. "Red," he said. "The color of the east, the place of the sun. Red, the color of the sacred fire, the color of blood. Life."

Sassa watched him put away the ochre, then rub his index finger in the fallen pine ash.

"White," Putiwa said. "The color of the south. Peace. Warmth. Happiness." Deftly feeling the bones of her face, he drew a white streak across each of her cheekbones.

Putiwa did not speak of the west, the color black, the place of the dead. Nor did he mention the north, the color blue, the color of defeat and distress. He painted her only with the good colors.

"The time of womanhood has come to you," he said. "With such status come all the rights, privileges, and duties. Listen and learn the lessons Nanta teaches you. Sew and do basketry. Prepare the coontie. Do a woman's work all day."

Sassa stared as Putiwa reached into the pouch again and this time withdrew a quahog shell. "At dusk each of the next three days, rub this shell across your lips. This will keep you from becoming a troublesome woman, a gossip."

He handed her the shell. She felt the rough ridges that banded the large clam shell and wondered if her lips would become raw.

"Why is everyone so afraid of moon blood?" Sassa asked.

Putiwa looked at the face of the young girl. He thought for a moment before answering. "A woman on her moon is feared not because the blood is bad, but because the blood is so powerful. Think about these things. If you touch a man's weapon, it will fail him the next time he uses it. If you eat with others, their food will become rancid. You cannot touch a medicine bundle during your moon cycle or all its magic is gone. If you do touch a man's weapon, the animals will smell the moon blood and they will flee. You may walk no hunt trails or they will become contaminated. And the first moon cycle is the most powerful of all. Do you understand?''

"Yes," Sassa answered.

"Good. This is a time of celebration. Be joyful."

What was so wonderful about this? Sassa questioned. She felt unclean all the time, she was quick to tears, her belly pained, and she was segregated and feared. She saw nothing to celebrate.

The shaman brushed the pine ash into a pile. Skillfully he urged it onto a seagrape leaf. He rolled the leaf closed, folding in the ends, then tied it closed with a thin piece of sinew. He handed it to Nanta for inclusion in her next tea.

14

Ramo poised himself on a deadfall that extended into the nut-brown water of the river. Here, the lily pad-thickened water seeped through cypress stands. The Panther cacique motioned for Banabas to come closer.

Banabas slapped at a mosquito as he crept under the tendrils of airplants that hung from the trees like the gray curls of an old woman's hair.

"There," Ramo said, pointing down the bank at the thick body of a sunning alligator.

"He is a big one," Banabas whispered. The creature was large, larger than a man, perhaps the length of two Jeaga men. The scutes on his back, the heavy armor of bone plates, collected the heat of the sun and stored it for the cooler night.

Ramo backed off the log onto the shore. He and Banabas stole through the thicket of grass and trees along the river toward the alligator.

Close to the creature, Ramo and Banabas raised their long poles. Ramo grunted loudly, simulating the bellow of a male alligator, tearing the animal out of its tranquility. The alligator swung its head around to see where the noise came from.

As close as he was, Banabas could see the algae that grew in sparse patches on the alligator's black hide. Yes, this was an old one, indeed. Banabas felt a fleeting flash of sympathy for the creature, having lived so long only to be killed in his old age. Then, as the massive alligator opened its mouth and hissed like the wind through the trees in a summer thunderstorm, the two men launched their poles down its throat, rendering the large-toothed jaws useless.

"Watch the tail!" Banabas shouted as the creature swung the heavy-muscled tail at them. One swipe could bring them both down, snapping a man's leg bone with a direct hit.

Ramo whooped with the thrill of the danger. "Flip him," he yelled.

Banabas released his pole, as Ramo jammed his even deeper. Banabas cautiously approached the alligator, grabbed its head and neck, and with a powerful torque, forced the creature onto its back, exposing its soft pale belly. Quickly Banabas drove his knife through the skin, then thrust upward, slashing the creature open.

The alligator thrashed, and Banabas jumped clear. The animal's entrails flagged out of the gash, blood spilling across the soggy earth, seeping into the soil, and trailing into the river. Ramo fought to control his pole. Then one last time, when the alignment was perfect, he thrust the rod, feeling it tear through more of the animal's gullet. The reptile convulsed. Then finally its eyes stared blankly, like dull, dark stones.

Banabas and Ramo sat on the ground, their breathing heavy from the struggle.

"He was too easy," Ramo said. "We were too much for even such a large one."

Banabas glanced at the dead creature, then at his own chest and arms which were smeared with the alligator's blood. "He was old," Banabas said. "Tired."

"Like you?" Ramo said, rearing back with a deep chuckle.

Ramo was right. Banabas felt the tightness in his back muscles. He *was* getting old. When he was younger, he could take on five of these creatures, one after the other, and never feel any aches or tiredness in his body. When had it happened? he wondered. When had he started walking instead of running? What day had his stomach gone flaccid instead of hard? What morning had he awakened to find cobbles of bone gnarling his finger joints? He didn't remember, and yet there it was. He looked at his hands. At just what moment had his body decided he was no longer a young man?

He was lucky his manpart still worked, he thought. At

least he knew it did when he slept sometimes, becoming so stiff that it awakened him, occasionally erupting with great ecstasy. And in the early hours it was often hard. He wondered how it would be with a woman. He had not been with a woman in a long time. Would his man-part work as it should? He thought of Talli, the delicate line of her neck, the gentle upswell of her breasts, the splendid curve of her hips. How might it be to nestle in her hair, touch her body, feel the dampness of her skin, stroke all those gentle smooth arches and indentations? There was a pulsing in his groin and a rush of warmth, even a small bit of swelling. That was a good sign, even though the response was not the same as when he was young. Just the thought of a woman used to make his manpart grow large and hard instantly. Now it took more coaxing.

"He is done bleeding," Ramo said, nudging the alligator with his foot. "Gut him."

Banabas opened the belly slit from throat to tail and cleaned the animal out while Ramo watched.

"Ufala has promised Talli to me," Banabas said, wiping his knife on the grass, then swirling it in the water.

Ramo lifted a brow. "Really."

"I have had an eye for her for a long time."

Ramo did not smile. "That has been evident."

"It will be a good union," Banabas said.

Ramo breathed out. "There may come a time the Panther and Turtle are in opposition."

"But we are all Jeaga," Banabas said. "One people."

"Times are changing, my friend. We must look out for ourselves. We cannot spend all our time worrying about our brothers or we may perish. As I have said before, we are thinning and have an inept defense against the Ais because we are so dissected. We must not sleep without one eye on the enemy."

Banabas sheathed his knife and stood up. "I am Jeaga first and then Panther."

"Of course," Ramo said. "Tell me, friend, if we can bind the two clans, do you not see how powerful we may become? Panther and Turtle as one!"

"And who will lead? Who will be the cacique? Yahga-ta is a strong cacique. His son, if he recovers, has his father's charisma and the skills it takes to be a good leader. He has the trust of his people."

Ramo rested his hand on Banabas's shoulder. "When the Turtle and Panther become one, we will need a vigorous, enthusiastic cacique. Someone with vision and the energy and determination to see the vision come to be."

"You speak of yourself, do you not? You see yourself as the leader of this consolidation."

Ramo's teeth gleamed in the sunlight as his lips broke apart in a smile. "And you as the war chief, my closest adviser. You will have great power, Banabas. Think of it. Not the Ais nor any other will be stronger than the Panther."

Banabas flinched. Ramo did not mention Turtle, he only referred to Panther. Did he see the Panther swallowing the Turtle and becoming a new, separate nation? If not Jeaga, then what?

"The thought intrigues you," Ramo said, noticing Banabas's concentration. "The river and its bounty will belong to us. We will multiply and spread along its banks." Ramo stared in the distance.

"I see the advantage in unification, Cacique, but I have my concerns."

Ramo sneered. "Doubts? Concerns?"

"For your plan to work, the unification must be a decision made by both the Turtle and the Panther. Both must want this. That is where I see the difficulty. Will Yahga-ta or his son wish to hand over all power to you, Ramo? How do you plan to bring that about?"

"You will see," Ramo said, one corner of his mouth turned up, his eyes alight. "Stand by me, friend, and you will be rewarded."

Ufala pinned his long black-and-silver hair to the back of his head with two raccoon bones. One stringy hank fell loose and he cursed it when he felt it swish along his cheek. He removed the pins and started over.

Ufala twisted his hair into a long rope, and then knotted it. He took one of the bones and shoved it through the tuft of hair. He anchored it with the other bone. He moved his head from side to side, testing the security. Satisfied, he fastened a raccoon tail to wave down the back of his neck when he walked. Tonight he offered a feast to the clan. Sassa was of age. He would also use this occasion to announce the betrothal of his eldest daughter to Banabas. This would be a most glorious evening. Every man of the village would forget about Ufala's maimed arm and see only his good fortune. He would be held in high esteem again.

At last he placed a large oval shell necklace about his neck. The gleaming mother-of-pearl was the perfect complement to his oiled, sun-browned chest.

"You are handsome, husband," Kitchi said. She wore a necklace of pierced freshwater pearls and red seeds. She also adorned herself with wooden ear-plugs inlaid with tortoise shell. Her lips shone with oil.

Ufala turned and looked at her. He appeared stunned as he saw her standing in the dusky light, as if he had not seen her for a long time. His mouth slightly opened.

"What is it, Ufala?"

He didn't answer. He shook his head and groped his right arm as he would an aching muscle. "Where is Talli?" he finally asked.

Kitchi turned away in disappointment. For an instant she thought she saw something in Ufala's eyes she had not seen since Climbing Bear's death. She had learned to do without those looks, to be numb to his indifference. But now, suddenly, with only the briefest of reminders, the flash in his black eyes, the way he looked at her for just that transient moment, old emotions had come flooding back. She missed her *husband*.

"She was here a moment ago," Kitchi answered. "I will send Sassa to find her."

"No! Sassa cannot be about. She is to be presented at the feast, not before." Ufala passed by his wife as he exited the lodge.

Where was her oldest daughter? Kitchi wondered. She would not dare seek Akoma. Would she?

Kitchi felt her skin prickle.

*   *   *

"Leave me," Akoma told his mother.

"But you are weak. You have not done much walking until now."

"I want to be alone, to thank the spirits for my recovery."

"Do not be long, my son. Yahga-ta is anxious to show the clan how you have recovered. He wants to reassure them his son is strong enough to become the next cacique."

"I understand," Akoma said.

Mora looked back once at her son as she returned to the village. She had accompanied Akoma into the wood. Yahga-ta would have disapproved, she thought. But Akoma had persuaded her. He needed the comfort of the earth, and he needed to express his thanks in a private sacred place, amongst the trees and birds, and the dark, rich loam. But he did not want his mother with him when he entered the place he and Talli thought of as their own.

Akoma proceeded alone. As he approached the special place, he paused. Someone was there. His vision was good, but the brush obscured what he could see.

Quietly, Akoma crept through the brush.

15

"Akoma," Talli whispered.

Akoma listened. Had he heard someone call his name?

In a moment he saw Talli moving through the brush.

Akoma embraced her. "I have missed you," he said into her hair, taking great handfuls and pushing his fingers through. "I cannot let you go. Banabas will not have you."

"How? I do not see any way." She looked up into his face and touched his cheek. "I will never be his . . . his woman. I will never allow him to lie with me."

Akoma pulled her close. "No. We will leave this place. We only need each other. I will take you away."

Talli's hand cupped the back of his head as she leaned into his shoulder. "We are chosen by the spirits. The Jeaga are threatened, and we are the answer. We are instruments of the peace that will be. And Ufala will regain what he thinks he has lost in stature."

"Ramo is the cause of all this."

"Everyone fears what he might do, but I have come to realize our fate is the spirits' design, not man's. Our task in life was decided before we were even born. There is nothing we can do to stop that. You were born to be the cacique, the leader of the great Turtle, to stand firm against the Ais. I was born to seal a peace between two Jeaga clans, so the Jeaga do not destroy themselves."

Akoma nuzzled in her hair. "But it is so wrong, Talli. Why would the spirits show us each other, let us feel like this just to take it away?"

"So we understand how important these things are that we must do. You will always be in my heart." She held his face in her hands. "The spirits want us to know each other. They do not deny us altogether. They have permitted us to love one another. They have given us a little time." Her voice softened. "We should not forsake this gift offered us." She paused a moment, searching his dark eyes. "I am to be Akoma's woman. It is meant to be."

Akoma touched his mouth to hers. His hand smoothed her hair against her back, then trailed on to the curve of her waist and crest of her hip. "Talli," he said, before exploring the sweet depths of her mouth again.

His tenderness, in the way he held her, touched her, his fingertips radiating his love, brought an unexpected stinging and welling to Talli's eyes. In a moment his hand was on her cheek, brushing away the tears.

Akoma eased her to the ground, cradling her as if she were something so precious and fragile he feared she might shatter.

His body was sleek and rippled with muscle. When the length of his legs came against hers, and the sheer hardness of all of him pressed against her, Talli wrapped her arms about him.

Akoma held a fistful of her hair, pulling it to the back of her neck.

She could feel his strength, and sensed the power constrained in his body. Since she had become a woman, this was the first time she *felt* like a woman . . . a woman in her lover's arms.

There would always be only Akoma, never anyone else.

Talli fought for air, taking great deep breaths. The heated cover of his body absorbed all the energy that flowed from her.

At his entry, she flinched. There was a quick piercing sensation inside her.

Akoma raised himself and looked at her.

"No," she whispered and pulled him back. "I am yours."

His tenderness was now tempered with raw urgency. A burst of breath came from him as he entered her again. All the sensations, his hands, his mouth, this fullness inside her, the warmth of his skin, the dewy sweat that broke out on his back, the intensity of his movement, overwhelmed her. Now she realized the affliction was also a gift, not just a burden. She was with him, feeling what he felt. How wonderful it was to feel the exquisite pleasure she was giving to him. The earth went dark, the world silent. There was only Akoma and this incredible feeling of completion.

Akoma stiffened, then fell against her. Talli shuddered and gasped. Her body was fantastically languid and content. She was certain not everyone was fortunate enough to love this way.

Talli held him close and still. She wanted to rock him as she rocked her baby sister, wanted to spread her love to him with every part of her body, melt him into her.

She stroked the back of his head, felt his mouth on her shoulder, and the gloriously heavy crush of his body. She never wanted to move. This was as close as you could get to another person. They were one.

.The sound of the brush moving interrupted her reverie and brought her harshly back to the world where she was going to have to give him up, live her life without him. For an instant she feared they had been discovered. But then she realized she didn't care. Had she not already told everyone this was the man who was in her heart, and they had denounced it? No one could take this moment from her. The spirits gave it.

She closed her eyes and waited to hear an outburst. But no one was there.

"I'm sorry, Talli," Akoma said slowly.

"Why? It is what I wanted."

"I thought only of me. Feeling you so close, I did not stop to think of you."

Talli trailed one finger down his back. "It will give me a memory to last a lifetime."

"But there was nothing for you. . . . I—"

"Shh." She wanted to tell him her secret so he would know that she had experienced everything he had. But she knew if he had knowledge of her affliction, it would be an unfair burden. She breathed in the scent of his skin. "You have given me more than I could ask for . . .

to be with you this way. I am complete. I *am* Akoma's woman."

His mouth again sought hers, this time delicately, sweetly as if tasting flower nectar. He moved to her side and onto his back, enfolding her with his arm so her head rested on his shoulder.

Akoma stared at the canopy of trees above him. His eyes hardened, and Talli knew he must have been thinking of their separation and Banabas.

"I told you I will never join with Banabas," she said. She sighed and snuggled against him. "See how we were meant to be," she said. "My body fits perfectly against yours. Your shoulder holds my head just so." She smiled and ran her hand over his chest.

Being so close, Akoma's thoughts and emotions flooded her. He would deny his destiny to be with her. He would leave the Jeaga and take her away. That was what he was thinking and feeling. Talli knew if he did not accept his destiny, one day, long from now, after the Jeaga fell to the Ais, he would question himself. No matter how much he loved her, there would always be that haunting guilt of failing the People. She wanted him to have no shadows in his heart.

Talli lifted her head so she could see him. Akoma started to speak, but Talli put her finger over his lips to silence him. "Do not make this too hard for me, Akoma. I know what must be and have resigned myself to it. If you object, I will fall apart. If you love me—"

Akoma rocked his head back and held her close.

Talli broke away and forced a smile. She feathered a finger over his lips. "The Turtle will have the finest cacique," she said. "It is you who will enable the Jeaga to survive. For generations the People will speak of Akoma, the grand cacique who led the Jeaga against the Ais. I will forever be proud that I am Akoma's woman. Even if no one else knows, I will."

Akoma took her hand in his and pressed his lips to her forehead.

Talli rested her head against his chest and closed her eyes. She wanted Akoma to keep some small hidden place in his heart that would belong only to her. "When you are an old man I hope you will remember this time we had," she said. "Do not ever forget. Do not forget me."

"Never," he answered.

"Watch me," Ufala said to his youngest daughter. He held a stick eye level and looked down it. "This is willow. But it is not straight enough," he said, holding it up to Nocatee's eyes. "See how it bends. This stick will not make a good arrow shaft."

Nocatee took the stick from him and inspected it herself. She nodded.

Ufala had cut the shafts during early summer and left them in the shade to dry out. Those he cut during other seasons seemed to dry straighter, but if he left the summer shafts in the shade, they did not crack or split as much. The best shafts were cut during the cold season. When the air chilled, he would show Nocatee how to choose the right wood.

"Try this one," he said, taking another stick from the bundle.

Nocatee held it up to her eye. "I think it is straight," she said.

Ufala examined the stick. "Umm," he uttered, looking down the wood shaft. "I believe you are right," he said. "We will cut this one."

Ufala held the stick against his forearm and measured to the end of his index finger. From that point he measured one more finger's length. "This is where we will cut it," he said.

As Ufala took his knife to the stick, Kitchi came up and took Nocatee's hand. "Why do you teach your daughter such things?" she asked. "She is not Climbing Bear."

Ufala scored the willow with his knife, not answering.

"Come Nocatee, we have preparations."

Ufala did not look up as he spoke. "I will show you how to cut the nock later," he said.

Kitchi led Nocatee away to help her prepare for the feast.

* * *

At dusk Putiwa draped himself in an array of elaborate skins and feathers. Shells dangled and tinkled around his ankles, wrists, neck, and waist. Radiating about his neck was a cowl of blue heron feathers. Fox and raccoon skins covered his head, with the fox face dipping over his forehead, the nose of the animal resting between the shaman's eyebrows. He polished his face with fish oil so he would gleam in the firelight.

Putiwa watched the hackberry tree, waiting for the right moment. At last when the moon rose between the two branches he had decorated with paints and shells and feathers, he entered the center of the village. His song issued the call for all to gather.

The people of the Turtle village collected about the central hearth and the man of the spirits.

Putiwa spoke, telling the legend of the Jeaga creation. "Our elders say the People were born out of the ground, coming up through the mouth of the Earth like ants. In those days they lived far to the west, where Earth jutted up to the sky like a giant backbone. There," he said, pointing to the northwest. "Earth became angry and ate many of her children. Those that were left journeyed toward the sunrise. In those days they had no clothing and no fire, but as they traveled, they learned herbal knowledge, how to cover themselves, and about fire. Then the Master of Breath spoke to the People, telling them that first the Earth was created. The second thing created was water, the third the trees and grass, and the fourth the things having life. All things, even the smallest, were created. Then the Master of Breath sent a great fog onto earth. The People could not see and wandered about in fear, calling out. They separated into small groups, and those groups stayed together, afraid to live alone. Finally, the Master of Breath felt compassion and began to blow away the fog. As the air cleared, the groups clung to one another and were joyful. They turned to each other and swore loyalty. They became as close as brothers and sisters. This was the beginning of the clans."

At the end of the tale, the people raised their voices in cheers and praise for the Turtle.

Yahga-ta came to the central hearth. As everyone noticed him, they hushed. When it was quiet, Yahga-ta said, "What Putiwa has said is so. That is how the Turtle and the Panther came to be. And the Deer, and Alligator, Wind, and Bear. All are Jeaga. Only the Master of Breath could separate the People. It is as it should be. The Turtle clan fights to keep the Jeaga spirit alive."

Yahga-ta turned, swinging his arm in a wide arc. "Akoma, come forward."

Talli strained to see through the crowd. Akoma came out of the darkness to stand next to his father. The crowd roared. Akoma was well! The spirits showed the Turtle clan great favor!

The firelight danced on Akoma's body, and Talli became transfixed, gazing at his image, recalling the afternoon. Her body flushed. He was wonderful to look at: strong jaw, black-as-charcoal eyes, hair black and shiny as the blackbird's feathers, muscular body, confident stature, and a gentleness she alone knew. Yes, he would be a fine cacique.

Yahga-ta's words tore at her heart.

"My son will lead us against the Ais. He has the youth, the new blood, and the energy to defeat the enemy. From the Panther he will choose a wife, one of a noble lineage. Together they will create the new generation of Turtle and Panther, a living bond of loyalty."

Talli felt her eyes fill with tears. Children! She had not thought of him having a child with someone else. They had often spoken of the children they wanted to have. She had promised him many strong and wise sons, and he had begged for at least one girl child that would look like her.

Talli swept her hand over her face and dug her fingers into the hair at her forehead. There was a sudden sick feeling inside her. She backed away and searched the crowd, looking at all their expressions. The people were smiling, their eyes filled with hope.

Ufala stood next to Putiwa, Yahga-ta, and Akoma. He said, "The peaceful understanding between the Turtle and Panther is a complex thing. Ramo is strong, a powerful leader with some strange ideas. Banabas, his closest adviser, is my friend. To him I have offered my eldest, Talli. He accepts. This will be a tether between the two clans and will influence the advice Banabas gives Ramo."

As soon as Ufala announced that Talli was promised to Banabas, the crowd stirred.

A man with a scar that ran down his leg from knee to ankle called out. "Ufala is a noble man!"

They cheered Ufala for his dedication and loyalty to the clan. Ufala's mouth twitched with the desire to smile.

Talli left the crowd and returned to the shelter, where Kitchi and Sassa gathered the last of the food to be brought to the central hearth.

"I think it is time," Talli said. "Father has told them I am promised to Banabas. He will offer the invitation to feast on his food next."

"He is proud to be the father of another girl that has become a woman. But most of all, he feels great pride that he was able to provide so much food, considering his arm. This is a good night for him," Kitchi said.

Talli didn't respond.

16

Banabas followed the marriage customs hoping Talli would soften to the ideas of marrying him. His obligation was to prove his skills as a provider before Ufala could accept the proposal for Talli. Banabas skinned deer and rabbit and gave Kitchi the pelts. He brought game from the hunt to Ufala, and in the Panther village he built a lodge. Ufala traveled there to appraise it. He told Banabas that he and Kitchi approved of the marriage and Banabas could have Talli as his wife.

Another cycle of the moon passed and the air was now crisp every morning, and damp and chilly at night. During the daylight, if one stood in the sun, there was warmth. But beneath the trees or on the water, especially when the wind blew, the air was uncomfortably cold. Still there was no rain and the earth dried out. Heavy concern enveloped the village.

Talli stood in shadows just inside her lodge. At first she had shivered, but soon there was a glowing coal of heat inside her. Kitchi stood behind Talli, chattering about the tasks of a wife. Talli wasn't listening. In a moment Banabas would come to the lodge and Ufala would accept his gifts in exchange for her.

Talli's stomach churned.

"You look beautiful," Sassa said.

Talli whipped around to face her sister. "No!" she said. "I do not feel beautiful."

Kitchi stroked her daughter's hair. The long braided strand, woven with beads and glistening shells, hung to Talli's shoulder. Sassa pushed it back so it trailed down her sister's back.

"You have not spoken much this day," Kitchi said.

Talli stared blankly. There was nothing to say. She could complain, but it would do no good. If she cried, her mother and sisters might cry also. She could express her deep love for Akoma, but that too would only do harm. There was nothing good to say. There were no good feelings inside her. So she remained silent. But deep within, she felt heated anger. She fought to keep the rage from rising out of her. The anger scorched the pit of her belly, and when it burned she felt the hotness surge all the way up into her face. She knew Akoma would recognize her frustration and outrage, and that would make his acceptance of their fate even more difficult for him . . . especially this day. She had to contain all her emotions, for the sake of everyone else. She wanted to scream, to rip the soft deer-hide cape from her shoulders and tear the shells and beads from her hair.

Talli swallowed and pressed her nails into her palms until the urge subsided to a more controllable level. If she were being tested, the spirits would not be disappointed. Maybe, if she did this right, Nocatee's and Sassa's children and their children would be forever free of the affliction. Perhaps she would indeed end it all. For that reason, and for Akoma, she wanted to be strong. There was one other reason she had to keep control. No one would see her cry. No one would see her lose her dignity.

"I would like some water," Talli said.

Nocatee was quick to bring her sister a ladle of water.

Talli sipped. Her head jerked up when she heard her father's voice. He greeted Banabas.

Nocatee kissed the top of Talli's hand, then hugged her thigh. "You will visit me?" she asked.

Talli bent over and brushed her hands along Nocatee's cheeks. "You know that I will. Am I not your sister?"

Nocatee smiled, but Sassa's face contorted.

"I will make certain the most handsome of the Panther come to visit," Talli said to Sassa. "I will tell them your name so they look for you." Talli forced a teasing smile.

Sassa hugged her older sister and whispered in her ear, "Say no, Talli. Tell them you refuse to marry Banabas. Do it now before it is too late."

Talli grasped Sassa by the shoulders. "Everything is as it is meant to be. Do not fear, sister. Father will not promise you to any other than the man you love. My fate was decided by the spirits."

"Talli, come out," Ufala called. "Banabas has come for you."

Nocatee whimpered and Talli put her finger over the little one's lips. She smiled at Sassa and faintly nodded.

Kitchi's hand covered her trembling lips.

"It is all right, Mother," Talli siad. "I will be fine."

Talli turned about and walked out of the lodge.

Banabas had brought Talli's family the final gift. He had hunted deer, squirrel, fish, and turtle. He had also prepared smoked fish.

"We accept your offering," Ufala said.

"I will be a good husband to her," Banabas said to Ufala.

Banabas lifted Talli's hand. He tied a shell bracelet around her wrist.

A moment passed in silence.

"Say something, daughter."

Talli shifted her eyes to Banabas. Expressionless, she said, "Thank you."

"It is a beautiful gift," Ufala said. "Tell him so."

Banabas let Talli's hand drop. "She does not need to say anything," he said. "You look lovely, Talli."

"Come," Ufala said. "Kitchi, Sassa, Nocatee. Let us get on with this."

Ufala led the way to the central hearth. Villagers gathered there to watch.

Putiwa chanted, and when Talli and Banabas stood before him, he painted white lines down Talli's face. He spoke in the spirit tongue. The lilt in his voice made Talli wonder if he was singing or if the spirit tongue was one of melody.

She was glad she had to keep her head bowed in respect. It would be painful to look about, to see her vil-

lage for the last time .. for her eyes to find Akoma in
the distance. And she did not want to look at Banabas.

Putiwa cupped her chin with his hand and tilted her
head up to paint another line on her forehead. He then
turned to Banabas and painted similar designs on his
face.

Ufala fidgeted. He leaned over to his wife. "She will
not do anything, will she? She does not plan to interrupt
the marriage or cause a commotion. You have talked
with Talli, have you not?"

Kitchi cocked her head. "You must believe you have
asked her to do something perhaps you should not have.
Do you think you have demanded too much of the girl?"

"What makes you say that?"

"If you knew Talli was happy, you would not fear she
might act inappropriately."

Ufala scuffed his toes in the dirt. "I do not understand
either one of you. Certainly not Talli. I cannot predict
the child."

"You call her a child now, but have promised her in
marriage. Look behind you. That is where her heart is."

Ufala looked behind him. Akoma glared from a
distance.

"Talli could not belong to Akoma. It was forbidden."

"You and Yahga-ta managed to break custom for her
to become Banabas's woman."

Ufala's face reddened. "I owe Banabas my life."

"Your life, not Talli's."

"This arrangement is good for the Turtle. Good for
the Jeaga!"

Kitchi laughed. "And good for Ufala. It is not good
for Talli."

Ufala glanced back at Akoma again. "Have you heard
any rumors that Akoma might try to stop this marriage
from taking place? Yahga-ta says his son is angry."

"Of course he is angry. He loves your daughter and
no one permits them to be together."

"Well, have you heard rumors?"

Kitchi let out a frustrated breath. "No, Ufala. I have
not heard anything. The spirits chose Talli and Akoma.
They understand better than you what is expected of

them. They will not disappoint the spirits or the Turtle. Their hearts are filled with the Jeaga spirit."

Still, Ufala watched Talli nervously. His left eye twitched, and he rubbed his injured arm.

When Putiwa was finished with the marriage blessing song, Yahga-ta led the procession to the river where Banabas had his canoe. Kitchi placed a basket inside the dugout.

"Things you might need," she said.

When Talli looked up at her mother, she saw Akoma by the trees. He put his hand over his heart and then extended his arm as if offering his heart to her. She repeated his gesture, placing her palm over her heart and then reaching out.

"We must go," Banabas said.

She was sure her new husband had noticed the gestures, but she didn't care. She loved Akoma, and she made no attempt to keep that hidden from anyone.

Talli sat in the canoe and stared through the crowd at Akoma as Banabas poled the canoe into the deeper water. When her husband took up the paddle, he turned the canoe and Talli no longer faced the village. She could still feel the warmth of Akoma's eyes on her back. As the water trickled past the canoe, she closed her eyes and held the image of her lover's face in her head.

"Take your wife to your lodge then meet with me," Ramo said to Banabas as soon as he arrived.

"Tomorrow," Banabas said.

Ramo clamped his hand on Banabas's shoulder. "Now," he said, one eyebrow arched.

Banabas carried Talli's basket. "Ramo must have something important to discuss," he said.

"Then go," Talli said.

Banabas took Talli's hand and walked inside his lodge. "This is your new home," he said. "Perhaps you would like to rest. Familiarize yourself with everything that is here. I have been a long time without a woman. Tell me anything that you need . . . for cooking, or sewing . . . women's things. I will see that you have whatever you want."

Talli nodded and sat down.

"I will not be long," he said. "Ramo is not a man taken to long orations."

"You need not rush," she said. "I think I will rest, as you suggest."

Banabas looked at his new wife, then left. Whatever Ramo had to say had better be important, he thought.

"Ah, Banabas," Ramo said, as Banabas walked up. "Come inside so we speak privately."

Banabas followed Ramo inside.

"I want to you to go with me tonight," Ramo said.

"What are you talking about?" Banabas said.

"Tonight. I go to find the Ais."

"For what?" Banabas said.

"We communicate. Sometimes if your enemy is powerful and worthy, it is better to become an ally."

"We are Jeaga," Banabas said.

"Of course we are Jeaga. That does not mean we must be stupid."

"No, I do not want anything to do with the Ais. They will kill us on sight."

"Not so," Ramo said. "There is a man. Chogatis. An Ais cacique. I know him."

Banabas turned in a half circle and put his hands on his head. "Ramo, do you tell me you have met with the Ais before?"

"I tell you nothing, my friend."

"Betrayal. Do you betray the Jeaga? The Panther?"

"Where is your vision, Banabas? Do not tell me you have gotten too old. Perhaps your young woman will be too much for such an old man."

"Enough," Banabas said. "You are—"

"Apologies," Ramo said. "But something must stir you. Tonight you go with me. Listen and then make a judgment."

"Not tonight, Ramo. Surely you must understand that."

Ramo smiled. "So you are not so old. You are right, my friend. I am selfish. Tonight is yours and . . ."

"Talli. Talli is her name."

"Yes, Talli. Tonight. But do not exhaust yourself, old

man. Tomorrow we will travel. Do you understand, Banabas?"

"Yes, Ramo. I do understand."

"Tomorrow you can tell me what she is like in the furs."

Banabas blew out a breath. "You do not even know when you encroach."

"You are sensitive about this girl. How did you get away with taking her as your woman? I understand she is not even eligible for marriage yet."

"Times are changing. Everything changes."

"I also understand Yahga-ta's son wished to speak for her. What a coup this is. You are so clever, Banabas."

"Ufala is my friend. I saved his life in the Ais attack. He offered his daughter as a way of expressing his indebtedness. Talli accepted."

"Mmm," Ramo said. "She chose you over Yahga-ta's son."

Banabas palmed his chin and rubbed. Ramo didn't know when to stop. Banabas was often the buffer when Ramo did this to others. Now he fended for himself. He did not want to lose his temper. Better that he just leave. "Tomorrow, then," Banabas said.

"Tomorrow."

Banabas walked away from Ramo's lodge. The breeze caught the shell ornaments that dangled from the cacique's lodge. They jingled.

What did Ramo have in mind? Banabas wondered. He would use the travel time tomorrow to talk to him. Then he would listen carefully to the conversation Ramo had with this Chogatis. Now he would return to Talli and not think of the Ais or the Panther or the Jeaga.

As he first entered his lodge, he saw her sitting near the back. It took a moment for his eyes to adjust. He was indeed a lucky man. How glad he was that he had managed to save Ufala's life.

"Talli, I am back," he said.

She looked up at him and put down the basket she was holding. "Do you want something?" she asked.

"Can I help you put your things away? Have you thought of things you might need?" He could not help but let his eyes fix upon her. Her beauty always astounded him.

"What space is mine?" she asked. "Is there somewhere special you wish me to keep my things?"

Banabas did not answer. He stared at her.

"Is there a place where you wish me to store my belongings?" she asked again.

Banabas blinked and snapped out of his daydream. "Anywhere. This is your home now."

Banabas sat next to her and put his hand on her upper arm and then gently stroked. Talli shifted so more of her back was to him.

He moved his hand to caress her hair. Talli tilted her head and leaned forward just enough to increase the distance between her hair and Banabas's hand. But he lifted a handful of hair and put it to his nose. He sniffed, then put her hair against his cheek. It was soft and smooth. He moved forward and put his face in the crook of her neck.

Talli stiffened and Banabas could feel the rigidity in her neck. He pulled back and massaged her shoulders. "You are so tense," he said.

"I am fine," Talli said.

"Lie down on the blanket and let me massage this tenseness out of you. It has been a long day for you."

"I said I am fine. I have no need of a massage."

Banabas continued to rub her shoulders. "I feel the knots in your muscles giving way," he said. "Look through the doorway. The sun is almost gone and the sky is aflame with its last colors."

Talli glanced at the sky. Banabas urged her to lean back, then guided her onto the sleeping skin.

17

Talli lay still, looking squarely at the sky. Banabas stretched out beside her.

"In a moment the sky will be black and all these magnificent colors gone. The hearth fires of our ancestors will slowly emerge and sparkle in the heavens. Is that not a grand design of the spirits? They give man something wonderful to observe each day, to remind him before he sleeps to be thankful. I do not believe every man understands that."

Banabas turned to his side. He brushed her cheek with the back of his hand. Talli turned her face away.

The light faded quickly as the sun sank beneath the earth. The lodge was quiet and dark. She could hear Banabas's breathing. Even her breathing sounded loud and coarse. Heat radiated from his body. He was too close. He was going to want to join with her. Her stomach turned over. Talli rolled to her side, putting her back to him.

In a moment, his hand slipped around her and came to rest on her breast. His fingertip fondled her nipple.

He tugged on her shoulder to bring her to her back again.

Talli looked up at him. In the darkness she barely made out his face.

Banabas loosed his breechclout and held his manpart in his hand. He stroked it several times, then took her hand and curled it beneath his. Talli felt him swell in her palm. Banabas released her hand and climbed astride her. With one hand he held his manpart poised to enter her. With his other hand he urged her thighs to separate, but Talli resisted. Again, he attempted to push one thigh to the side, but she did not allow her leg to move.

"You are my wife," he said.

"Yes," Talli said. "I am your wife." She felt the hardness of his manpart straining against her.

"What is wrong?" he asked.

Talli didn't answer. She just lay still. She felt his disappointment and his frustration. She was glad she had the affliction . . . glad that Banabas suffered a lack of fulfillment and could not satisfy his yearning for her.

Banabas's head dropped, and he rolled off her.

Talli closed her eyes and turned to her side. She tucked both her hands under her cheek. She was Akoma's woman.

When the sun lightened the sky on the eastern horizon, Banabas sat up. He had not slept much during the night.

The air was cold. He took another sleeping skin and covered Talli. He wrapped a fur around his shoulders, then went outside to greet the day.

When he finished his morning prayers, he started his fire and warmed some dried fish. He wanted to leave her with something fresh to eat. Winter had arrived. This was the season for turkeys. The Jeaga did not hunt turkeys when the weather was warm for fear of killing too many hens. If too many hens were killed, then the turkeys would eventually become scarce.

Banabas took his bow and some arrows and his turkey call made from a small turkey wing bone. He trekked off into the woods. If he had been smart, he would have looked for their roosting place the night before. But last night was not supposed to be for turkey hunting.

Banabas watched for signs like scratchings in the dirt where turkeys fed on acorns or grapes. In a cluster of oaks he detected evidence that the large birds had been about recently. Turkeys were curious animals, he thought. Like the Jeaga, they also faced the east at sunrise and greeted the day.

Moments later he spotted a flock. He propped his back against a tree, facing the turkeys. If a man stayed

on the side of a tree facing the fowl and didn't move,
the turkeys would look right past him and he would have
a clean shot.

Banabas nocked an arrow, put his turkey wing bone
in his mouth, and sharply sucked air through it. The
sound imitated a turkey yelp. He used the call several
times, and when he saw one begin to approach, he
took aim.

The male turkey strutted toward him. Banabas's first
shot brought down the bird. When he returned to his
fire, he cut off the head and feet. He hung the bird
upside down to bleed while he heated water in a large
pot. He cut up the middle of the bird from the legs to
the breastbone and removed the entrails, then halved
the turkey. He cut off both wings and spread them open
to dry in front of the fire. They would make nice fans.

When the water roiled to a boil, he put in as much of
the turkey as he could, scalding a piece at a time. When
he removed them, he plucked the feathers, then singed
the fuzz off in the fire. When the turkey was clean, he
skewered some pieces of it and cooked it above his fire.
A few pieces he placed on a grate to smoke. The smoked
meat would keep longer.

Ramo came up. "You are busy early this morning,"
he said. "Are you ready?"

"I will be. I still disapprove."

Ramo laughed. "That is why you are my adviser. You
do not agree with me just because I am cacique. You
are not afraid. I listen to you. I do not necessarily do
what you say, but I listen."

Banabas stirred the fire. "I am going with you, and I
will listen. Perhaps something will change my mind."

"There, you see. You have an open mind and you
analyze everything. So when you speak and offer advice,
it is wise to listen."

"Why are you flattering me, Ramo?"

"I speak the truth. Now, friend, tell me how was she?
Where is she?"

Banabas clenched his teeth. "She is still sleeping."

"You must have worn her out," Ramo said and
laughed. He slapped Banabas on the back.

"Let me get my things. I will meet you by the central hearth."

Banabas turned the smoking turkey, then rose and went into his lodge.

Talli was sitting, the rolled-up sleeping skin in her lap. She combed her hair with her fingers.

"There is turkey cooking," he said. "Look in the baskets for other things to eat. Take whatever you like."

"Thank you," Talli said.

Banabas stepped closer. "I am leaving with Ramo. I am not certain when we will return. It may be two days."

"All right," Talli answered.

"Is there anything you wish before I go?"

Talli shook her head.

Banabas stared at her for a moment. The morning light filtered into the lodge giving everything a hazy golden cast. He longed for her to rise and put her arms around him, hold him close, and tell him she would miss him.

Ramo and Banabas left on foot, heading in the same direction as they had the day of the hunt when the Ais attacked.

"What is it you want to talk to Chogatis about?" Banabas asked.

"It is wise to have conversations with those who could be your enemy. The Ais are strong."

"They *are* the enemy. There is no question about that."

As they journeyed, the grand laurel and live oaks cast cold shadows. Banabas shifted his wrap about his shoulders. By midafternoon, the wind picked up. By late afternoon, even his insides were chilled.

"Let us make camp here," Ramo said, "while we still have some light."

"Look there," Banabas said.

Ramo looked where Banabas pointed. Long claw marks streaked down the bark from high on a tall pine.

"Bear," Ramo said.

"This is a big one. Smaller males will stay away once they see how high he scratches." Banabas walked up to the tree and Ramo followed. The older man pulled several black hairs from the rough bark. "Probably foraging last night. I am surprised, with the air this cold."

"It has grown colder all day. Last night was not that uncomfortable. He is still trying to fatten up."

"We should not take a chance and make camp right in his path. We should move on just a little."

"Good idea," Ramo said.

They stopped in an area where the dark soil turned sandier. The oaks were scrub. Palmettos and pines ate up the landscape.

Banabas started a fire with his bow drill just as the sun went down. "So where is this Chogatis?" he asked. "Why did you think you would find him?"

"I have heard he comes close."

As darkness fell over them, they ate dried fish and dried turtle meat.

"Should have looked for a rabbit," Ramo said. "This meat is too old. Tough and tasteless."

"Shh," Banabas said. "Listen."

Both men stood without moving. "The wind," Ramo whispered. "I only hear the wind."

Banabas shook his head, put down the remnants of his fish, and held his hand up, palm out, signaling Ramo to be still. "Sounds like a call. Someone imitating a bird."

"Ais?"

"Maybe."

Ramo and Banabas crouched, turning their heads to catch sound from any direction. Banabas threw dirt over the fire, extinguishing it.

The sound came again. "I heard it," Ramo whispered.

"Closer, and from a different direction. There are two of them. Is it your Chogatis?"

"I have no way of knowing. We should take no risks."

Banabas and Ramo drew out their knives, held them in their teeth, and crawled on the ground to a thicket of palmettos. The serrated edges of the branches sawed their skin as they backed in for cover.

"It may be too late to hide. They may have spotted our smoke."

With the loss of the sun, the wind died to an occasional breeze. The earth was dry and brittle from the drought.

The cracking of a twig and the barely audible crunching of the ground alerted both men. The sound was close.

"It is either the bear or the Ais," Banabas whispered.

"Either way, I do not want to be trapped by these palmettos," Ramo said, jumping out of the cover. "I am here!" he shouted.

Ramo was insane, Banabas thought. But he did have a point. If an enemy party or the bear found them, they would be at a disadvantage because of the palmettos. They would only be able to move forward and toward the enemy. If it was Chogatis, he hoped there was no danger.

Banabas bolted forward also and gave a loud whoop.

In an instant, two men darted out of the darkness, one wielding a lance and the other a knife. They came shouting battle cries at Banabas and Ramo.

"Neither is as big as the bear," Ramo shouted, lunging to the side as the first man threw his lance at him.

Banabas took on the warrior with the knife. He was larger than the Ais, but he was also older. The Ais warrior slashed at Banabas's chest, but Banabas hopped backward. He caught the Ais man's wrist, twisting the arm behind his back. He was ready to put his knife to the warrior's throat when the Ais thrust his elbow back and up into Banabas's ribs.

Banabas recoiled and stumbled back. The Ais came at him again. Banabas raised his weapon. He blocked the Ais's stabbing knife, catching a knick in his forearm. Banabas slashed and opened a gash in the man's side. The Ais clutched his wound. Banabas grabbed the man's hair and pulled him toward him, then kicked his feet out from under him. The man went to his knees. Banabas maneuvered to the man's back, yanked the Ais's head by the hair, and held the beveled edge of his shell blade to the exposed throat. The Ais did not move.

Banabas heaved for air as he looked to see what had happened to Ramo. Ramo sat astride a bloody Ais whose eyes stared blankly.

Ramo stood up and spoke to the Ais that Banabas held. "I am Ramo, cacique of the Jeaga Panther clan. I was in search of Chogatis. He will not be happy to hear of your attack."

The Ais warrior smiled. "He will not want to see you."

"He will want to see me. We have great visions together."

The Ais laughed loudly. "Your visions are dung, Jeaga. You have just killed Chogatis's son!"

Ramo's head shot up to look at Banabas. "Do it."

Banabas pulled the knife across the warrior's throat, cutting deep into the artery. He pushed the man's head down, then kneed his back so he fell on the ground.

"We could not release him. He would have gone to Chogatis and told him we killed his son," Ramo said. "There would be untold vengeance unleased on the Panther."

Banabas nodded. "There is to be no negotiating with the Ais, Ramo. Let this incident speak for that."

"Chogatis will never know who did this."

"Of course he will know they were killed by Jeaga."

"Turtle Jeaga," he said. "Not Panther."

Banabas swept his hand over his face, and then wiped his knife on the fan of a palmetto.

"Dig a hole to put the bodies in," Ramo said. "They should not be found right away."

Suddenly the two men were aware of a rustling in the brush.

"Another?" Banabas asked.

Ramo cocked his head to one direction, indicating that Banabas go in the direction he gestured. Ramo went in the other direction so they circled the area where the noise came from.

Banabas crept as silently as he could on the dry ground. He cringed with each step. A cloud came across the moon, making the night grow even darker. Where was this Ais? Or was he stalking the bear?

Banabas heard commotion and sprinted toward it. He jerked to a stop when he spotted Ramo, shocked at what he saw.

18

"Ramo, stop. No!" Banabas screamed. "Stop!"

Ramo knelt, straddling a young boy, his knife pressed against the boy's throat. "He is Ais."

Banabas ran beside them. "Ramo, you cannot kill him. He is only a boy."

The boy arched his neck, offering even more of his throat to Ramo.

"He is a feisty one, this Ais boy," Ramo said. "So you want me to kill you, too?"

"Leave him," Banabas said.

"We cannot leave him. He will go straight to Chogatis. He has heard you call my name."

"No," Banabas said. "I cannot justify killing a boy."

"Then what do you suggest?" Ramo asked. "Tie him to a tree and let the bear finish him?" Ramo flashed a taunting smile at the boy. "That would be more cruel than getting it over with right now."

"Bring him with us," Banabas said.

"You have crazy thoughts, old man—an Ais living with the Jeaga. How old do you think he is? How old are you boy, seven, eight summers?"

The child didn't answer.

"My guess is eight," Ramo said. "He is old enough to know he is Ais and we are Jeaga. And who do you think will want to take care of an Ais after the recent skirmish? Jeaga still grieve for lost ones. We have no choice."

Ramo placed his knife over the child's right cartoid artery.

Banabas could see the boy's chest rapidly rising and falling as he breathed. His heart pounded in his neck.

The boy was frightened, but he didn't cry out. He was a brave one. "I will take care of him," Banabas said. "Take your knife away, Ramo."

Ramo sat back and sheathed his knife. "You are a lucky boy," he said. "This fool does not want me to spill your blood."

"Ais!" the boy whooped as he attempted to get up.

Ramo put his forearm across the boy's chest and leaned on him, pressing the boy flat on the ground.

"You have a lot of courage. A lot of spunk for an Ais." Ramo looked up at Banabas. "Do you believe what you see? He does not give up so easily. I think he would rather die than be amongst the Jeaga." Ramo laughed aloud.

"Yes, he is a brave one," Banabas said. "Get him up and we can get on our way."

Ramo grasped the young boy's upper arm. He stood and jerked the boy to his feet.

"What is your name?" Banabas asked.

The boy spit at him.

"Just like an Ais," Ramo said. "Who cares what his name is? Call him whatever you want. Call him raccoon dung." Ramo sniffed. "He smells like raccoon dung and behaves no better."

"Give him time. He will tell us his name when he is no longer afraid." Banabas touched the boy's shoulder. "Do not be afraid. No harm will come to you."

The child shook his shoulders to free himself of Banabas's hand.

Ramo pushed the boy toward Banabas. "You drag him. You are the one who wants to take him."

The boy looked hard into Banabas's eyes, then bolted.

Banabas and Ramo ran after him. Suddenly the boy stopped. He stared at the two Ais bodies that lay on the ground in front of him. He spun around. Banabas and Ramo were almost upon him. He dove next to one of the bodies and retrieved the knife. The boy stood up straight, whooping as he drew his arm back, then hurled the weapon at the men who chased him.

The knife wobbled through the air. Banabas and Ramo avoided it without any difficulty.

"Ais!" the boy screamed, thrusting a brown arm into the air. "Ais!"

Ramo lunged and grabbed the boy. "You are making it very difficult for me to save your life," Ramo said. "Come here, Banabas. Hold on to him."

Ramo released the child to Banabas. "Wait here," he said.

Ramo wandered off.

"You need to cooperate with us," Banabas said.

The child stared at one of the bodies.

"Tell me who they are," Banabas said. "Your uncle?"

It was common for the uncle to take part in teaching his sister's male children hunting and fishing skills. He looked at the boy's face, and then at the man Ramo had killed. There was a strong resemblance. "Your father?" Banabas asked. "Is that one your father?"

The boy did not speak.

"Why do you not talk?" Banabas asked. "Is 'Ais' the only word you know? Our languages are nearly the same, so I know you understand me. Are you stubborn?"

Still the child did not answer.

Ramo returned with handfuls of sabal palm fiber. He had gathered it from the leaves where the leaf splits. He sat on the ground and took two separate bundles and laid them across his upper thigh two fingers' width apart. With his left hand he held the bundles. His right hand pressed the bundles against his thigh. He rolled them smoothly down to his knee, twisting the fibers tightly.

"He will not be so happy," Ramo said. "This will make our journey less troublesome."

Ramo took the two bundles and placed them snugly against each other and rolled them back up his thigh. He repeated this several times, moving his hold on the bundles to grasp where they were not twisted. The finished twine fell between his legs.

"There," he said, admiring his work. "If we bind his legs and make him hobble, he will slow us down. If we bind his wrist, he can still run, and I think he will run again. But, if we bind one of his wrists to one of yours, I think we have a solution."

"I have no objection," Banabas said. "Ramo, look at the face of the man you killed, then look at the boy."

Ramo did as Banabas suggested. "I see what you mean," he said. "They do look alike. Is that man his father? Is this Chogatis's grandson?"

"I think so."

"We must keep this quiet. I am not sure yet how we will take care of this. The boy may be a good bargaining tool or he may squelch our plans. I do not know how Chogatis will react."

Ramo stood up and tied the boy's wrist to Banabas's.

"You will not regret sparing the boy. It is not the Jeaga way to kill children or women," Banabas said.

"We will talk more after we get back to the village. I do not want the child to hear everything."

Banabas nodded that he understood.

Talli sat next to the small hearth. The warmth was comforting. She had not felt good most of the day. Her stomach churned. She sipped some tea hoping it would settle her stomach.

She was so intent looking at the fire she didn't see Liakka approach.

"So you are the Jeaga woman."

Talli startled and spilled some of her tea. "I was day-dreaming," she said.

"I did not mean to surprise you. I am Liakka." Liakka circled Talli, then sat across the hearth from her. "I heard you were attractive and young. I was surprised."

"Banabas saved my father's life. I was promised to him. To become his wife was not my choice."

"Banabas is a good man," Liakka said. "He will make a good husband."

The nausea that plagued her most of the day returned. Her hand went to her stomach.

"You do not feel well?"

"I have been through a lot of change in a little more than a cycle of the moon. My stomach is unsettled. But I will be fine."

Liakka tilted her head to the side as if curious. "There

is the rumor that you had your heart set on Yahga-ta's son. Is that so, or do the old women just babble?"

"It does not matter now."

"Custom was broken so you could become Banabas's wife. Why was that?" Liakka asked.

Talli glared at her. "You are very forward. Why do you not tell me more about yourself?"

"Ramo has interest in me. My grandmother was the wife of a cacique. The Deer clan."

"A noble line," Talli said. "Then you are eligible if Ramo wants you."

Liakka grinned. "I do not know if I want him." She looked past Talli. "Ceboni comes."

Ceboni was shorter than Liakka and heavier. But she did have a friendly face, cheeks a little too round, and a mouth that seemed to be on the verge of a perpetual smile. She pulled her dark hair into knot on top of her head. She wore a strand of shell beads.

"Hello," she said. "I am Ceboni. You are Banabas's woman, yes? I have some things to share with you if you need them. There was an abundance of grapes in the summer. I dried so many I fear they will become food for the animals before we can eat them all. I am going to dig some greenbrier roots today. Would you like to go?"

"You have not given Talli a chance to answer," Liakka said. "You go on and on."

Ceboni laughed, almost a giggle. "I am sorry. I do that a lot. I just have so many things to say."

"Ceboni, this is Talli. I think it best if you start with her name."

"Talli. Nice," she said. "Would you like to gather greenbrier root with me?"

Talli had not thought of making friends, but she was lonely. These weren't the Ais, they were Jeaga, and her job was to help keep the Jeaga united.

"Perhaps later," she said. "I am not feeling well this morning."

Ceboni winced as if it were she who was not feeling good. "What do you suppose is wrong? I have good medicines. I am sure you do, too. I only wanted to offer to prepare some if you do not feel well enough to do so yourself."

Liakka yawned. "When does Banabas return?" she asked.

"He was not certain how long he and Ramo would be gone."

Ceboni asked, "Where did they go?"

Talli shrugged. "I did not ask."

Liakka smiled faintly. "I have heard a few of the men talking. They speculate on where the two have gone. Some even say to talk to the Ais."

"If the drought would end, then the Ais would stay put and leave the Jeaga territory alone," Ceboni said.

"I do not think so," Talli said. "I have listened to the men, also. The Ais recall the last drought. They want the river, and that means displacing the Jeaga."

Liakka folded her arms across her chest for warmth. "There is a lot of river."

"The Jeaga are all along the river, to the mouth of the Big Water," Talli said. "And there are other people on the banks of other rivers. The Ais come from the north, the Calusa and Tocobaga are to the west, the Tegesta to the south of us. Some of the Ais do not have enough access to fresh water when there is drought. They have decided it is the Jeaga they must deal with. I do not like it, but it is logical. We are the closest to them, and we are on the river."

"Well, I do not like to think about it," Ceboni said. "I feel frightened every time it is discussed. My husband says it is not a woman's concern anyway."

"I think women take more of a part in such political discussions than they used to," Liakka said. "We may not sit in council, but there are private times when wives speak to their husbands. Then their husbands think about the discussion, and then they speak to other men. Some of the woman's influence gets tied up in their thinking."

Ceboni frowned. "I do not think I want to be involved. Let him do the man's work, and I will do the woman's. Women do not carry weapons or know how to fight, so why should we speak on the subject?"

Talli stirred her tea with her finger. "I think women carry a lot of the responsibility for the well-being of the People. In a different way, of course. Perhaps they carry the deepest burdens."

"You look so pensive, Talli," Ceboni said.

Talli took a deep breath and looked up. Her first impression was that she liked Ceboni. Liakka was different. Ceboni bore some childlike innocence. Liakka, however, seemed quite capable of deception. Even as near to Liakka as Talli was, she could not understand all the feelings this woman was having. She felt mixed feelings inside Liakka. Intuitively, she did not trust her.

"Come for me later. I will feel better then, I hope," Talli said to Ceboni. "I think I will lie down for a while. Perhaps I did not sleep enough last night. And Liakka, thank you for introducing yourself."

"I will see you again, soon," Liakka said, then left with Ceboni. Talli watched the two women walk away. Ceboni was chattering, and Liakka appeared to be paying no attention. Instead, she was surveying the village.

Talli pulled her wrap tighter, put down her cup of tea and went into the lodge. She wished she felt better. She lay down and fell asleep.

"Are you in there? Talli, it is Ceboni. Are you coming with me?"

Talli was reluctant to relinquish her dream. In her sleep she had been with Akoma, drifting down the river in his canoe. She sat with her back against him, her head resting on his chest.

Ceboni's silhouette appeared in the doorway. "Are you very sick?" she asked. "What can I do?"

Talli sat up and swept the hair from her face. It took her a moment to orient herself. "I was sleeping."

"Yes, I see that," Ceboni said, entering the lodge. "Is there something wrong? You are still sick?"

"I am not sure. Oh," she said remembering, "I was going with you to dig greenbrier roots."

"You do not have to. I can gather enough for both of us if you like."

Talli stretched her neck back and then from side to side. "I think it will be good for me," she said.

Talli took the basket her mother had given her and went with Ceboni in search of the greenbrier roots. She shivered when a puff of wind caught under her wrap.

"Ah," Ceboni said. "There are some." Deeper in the damp woods she pointed to spiny vines climbing the trees.

When next to the greenbrier, Talli bent over with her digging stick. Without warning the world distanced itself, growing darker, and the sounds grew fainter.

"Talli, are you all right?" Ceboni asked.

Everything closed in black.

Talli realized she was on the ground. Ceboni's face slowly came into view.

"What happened?"

"I was bending over. I got dizzy. I must have fainted."

"What should I do?" Ceboni asked. She paced.

Talli pushed up on one elbow, but as soon as her head came off the ground, the dizziness returned. "Give me a few moments," she said.

"I think I should go for Ocaab."

"Who is Ocaab?"

"The shaman. He will know what to do. What is wrong with you?"

"Wait," Talli said. "I will be all right in a moment."

"How long have you been sick?"

"I have not really been sick. My stomach has been queasy on and off for a few days. Nothing serious."

"Except now you have fainted."

"I did not eat today because my stomach needed a rest from food, I thought. I sipped a little tea. And I did not eat yesterday. Only tea. I am weak from not eating."

Ceboni jabbed her fingers into her hair, scratching her scalp. "What to do? What to do?"

Talli pushed herself up again on one elbow. This time she came up slower, and there was less dizziness. "You do not have to do anything. Look, I am sitting up now."

"It is too soon for you to be pregnant. You have only been his woman for a few days. Oh my goodness, what if that is what is wrong? I have never heard of anyone feeling sick so fast, though some women suffer so much more. I was only sick with my second. Do you think that could—?"

Talli's face paled. What if she was pregnant? She had been with Akoma a little more than a moon cycle ago. She thought the delay in her moon cycle was due to all the change. What if it was not from that at all, and she did carry a child? *Akoma's* child!

"Talli, do you think you could be pregnant already?"

"I suppose that is possible," she managed to scramble out of her mouth. "It is too early to tell." If she was pregnant, she had to make sure people believed she carried Banabas's child. The only one who would know that was impossible was Banabas.

Talli held her forehead in her hand. "My mother was sick very early with all her children," she said.

"Let me walk you back to your shelter. I will gather the greenbriers later. I will bring you some."

"Yes," Talli said. "I do not think I feel up to digging right now. I am sorry."

"No, do not be sorry. Think . . . a baby! Banabas will be so thrilled to be having a baby at his age. Men are proud that way."

"No," Talli said. "I do not want to tell him yet."

"Why not? The possibility is so exciting."

"I would not want him to suffer the disappointment if there is no baby. Promise me you will keep this a secret. Do not mention it to anyone. Will you promise?"

"I can keep the secret if that is what you want," she said, helping Talli to her feet.

"For now I think that is best." She did not know what kind of woman Ceboni was. Was she a gossip who would spread the suspicion of her pregnancy? Would Banabas find out? She had to think of something!

19

Near the Panther village, Banabas stopped. "I think we should decide how we will explain the boy. What do you plan to tell the people?" Banabas asked.

"We will say we found him hiding. We came across a bloody site. Found two slain Ais. He must have been with them." Ramo paused before he continued. "We are fortunate the boy does not speak."

Ramo took the boy's chin in his hand and raised his face so the boy would look at him. "Do you talk, boy? Can you?"

The child glared at Ramo.

"He does say Ais," Banabas said. "He has a voice."

The thick forest obstructed the view of the village until right upon it. When the woodland finally allowed sight of the village, the boy hesitated.

"Welcome to the Panther Jeaga village," Banabas said to the child.

As they walked through the village, the people took notice. Liakka approached Ramo. She playfully slid her hand across his chest. "Who is that?" she asked.

Ramo took her hand and rubbed it against his nipple. "An Ais boy. We found him."

Liakka leaned around Ramo as they walked to get a better look. "What do you mean you found him?"

Banabas watched Ramo's face as he explained to Liakka. "Turtle killed the party he was with," he began. He lied with no trace of deceit showing in his expression, nor in the tone of his voice.

Talli stirred the fire, bringing up more of a flame. The warming turkey didn't pique her appetite. Instead, she found the smell made her feel ill. The preparation of food across the village doused the air with a mixture of aromas. The rich combinations floated through the village and seeped out into the woods.

Suddenly Talli felt a rush of heat travel through her. Her hands trembled, and she was overwhelmed by a sense of fear. She didn't understand. What was happening? Perhaps she was going to get sick, but it felt more like the affliction. Her heart raced. Her body broke into a dewy sweat. Her hands and feet were cold, yet she was steeped in perspiration. Tightness in her throat made her clutch her neck. Where was this awful feeling coming from?

Talli looked across the fire at the rest of the village. Her husband approached . . . with a child. She focused on the boy and realized he was the source of the panic she felt. His fear was so intense, she was able to experience it, even from a distance.

Talli stood and looked inquisitively at her husband. "Banabas?"

"Ramo and I found him. There were two dead Ais, and the boy was hiding. We could not just leave him."

"No, of course not." Talli still trembled. "He is so frightened." She touched the cord that bound the man and the boy at the wrist. "Loosen the tether," she said.

The child stared up at her. His wide dark eyes brimmed with tears. He was not only scared, but extremely sad. She crouched in front of him. "Do not be afraid, little one," she said. Talli stroked his head, then held his hands in hers as Banabas cut the rope. "What is your name?"

"He does not talk," Banabas said. "He only says 'Ais.' That is all."

Talli put her hands on the boy's head. "Can you not speak?"

The child blinked, and a tear trickled down his cheek, leaving a fair trail through the dirt on his face. Quickly he brushed it away and straightened his back. "Ais," he said, but this time he spoke softly.

"My name is Talli," she said, pointing to herself. "Can you tell me your name?"

Banabas shook his head. "I tell you, the boy does not talk. Do not press it."

She watched the child's face. Her trembling ceased. There was less horror in the boy now. She wished the affliction allowed her to know what someone was thinking instead of only how they were feeling.

"Sit," she said, speaking to Banabas and the boy. "I will feed you both."

Talli prepared the turkey and some fish stew. She ladled the stew into a bowl that glistened with sand crystals imbedded in the dark pottery. "When you are finished, I will take you to the river to bathe," she said. "I suppose I need to call you by some name. If you cannot tell me what it is, then I will have to give you one."

Talli felt Banabas's eyes on her. He watched her closely and appeared intrigued with the ease she exhibited in dealing with the child.

"He is not much older than Nocatee," she said. "I can imagine how frightened she would be in the same situation. I want to help him."

Banabas took a bite of turkey off the bone. The boy did not touch his bowl or the turkey meat.

"You must eat," Talli said. "A man must be strong in his body as well as his mind. If you do not eat, your body will not be strong."

The boy lifted the bowl of fish stew to his lips and sipped.

"Better," she said. "You know what a man must do."

In a few moments the child had finished all the stew and meat. He wiped his mouth with the back of his hand.

"Joog," Talli said. "Until we know your Ais name, we will call you Joog. Now come with me to the river."

"The boy tries to run," Banabas said. "I do not know how you will secure him. You must stay with him."

"He will not run tonight. It is late, and not long from now he would not be able to see where he was going. And he is tired." Talli looked away from Banabas and at Joog. "His belly is full now, which is the first thing a man must do to keep his body strong. The second thing is to make sure the body has time to rest. He should have a good night's sleep, rest his body. Is that not so, Joog?"

Banabas gave Talli an approving expression. "Take him now, then, before darkness."

Talli walked the boy to the edge of the river. "You must take your clothes off. I will cut you a new breechclout from clean hide."

The boy shook his head.

"If I turn away, I risk that you will flee. My husband will be very upset with me if that happens. What should I do, Joog?"

Talli shuddered and quickly felt Joog inside her, or her inside Joog. She was never sure just how the affliction worked. "You want to speak, but cannot. You have lost your speech . . . ever since—"

Joog's face contorted as if he fought back the urge to cry. His chin trembled.

"Oh, my," Talli said. "Banabas has not told me all the truth. You saw what happened and that is when you lost your speech." Talli reached for the child and pulled him to her, wrapping her arms gently about him. She hugged the boy and felt his shoulders shake. He was crying. She waited for signs that his crying had ended before she urged him away.

"You must not run from me, Joog. Do you understand? You will be safe with me. I will do what I can to have you returned to your people. Now, cleanse yourself in the water. I will face the other direction."

Joog sniffed and swiped the tip of his nose with his hand.

"Go," she said.

Talli heard the movement of the water and the splashing as Joog washed. She listened closely to make sure he was still just behind her as she cut the new breechclout and sash. If the boy did run, she was not sure what would happen. She didn't fear Banabas, but Ramo was a man she did not understand. From the little she knew of him, she thought him unpredictable. She finished the breechclout and laid it behind her.

The sound of the water splashing stopped. "Joog, are you there? I am waiting. I am trusting you."

A moment later Talli felt a tap on her back. She turned. Joog stood before her, his hair still dripping, the streaks on his face cleansed away.

"Good," she said. "The sun is setting. You do not want to be in the water when it is dark. The alligators are fierce."

She felt the exhaustion sweeping over the boy, both mental and physical. He had witnessed something terrible, so horrifying he had lost his speech. It had probably been his first outing with his father. He was about that age. What a horrible thing for a boy.

Talli tousled his hair, flinging water droplets into the air. "You are safe with me, Joog."

She wondered about Joog's mother. Did she realize her son was missing yet? Talli's mind tripped over the word "mother." What if she really was pregnant with Akoma's child? What was she going to do? When everyone was sleeping, she would think about it, try to devise a plan of some kind, evaluate her options. She couldn't think about it now. Later.

They walked up to Banabas's hearth with only a thin orange line on the horizon. The sun was gone for the day. The moon rested in the eastern sky, surrounded by a translucent halo. There were no stars inside the ring.

"The promise of rain does not look good," she said to Joog. "When there is a ring around the moon like that, if you count the number of stars in the halo it will rain in that many days. But the halo has no stars."

She could tell by the boy's expression that he understood the importance of rain, what it meant to the Ais and the Jeaga.

"I wish the drought would end, also," she said. "There would be less trouble between our people."

Banabas crouched by the fire. He scooped together nearby leaves and sticks, then sprinkled water on them. "Put a thin layer of this on the fire," he told Joog.

The boy shoveled some of the damp debris in his hands.

"If the smoke goes to the ground, it will rain soon," Banabas said. "Put the fresh tinder on the fire."

The boy laid the debris atop the glowing embers. The

smoke hissed. All three watched the tendrils of smoke spiral up like a lazy snake.

"The signs are not there," Banabas said. "Have you noticed how high the birds fly? Watch them tomorrow and you will see. They do not fly low as if expecting rain. The drought is not ending yet, and the Ais and Jeaga have not ended their dispute."

Talli escorted Joog inside the lodge. "Rest for the night. Grow strong. You are a good boy," she said. "A brave boy your people would be proud of." She rolled out a sleeping skin and blanket. "Sleep well, little man."

Talli touched his forehead, then went back out to the fire.

"You are a kind woman," Banabas said. "Tender and gentle."

"He is just a boy. A very frightened little boy. He has every reason to be so afraid. Why did you not tell me the truth about what happened? You and Ramo killed the two Ais men. Joog saw it all. He was so horrified, he lost his speech."

Banabas tossed a stick into the fire, then rocked back on his haunches. "How do you know this?"

"I asked the right questions. The child let me know with his expressions and gestures. What really happened?"

"Talli, you are my wife and anything I tell you must be kept in confidence. You should speak of this to no one. Do you understand?"

"No," Talli answered, "I do not understand. That is why I ask you to tell me the truth."

Banabas sighed and took her hand in his. "This marriage has enough complications. I cannot add to it with untruths. That is a poor foundation. So, I will tell you, but you must let me know that you value the sacredness of marriage and will abide by that. You must not relate to anyone the things I tell you."

Talli nodded. "I will tell no one," she said.

"Ramo went in search of Chogatis, the leader of the Ais clan that recently attacked us. Ramo wants to negotiate something. We had a confrontation with two Ais. One of the men we killed is the son of Chogatis, the leader of an Ais clan. When we were leaving, we heard a noise in the brush. We thought it another Ais warrior, but it turned out it was this boy. Chogatis's grandson. We could not release him. Ramo was ready to kill him, but I could not justify it. So we brought him back with us. It is a good thing the boy does not speak. We cannot let word sneak back to Chogatis."

"But at some point the Ais will realize that the men have been killed and the boy is dead or missing. They will certainly assume they died at the hands of the Jeaga."

"Turtle."

Talli squinted in confusion.

"Ramo has a connection with Chogatis. He will imply to Chogatis that his son was killed by a Turtle, not a Panther."

Talli clenched her teeth. "We are all Jeaga. Why does Ramo insist on putting the knife in his brother's back? He will destroy the People—especially the Turtle. I have to stop this."

Banabas grabbed Talli's shoulder. "You cannot do anything. You must not speak of this to anyone. You gave me your word."

"That was before I understood what Ramo planned to do. He betrays the Jeaga and offers the Turtle as sacrifice."

"What would you do, Talli? How would you stop this?"

Talli cleared her throat and thought for a moment. "I would tell Yahga-ta."

"To what end? Yahga-ta would not go to Chogatis to discuss this. They have no relationship. Chogatis would believe Ramo. There is nothing that can be done, except to protect the boy until such time as we can find a way to return him to his people. Perhaps, if he grows fond of us, he will carry that message home with him. If you and I do this right, Joog may be the answer to ending the animosity between the Ais and the Jeaga."

Talli did see Banabas's point. Maybe finding this boy was the best thing that could have happened. She would enjoy taking care of him. He helped fill the emptiness she had from missing Sassa and Nocatee.

"I am quite tired," she said.

"I am, also."

Banabas made sure the area around the hearth was clear and that the embers were burning low before he followed Talli into the lodge.

Joog was sleeping soundly. Talli adjusted the blanket over him, then lay down on her side on her sleeping skin. Banabas lay next to her. His fingers ran down her spine. It did feel good and made her more relaxed. His hands were warm, and his touch firm enough to knead the muscles in her back.

She felt Banabas snuggle against her, his knees bending in the fold of hers. Then his arms went around her, and one hand sought her breast, the other her thigh. Talli pulled away. Banabas stopped his fondling and submitted to just holding his arms around her. In a few moments she heard his deep breathing, bordering on snoring. Joog slept and so did Banabas. It was her time to think.

She lay there remembering what it was like with Akoma. Now, when she had time alone in the dark, she could make herself be with him, even if it was only her imagination. She put her hand on her abdomen. Had that wonderful time of joining with the man she loved created a new life inside her? Instead of feeling panicked as she had earlier, she experienced a remarkable peace. She became more certain that she did indeed carry a child, a beautiful consummation of their union. Now all she had to do was not let Banabas or anyone else know she was pregnant with Akoma's baby. How was she going to do that?

Suddenly her eyes flew open. She had a plan.

20

Talli was at the hearth before Banabas awakened. The sunrise blushed the village with golds, yellows, lavenders, and pinks. The Panther village was beautiful, just as the Turtle village was. She wondered how her ancestors used to feel about moving with the seasons rather than staying put permanently. It may have been quite an adventure to go and see new places. Or perhaps they did not look forward to uprooting all they had worked so hard on. She would have to ask the elders what stories they knew about such things. The daily living of the ancestors should not be forgotten.

The thought troubled her. As evidenced by the ease with which custom was broken for her to marry Banabas, there grew a great lack in respect for tradition and heritage. Maybe it would not be the Ais at all who would eradicate the Jeaga. The Jeaga might do it to themselves.

Talli stirred a stew thickened with the flour made from coontie root. Her stomach churned, but she didn't mind. It was a reminder that a part of Akoma was with her.

She shivered from the cold and fed the fire a little more fuel. With a stick, she prodded the clam shells which were filled with baking berry cakes. She rotated them so they cooked evenly.

A few more villagers appeared about their hearths, and aromatic smoke began to permeate the air.

Ceboni padded across the plaza to Talli. Her eyes were still puffy from sleep, and a crease appeared in her face where the sleeping mat had wrinkled beneath her cheek. "It is a good morning," she said, running her hands through her disheveled hair.

Talli smiled.

"How are you feeling? Have you told Banabas?"

"No. It is much too early."

A deep voice surprised them. "Told Banabas what?" Banabas asked, emerging from the lodge.

Talli jumped up. There was a brief silence, and Talli scored her bottom lip with her teeth. "Ceboni wondered if I had told you of the fine breakfast I was preparing for you. I thought it was too early to wake you."

"Yes, that was it," Ceboni said. "Look at the berry cakes she bakes for you. You are a lucky man to have such a wife."

Banabas stood next to Talli. He put his arm around her waist. "You are right, Ceboni, I am a very lucky man."

Talli stiffened, but then forced herself to relax and let his arm embrace her.

"I'd best be going and prepare my family something to eat, also," Ceboni said. "Iquan enjoys his morning meal. I will visit later, Talli, if that is all right."

"I would like that," Talli answered.

"I am glad you have made a friend," Banabas said. He moved directly behind her and wrapped his arms around her waist. She felt him press his body softly against hers. She stood still, fighting the urge to pull away. She couldn't do that, not if her plan was to work.

Banabas reached a hand under the fall of her hair and the blanket and stroked her back.

"Oh, the cakes are going to burn," she said as an excuse to move away. She bent over the clam shells and poked them with the stick.

"Talli . . ."

She turned her head to look up at him. Bent over, her eyes were level with his thighs. Immediately she saw the distension of his breechclout. He was aroused.

"Yes," she said. "What is it?"

Banabas massaged his shoulder. "Nothing," he said. "You are quite lovely. I am happy that you are my wife. I will be a good husband."

Talli realized that her perception of Banabas had changed. He was a kind and gentle man. He had not pressed her to join with him and had not even spoken of it. He was patient. She assumed most men would be outraged if their wives refused the wifely duty. She smiled at him. "Greet the day," she said.

"I will do it at the river," he said.

As Banabas walked away, Talli watched him. There was nothing arrogant in his gait. His gray-streaked hair blew back from his shoulders as he walked. She thought of the pouch he kept of his wife's things. He was a sentimental man who felt things deeply, she thought. Not only would the knowledge that she carried Akoma's child be devastating to the relationship between the Turtle and the Panther, it would also be destructive to Banabas. She was glad she had figured out a plan. Last night she had wondered if she could go through with it, but now those reservations faded.

Talli peeked in the shelter. Joog was still curled up beneath the blanket. She had checked on him several times during the night. She'd wake him when Banabas returned.

Banabas, Talli, and Joog ate breakfast together.

"You will help me with the canoe," Banabas said to the boy. "There is still much to be done. I am glad to have help."

Banabas disappeared inside the lodge, then came out with a long coil of cordage. "Stand up, Joog."

The child obeyed, but a distraught expression came over his face.

"Banabas, must you do that?" Talli asked as he looped the rope around the boy's waist.

"I am afraid he will try to escape."

Talli walked over to the boy. "Promise you will not try to run," she said, taking his face in her hands. "You do not know your way, and it is dangerous for anyone to wander without weapons or companions. Men do not travel alone."

Joog didn't answer.

Talli continued. "We will work hard on returning you to your people, but you must not run away. You will never get home that way. Do you understand?"

The boy nodded.

"Do not tie him," Talli said.

"It would be extra security. There is much at risk."

"He will not run. For me. Please do not tie him to a tree like a captured animal."

Banabas unwrapped the cord from the boy. "Come, then. Let me find you a tool to smooth the inside of the canoe."

When Talli finished her chores, she told Banabas she was going to stroll about the village and then visit with Ceboni.

"We will be here," he said.

Talli forced a smile, then left.

The village was very similar to her own. Ramo's lodge was more ornate than Yahga-ta's. But then Ramo was more pompous than Yahga-ta. As she passed, she saw Liakka standing just inside the doorway of Ramo's lodge. Liakka ran her hands up the cacique's sides, then wiggled her hips against him. The woman was quite bold, she thought. Ramo nipped at her neck. Liakka playfully pushed him away and promenaded out of his lodge.

Talli realized she had paused and was staring. Quickly she turned away and continued to look for Ceboni.

Halfway across the village she saw Ceboni plaiting palmetto, making a new mat. A girl played with a doll made from sabal palm fiber and an older boy sat next to Ceboni, sharpening a stick.

When Ceboni spotted Talli, she put her handiwork down and jumped up.

"I am happy you have come."

Ceboni's daughter came next to her and latched on to her skirt.

"This is Zowhi. She is shy. Say hello to Talli, Zowhi."

The girl buried her face in her mother's thigh.

"I was timid when I was a child," Ceboni said. "You would not know that now. I guess Zowhi will grow out of it like I did." Ceboni patted her daughter's head. "Go play," she said.

The child eased away, holding her doll to her chest.

"I have the greenbrier for you," Ceboni said. "I should have brought it to you. How do you feel?"

"My stomach is still unsettled. It comes and goes."

"Yes, that is the way the pregnancy sickness is."

Talli shifted her weight, half listening to Ceboni. She waited for the right opening in the conversation.

"Is that how it is for you?" Ceboni asked.

"What?" Talli realized she had missed part of the conversation.

"Worse in the mornings and when you are hungry. Is that how the sickness is for you?"

"Yes. I think so." Talli drew in a breath before speaking again. "Ceboni, I have a favor to ask of you."

"Certainly," the woman said. "Sit down. Tell me what you want."

Talli lowered herself to the ground and sat facing Ceboni. "The Ais boy stays with my husband and me."

"Ais!" Ceboni said. "Who would have ever thought an Ais would live among the Jeaga? I never would—"

Talli interrupted. "My husband and I are just married."

"Ohhh," Ceboni said with a grin. "You have no privacy."

"That is right," Talli said. "I would like to plan a special night for him tonight, but I cannot with the child there. I want us to be alone."

"Ahh, are you a noisy one? It is difficult to be discreet if you are one of the noisy kind."

"He is not our child. I find his presence inhibiting. Banabas and I are still learning about one another."

"Tonight," Ceboni said, looking up and pondering. "Why do you not let him stay with us for the night? He is about the age of my son, Tawute."

"I would appreciate that. We will have this one night."

Ceboni's face lit with an impish grin. "You have made me think. It *is* different with children about."

"Perhaps I can return the favor. You should do that for your husband," Talli said.

Ceboni giggled. "What would Iquan think of me if I sent the children away for a night? Oh my goodness, Iquan would be so surprised." She giggled again, her face blushing.

"He would probably think you are wonderful."

"One night like it used to be! When the children were

babies it was easy, but they are older now. Iquan and I have no real private time anymore."

Talli raised an eyebrow. "Plan on letting me keep your children one night. You let me know when you are ready."

"Joog was helpful to me today," Banabas said. He sipped his tea. "I know in his heart he wanted to run, but I think he listens to you. He is frightened, and he has had hatred of the Jeaga ingrained in him. I am sure he feels confused."

"I know," Talli said. She looked up at the moon. "There is no halo tonight." She put her hand on his thigh.

Banabas's forehead furrowed with bafflement.

"I have not been a good wife," Talli said. She lowered her eyes. "I am sorry."

Banabas rested his hand on top of hers. "Talli, I am a patient man. I do not want to rush you into anything you are not ready for. When the time is right—"

"The time *is* right," she said. "Joog is with Ceboni, and we are alone." Talli stood up, still grasping his hand. "Come inside, husband."

Banabas got to his feet and followed her into the lodge.

Talli shook her hair to her back, then slowly lowered her skirt to the floor. She stood naked, highlighted in a slice of moonlight that pierced the entranceway. Her black hair shone as if fire polished as it spilled over her shoulders.

Banabas moved only his eyes.

"Is something wrong?" she asked. "Do I not please you?"

"You please me very much," he said. "I am stricken with your beauty."

"Come," she said.

Banabas moved to her and put his hands on her shoulders, then slid them down her arms and onto her waist, over her ribs, pausing at each curve. His eyes closed, and his hands feathered across her belly and up to her midriff. He stopped short of cupping her breasts.

Banabas sighed, a sound that came from deep inside him. He ran a hand up the nape of her neck and then buried his fingers in her hair. Talli arched her neck and Banabas put his mouth in the hollow of her throat. His breath was warm and moist.

Slowly, Talli slipped down and lay on the sleeping skin. "Husband," she whispered.

For a long time, Talli lay awake. Banabas had been exceptionally gentle, and he had spent a long time touching her and caressing her before he actually joined with her. She tried to imagine he was Akoma and several times found herself responding to him. Then she would catch herself and the fantasy would be spoiled.

Banabas slept deeply, his breathing heavy and even. If she had loved this man, she supposed the joining with him would have been very pleasurable. She would not do it again. She had promised Akoma she would never be Banabas's in that way. But she had to, just this once. In a few weeks she would tell Banabas she was pregnant. He would believe it was his child. Akoma would understand.

21

Two sets of ten days passed. Joog remained mute, and Talli and Banabas became confident he was not going to attempt to run away. They told him often that they would make every effort to get him returned to his home, but it would be unwise for him to try to make it alone. Joog appeared to understand. He was a bright boy, they concluded.

One late afternoon the sky became overcast. The people anticipated rain. When the darkness came, they saw no stars. They were certain the rain was coming. Late in the night a mist of rain fell, enough to dampen the air so it chilled people to the bone. But no real rain fell. The drought continued.

Talli didn't allow Banabas to join with her again. She found many excuses to deny him. After several attempts, he discontinued his efforts. Banabas remained patient, but confused. At last enough time had passed that she could tell him of the pregnancy.

Talli sat weaving a basket and watched Banabas teach Joog how to strike flakes from chert.

"The pit is cool," Banabas said, digging his hand into the sand of the fire pit. He dug down, removing alternate layers of sand and coals until he reached several stones he had buried and heated the day before.

He withdrew the cobbles. "Some of the color has changed from the heat," he said to Joog. Banabas sat on a log near the hearth. He patted a spot next to him. "Sit next to me and watch. Be very careful. The flakes will be extremely sharp, and it is easy to get cut."

Banabas put a leather pad over his left thigh and one over Joog's leg. He placed a nodule of chert on each pad. "Study it," he said. "Listen to what the stone tells you. Notice the ridges. Always follow the ridges, the stone speaks to you that way."

Banabas rolled the nodule in his palms. "All things speak to you if you know how to listen."

Joog picked up his cobble and felt it.

"Put this on your left hand," Banabas said. He handed Joog a leather pad like his own, only smaller to fit the boy's hand. The pad had a hole in it through which he put his thumb, laying the rest of the leather across his palm. "This will protect your hand," he said.

Banabas placed the nodule on his left thigh. "Do you know where you will strike the stone?"

Joog nodded.

"Put the striking platform facing to the right," Banabas said. "The first thing you are going to learn is how to detach usable flakes. It will take practice."

Banabas swung his arm. "See how I do this? You are going to swing your arm in an arc. Do not stop when you hit the stone, keep your arm moving. Follow through. Do like I do."

Joog swung his arm, copying Banabas. After several swings, Banabas retrieved a piece of antler about two hands long with the base still attached. "I use antler because it is hard enough, yet the core is soft enough to grip the nodule and not slide off when I strike. Some prefer coral or shell. I like antler."

Banabas closed his eyes. "Picture the flake you want." He lifted his arm, then swung down, striking the nodule with the antler billet. A feathery, sharp-edged flake flew to the ground. He picked it up. "Watch me do several of these," he said. "Then you try."

The boy watched, studying and observing all the finesse with which Banabas knapped the stone.

"These are blanks," Banabas said, picking up the flakes. "You shape these into the tool you desire. That will come in time, but first you must learn to produce good blanks. Let me see you do it. Concentrate."

Joog closed his eyes, as Banabas had, then swung his antler billet and struck the stone. A flake fell away.

"Well done," Banabas said.

After the boy produced several flakes, Banabas had him gather them from the ground and put them in a pouch. "Be careful of the waste. Clean it up so you do not step on it."

The boy did as he was told. "Now I will show you what to do with a finished piece." Banabas opened a pouch that lay at his feet. He pulled out a long, worked chert blade. "I want to make a knife with this blade," he said. "Would you like to learn how to do such a thing?"

Joog nodded.

"He has learned a lot in one day," Talli said. "Let him go and play with Tawute." She was anxious to tell Banabas that she carried a child. She'd been apprehensive all day.

"Soon," Banabas said. He turned to the boy. "Melt this pitch over the fire while I grind some of this burned wood into a powder." He handed Joog a lashed pot with a ball of pitch inside. "Do not let it boil, just heat it until it melts."

Talli strung the pot over the fire for the boy.

"You have to watch it," Banabas said.

After the pitch melted, Banabas stirred in the charcoal he had ground up. He held a notched piece of antler that would be the knife handle and dabbed some of the pitch glue in the notch. He pushed the butt end of the blade into the notch, then spread more glue around the base. He waited a few moments for the pitch to cool a little, and then he smoothed the glue with his fingers. He propped up the knife. "When the pitch is set, it will hold the blade securely," he said.

"Now," Talli said. "Let the boy play. Find Tawute," Talli said.

Banabas kept an eye on the boy as he crossed the village. "We let him go alone," he said. "If he runs, Ramo will find no favor in me."

"Do you want me to follow?" Talli asked.

"No," he answered.

Talli swirled the tea she had prepared. "I have something I wish to speak to you about."

"What is it?"

"Sip your tea first," she said. She had practiced many ways of telling him. None seemed right.

Talli touched her abdomen. He had to believe that the single time they joined had produced this child.

"I will show you the rub," Tawute said to Joog. "The bear was close, you will see."

Joog followed Tawute into the forest. "It is not too far from here," Tawute said, leading the way deeper into the wood.

They passed a lowland where cypress grew, and then moved on to higher ground. Tawute stopped next to a huge, spreading laurel oak. "Look," he said.

Joog wrinkled his nose as he looked close where Tawute pointed. A swatch of bear fur stuck to the oak bark.

"Look up," Tawute said. "See how big he is. His claw marks are so high."

Joog's eyes widened.

Tawute paced the area. "I wish the ground was wet so we could see his tracks. Bears walk just like we do. They put the heel of their back foot all the way down. Raccoons do, too. And you can see all five of his toes. I want to find him," Tawute said. "He is lazy because of the cold. I am surprised he is even about. When it gets colder, he will not come around. He will sleep."

Joog shook his head.

"Are you afraid? Jeaga are not afraid of an old bear."

Joog straightened at the insinuation that his people were not as brave as the Jeaga.

"We could probably kill him if we wanted to," Tawute said. "I could take my father's large spear—"

Tawute danced and pretended to hold a spear shaft in his hand. "Come on, fat lazy bear," he said, taking a wide stance. "I am not afraid of you."

Tawute finally stopped. "We will go get the spear now, then look for more signs of him. Everyone will be surprised when two boys bring home bear meat!"

Joog followed Tawute back through the woods. The earth was dry beneath the pines, and the needles and leaves crackled under their feet as they walked.

In his excitement, Tawute paid little attention to where he walked. His father had taught him to always be alert, never take for granted a single step. All that teaching was lost to Tawute's anticipation of finding the bear.

"I do not know how much your father has told you about me," Banabas said. "My wife died a very long time ago. She crossed over to the Other Side while giving birth. The child was stillborn, and my wife did not live to see the next sunrise. Regretfully, I have no children. I did not think of another wife until you. Joog has become like my own. He is the child I never had. All this time I find myself becoming attached to the boy and I know I will eventually have to give him up. He is Ais."

Talli tilted her head and smiled. "It is admirable that you find a place for Joog in your heart. I have also grown quite fond of him."

"For now, he is our son," Banabas said. "I do not think of him as Ais. I only think of him as a child. I wondered how you might feel about that."

"I feel the same as you," she said.

Banabas set down the gourd that contained his tea. "All right, I have finished. The tea was very good, too. Now tell me what it is you want to talk to me about."

"I am hopeful it will make you happy," Talli said.

Banabas suddenly stood up. Talli looked where his eyes focused. Ceboni was running toward them. Tawute ran beside her.

Talli dropped her tea and rose to her feet. "It is Joog," she said. "Something has happened. Has he run away?"

Breathless, Ceboni spat out the news. "Rattlesnake," she said. "Tawute says a big one . . . diamondback."

"I did not see him until after he bit Joog," Tawute wailed. "I stumbled over it. It is my fault. I awakened him or made him mad and he bit Joog. He was as long as my arm and bigger around."

"Where?" Banabas said. "Where is Joog?"

"In the forest. I told him to lie down and be still."

"Tawute, take me to him. Hurry," Banabas said, picking up the knife he had made earlier.

Tawute took off in a run, Banabas behind him. Talli started to follow.

"No," Banabas yelled back to her. "Prepare the medicines. Have them ready when I bring him back."

"I will help you," Ceboni said.

"I cannot think," Talli said. "Button snakeroot, thorn apple, hood-wort."

"I have some snakeroot," Ceboni said. "And I know where to find black haw. That is also good for snakebite."

"Ceboni, gather what you can. I know where there is thorn apple. I will go and get it."

"Yes," Ceboni said. "I will be right back."

Talli sprinted into the woods. She had noticed the thorn apple before. Putiwa used an elixir made from the plant to help induce his visions. And she'd seen him make poultices for wounds. Her mother told her it was useful for snakebite.

Quickly she gathered the leaves from the thorn apple, then fled back to the village. With her oak pestle, she pulverized the leaves, then started them steeping in hot water over the fire.

Ceboni returned with a basket of plant parts she had collected. "We have everything," she said, panting. She ground the button snakeroot and then scraped the result into a pot of water she hung over the fire. She held up a hood-wort. Its yellow fibrous roots dangled.

"Use it all," Talli said. "The whole plant."

Ceboni crushed the plant with the pestle, put it to boil, then took the bark of the black haw and put it in a separate pot. "I used a decoction of black haw while I was carrying Zowhi. I kept having a little bleeding with her. Ocaab told me to drink tea made from black haw bark. It worked."

"Here they come," Talli said, spotting Banabas. He carried Joog, and Tawute ran beside him.

"Take him inside," Talli said. "We are almost ready." She turned to Ceboni. "Will you get Ocaab?"

Ceboni hesitated.

"What is wrong?"

"Nothing. I will go get the shaman now."

Talli watched her with curiosity, wondering why Ceboni had hesitated. She would ask her later. She turned her attention to the medicines. They could probably cook a bit longer, but there was no time.

How was she going to care for Joog without giving away her secret?

"Talli, bring the medicines," Banabas called.

She removed the pots from the fire, put the lashes over her arms. She stood rooted in the entrance to the lodge. Her hands trembled and she felt a wave of heat begin in her chest and roll through her body.

"Bring them," Banabas said.

The elixirs sloshed out of the pots as her arms shook. The buzzing noise that often accompanied the onset of the affliction grew loud.

"I cannot," she said, feeling herself losing touch. There was great pain in her leg, and she felt Joog's thirst in her throat.

"Talli, what is wrong?"

Banabas slipped the pots off her arms and put them on the ground. His arms went around her to guide her into the lodge.

Talli shook her head and resisted, pulling back.

"Come sit down," he said, again encouraging her inside the lodge.

"No. No." Her voice was weak and shaky. "I need fresh air."

She backed away, her face pale, her knees unsteady. Talli dropped to the ground in front of the log Banabas used to sit on. The sharp edge of a flake fragment, one that was missed when Joog cleaned up the waste, bit into the flesh of her leg. She held her face in her hands.

"Ceboni, come quickly," Banabas said, seeing the woman on her way.

"Take care of her while I tend to Joog. I think she became sick at the sight of the boy's leg."

Banabas went back inside the shelter.

Joog moaned. Trails of dried blood streaked his leg from where Banabas had slashed the punctures with his knife in an effort to bleed the poison out.

Banabas soaked a strap of deer hide in the button

snakeroot and then dipped it in the thorn apple medicine. He held it up to cool so it would not burn Joog's leg. Still warm, he tied it around the boy's wound. Joog groaned.

"I will get Talli to give you the medicines," he said before passing through the doorway.

Banabas sat next to his wife. "You have cut yourself," he said, wiping away the string of blood that ran down her leg. "Are you all right?" he asked.

Talli still hid her face in her hands.

"She will be fine," Ceboni said. "This happens to some women."

Banabas looked up at Ceboni. "What do you mean?"

Ceboni's expression told of her regret over her comment. She fidgeted. "Well, some women get very upset when someone they care about is injured."

Banabas massaged Talli's shoulders. "Joog needs you," Banabas said. "His leg is already swollen. I have dressed the wound. You will not have to look at that. Take it slow and easy. You will be fine."

Banabas helped Talli to her feet. "Let me go in alone," she whispered. If she could not control the affliction, she didn't want Banabas and Ceboni to witness her. She prayed that the worst was over. Usually the affliction happened when she was first exposed to the situation, then it lessened and went away. She hoped that all that was going to happen had already happened.

Talli entered the lodge. She stood just inside the entranceway. There was the slightest pain in her leg . . . Joog's pain. She waited to see if the symptoms would grow worse. When they didn't, she stepped closer to the child. For an instant she felt dizzy, and the buzzing returned, but then it dissipated.

"Banabas," she called. "Come inside."

Talli ladled out a very small portion of the hood-wort decoction in a clam shell. While Banabas held the boy's head up, she kept Joog's mouth open and dribbled ten drops onto his tongue. Then she gave him a full shell of black haw elixir.

"Maybe a small dose of thorn apple would make him rest better," Talli said.

"Be careful with that. Too much can be harmful. It could make the child crazy."

Joog writhed on the mat.

"He is so fitful," she said.

Talli knew the affliction could return at any moment. At the first sign, she would leave Joog until it abated. Caring for him was going to be difficult.

Ceboni called from outside the lodge.

"Enter," Banabas said.

"Where is Ocaab?" Talli asked.

"He is not coming," Ceboni said.

"Why?"

"Joog is not Jeaga."

So that was why Ceboni had hesitated when asked to go get Ocaab. She must have suspected there would be a problem.

Banabas threw his knife across the lodge. "Joog is a child. He is not the enemy. He is just a boy. A good boy."

Ceboni shrugged.

Banabas stood up. "I will be back," he said.

22

Banabas stomped out. What was wrong with Ocaab? It did not matter if Joog was Ais or Jeaga, he was a boy and in his charge.

"Ocaab," Banabas said when he found the shaman. "Speak to me."

"I cannot help the Ais boy," he said. "He is not Jeaga."

"Why does it matter?"

"The spirits are not the same."

"You call upon the Jeaga spirits to intercede for you. You can ask them to do anything. You ask the favor. They answer you. The boy is not calling the spirits. You are."

"No."

Banabas seized Ocaab's shoulder. His head dipped in anger, and his eyebrows pitched toward the bridge of his nose. "He is only a boy. Our cacique brought him here. The child did not come on his own. He is no threat! There is no reason you cannot help. He might die. Do you understand?"

"Yes, I do," Ocaab said, removing Banabas's hand. "Joog is a boy now, but he will grow to be a man. An Ais man. The enemy."

"You are supposed to be wise, shaman. I think you are blind!"

Banabas spun around and returned to the lodge.

"Banabas, is Ocaab coming?" Talli asked.

"No. And his reasoning is all wrong."

"Talk to Ramo. Can he intervene? Look at him," Talli said. "His leg is already so swollen. He moans."

"Ocaab says Joog will grow up and be the enemy."

Talli raised Joog's head and put it in her lap.

"No one knows the boy like we do," Banabas said.

"Even so, how can a spirit man deny help for a child?"

Banabas removed the dressing and wrung it out. Talli grimaced.

"The skin is so tight and discolored," she said.

"We will have to cut some of the flesh away. Maybe you should give him a little of the thorn apple decoction. Let me burn my knife so the skin will seal."

Talli cuddled Joog's head and gently rocked. "Do you have to do that?"

"The flesh will die, and he will get sicker."

Talli sang softly to the boy. She sang a song her mother had sung to her and her sisters. She had always found it soothing.

"You must fight the poison," she whispered when the song was done. "I will get you home one day, Joog. Fight hard."

Ocaab was right. One day Joog would be an Ais warrior. But she could never imagine him as the enemy. Perhaps this was as it was meant to be, as all things were. Maybe Joog would be an instrument of the peace. His grandfather was a leader. Joog would be also.

"You will have to help," Banabas said. "We will give him a small bit of the thorn apple. It will be easier on him."

Banabas put some of the elixir in a shell spoon. "Hold his head up so he does not choke."

Talli pulled the boy higher in her lap, and Banabas put the spoon in Joog's mouth. "Just a little at a time. Swallow, Joog," he said.

When Joog finished the medicine, Banabas went out to heat his knife. "There will be bleeding," he said. "Are you prepared for that?"

"Yes," she answered. "Let us get this done."

When Banabas returned, he had Talli hold Joog's leg still. "He may flinch," Banabas said, "but you must keep the leg from moving." Banabas examined the boy's eyes. "Good, the thorn apple works. Are you ready?" he asked Talli.

She nodded, and Banabas pressed the edge of his knife to Joog's leg.

"That much?" Talli asked, seeing how far from the wound Banabas put his knife.

"Two finger-widths is good," he said. "We may have to take even more. We will see how he does."

Banabas cut away a chunk of flesh. The wound oozed blood, and Banabas instructed her to dab it up. Talli felt her stomach turn over with a wave of nausea. So many women only felt sick in the mornings when they were pregnant. Talli felt ill on and off all day. The sight of the blood-soaked bandage added to her discomfort. She had never shied from injuries, no matter how bloody. Of course, she usually kept her distance from such situations because of the affliction.

Banabas glanced at Talli. "Are you not feeling well?" he asked, dressing the wound. "Your face grows pale. Even your lips. Go out, I will tend to Joog."

"No, it is not that, Banabas." Talli stumbled over her words. "I . . . um."

"What is it?"

"I have to tell you something." Talli was surprised to hear her own voice. "It appears I carry your child," she blurted out.

The surprise on his face made Talli relax. She was doing the right thing for everyone. If anyone ever thought she carried the child of the next leader of the Turtle, there would never be harmony amongst the Jeaga. In addition, the humiliation Banabas would suffer would be horrible. Her husband did not deserve that. Such knowledge would not serve Akoma well either.

"Are you pleased?" she asked.

Banabas touched her cheek with his fingertips. "Very pleased."

"I know there has only been that one time when we . . . I will be a better wife."

"You are a fine wife. I know you do not love me, Talli. I realize you are a gift. Maybe I should not have accepted Ufala's proposal. It seemed right at the time."

"All things are designed by the spirits. I have come to believe we have little control over our lives."

"And this child you carry, is that what has been making you sick?"

"Yes, I believe so. I confided in Ceboni, asking her questions about what is normal. That is why she made that remark this morning about how this happens to women sometimes. I hope you are not angry that I did not tell you first. I was not sure."

Banabas grinned. "Angry? No, I understand. Do not ever be afraid that you might anger me. I am your husband. You can always be truthful with me."

Joog groaned and shifted.

"Do you think he will be all right?" Talli asked.

"I cannot tell." Banabas wrapped his arm around his wife's waist. "Tawute speaks of how large the snake was, but I do not know how much poison it delivered. Joog is not very big."

Liakka suddenly appeared in the doorway. "I have heard what happened. How is the boy? Is there anything I can do to help?"

"Yes," Talli said. "Let me come outside and talk to you so Banabas can finish and Joog can rest. I need you to do something for me."

"What are you asking Liakka to do?" Banabas asked.

"A favor," she answered.

Ramo's white teeth gleamed in the moonlight. "There is a halo around the moon tonight. And there are stars in it," he said. "The rain will come, Liakka. That is not good."

"What do you mean?" she said, sliding her hands down his sides beneath his wrap.

"The drought needs to continue to pressure Chogatis until my plan is in place. I may have to request a great favor of you. In time you will be liberally rewarded."

"Everyone wants a favor from me today. What do you wish?"

Ramo put his mouth to her hair over her ear and whispered, "Who else asks a favor of you?"

"The Turtle woman," she answered. "But let us discuss that later." Liakka feathered her hands along his thighs. "You are so strong, Ramo. So smart and so strong." Her damp mouth touched his nipple.

"You have stirred my curiosity. Tell me what the Turtle woman wants from you."

"Wait," she said, rubbing her face against his chest and wrapping her hands about his neck.

Ramo put his hands over hers and pulled them apart. Liakka looked up and sighed. "It will spoil this moment we have," she said.

"Tell me, Liakka. I am already distracted, so the moment is ruined until I have my curiosity satisfied."

Liakka slowly opened and closed her eyes, cocking her head to the side in disappointment. "You have heard about the snake and the Ais boy?"

"Rattler bit him."

"Ocaab will not minister to him because he is Ais, not Jeaga. Banabas and the Turtle woman fear he will die without the shaman's help."

"What are you supposed to do about that?" Ramo asked.

"She wants me to persuade you to step in and demand that Ocaab use his medicine on the boy."

"And you agreed?" he asked.

"I told her I would ask."

"And that is why you come after me tonight, slithering in my lodge like a snake yourself?"

Ramo grabbed her and pushed her against a support post. His hand tore at her skirt. "What did you come for?" he asked. "This?" He lifted her and then was suddenly inside her, pushing hard and rough.

The back of her head scraped the support post. "Stop," she said.

"You wanted to use our joining, did you not? Wanted to ask me for a favor at my weakest moment?"

Ramo thrust into her again.

"Stop, you are hurting me," she said.

"No, you like it like this. I know what makes a woman like you scream like the panther."

"No." Liakka pushed on his shoulders, but he pinned her to the post. The bark scratched her back.

"Admit why you came here tonight. You want to take advantage of the cacique?"

"You know that is not so," she said. "Let me go,

Ramo. I told you if we discussed this, the evening would be spoiled."

His sweaty body pulled away from hers, and he released his grip. "And so it is," Ramo said. "Tell this Turtle woman that I do not interfere with the man of the spirits' decisions. He speaks with the spirits, not I. Also inform her, if she seeks a favor from the cacique, she should do her own bidding. I never answer to anyone secondhand."

A low rumble of thunder made them both look out of the lodge. Maybe this was the end of the drought.

Liakka straightened her skirt.

"The Panther may need you, Liakka. I will let you know," Ramo said. "It will not be a favor just for me, but for our people."

Liakka turned and glared at him. She raked her hair back from her face and left.

The thorn-apple elixir allowed Joog to sleep more peacefully. Banabas lifted his head from his mat at the sound of thunder. In a moment the splatter of rain rattled the thatch of the lodge.

Banabas's head dropped onto the sleeping mat. He lay on his back. "Are you awake?" he asked Talli.

"Yes," she answered. "I hear the rain."

"A beautiful sound," he said. "Especially when you have not heard it in a long time."

"Banabas," she said, "do you think the rain will end the trouble between the Turtle and Panther and the Ais?"

Banabas ran his arm under her neck and drew her near. "The trouble between the Panther and Turtle runs deeper than the drought. There are issues between the two that will take time to resolve, whether or not the rain relieves the Ais."

"Do you see that happening soon?"

"I see it taking generations. I doubt our child will know the sincere unity between the Panther and the Turtle," he said, touching his fingers to her belly. Softly, he brought his hand to rest. "It is unfortunate. There are deep differences in our ideas of ourselves. We are both Jeaga, but *how* we should be Jeaga is the question that separates us."

Talli sighed. She wanted the Turtle and Panther to end their differences. If they did, she could return to her village. But it did not sound as if that was going to happen. Maybe Banabas would give her up if she begged, and she could return home. Maybe Akoma would come for her.

"And what about the Ais?" she asked.

"The Ais are already committed to their cause. The last drought hurt them so badly they will not forget. Chogatis will not allow his people to suffer again."

"Do you blame him? Yahga-ta would do the same."

"No, Chogatis does what a good cacique does. His objective is to save his people. But it threatens the Jeaga, and so we also must take a stand."

Talli yawned, recalling all the stories she had heard about the Ais. "But the Ais are different than the Jeaga. The People believe that negotiation and compromise are the way. That is our tradition. The Ais tradition is war."

Banabas stroked her arm. "These are not the worries of women."

"But they are," Talli said, sitting up. "We are just not permitted to participate in the decisions and discussions the men have on such matters. The Ais, the traditions of the Jeaga, those things affect us. We lose our fathers, brothers, sons, and husbands. The women grieve, and if the husband is lost, we wonder what will become of us and our children if there is no one to provide."

Banabas smiled. "You speak with such ardor, like a fanatic in council."

Talli lay down again. "You do not understand. Men do not understand."

Banabas rolled to his side. He swept his hand over her face, then to her throat and to her breast. In a moment, he was atop her and making entry.

Talli squinted her eyes closed. She had to keep her promise to Akoma. She groaned and grimaced.

"What is wrong?" Banabas asked. "Do I hurt you."

"A little," she said, sounding as if she did not want to tell him.

Banabas withdrew. "I am sorry," he said.

"It must be because of the baby," she said.

Banabas rolled onto his back.

Talli waited until her husband slept, and then slipped away from him. She felt relieved. Perhaps he would not attempt to join with her again for the rest of the pregnancy.

She changed Joog's dressing and gave him some water to drink.

The boy whispered something, and Talli leaned closer. "What, Joog?"

"Mother," he whispered.

She stroked his forehead, drawing back his hair.

Talli knew the affliction was going to happen again. Joog's mental and physical pain were so great. She did not back away. Instead, she pulled his head into her lap and closed her eyes. Banabas was sleeping, and there was no one to see.

The dizziness came quickly, but for the first time in her life she did not fear what was to happen. She let the blackness roll over her as she had allowed the waves of the Big Water to sweep over her when she was a child playing on the beach. She didn't fight the buzzing. Bizarre sounds echoed as the breath of the spirits whisked her through the air and sucked her through a tunnel of clouds. She felt the moisture dampen her skin and the wind blow her hair back from her face. The chill in the air made her shiver. Strange images tumbled before her. She saw a village. Not Panther. Not Turtle. Different.

She soared over the village. It was night, and a fire blazed in the center of the village. The people were dancing and drinking the black tea. She heard the music, the striking of sticks, the jingle of shells, the deep bellow of the drum. The men chanted, stepping, bending deep with each footfall. They were part of the music, one with the fire, the music, and the night.

Near the circle of dancing men a woman stood with a baby in her arms and a boy child at her side. The boy imitated the men, stepping in place, wobbling his head to the beat of the drum. It was Joog.

The image suddenly changed. Joog was in the woods. In his hand he held a leaf between two flat sticks. He held it to his mouth and blew. He was calling a deer. She felt his excitement as a buck approached. A man behind him praised him. Talli assumed the man was his father. They looked alike.

Again the picture in her head changed. Joog sat next to his father. The man spoke. "An Ais boy must learn to endure hardship without complaint. A boy must learn to go without food or water for two or three days without growing weak. Tomorrow you will accompany your uncle and me to learn the ways. You will not eat or drink. We will teach you the ways of being a man. The lessons will begin."

Then came the sight she had seen before, Joog hiding in the brush, witnessing the death of his father and uncle. She felt the boy's sheer panic, the sense of devastation, and the denial of his want to scream. A man would not cry out! That was the moment he lost his speech.

Talli suddenly returned to the natural world. Joog moaned in his sleep. Those were the dreams Joog was having. He was remembering home and his journey to becoming a man. How tragically that journey had been interrupted. The Ais and Jeaga had more in common than she had thought.

"Mother," Joog whispered again.

"It will be all right," Talli said. "I promise you will become a man no matter if it be Jeaga or Ais." She brushed his hot cheek with her hand. "Shh," she whispered.

Talli waited until she was sure Joog had quieted and then returned to her sleeping skin. She lay awake listening to the rain. She thought of Joog and how stalwart he was. She thought of Akoma and wondered if she would ever lose his image and not be able to recall what he looked like, how he smelled, what his skin felt like.

Talli turned onto her side and looked at her husband. It was unfortunate she did not love him. He deserved a good wife. She turned again onto her back. She would never betray Akoma. Perhaps Banabas would not try to join with her again until after the child was born. She would have some other plan by the time she delivered the child. Maybe she would even be home by then.

23

Four more cycles of the moon passed. Talli continued to give Joog the medicines she and Ceboni prepared. She fed Joog gruel made from pounded, dried venison and fish that she had soaked in water to extract all the nourishment. She mixed that broth with a small amount of coontie flour to give it some texture. Every day she made Joog drink her concoction, praying that it would give the boy strength. Joog recovered, though slowly, even without Ocaab's help. He still limped because of the missing chunk of flesh and muscle. But even that seemed to be diminishing.

Talli's abdomen swelled with the child she carried. Banabas was understanding and sensitive. He made no more attempts to join with her.

Liakka paid frequent visits to Ramo's lodge. Everyone was aware of their relationship. Talli felt some sympathy for Liakka. Ramo took from her and gave nothing back in exchange. Ceboni thought Talli naïve and told her so. "Liakka knows what she is doing," she said.

Ceboni often spent time with Talli, telling her stories of her own pregnancies and assuring Talli that all her symptoms were normal. Once Ceboni mentioned that she thought Talli was inordinately concerned. Talli denied she worried excessively, but admitted to herself that she was obsessive over the baby. This child was the only strand of connection she would ever have with the man she loved. Her nightmare was that this child would be ripped from her just as she and Akoma had been torn from each other. Any little twinge made her panic. Ceboni did her best to convince Talli that her pregnancy was quite normal.

*   *   *

The Turtle village perched on the brink of change.
Yahga-ta was eager and proud to turn over the leadership of the clan to his son. Akoma had gained the repu-
tation of being a man of courage and vision. The
villagers were enthusiastic that Akoma, a young and vigorous man, was ready to become their cacique.

Akoma spoke of Talli only when prodded. What appeared as stoic was actually his way of dealing with the
pain of losing her. He could not think or speak of her
without a knife of pain slashing through his heart. The
People would not tolerate a cacique with such a fragile
component to his spirit. And so he kept that part of his
spirit hidden from others, buried deep inside.

"I am going to seek a Panther wife," Akoma said to
Bunta. "That is my obligation."

"Then Yahga-ta is ready to step down and you are
ready to become cacique. When?"

Both men stepped in the water. The fish traps were
full.

"Soon," Akoma said, filling his satchel with fish. The
fish flopped about, making the hide bag seem alive.
"Perhaps in several days I will travel there. When I visit
the Panther, do you wish to go, also?"

The war chief laughed. "I already have a wife."

Akoma returned the laugh and then took on a serious
tone. "I think you should go. Not only do I seek a
woman, I think Ramo has been too silent. We should
pay him a visit."

"I agree with that," Bunta said. "Tell me when we
plan to leave and I will be ready." He leaned over and
scooped up as many fish as he could in his hands.

"Even with the promise of the return of the rains,
Ramo seems more dangerous than the Ais."

Bunta rubbed one thumb over his chin. "Several
mornings ago I smelled smoke from the west. The muck
is still dry and the lightning ignites it like kindling. The
rain we have had has not replenished all the water, but
even if it had, I do not believe the Ais would back off.
Neither will Ramo. He seeks power. He takes advantage

of the situation. As the drought continues, it fuels his power, and power is what feeds the man. He is a blemish on the Jeaga. I cannot believe so many listen to him."

Akoma filled his satchel and closed it. "He is charismatic. He is handsome, energetic, and has the ability to bring out tremendous passion in most men. That is not only a quality of great leadership, it is a talent. He is a master."

"Unfortunate that that talent is spent on someone who does not harbor the well-being of the People in his heart."

Bunta also closed his bag, and the men stepped on shore again. "Tell me, Akoma. You say you are ready to seek a wife. Has your heart healed from Talli?"

Akoma looked down the bank. How was he going to answer that? His heart would never heal. That was why he was going to visit the Panther now. He had no interest in a wife, but if seeking one in the Panther village was what it would take to see Talli again, then that was what he would do. Akoma's eyes caught something. "Look there," he said, pointing.

Bunta squinted. "I cannot make it out. I need to be closer."

"I think it is a man," Akoma said. "There, lying by the edge of the water."

The two men slid their satchel straps from their shoulders and put the bags on the ground. They left the bank and skulked through the heavy brush until they were close enough to make out just what they had seen from downriver.

"It is a man," Bunta whispered. "Is he dead?"

"Wait here."

Bunta nodded, and Akoma crept up to the man, who lay facedown. The man had cuts, bruises, swollen places, all over his body. The side of his head that faced Akoma was swollen, and his eye was discolored. There was a dent in the side of his head and a cut that had already stopped bleeding. Akoma could see the bloody bone beneath the split in the scalp.

Akoma nudged him with his foot, gripping his knife in a ready pose. The man did not move.

Again, Akoma jostled him with his foot. The man
groaned. Akoma knelt next to him. Keeping his knife at
the man's throat, he flipped the man onto his back. The
downed warrior's hair clung to his sweaty face in stringy
blood-crusted mats. Fissures in his lips were caked with
traces of blood.

"He has been down for a while. The blood is dry,"
Akoma said. He looked the man over. "He is Jeaga!"
Akoma called to Bunta. "Come help me."

The markings the man bore on his skin, tattoos made
with plant dyes and thorns, were distinctly Jeaga.

"Do you recognize him?" Akoma asked.

"No."

"Help me with him," Akoma said, raising the warrior's head.

"What has happened to him?" Bunta asked as they
lifted him to Akoma's shoulder.

The man's torso hung down Akoma's back. "We will
have to wait and ask him. Kitchi can care for him. She
has much experience in healing and seems to have a
talent for it."

Bunta's eyebrows arched. "Ufala is proof of that. I
wonder if she ever wishes Ufala had not recovered from
his wounds?"

Akoma laughed. "He is cantankerous. You would
think he would be more grateful for his health."

"At least he hunts again. The maiming of his arm
humbled him, perhaps too much. But with the marriage
of Talli to Banabas, he believes he regained his worth.
I think it has gone to his head. The stories he tells! At
first they were entertaining, but I believe we all grow
weary of hearing him boast."

"Time will help. His arm has healed, such as it is,
nearly useless, but it takes longer for the mind to heal."

"Akoma," Bunta said, "you do not sound as if you
resent him."

Akoma cleared his throat before he spoke. "Talli
helped me understand. The decision to offer her as part
of the strategy to maintain the unity of the Jeaga was
not really made by Ufala or the Turtle Council. Oh, the
men take pride in their shrewdness, but really it was

determined by the spirits." He turned to look at Bunta. "We are all here as part of an elaborate design. It is like we are all part of a spider's web. It is important that each of us performs his duty. If we do not, a single, fine strand of the web breaks. Unimportant as that strand may seem, the web is weakened and does not function as it should."

Sassa's small feet padded hurriedly across the damp ground of the village to Akoma's hearth. The rainy season was going to come this time, she was certain. The stench of fires burning to the west was not in the air this morning. A good sign. She thanked the spirits.

Akoma acknowledged her with a nod.

"Come quickly," she said. "The stranger speaks. Ufala says you must come right away."

"Who speaks?" Akoma asked. "Settle yourself and tell me why Ufala has sent you."

Sassa drew in a deep breath. "The injured one. He has been lucid sometimes, and he talks. Ufala thinks what he says is important and wants you to hear." Sassa beckoned him with her hand. "Ufala is waiting. Please hurry. He will be angry with me if I do not fetch you right away." Sassa nervously tapped her lips with her fingertips.

"All right," Akoma said. "Go ahead and I will follow."

Sassa took off in a run, and Akoma followed her to Ufala's lodge. He peered inside. Kitchi swabbed the warrior's forehead with a damp piece of hide, and Ufala sat at his side.

"Come," Ufala said. "He is mumbling again."

"He says his name is Cunpa," Kitchi said.

Ufala nodded. "Deer clan. Says he was captured and tortured by the Ais, but he managed to escape. Appears his injuries have been too much for him."

The man's parched lips moved, cracked, and bled. Kitchi dampened them.

"Chogatis—" His voice seemed to dry up. Kitchi lifted his head and gave him water to drink.

"Chogatis? Is that what he said? He speaks of the cacique of an Ais clan?" Akoma asked.

"Yes, he has repeated that name several times."

Akoma squatted to be closer. "What do you want to tell us about Chogatis?"

"Turtle," the man whispered. "Turtle murdered his son."

Akoma shot a look at Ufala. "What is he talking about? Whose son?"

Ufala shrugged and shook his head.

"Chogatis's son," the man said.

"Cunpa," Akoma said, "tell me more. Chogatis believes a Turtle man killed his son? There was a lot of bloodshed in the skirmish?"

The wounded man shook his head and coughed, coiling his body into an agonized ball as the spasm wracked him.

"When then?" Ufala asked. "When did this supposedly happen?"

"Leave him be, now," Kitchi said. "He cannot talk. Come back later," she said looking at Akoma.

Ufala snatched the sponging hide from his wife. "Get away, woman."

"No, she is right," Akoma said. "We will learn more from him if he recovers. He needs rest."

Kitchi shook her head.

Akoma understood. She did not believe the man was going to recover.

Kitchi took the man's head in her hands and turned it to the side so Akoma could see. The gash to his head had festered and swelled to the size of Akoma's fist. Bad spirits had gotten inside despite Kitchi's attending him.

"Let me know if he says anything else," Akoma said.

Ufala left the lodge with Akoma.

"I think we need to ask Cunpa more questions," Ufala said. "He wants to tell us something."

"If Chogatis believes a Turtle killed his son, especially if it was not during our confrontation, then what? What has happened?"

"That is what I mean," Ufala said. "We need these questions answered. Chogatis could be heading this way as we speak, preparing to make war on the Turtle. We would be caught by surprise!"

"Get Putiwa to the man's side," Akoma said. "Perhaps he can provide a medicine that will relieve some of Cunpa's discomfort so he can talk."

"Yes," Ufala said. "That makes sense. If the man dies before we get anything out of him . . ."

"Get the shaman," Akoma said. "I will tell Yahga-ta."

Later, Putiwa accompanied Ufala to his lodge. Yahga-ta and Akoma were also there. Putiwa shook his rattle, painted the stranger's body with yellow ochre and red juice from the rouge plant. Yahga-ta, Akoma, and Ufala stood in the back corner of the lodge.

Nocatee hugged her mother's leg and watched as Putiwa lit the end of a bundle of pine needles and pitch. The green needles crackled and spit red sparks through the pungent gray smoke. The shaman chanted and waved the burning cluster of needles, issuing the smoke throughout the lodge.

"He slips away," Kitchi said.

Cunpa's eyes fluttered, then closed.

Finally, Putiwa stopped. "He can tell you no more," he said.

Nocatee turned her head into her mother's leg. Kitchi stroked her hair.

"He is dead," Putiwa said.

"What did Cunpa mean?" Yahga-ta asked aloud. "Why would Chogatis think one of us murdered his son?"

24

The rising sun's light bounced off the edges of the clouds and polished the Panther village with a flaxen glaze. The oaks and sabal palms caught the luster, played with it in their leaves and fans, and then sprinkled the light down across the thatch huts in patches and ribbons.

"A man must rise early," Banabas said to Joog. "As a hunter, that is when he will find the most game. As a warrior, he must be alert at sunrise, as that is when most enemy attacks occur."

Banabas was careful not to mention either Jeaga or Ais, though it would have pleased him to instruct the boy in the traditional way, telling Joog what a *Jeaga* man must do, or explaining when the Ais most often attack.

"Today is going to be a special day for you, Joog," Banabas said. "We are going to spend a day in the woods. You will fast," he said. "Even when there is plenty to eat, it is good to practice fasting. It prepares you for a time of famine. Also, when a man fasts, he sharpens his senses. He is more receptive to the spirits' voices."

Banabas handed the boy a piece of charcoal from the fire. "Blacken your face so that the people and the spirits will see that you fast."

Joog smeared the charcoal across one cheek, beginning under his eye.

"Do not be afraid," Banabas said. "Cover your face with the charcoal."

Joog smiled and more vigorously rubbed the charcoal over his entire face.

"Will you be all right?" Banabas asked Talli.

"Yes," she answered, her hand on her distended belly. "You worry too much about me."

"I have asked Ceboni to keep watch over you."

"Go," she said, "while it is still early."

"Get the water," Banabas told Joog.

Joog retrieved the water pouch, which was made from the dried pericardium of a deer. He tied it to his belt, next to the sheath that held the knife he had made like Banabas's.

The two of them trekked out of the village and into the forest.

"Let the river be our guide," he told the boy. "Follow it and you will find your way back."

The day was warmer than previous days, and by the time the sun was high overhead, both had broken into a furious sweat. Joog stopped for a drink of water.

He looked at Banabas as if to ask why he carried this pouch of water when they followed the river. All the water they could ever want was there in the river.

"A man cannot always find water on a journey," Banabas said. "We follow the river now, but what if the spirits spoke to you and told you to take another route? Then what would you do? Would you tell the spirits you were unprepared for the lesson they were ready to teach you?" He squatted in front of the boy. "This is why I take you on this journey, so that you may ponder, and wonder, and ask questions. it is a good thing. Do you see how clear your mind is? It is already in search of truths."

Banabas tousled the boy's hair and Joog grinned, flashing a missing tooth.

"Listen," Banabas said. "Do you hear that?"

Joog inclined his head to the side, concentrating on the sounds around him. He heard a deep, guttural grunt.

Joog flapped his arms like wings.

"That is right," Banabas said. "A bird. But do you know which one?"

Joog shook his head.

"I will give you some hints," Banabas said. "He is a large, dark bird with a slender body and lives on the river."

The boy still could not identify the bird by its sound.

"It has an orange throat pouch. He stands upright when perched. He is a good fisherman."

Suddenly Joog nodded. He dropped to the ground and hurriedly cleared the leaves and debris away, making a clear spot in the earth. Quickly, he patted the earth smooth for a canvas, then scribbled in the dirt the head of a bird with a hooked bill.

"Yes!" Banabas said. "Cormorant. Very good. you should be able to identify the birds by their sounds. What if you heard that sound deep in the forest, far from the river?"He let Joog think for a moment. "You would be suspicious. The cormorant is a water bird. The sound might really be a hiding warrior communicating with another of his party."

Joog grinned in understanding.

"You are such a bright boy," Banabas said. "The smartest in the village. You are going to be the wisest Jeaga—"

Joog looked up at him.

Banabas started over. "You will be the wisest young man I know."

An explosive, rasping *skyow* captured their attention.

"What about that one?" Banabas asked.

Joog closed his eyes. He knew that same bird croaked and cackled.

Banabas held out two hands. "This one," he said, waving his right hand, "is an egret." He showed Joog his left hand. "And this one is a green-backed heron. Which one do you hear?"

Joog tapped Banabas's left hand.

"Excellent!" Banabas said. "The heron. There will be nothing left for me to teach you."

The boy's smile spread across his face and through his large dark eyes.

"I can see you are proud of yourself," Banabas said. "You should be. You are learning how to pay attention to all the things around you."

Banabas started walking and motioned for Joog to keep up. "Since we are learning about birds, I will give you this last lesson. There are seven events in a bird's

life that influence what it says and how he chooses to
say it. Do you want to know what they are?"

Joog nodded.

"First, when a bird hatches from the egg, he is hungry.
He opens his mouth and cries for his mother or father
to feed him. You see, that is the same with people also."

Joog skipped alongside. When Banabas paused, Joog
stopped to let him know he was listening and paying
attention.

"Then," Banabas continued, "as the bird grows and
gets his feathers, it comes time for him to fly. He knows
how to fly, but he is afraid. The parents encourage him
and call to him. If the young bird is stubborn, the parent
will push him out of the nest so he has to fly. The young
bird will cry, but finally he makes the leap and flutters
his wings. He is awkward at first, but quickly learns. It
is the same with children.

"The third thing that happens in a bird's life is he
must now learn to hunt on his own. Birds often call to
others of their species when they feast.

"Now the bird is grown and finding food on its own.
He wants a mate. Different birds have different rituals,
but there are basic behaviors they all have in common.
The male likes to show off. Just look at the difference
in plumage between the male and female. The male is
much more colorful. He is the aggressor. Like men,"
Banabas said with a chuckle. The boy also laughed.
"And like women, the female acts coy. When a male
songbird declares territory for a nest, he sits in the very
top of a tree and sings as loudly as he can to warn all
other males that this is his spot. The female comes and
looks over the male and the chosen spot. If she is im-
pressed, she accepts the male as her mate.

"Next, of course, is the wonderful event of egg laying.
When the female lays the eggs, she celebrates in an excited song. The male announces to the world with his
cries of excitement that his mate has laid eggs.

"And last is the care of the offspring. Both the male
and female feed the young and converse back and forth,
constantly informing each other of the situation. If an

intruder comes too near, you will hear the loud angry cries of the parents.

"Those are the sounds you should listen for, as each one is different. Know who sings and what makes him sing."

They had traveled a great distance by nightfall. Banabas gave lessons all along the way, and the boy appeared to drink them in.

"Tonight we sleep under the stars," Banabas said. "Tomorrow we will return home and celebrate the end of your fast at sundown. Drink some water," he said. "Water is more important than food."

Talli put down the birthing mat she was weaving. When she was finished with it, she would put it in the birthing hut so it would be there when she was ready to have the baby. She looked at Ceboni.

"I feel heavy here," she said, placing her hand low on her abdomen.

"Not to worry," Ceboni said. "As the baby grows you will feel that more and more."

"And my back aches. Do you think anything could be wrong?"

"Talli, relax. Everything is fine. What you feel is normal. Why not let Ocaab tell you what he sees? You might find some relief from this worry if the shaman confirms what I am saying. Let me take you to him."

Talli breathed deeply. She wondered if anyone could quell her fear of losing this child.

"Not now," Talli said. "Perhaps tomorrow when Banabas returns."

"You miss him, do you not?" Ceboni asked.

"The lodge is empty without him and Joog."

"I am not sure how you feel about your husband," Ceboni said. "I watch you. I see him offering affection, but I also see you having a difficult time accepting it. I suppose it is none of my concern, but I want you to know I am your friend and you can speak to me about anything. I keep secrets."

Talli was silent for a moment before she responded. "Thank you, Ceboni," she finally said.

"I suppose I had best get back to Iquan. He and Ramo and a few of the others prepare for tomorrow. They talk and plan. They are worse than old women."

"What are you talking about?" Talli asked.

"Tomorrow. The visit."

"I am sorry," Talli said. "I have no idea what you are referring to."

"I guess Banabas did not tell you before he left. Akoma, of the Turtle, comes tomorrow. They say he comes in search of a wife. He is to become cacique very soon."

Talli felt the air sucked from her. Her mouth dried up, and her tongue became glued to the roof of her mouth. As if her blood had been heated, it flooded through her. She felt her face redden, and her palms grow cold and sweaty.

"Akoma comes to seek a Panther wife?" Talli asked. Her voice was tremulous and so quiet Ceboni had to strain to hear what she said.

"Yes. It is another offering of goodwill between the Turtle and Panther. A messenger came yesterday and requested that Ramo grant Akoma hospitality."

Talli twisted a lock of her hair.

"Is something wrong?" Ceboni asked. "Do you feel ill, Talli?"

"No," she answered, her voice distant and barely audible. "I am going to rest for a while. I will speak with you tomorrow." she said. "I just want to rest now."

"If you need anything, let me know, Talli. I promised Banabas I would look after you."

"No, I do not need anything. Just some rest."

Ceboni gave Talli a curious stare, a quick hug, and then left. Talli went inside the lodge and sank to the ground. *Akoma was coming!*

Talli didn't lie down. She sat on the floor and bundled the sleeping skin into a roll and held it to her chest. *Seeking a wife,* she thought. In her head she had known Akoma would take a Panther wife, but until now that knowledge had not penetrated her heart. She could not imagine him with another woman, his hands on someone else, someone else hearing his breath close to her ear.

Would he tell this woman the kinds of things he whispered to her?

Talli felt sick. She wasn't sure if it was from the pregnancy or her thoughts of Akoma with someone else. She had a deep ache inside.

Talli dropped the sleeping skin and stood up. Perhaps Ocaab could give her some peace of mind. She had to know the child was all right. Knowing that the baby grew safely inside her would give her strength tomorrow when she saw Akoma. How she longed to hear his voice and to once again tell him how much she loved him. She would tell him she carried his child!

The village was growing still and silent. Embers in the cook fires burned low, and the people performed their end-of-the-day chores. When darkness fell, if there was no feast or celebration, the Jeaga entered their lodges and welcomed sleep so they could rise early the next morning. Tonight was a quiet one.

Talli crossed the plaza and proceeded on to Ocaab's hearth. She had a flash of a memory, for just an instant thinking she should not be about the village alone after dark. The thought was almost incomplete, it vanished so fast. She was a married woman, and the taboos associated with unmarried women no longer applied.

Ocaab was a man of the spirits and did not adhere to the same customs as others. Visions and voices of the spirits dictated his life. He sat by his hearth, legs crossed, palms up in his lap, back erect, eyes closed. Talli heard his low chanting. She wondered how a shaman learned the old tongue, the language of the spirits.

"Turtle woman," Ocaab said without even opening his eyes.

"Yes," Talli answered. "I have come to seek your wisdom, shaman."

Ocaab continued his chant as if he hadn't heard her. Talli felt the hair on the back of her neck prickle. Perhaps the gifts of the shaman were not so unlike her affliction.

"Your husband is away and you have a heavy burden," Ocaab opened his eyes. "Sit and we will talk. Tell me more."

Talli put the back of her hand to her forehead and lowered her head in respect. "I wish to speak of the child I carry."

Ocaab took her hand and pressed a stone in her palm. He curled her fingers and closed her fist. "Let the spirit of the stone come into you. Open yourself."

"I am not sure I know how," Talli said.

"Clear your mind. Let go of your thoughts. Create an open field for the spirit of the earth so it may enter you. Let the stone speak."

Talli closed her eyes. There were too many thoughts. The more she tried to ignore them, the more thoughts swamped her mind.

"I cannot do it," she said, opening her hand.

"Give me both hands, Turtle woman," Ocaab said.

Talli dropped the stone and extended her hands. Ocaab took them in his. "Think of the warmth of the joined hands," he said. "Feel nothing but the soothing warmth that flows from me into you. My body heat becomes yours and yours mine."

Talli felt a pulse of warmth in her wrists. It traveled up her arms and spread through her chest.

"Good," Ocaab said. "The joined hands have opened a doorway, a cleft so that I may see inside you."

Talli no longer felt Ocaab's hands. She could not tell where her hands ended and his began. Their contact made her think of melting pitch.

"Speak of what troubles you," Ocaab said. "It is the child, is it not?"

"Yes," Talli said. "I have a great fear that something might go wrong, that I might lose this child. I need those fears put away."

Ocaab let go of her hands and placed both of his hands on her abdomen.

"There is more to your fear than you have said," Ocaab said. "Why do you have such apprehension?"

Talli swallowed. She didn't know how to answer.

"It is an exceptional fear. But the basis for it is unclear. What is it that fosters such anxiety?"

"I . . ." Talli started again. "My husband has no children. He will suffer enormous disappointment if something happens to this baby."

Ocaab was silent. He appeared troubled, and it disturbed Talli. She thought that perhaps she should not have come. Ocaab asked too many questions that she didn't want to answer.

"I suppose my fears are unwarranted," she said. "Even Ceboni has told me that. I should have listened to her. I am sorry I have wasted your time," Talli said, attempting to get up.

Ocaab's jet eyes flashed open. "You do not speak the truth, Turtle woman. Whose seed have you nourished?"

25

A chill charged through Talli's body. What had Ocaab seen?

"I do not know what you mean, shaman," Talli said. "My body nourishes my husband's seed."

"That is not what I see," Ocaab said. His voice was soft, almost consoling. "The child inside you does not belong to Banabas."

Talli sprang to her feet. "You do not know what you are talking about," she said, backing away. "Banabas is my husband!"

"Sit down, Turtle woman," Ocaab said.

Talli took another step backward. "No, I will hear no more of this," she said.

"It does not matter whether you hear it or not. That changes nothing."

"Ocaab, please," she said, her voice cracking. "Forget that I was here. Will you do that? I am sorry I took up your time. Please." Tears welled in her eyes and sparkled in the firelight.

"Turtle woman, I am a shaman. I see all. There are secrets that everyone keeps. It is not my place to divulge them. I only offer myself as a channel to the spirits."

Talli stopped backing up. She bent forward, her arms wrapped around her middle. "Please, Ocaab. Say nothing of this. For Banabas's sake. For the harmony between the Turtle and the Panther."

"Turtle woman," he said. "You came to me with a question." He paused, then said, "The child is healthy."

Talli turned and ran back to her lodge.

She flung open her sleeping skin and lay down on it. Ocaab knew Banabas was not the father of this child!

What else did he know? Did he know that the child was Akoma's? Whom would he tell?

"Banabas," Ramo called, seeing his adviser and Joog return from their journey. "Send the boy on, I wish to speak with you."

Banabas rested his hand on Joog's shoulder. "Go on to the lodge. Talli will be waiting for us. Tell her I will be along in a moment."

Banabas gave the boy a pat, and Joog did as he was told. "What is so important, Ramo?"

"I expect Akoma before the sun sets."

"Yes, that seems about right. Do you want me to pass the word for council to meet upon their arrival?"

Ramo reared back and gazed at the sky, then back at Banabas. "He says he comes seeking a woman. I question his motives, but we will proceed as if all he comes for is to examine our women."

"All right," Banabas said. "What else do you have on your mind? You did not stop me just to tell me that."

"Tell your woman to keep the boy out of sight while Akoma and Bunta visit. We would not want them asking questions. You do understand, do you not?"

"I understand," Banabas said.

"I called the council together while they were off with the boy," Ramo said. "They will not mention that an Ais boy lives amongst us."

Banabas gave an acknowledging gesture with his head and hand and proceeded on to his lodge. Talli waited outside.

"Welcome home, husband," she said.

Banabas put his arm around her shoulders. "We had a good journey. He learns quickly. You would be proud of him."

Talli found herself biting the inside of her cheek. "Whom did you stop and speak with?" she asked. "Did Ocaab stop you?"

"No," Banabas answered. "Ramo detained me. Why would you think of Ocaab?"

Talli rubbed both her upper arms as if she were cold.

"I thought I saw him going in your direction. That is all. No special reason. What did Ramo want?"

"He wants me to tell you to keep Joog out of sight while Akoma and Bunta are here."

"You mean I have to stay with him in the lodge? I cannot speak with my people when they visit?"

"Ramo does not want them asking questions. The fewer who know what transpired with the Ais the better. It does not take but one man to betray a trust, and Chogatis will come after us with a vengeance. Even the Panther Council does not know what happened. I confided in you because you are my wife."

"But I want to ask about my family," Talli said. "I wish to inquire about my mother and sisters."

Banabas looked at her. "I am sure you do," he said. "I will ask for you."

"But, Banabas—"

"Ramo is right. Joog must be kept out of sight."

Talli hung her head. She wanted the opportunity to see and talk to Akoma. She didn't know when that chance might ever come again.

"They are coming!" Tawute screeched. He ran from the river into the village hailing the news that the Turtle visitors were arriving. Ramo and his entourage of advisers met the canoe at the landing.

Akoma wore full dress. His thick, straight black hair gleamed, and the braid at the side dangled with feathers. Strands of white shells hung around his neck and rested in magnificent contrast against his oiled brown skin. The shells winked in the late afternoon sun. Other heavy bands of shells around his ankles and upper arms clinked when he moved.

"Welcome, Turtle brother," Ramo said.

Akoma and Bunta banked the canoe. Akoma gave the dugout a few shoves, testing how well it was grounded. Satisfied, he turned to Ramo. "We appreciate your hospitality, Cacique."

"And, Bunta, it is good to see you again," Ramo said. "Does your woman approve of such a visit?"

All the men laughed.

"My woman would be relieved if I brought another home to take over some of her duties," Bunta said.

Again there was laughter.

Ramo escorted the visitors to his lodge. "Come and sit. Let us talk a little before you exert yourself looking over my women."

Akoma and Bunta sat on the benches.

"Would you like to stay, Banabas?" Ramo asked. "You might query about your friend Ufala and the rest of your wife's family." Ramo's face squirmed into a malevolent grin. "We do not see much of Banabas these days. His new young wife keeps him much too occupied. I am surprised the man can walk!"

Akoma's body tightened, and his jaw muscles contracted, then relaxed.

Ramo continued. "Banabas has been without a woman for so long, I think he makes up for all that lost time."

Banabas shifted uncomfortably. "Tell us about my friend Ufala. How is his arm?"

Ramo broke in. "Ah, Banabas, I have embarrassed you. Akoma, can you imagine what it must be like to be without the pleasures of a woman for so long and suddenly have those firm round breasts at your lips and hands night and day? Like delicious fruit, are they not, Banabas? Yes, you must think of her like a succulent fruit . . . ripe, sweet, and juicy."

Akoma balled his hands into fists.

"Enough, Ramo," Banabas said.

Akoma rose to his feet. His eyes were as piercing as an eagle's, his brow angled sharply with rage.

Bunta stood up. "Perhaps we will discuss the concerns of the Turtle and Panther later."

"Sit down," Ramo said. "I cannot keep this conversation up. I am afraid if I continue, Banabas will get so aroused just thinking about it, he will bolt from the lodge, run home and mount his woman. So, we will get on with business."

There was a moment of uncomfortable silence. Akoma wanted to smash Ramo's teeth down his throat. It would give him enormous gratification to do so.

"We have some things we would like to bring to your attention, Ramo," Bunta said. "Is that so, Akoma?"

Akoma lowered himself to the bench. When he spoke, his voice was hoarse with anger. "We had an interesting thing happen recently," he said. "A man from the Deer clan has been with us. He was captured by the Ais and tortured, but he managed to escape. We found him and brought him back to the village. He succumbed to his injuries. But before he crossed over, he spoke of Chogatis."

Ramo's cheek twitched. "What did he say about Chogatis? Was the man lucid?"

"Oh, he was quite lucid at times," Bunta said. "The man's name was Cunpa. Do you know him?"

"No, I do not recognize the name," Ramo said. "Deer clan?"

"Cunpa told us that this Chogatis, the Ais cacique, believes a Turtle man killed his son. Where do you suppose he got such a notion?"

"We have also heard that rumor," Ramo said. "The Panther were very disturbed that a Turtle man would provoke the Ais in such a way. I have done my best to assuage them. They are still riled, even though I have told them this accusation is false."

Akoma rocked back. "Where did your people hear this?"

Ramo waved his hand in the air. "I am not sure."

The veins in Akoma's temple bulged and pulsed. "I cannot make sense of this accusation. Where did such an idea get started? Think about it, Ramo. Perhaps something will come to you."

"Perhaps the man from the Deer clan hallucinated," Ramo said. "You said he had grave injuries."

"I do not think that the case," Akoma said. "How then would such a rumor reach your village?"

Ramo shrugged nonchalantly. "Rumors, you know how they spread. Panther and Turtle men have contact." Ramo stood up. "Come now. Let me walk you about so you can see what beauties the Panther have to offer the cacique."

"Yahga-ta is still the cacique."

"Ah, a formality. Within a cycle of the moon you will take his place. Everyone knows that."

"It is no secret," Akoma said. "But while my father is still the cacique, I should not be addressed as such. It is a matter of respect."

"Can you watch him for just a few moments?" Talli asked Ceboni.

"What are you going to do?"

"I want to see my people. Banabas told me to keep Joog out of sight. Ramo does not want questions asked."

"What did you tell the boy?" Ceboni asked.

"I have not told him anything."

"Does he not ask why he is being kept in the lodge?"

"I have been entertaining him. I suppose you are right, he will ask soon." Talli glanced at the doorway of the lodge. She could see Joog just inside. He sorted antler and bone—Banabas's raw material for tool making.

"All right," Ceboni said. "I will take both Tawute and Joog to the river to catch fish."

"Not close by."

"No, we will go downriver."

"Thank you, Ceboni. What would I do without my friend?"

Ceboni grinned. "Let me get Tawute. I should hurry before it gets too late and the sun goes down."

Ceboni soon returned with Tawute. "I hear there are a lot of fish downriver," she said. "If we go right now, we will still have enough daylight."

Joog grasped his three-pronged fishing spear. He had gotten quite good with it. Banabas had spent a lot of time with him showing him how to harpoon fish.

Once they were out of sight, Talli finger combed her hair. She pinched open a berry from the rouge plant and lightly stained her cheeks. She rubbed crushed yellow jessamine flowers on her arms and on her throat. The fragrance was sweet.

Talli stole behind the lodges. Finally, she spotted a group of young girls in the central plaza. They giggled and displayed their most coquettish demeanors. Ramo showed them off, taking one by the arm and turning her in front of Akoma.

One of the young women deserted the knot of giggling girls and slinked toward Akoma. Talli's eyes widened. She could not believe who it was!

26

Liakka moved sinuously toward Akoma. Her hips moved with a deliberately provocative sway. When she stopped in front of him, she tossed her head, swirling her hair back. Boldly, Liakka reached out and touched Akoma's necklace. She toyed with the shells, then let the necklace drop back to his chest.

Talli looked at Ramo. He was distant, but she clearly made out a wide grin on his face. How peculiar, she thought. He seemed pleased Liakka was so brazenly flirtatious with another man. Ramo was indeed unpredictable.

Akoma removed the woman's hand from his chest. Again she touched his chest and let a finger snake down the center of his torso. When she reached his breechclout, she stopped.

Talli's stomach turned over. It was difficult for her to see another woman touching Akoma in such an intimate way.

She wanted to speak to him and had hoped she would find him, but not like this, when he was appraising women of the village. Perhaps later Akoma would break away from the crowd and they could talk.

The sound of the men laughing made Talli feel even more ill.

Akoma smiled at Liakka. He appeared flattered by her attention. The sick feeling in the pit of Talli's belly persisted. Perhaps he had forgotten her. Had he even asked for her? She watched as Akoma continued to respond to Liakka's enticement.

Talli backed away, her hands cradling her abdomen. She changed her mind about seeking him out. He knew she was here, and if he still loved her, he would find a way to see her. Her eyes stung as she thought of his heart embracing another. Maybe she had been wrong all along. Maybe she loved him much more than he loved her. Finally, she turned and ran back to the lodge. She huddled inside. Tears streamed down her face.

Akoma slept in the open. He told Ramo he preferred it that way. Bunta, however, chose to be a guest in Ramo's lodge.

Akoma lay on his back looking at the stars. He wondered where in the village Talli might be. He was not sure where Banabas's lodge was located. He thought of wandering about, maybe catching a glimpse of her somewhere.

His heart ached. Surely she knew he was here, yet she had made no effort to contact him. It would have been wonderful just to see her, be near her, and hear her voice. What if something had happened to her? Could she be ill, or worse?

Akoma turned onto his back. He was restless and sleep seemed as if it would not come on this night. He had not had much appetite, and so had eaten very little of the evening meal. He had come here to see Talli, even if for only a brief conversation. He would only be here one more day and night. Maybe she would come to him tomorrow. He could not ask for her, she was another man's wife. Somehow he would find a way to see her.

Akoma envisioned her, her long black hair blowing in the sea breeze. He imagined her in his canoe, the brightness of her dark eyes shining in the sunlight. How would he ever bear it if he found she no longer loved him? What if all those words she had spoken were forgotten?

The stars glistened in the sky, and slivers of silver moonlight knifed through the trees. Akoma closed his eyes and remembered the time he and Talli had joined. He could even smell her skin if he breathed deeply. Finally sleep came, a relief to the heavy sadness he felt.

In the morning Akoma greeted the day at the river. The sky was a dazzling brilliant blue without any clouds.

He wondered what he would thank the spirits for today. If he were to see Talli, then he would be grateful. Now, he felt appreciative of nothing. Always he let the spirits know he was thankful, but today he felt empty and had no energy. He sat with his legs crossed, his back straight, his palms up. The body was in the right position, but the heart was not. After some time of introspection, Akoma got to his feet. He removed his breechclout and walked into the river water. The flowing water felt cool against his skin. He sank below the water, then came back to the surface. He rubbed his face and ran his fingers through his soot-black hair. Cleansing usually brought on energy.

"Akoma," a voice called.

He looked to the bank. Liakka stood on the edge of the water, his breechclout in her hand.

"What are you doing, woman?" he asked.

"Do you want me to bathe you or dress you? I would like to do that. I could slide this breechclout between your thighs, then go through the sash at your waist. You would not mind if I took a little detour along the way, would you?"

"You are a brazen one," he said.

"I know when I like something or someone," she said. "Why should I not speak what I feel, or act upon my feelings?"

Akoma laughed. "I am intrigued, but I think you should put my breechclout back on the limb where you found it and be on your way so I can get dressed."

Liakka cocked her head, a playful smile swimming across her lips. "Are you embarrassed? Do you have something to hide?"

"Do you behave like this around many men?"

"Not really," she answered. "Ever since you touched me yesterday I have wondered what your body . . . your whole body looks like. You were quite brazen yourself," she said. "I have had fantasies."

Akoma rose out of the water. He twisted his hair and wrung it out.

"You surpass even my fantasy," she said.

He approached her and reached for his breechclout. "Liakka, you are a beautiful woman, but—"

"You like me," she said. "I can tell."

Akoma tied the sash around his waist and then threaded the panel of soft deer hide through the front and back of it.

"Tell me," he said. "There is a woman here from my village. She is Banabas's woman. I am curious about how she is faring. Her father would want me to ask."

Liakka's posture changed. Her shoulders were not quite so high, her head not held quite so confidently. "She is feeling better."

Akoma's head shot up. "Is she ill?"

"Just the normal sickness that comes with pregnancy."

Akoma felt his stomach lurch into his throat.

"You look surprised," Liakka said. "Banabas was also. He is quite proud to be fathering a child at his age."

Akoma clenched a fist at his side.

When night fell, Akoma declined to sit with the other men. He told them he was exceptionally tired from all the attention the Panther women had shown him. He chuckled and told them he wore himself out just thinking about it. The men laughed, and Akoma left.

He wandered about the village. The women completed their evening chores and one by one disappeared inside the lodges. Somewhere an infant cried briefly, then was quiet.

Suddenly Akoma halted. Illuminated only by a dying fire and the moonlight, he saw her.

Talli stood just outside a lodge, looking up at the moon. Akoma saw her swollen belly and a wave of nausea swept through him. She had betrayed him, not kept those words that he had treasured and heard over and over again in his head. She had been with Banabas, and from the look of her, she had wasted no time in doing so.

Akoma stared, not understanding just what he was feeling. There ran such a deep current of love, yet he could not separate that now from the fury he felt. He recognized the overwhelming passion raging inside, but could not tell if it was love or hate.

Talli dropped her head, chin close to her chest, and went inside her lodge.

Akoma couldn't move. He felt heavy and sick.

"Do you wish to stay under cover tonight?" Banabas asked, coming up behind him. He scanned the sky for signs of rain.

"No, no," Akoma said.

The two men stared at one another in silence.

Akoma finally spoke. "Be good to her," he said, so quietly that Banabas almost could not hear him.

It had not been easy for Akoma to fall asleep. The image of Talli in the moonlight blazed in front of his closed eyes. She carried Banabas's child. She had joined with him. Banabas had touched her, put his mouth on her, felt her nakedness.

When sleep did come, it was filled with dreams of Talli, both good and bad. He stirred. A warm hand kneaded his shoulder, then a body curled against his. "Talli," he whispered, turning to her.

"No," Liakka whispered. "But I will make you forget her," she said. Her hand played down his belly, reaching to his thigh, then beneath his breechclout. Her mouth pressed against his, wet and warm.

Akoma stared at her as he permitted her to fondle him. He had no immediate physical response.

"Relax," Liakka said. "Let me make you feel good."

"Liakka," Akoma began, taking her wrist and guiding her hand away from him.

"Say nothing," she said. "Just enjoy the pleasure I give to you. There is no harm, no reason to deny yourself."

Liakka wrenched her arm free and untied his breechclout. "Shh," she whispered, aiming her warm breath at his lower belly.

At first he attempted to push her away, but Liakka persisted. He closed his eyes. She was right, there was no reason to deny himself this opportunity. The covenant between him and Talli no longer existed.

He shoved his fingers up through her hair and let out a low moan.

Talli also found it difficult to sleep. She tossed. She could tell that her husband slept. He breathed slowly and deeply, sometimes snoring.

She got up and stepped outside the lodge.

She let out a mournful, troubled breath. "Akoma," she whispered. He was here, so close. She had to see him, no matter if he loved her or not. She had to tell him he was still in her heart and would be forever. She wanted to tell him that she loved him, and her words had been true even if his had not. Even if he did not speak, she could touch his face with the palm of her hand, imprint the contour of his cheek and jaw in her mind forever. She could stand close enough to hear his breathing and smell his skin. She had to see him, if only for a moment. She caressed her abdomen as she thought of telling Akoma she carried his child.

Careful not to wake Banabas and Joog, Talli slipped out of the lodge. The village was still. Everyone was sleeping except her.

She wondered where Akoma slept. She would have to dare to look inside Ramo's lodge, and if Akoma was there, wake him.

Talli swallowed as if that would devour the fear.

As she approached Ramo's lodge, she felt her spine tingle with apprehension. At the lodge opening she hesitated. Beneath the curtain of her black hair, perspiration flowed.

A breeze swept through the village, and the shell ornaments hanging on Ramo's lodge jingled. The sound was melodic and gentle, but Talli jumped and sucked in a breath. She was sure if Ramo slept, the sound of the shells stirred him.

She waited a few moments, flattened in the shadows, barely breathing. At last she made herself move. Cold-hot blood coursed through her veins. Just inside the shelter, she squinted, striving to make out the sleeping bodies. There were two. One was clearly Ramo, but she was uncertain of the other near the rear of the lodge.

Talli touched her left breast in response to the skipping beat of her heart. She kept her eyes on Ramo as she moved past him, taking a single small step at a time. She moved toward the man sleeping in the back of the lodge. It was so dark back there. She couldn't make out any detail.

Talli edged closer until she stood next to the man. His back was to her, and the deerskin blanket crept up behind his back. Carefully she leaned forward.

It was Bunta.

The shells pealed once again. Talli's top teeth bit sharply into her lower lip. Ramo turned to his side and cleared his throat. Bunta shifted.

Talli stood rooted in fear. She could think of no explanation she could give for being there if either man awakened.

The more she stared at Ramo in the darkness, the more certain she was that his eyes were open. She thought she could see him looking at her, but he didn't say anything. She waited, blinked hard, and looked again. His eyes were closed.

Talli moved quickly, without as much stealth as she had when she entered the lodge. She wanted to get out fast. Sweat soaked her skin, and her hair clung to her back.

At the opening of the lodge, Talli darted out and ran for the brush. Breathless, more from the fear than the sprint, she hunkered low, hiding in the thicket.

Where was Akoma? If he didn't sleep in Ramo's lodge, then where? How many shelters would she need to investigate?

She heard a disturbance in the brush, the rattling of dead brittle twigs.

Talli shrunk into a ball.

A voice startled her, and she flinched.

"Why are you hiding in the brush like a wounded bird?" Ocaab asked.

"Oh, you scared me," Talli said, jumping to her feet. "I am not hiding," she answered, dusting herself off. Talli raked her hair back. "I could not sleep, so I took a walk. I thought if I sat awhile—"

"You chose to sit in the middle of the weeds?"

Talli did not respond.

"You have many secrets, Turtle woman. I think it may be that way for all the Turtle. To me, the people of your clan behave strangely."

Talli fidgeted. "I guess I will try to sleep now," she said.

Ocaab arched a brow. "Even the man who will be cacique sleeps in the open instead of accepting the hospitality of the Panther. That is peculiar."

"Oh," Talli said. "I do not think a man wishing to experience the beauty of the night is peculiar."

"Perhaps not," Ocaab said. He cocked his head in the direction where he knew Akoma chose to sleep. "Perhaps he sleeps well there. We would not want to disturb him."

Ocaab seemed to know she was looking for Akoma, and he discouraged her.

"There is something different about you," Ocaab said. "Special. The spirits tell me that, yet they do not tell me what. I am to keep watch over you. Help you." Ocaab stared at her as if he wanted her to explain.

"I am glad I have a friend in you," she said.

"Can you tell me more?" he asked.

Talli didn't answer.

"Perhaps another time . . . when the time is right," he said. "Go back to your bed, Turtle woman. Wander no more."

Talli felt it was a warning of some sort. She would have to give up on her search for Akoma.

27

Suppose Akoma was with someone, perhaps Liakka? Was that why Ocaab discouraged her?

Suddenly she was thankful she had not had the opportunity to talk to Akoma. She couldn't have stood hearing the words come from his mouth that he no longer loved her.

Before the next cycle of the moon, Akoma returned to the Panther village again. He courted Liakka exclusively, though he constantly scanned the village for a glimpse of Talli. Talli stayed out of sight. She heard the women gossip and the men joke about how Liakka made the new Turtle cacique wild with want. Talli knew if she talked to Akoma, she would cry. She couldn't shame Banabas that way. And there was nothing to say to Akoma. She was no longer in his heart.

Through the cover of trees or from a distance, she watched him. Though seeing him tortured her, especially when he was with Liakka, she couldn't fight the compulsion to be near him. She ached to touch his face with her fingertips, to lay her head on his shoulder, and feel his arms surround her.

When Akoma prepared to leave, she felt a great shadow swallow her. "Your father," she whispered to her unborn child as she watched Akoma board his canoe to return to the Turtle village. "Good-bye."

Nearly a complete cycle of the moon after Akoma's last visit, Talli woke up in the middle of the night. A twinge across the small of her back and a tightening in her abdomen made her wince. She lay awake, eyes open.

The discomfort occurred again. Through the opening of the lodge, she watched the track of the moon as it crossed the sky. Each time she slipped back to sleep she soon awakened from a pain. For a long time she tossed, not wanting to awaken anyone too soon. Near dawn the pains grew strong and frequent. She decided it was time.

"Banabas," she finally said, tapping him.

He turned to face her, one eyelid open.

"I think the child comes."

Banabas sat upright. "Joog," he called. "Wake up."

Joog rolled over.

"Go get Ceboni to go to the birthing hut."

Joog jumped to his feet.

"Hurry," Banabas said.

The boy flew out of the lodge.

"What should I do?" Banabas asked, palming the side of her head. "Should I carry you?"

"I can walk," she answered.

"Are you all right?" he asked.

"I am fine," she said, then put her hand on her abdomen as she felt another contraction. She stood perfectly still, eyes closed until it passed. She wished her mother and sisters were with her. She wanted to hear her mother's reassuring voice.

"I will take no chances," he said.

Banabas swept his arm under her knees and his other arm around her shoulders and lifted.

"You do not need to carry me," she said.

"No," he said, ducking through the opening as he carried her outside.

The birthing hut was a small structure on the perimeter of the village. Banabas lowered his wife to the ground inside the hut.

"Where is Ceboni?" he asked, looking over his shoulder. "What keeps her?"

"She will be here," Talli said.

"Lie down," he said. "Rest."

With a flurry, Ceboni and Joog rushed into the hut.

"She is in pain," Banabas said. "Do something."

Ceboni waved her hands in the air, shooing Banabas

and Joog out of the hut. "Wait outside. I will tell you when it is over."

"Do you want me to stay with you?" Banabas asked.

Talli shook her head and smiled at him. "What would a man be doing in a birthing hut?"

"I do not care about custom or what someone would think," Banabas answered. "If you want me here—"

"Out!" Ceboni said. "You and the boy, go. I have brought many babies into this world. I will look after her. Nothing to worry about."

"I will be fine," Talli said. "Go ahead."

Joog left, and Banabas slowly backed out of the hut.

"You are a lucky woman. He loves you very much," Ceboni said.

"I know," Talli said. "He is a good man." She held her breath with the next contraction.

"No, no. Breathe," Ceboni said. "Lie down and let me see where this baby is."

Talli realized the contractions were growing stronger still. How long was it going to be before the child was born? How much worse were the pains going to get?

"You need to rest and save your strength."

Talli lay down on the birthing mat she had brought here not long before. At last, she thought, I will hold in my arms a part of Akoma.

Ceboni held both hands firmly against Talli's abdomen. She pressed, feeling the contour of the child inside. Her hands molded the shape of the baby. "Not yet," she said. "But soon."

Ceboni started a small fire so they would have light and heat. The predawn air was cold. The smoke spiraled through a small opening in the roof.

In the center of the hut was a wood pole, worn smooth from the many hands that had held it. Talli stared at it as another pain coursed through her. This one was significantly more powerful. It began in her back, then squeezed like a band all the way around her. The pain had its own rhythm, beginning as a twinge, increasing in intensity till it reached a peak that she thought if it lasted any longer she would beg for the child to be cut out of her. Then just as she could bear no more, the pain began its decline until at last she felt relief.

"How long, Ceboni?" she asked.

Ceboni knelt next to her and again put her hands on Talli's belly. She pressed hard, feeling the baby's position.

"A little bit yet," she answered. "You are doing fine."

"No, I am not," Talli said, desperation tingeing her voice. "Make it get over with. Help me!" She squinted and held her breath as a new contraction started.

"A strong one," Ceboni said, feeling the tightening. "Do not let the pain sweep over you. Find something to look at, focus there. Do not close your eyes or you get lost in the pain. Breathe."

Talli nodded and drew in a deep breath.

"Let it out. Do not keep the breath inside. Make yourself breathe through the pains. It will help. And remember to focus on something."

The pain was so unbearable and the pressure so strong! Talli grunted and bore down.

When the contraction ended, she took in a big breath and then expelled it. She clutched Ceboni's hand. "Can you tell if the baby is all right? He is, is he not? The baby is all right!"

"Everything appears to be fine," Ceboni answered. "Relax between the pains. Let your body go limp, let your mind clear."

Talli squeezed Ceboni's hand and balled her other hand into a fist. "I cannot," she said. "Get the baby out," she cried. "Please!"

Her face reddened as she pushed.

"I think it is time," Ceboni said. "Get up and hold on to the pole. Use it for balance. Squat and push. Do you understand?"

"Leave me alone," Talli said, heaving out a breath, then panting.

"Up," Ceboni said. "Grab the pole."

Talli moaned and closed her eyes.

"You want this child? Help it be born. Get up!"

Talli struggled to her knees with Ceboni's help, then used the pole to get into a squatting position.

"Keep your knees flexed, and when you feel the need to push, push hard."

With the next pain Talli gripped the pole, leaned her forehead against it and bore down with a deep groan.

"That's it," Ceboni said. "Good."

Talli cried out in soft sobs. "This cannot be right. What is wrong? What is wrong?"

Ceboni wiped Talli's forehead. "You are doing fine. It will not be long now. A few more pushes, Talli."

Even before Ceboni finished, Talli felt the onslaught of another contraction. She strained, feeling as if the pressure would make her eyes explode from her head.

"Keep on. Good. Good," Ceboni encouraged, slipping her hand beneath Talli. "I feel the head," she said. "The baby is coming. One more good push, as hard as you can."

Talli bore down with all her strength. She felt she would split in two. "Akoma!" she cried out.

Ceboni's head shot up.

28

"Talli!" Ceboni said, glancing at the opening of the hut to see if Banabas stood there.

"The baby!" Talli called out. "My baby," she sobbed.

"Ahh," Ceboni said, feeling the child slide into her hands.

"Show me," Talli said, crying tears, her body shaking, her shoulders slumping. "Show my son to me."

Ceboni held up the white-coated infant. "How did you know it was a boy?"

"I knew," she said, her voice weary with exhaustion.

Ceboni cleaned the baby's face and swabbed his mouth with a soft deerskin rag. The child began to wail.

"Ohhh," Talli cried, reaching for the squirming infant.

"A fine boy," Ceboni said. "Lie down and I will give him to you."

Talli lowered herself to the ground.

"Let him suckle. It will help expel the afterbirth," Ceboni said.

Talli put the newborn to her breast.

Banabas appeared in the opening of the hut. "Is she all right?" he asked.

Ceboni whipped around. "Out! Your wife is fine. Give us a few moments, then I will tell you to come in."

"Talli?" he called.

"I am all right, husband."

Banabas exited.

"He worries," Talli said. "He did not even ask if the baby was a boy or girl."

"That is not important to him."

The baby's mouth gently tugged at her breast. She felt so whole, so wonderfully complete, much like the contentedness she had experienced when joining with Akoma. She had not experienced anything like that since Akoma lay spent upon her.

"He is beautiful," Talli said.

"Yes, he is." Ceboni cleared her throat. "Talli . . ." Ceboni hesitated.

Talli looked up and saw the puzzled expression on Ceboni's face. "What is it, Ceboni?"

"You called out Akoma's name."

Talli's gaze dropped back to the child.

Ceboni waited for Talli to respond, but she did not. Ceboni decided not to pursue her curiosity.

"The afterbirth is wrapped inside this bundle," she said. "At dawn tomorrow, you must take it away and bury it."

Talli nodded and closed her eyes, nestling closer to the baby.

"I will go now. Your husband and Joog are anxious to be with you."

"Yes," Talli said.

A stream of lemon light followed Banabas and Joog into the hut.

"A son," Talli said.

Banabas sat next to her, and Joog stood behind him.

"He is perfect," Talli said.

Joog knelt and touched the baby's head, swirling his finger in the mat of thick, damp, black hair. He grinned.

Banabas put his hand over Talli's. When she looked up at him, she saw that his eyes were laden with tears.

Banabas sniffed and wiped his eyes. "The smoke," he said.

A jab of guilt struck her. But how could she tell him this was Akoma's child, not his? In a way she loved Banabas. She didn't love him as she loved Akoma, but she did care about him. Let him find happiness in this child as if it were his own, she thought. Maybe the child was all the happiness she could bring the man, and he did deserve that.

Suddenly Banabas's face darkened.

"Joog, let us leave and let Talli rest for a while," Banabas said.

Quickly Banabas got to his feet. "Come, now," he said, ushering Joog out.

"Is something wrong?" Talli asked. "What is the matter?"

"I will be right back," Banabas said. "Rest."

As soon as he was out of the hut, Banabas told Joog to go back to the lodge and wait for him. The boy looked confused.

"Do as I say. I will explain later."

Banabas hurried across the village until he was near Ceboni's dwelling. She stooped by her cook fire.

"Come," he called to her. "Something is wrong. Hurry! Hurry!"

Ceboni dropped her stirring stick. "What is it?" she asked, straightening.

Banabas was slightly out of breath. "Talli! Blood pools beneath her!"

"I am sure she is all right," Ceboni said in an effort to calm him. "There is always a lot of blood after a birth. I will check on her. Go and get Ocaab, just in case."

"Yes. Yes," Banabas answered.

Ceboni abandoned her cooking. As she passed Ramo's lodge, she heard laughter. Liakka. Ceboni couldn't understand the relationship the cacique had with that woman. Nor did she understand Liakka. Whenever Akoma visited, Liakka flaunted herself, and Akoma appeared to bask in her attention. Ramo seemed to approve, almost encourage the relationship. Strange indeed, Ceboni thought. There was something else she didn't like about it. The entire situation had an air of deceitfulness and wrongdoing. But it was none of her business, just as her husband had reminded her when she spoke of it to him.

At the opening of the hut, Ceboni stopped. "Talli," she called. "It is Ceboni."

"Come," Talli said.

Ceboni retrieved a stack of absorbent hide swatches from the corner of the hut. She knelt beside Talli.

"He sleeps so peacefully at your breast," Ceboni said, looking at the infant. "I hate to disturb him."

"What do you mean?" Talli asked.

"I need to clean you up. There has been a lot of bleeding. Roll onto your back," she said.

Talli kept her son in the crook of her arm and slowly turned flat on her back. Ceboni pressed on Talli's abdomen. "Too soft," she said, plunging her hand deeper and then squeezing.

Talli felt blood gush from her. She shrieked from the pain and grabbed Ceboni's wrist. "Stop!"

"I know it is uncomfortable," Ceboni said, halting for a moment. She pressed hard with her fingertips and rubbed in a circular motion. "This is necessary or you will bleed to death. Feel this," she said, taking Talli's hand in her own. She pressed Talli's fingertips deep into the flesh until Talli could feel her womb, about the size of her fist, drawn into a taut ball.

"That is the way it should feel," Ceboni said. "We must keep it tight like this to control the bleeding. Massaging it will help. Can you do it yourself?"

Talli nodded.

"You must pay attention to what I say. You will massage as I have told you?"

"I will," Talli answered.

"Now give me the child," Ceboni said. She took the new infant in her hands. Ceboni stared at him. "He is beautiful," she said, placing him on a blanket.

"I want my mother to see him."

Ceboni smiled. "That can wait a little. In time, you can journey to your village."

Ceboni pulled the mat from under Talli and replaced it with a fresh one. With wet swatches of hide she cleaned the blood from her friend. "The bleeding is not too bad," she said. "Enough to frighten Banabas. If you keep doing as I told you, the bleeding will not be so heavy, but do not expect it to go away."

Talli sighed. Though the bleeding was a nuisance, as long as it continued, Banabas would not attempt to join with her. She no longer had the excuse of carrying a child. Talli wondered what she would do when the bleeding stopped, or how long she could fake her moon cycle after it did stop.

A rustling made her look to the doorway. Banabas stood there with Ocaab at his side.

"Is she all right?" Banabas asked.

"Talli is fine, and so is your son," Ceboni said.

"But the blood! There was so much!"

"It is taken care of," Ceboni said.

"Husband, you worry too much." Talli felt a twinge in her lower abdomen as she massaged her womb. "I will be fine."

Banabas entered the hut. "Ocaab has brought some medicine."

The shaman stepped inside, medicine pouch in hand. He closed his eyes and drew in three deep breaths through his nose and blew them out through his mouth.

"Let us leave them alone," Ceboni said, bundling the soiled materials.

"Yes," Banabas agreed, stepping out the entrance.

Ceboni put the baby in Talli's arms and joined Banabas outside.

Ocaab lowered himself to the ground, crossing and folding his legs, knees out and heels tucked under him. He closed his eyes and, for a few moments, there was no sound other than the child's suckling, sweet and soporific. Talli let her eyelids close. Then, she heard Ocaab's soft chant. His song tangled with the delicate breathing of the newborn as if they were one. He was a gifted shaman, she thought. Talli felt the spirits swirling about in the air, brushing her cheek, touching her eyelids, and telling her to be still and to trust. The hut swelled with a mystical melody, faint, yet permeating.

"Another spirit comes to Mother Earth," Ocaab said.

Talli looked down into the baby's face.

"The bear spirit watches over him. Climbing Bear."

"What did you say?" Talli asked.

Ocaab didn't flinch. His eyes stayed closed.

"You said 'Climbing Bear,' " Talli said, tugging on the shaman's arm. "Where did you hear that?"

Ocaab remained subdued. "The spirits have spoken. Again a soul comes to the earth. He is a gift from beyond. Look in his eyes and you will see another lives through him. You are chosen, Talli. The spirits do not tell me all, yet. I see double images. I cannot interpret the vision.''

Talli traced her finger along the child's nose. It was straight, and the eyes were definitely his father's, deep black like burned coals. His cheeks were outlined in strong bone lines, the profile of a cacique—so obvious in his features. Talli feared someone else might also notice. She stared into her son's eyes. He looked back with an ethereal sparkle. He was the essence of two deep meanings in her life: Climbing Bear, whose death severed her father's ability to love her, and Akoma, the love of her life.

Talli cringed at the thought of this child ever going into battle. She would do whatever she could to strive for the end of conflict.

"Whose child is this?" Ocaab asked.

Talli's throat suddenly dried, and her tongue grew confused so she stuttered when she spoke. "What . . . what do . . . what do you mean?"

"The child is guarded by the spirit of Climbing Bear. It is a close spirit. Who is he?"

"My brother," Talli said, sinking onto the mat with relief.

"I see," Ocaab said, again closing his eyes. He hummed softly and the melody made Talli uneasy.

"What are you doing?" she asked.

Ocaab continued to hum as if he had not heard her.

Talli rubbed her dry lips together. "He died as a small child. I did not know him."

The loud musical chirping of an osprey rang in the air. "The fish hawk hunts this morning," Ocaab said. "His song is distinct. He is happy. His belly is full and the sun is on his wings. Do you hear him?"

Talli shook her head. She had been too distracted to notice the bird's cry.

"You see," Ocaab said. "You must pay attention to what is now, to what you have. If you focus on what is not now, what you do not have, you will miss all the beauty of the day the spirits have given you." Ocaab's face appeared lined with ridges and creases of wisdom. His eyes were deeper set than most, his voice almost hypnotic. "All will come to you that is due," he said. "Does what I say have meaning to you?"

"Yes," she whispered.

"I see great shadows in your heart," he said. "One dark corner is your birthright, and another is from pain and sacrifice. This child brings joy and sadness."

Talli felt the tears begin to well in her eyes.

"Will you tell your husband of either shadow?" he asked.

Ocaab knows! Talli thought. He knows everything. She pulled her child closer and squeezed her eyes shut in fear. What would become of her now? She didn't care about herself, but her son!

"There is nothing to fear," Ocaab said. "This is the work of the spirits. I am not to interfere."

Suddenly, Talli realized she felt a sense of relief that someone knew all about her. A heaviness lifted from her. "Should I tell Banabas?" she asked.

"There is a time for all things," the shaman answered. "You will know when the time is right."

Ocaab put his hand on top of the child's head. "Climbing Bear is his spirit," he said, "Mikot, his name."

Talli smiled, liking the sound of the name. It suited the child for some reason. She said the name aloud. "Yes," she said. "The spirits have chosen a good name."

Ocaab sprinkled yellow powder on the child's forehead and with his fingertip, he drew lines with it. Then he withdrew several leaves from his pouch. "Chew on these, one now, and one when the moon is out."

He put the leaves in Talli's hand, then stood.

"Ocaab, I am safe, am I not?" Talli asked. "Banabas does not need to know yet. The time is not right. You will keep these things to yourself?"

Joog peeped through the opening of the hut, and Banabas stepped forward. "What secrets does a wife keep from her husband?"

29

Two full moons had passed since Akoma had last visited the Panther village.

Yahga-ta put his hand on his son's shoulder. "It is time for you to make a decision," he said. "Choose a woman. Ramo delights in the notion that a Panther man has the woman you desire. He likes to think the Panther make the Turtle squirm. Take Liakka."

"She confuses me," Akoma said. "Ramo confuses me. I thought Ramo—"

"Liakka is not really Ramo's woman. I do not think Ramo wants any one woman. I do not believe he knows how to love anyone. Does she make you happy?"

Akoma waited before he answered. Liakka had her ways, but he wondered if that was true happiness. She certainly had some expert physical ways of pleasing him, but even though the intimacy with her was exciting, there was some element missing.

"She pleases me in some respects."

"It is time, Akoma. You are the cacique. There is talk amongst the people. They wonder why you cannot find a woman. Suspicion hovers that you yearn for Talli. Let the Turtle and the Panther see no weakness in you."

Akoma acknowledged his father's advice, then returned to the lodge the villagers had built for him, their new cacique.

The brilliance of the moon glossed the village with silver light. Akoma reclined on his sleeping skin. He knew in his head that his father was right, but he didn't accept it in his gut.

Shortly, he was sleeping. In his dream he stretched out on pillows of green moss, the light of the sun penetrating his skin, going deep, even into his muscles and tendons. Warm. Talli was next to him, her skin soft against his, her hair sleek, gliding over her shoulder as he touched it. Then the image disappeared, fading into nonsense currents of thoughts.

On and off through the night his dreams snaked through his head like streams of smoke. They were vivid only for short moments, and then they became vague and fragmented. Once he awakened in a sweat. The dream was of Talli with Banabas. She told Akoma she loved her husband, for Akoma to go away, she had no feelings for him any longer. Akoma pleaded with her as all the village looked on. Talli turned her back to him and walked away holding Banabas's hand. Akoma was calling her name aloud when he awakened. It was difficult to let go of the feelings of anger and devastation he experienced in the dream.

Akoma turned over with a sigh. He supposed it was near dawn. He couldn't sleep. He lay awake, eyes closed, listening to the near-dawn sounds. There was little rustling of leaves. The wind wouldn't pick up until later when the sun warmed the air.

He did hear the crickets chirping and the flutter of a bird's wings. An owl perhaps . . . a bird that hunted in the darkness. Owls were not good omens. They could carry a man's spirit away. An alligator bellowed in the distance. Akoma shifted. He felt uneasy, but couldn't understand why. His restlessness escalated until finally he sat up and stared out into the indigo sky. Stars were rapidly losing their brightness as the sun pricked the horizon.

The silhouettes of trees stood erect, rippling only with the breath of an occasional soft breeze. There was another movement Akoma thought. He strained to see better.

A birdcall captured his attention. The sound had an odd pitch or something. He wasn't sure what it was he didn't like. It almost sounded like a blue jay's, but not quite. And it was still too dark for the birds to start their songs.

Akoma stood, took his knife from its sheath, and retrieved his lance from the corner of the lodge where it leaned against a sabal palm support bole. He stole out of the lodge and hunkered down. He heard that same bird sound. He focused in the direction from which it came.

Hearing a return birdcall from behind him, Akoma twisted around. These were not birds, he was certain. He needed to alert the Turtle men before an attack came. Ais had to be waiting for the sunrise. They surrounded the village, communicating their positions with the birdcalls.

Akoma knew there was not much time. Stealthily, he crept to Bunta's lodge.

"Bunta, wake up."

As soon as Akoma saw Bunta move, he whispered, "The Ais are here! Get up. Help me tell the others."

Bunta shot upright, clasping his hand over his wife's mouth. "Shh," he whispered to her.

Both men crawled outside, moving slowly, keeping in the shadows.

The word spread quickly, but the earth was brightening quicker than the Turtle could alert all their men. Suddenly, the blaring of war whoops rang out, and the Ais bolted into the village. Akoma spun around just as an Ais warrior sprang at him. He blocked so the enemy's knife caught his upper arm, tearing a gash. Akoma dropped his lance and swung his arm up, knocking the knife out of the Ais's grip. With his other hand, he plunged his knife blade into the man's stomach. Akoma angled the tip upward and shoved, twisting the knife. He heard the flesh and entrails snapping and ripping as he felt the resistance against the blade of his knife.

Akoma pulled his weapon out as the Ais warrior slouched to his knees. As soon as the man's body cleared his view, Akoma saw Putiwa on the ground beneath a large Ais warrior. He grabbed his lance and ran toward Putiwa, shouting a war cry. Akoma balanced the lance shaft near his right ear, and with a powerful lunge and thrust he hurled it.

Without the slightest wobble of the long shaft, the point of the lance penetrated the Ais man's back. The

warrior jolted upright, throwing his head back in reaction to the pain in his back. Putiwa's eyes, bright with
fear, focused on the man's face. Then, the Ais listed to
his side and slumped over.

Putiwa pushed the body of the dying Ais off him and
scrambled to his feet.

Akoma heard the cry of an Ais, perhaps their war
chief.

"The Turtle will pay! Your blood will soak the earth!"

Then, at the sound of another cry, like ants scurrying,
the Ais retreated into the forest, whooping and shouting,
denying defeat.

Akoma saw Bunta coming toward him, the pink
clouds of sunrise glowing behind him.

"We were ready for them," Bunta was saying. He
punched his lance in the air and let out a proud victori-
ous cry. He threw his arms around Akoma, then Putiwa.
"They thought they had us by surprise!"

"Where is Wabashaw?" Akoma asked. "It was his
watch."

Bunta's expression switched from exhilaration to
gravity.

The three men walked in silence to the area where
Wabashaw should have been standing watch.

Their fears were confirmed. Wabashaw lay in a puddle
of blood, his throat gaping from ear to ear, nearly
decapitated.

Akoma closed Wabashaw's eyelids, keeping in the
soul of the man that was the pupil of the eye. This one
remained with the body after death. The other two souls,
the shadow a man makes, and the image one sees in
clear water, left the body and crossed over when a
man died.

The fire blazed in the darkness. Council gathered at
the central hearth.

"Wabashaw and another are our only losses," Yahga-
ta said.

"That is true," Akoma said.

"We drove them away quickly," Ufala said, wielding
his good arm in the air.

The other men, some with bandaged wounds, cheered in response.

"They will come again. Again and again," Bunta said. "This is not over. Only a skirmish."

The men fell hushed.

Akoma stirred up the coals and tossed more wood on the fire. The men grew still and attentive. They knew Akoma had something to say. When he spoke, his voice was calm, but clear, reaching out into the dark shadows like a light.

"Did you not hear?" Akoma asked. "The Turtle will pay. Chogatis believes we are responsible for the death of his son. The man from the Deer clan knew of what he spoke." Akoma leaned forward and picked up a handful of dry earth. "It does not matter if the rains return. The Ais no longer yearn for the soil to soak with rain, they strive for the earth to drown in Turtle blood."

A man beside Bunta, creased and folded with age, rubbed his chest as if it ached. The bony hand, skin thin and translucent, pushed hard at the breastbone. "But when the rains do return," he said, "the pressure will ease on the Ais. Perhaps with the passage of time—"

"No," Akoma said. "Like those who live to our far west, these are a bellicose people. They think differently than we do. I have heard that their man of the spirits requires the sacrifice of men, and victims' heads are carried about in dances, then placed beneath a tree. He eats human eyes."

"He is a sorcerer, not a man of the spirits," Putiwa said. "What spirit, other than an evil one, would guide a man to do such a thing?"

The men mumbled, agreeing with Putiwa.

"It does not matter how we argue their beliefs, it will not change anything. That is the nature of our enemy, and we must know *who* our enemy is," Akoma said. "Let me tell you a true story my grandfather told me."

Yahga-ta smiled at Akoma's ability to gather the people to him. They leaned toward the cacique, waiting to hear what wisdom Akoma had to share.

"Before the Earth existed there was only water," Akoma began. "Far above was the other world in the sky. There, in the world above, was an ancient and great tree. No one knew how long the tree had existed. It had many roots which stretched in each of the directions, and from its branches all kinds of fruits and berries grew."

Akoma held his hands out and spread his fingers like the roots of the tree. "Can you see the tree?" he asked, soliciting the men to visualize the story he told, to become a part of it.

He continued. "There was an ancient cacique in the world above. One night his wife had a strange dream that she saw the Great Tree uprooted. She did not understand the dream and was troubled by it. The following morning she told her husband her dream.

"The cacique stroked his wife's hair and told her he was sorry she was troubled. He believed the dream was clearly a dream about power, and when one had such a dream, everything should be done to make the dream come true. 'The Great Tree must be uprooted!'

"The cacique called all his warriors together and told them they must pull up the tree. But the roots of the tree were so deep and so strong that they could not budge it."

Akoma paused. "That is how it is with the Ais. Even the Jeaga and Tegesta. Each of us is an ancient tree with roots. We are the fruit of the tree that has made us."

"The cacique speaks the truth," Bunta said. "The Ais are what they are and always will be. We cannot change that—uproot them. We must accept that they will never behave as we do. The spirits and traditions that guide them, what have made them what they are, are not the same as the Jeaga's. We cannot anticipate that they will respond to situations the way the Jeaga would."

"How do we prepare ourselves then?" the old man asked.

Akoma stood. "We go on as Jeaga."

A tall, thin man in the back called out. "We need the head of our cacique concentrating on nothing other than the well-being of the Turtle."

The statement stunned Akoma.

"What do you mean?" Akoma asked. "Speak." His

face was tight, slightly intimidating, his eyes burning like the embers of the fire.

The man stood up, the firelight barely flickering on his face. His posture indicated respect. He placed the back of his hand to his forehead to express his subservience. "I do not mean to offend, but—"

"No apologies need be spoken. Be forthright."

The man walked closer, moving through the other men. "There is a concern that you are preoccupied, that perhaps you cannot give all your attention to the troubles with the Ais and the Panther. We were led to believe you would quickly take a Panther wife to encourage the unity between the Turtle and the Panther."

The council grew deathly silent.

30

Banabas waited for Talli to answer. "Well," he said, "what do you ask the shaman to keep to himself? Is there something I should know?"

"I wanted to tell you myself," Talli said. "I did not want Ocaab to tell you before I did."

"What?" Banabas asked.

"Our son . . . Climbing Bear is his guide spirit." Talli looked briefly at Ocaab, then at the baby.

"Take the medicines I have given you," Ocaab said as he left.

"I will," Talli said.

Banabas knelt next to her and stroked her hair. "How wonderful," he said. "I am certain that knowing Climbing Bear is our son's guide spirit makes you very happy. My heart smiles as well. Kitchi and Ufala will be most pleased."

"I am anxious to tell my mother. I hope word does not get to her before I have the chance to tell her."

"Talli," Banabas said. "I must leave you for a day or two. Ramo has arranged to speak to Chogatis. He asks that I accompany him to meet the Ais at a place on the river."

"Meet with Chogatis? He is the enemy!" She recalled the day of the attack, seeing Akoma near death. She shuddered. "Do not go," she said.

"I have to go," Banabas said. "And Talli, do not say anything to anyone. No one knows where we go. Especially keep it from Joog. Do you understand? Ceboni has agreed to watch over you."

Akoma sensed the men were taut with the urge to speak up. He maintained enough of their respect to keep them silent. He needed to allay their concerns. There were enough worries. They should have confidence in their cacique.

"The plan is made," he said.

Yahga-ta's head snapped to the side as if to hear better.

"My father and I have discussed the matter at length. Soon I will travel to the Panther village. There is a woman there named Liakka. Bunta knows her. She is from a noble heritage, suitable to be my wife. Your cacique remains focused on the concerns with the Ais and the Panther. The marriage to Liakka will further seal the unity between the Panther and Turtle."

Mumblings of approval echoed through the men.

Putiwa stood. "Chogatis will keep coming at us, Akoma. If we are not one with the Panther, the Ais will eventually have us and the river. Ramo will find a way to protect himself. His solution for unity is unacceptable. The Turtle want unity, but not loss of independence. We do not want to be swallowed by Ramo! He is as dangerous to the Turtle as Chogatis. I think your decision to take a Panther woman at this time is good. But still we have the Ais."

"I say we go after Chogatis," Ufala said. "We are no different than the deer we hunt. Chogatis is the hunter, and we the prey. This should not be. We are Jeaga! We are strong!"

Ufala's short speech riled the men. Cries of agreement rang out.

"That would be foolish," Yahga-ta said. "We are a small group. Chogatis has many, and all the Ais would join him. We do not even trust our closest Jeaga neighbor."

Ufala held up his maimed arm. "The Ais took the use of my arm. I will not let them have my pride!"

Akoma held up the talking stick to bring order to the group. "We must keep our heads. Bunta, what do you say?"

Akoma handed the talking stick to the war chief.

Bunta used a moment to look at each man's face. His eyes made contact with each man's. "Chogatis provokes us. He believes we are responsible for the death of his son. Not only does he want the river, he wants Turtle blood. I think it would be unwise to offer ourselves to him. If he wants our blood, then make him come for it. We should not get so emotional that we make unwise decisions."

Several of the men who had sided with Ufala grew calmer and nodded their heads.

"Bah," Ufala grumbled. "Are we a bunch of women? What has become of the Jeaga?" He turned his back on the group and walked away.

Kitchi put down the basket she worked on when her husband approached. "What is wrong? Council still gathers."

"The central hearth is no more than a woman's cook fire."

"What do you mean?" she asked.

"I think there are no men left amongst the Turtle."

Ufala stopped for a moment as a thought passed through his mind. "We will see," he said. "Perhaps there are a few men with courage."

Kitchi looked up at him. "What stirs in your head?" she asked.

Ufala leaned his head back and stared at the sky, then looked back at Kitchi. He blew a long slow breath out his mouth. "I have not worked this hard to restore my skills for nothing. I would rather be the hunter than the hunted. Even with this bad arm, I could take Chogatis. He thinks he wants Turtle blood. I dream how it feels to draw my knife across his throat, to feel his warm blood flow over my hand."

"You need to let go of that hate," Kitchi said. "It serves no purpose. You are lucky you have healed as well as you have. Be thankful."

Ufala threw a rock. "Do you have any idea how difficult it has been for me to learn to do that with the other arm? Every day I practice until the arm shakes with exhaustion. There are things I will never be able to do again, no matter how much I practice. The Ais took that from me. They left me alive, yet dead. I will taste their blood."

Ufala's feet pounded the ground as he walked away. Kitchi watched. His strides were long and angry. His shoulders sat at an angle, the bad arm sagging slightly. "Where do you go?" she called.

Ufala did not look back.

Kitchi got to her feet. Suddenly she stumbled sideways. She put her hands to her head. She was so dizzy! Her hands trembled.

The same thing had happened yesterday, and then a few days before that. Sometimes her hands trembled so that she could not weave.

Sassa came to her. "Mother, what is wrong? Are you all right? Your face is pale."

Kitchi held Sassa's hand. "I am just tired," she said. "Help me inside. I think I will rest awhile."

Akoma's canoe glided over the water. He hoped he would have a vision that would help guide him in his life. His charcoal-painted face indicated he fasted. His belly didn't knot with anger. The vision was much more important than eating.

With each pull of the paddle, a little more of his frustration flowed from him. Over the last few days, he had sensed an undercurrent in the village. Occasionally, when he approached a small group of men, their conversation ceased and they dispersed. Ufala was usually among those groups. Akoma didn't like it.

Near the Big Water, Akoma detoured, paddling up a small mangrove-lined branch. Startled by Akoma's presence, a large alligator slithered off the muddy bank into the water. At first Akoma thought it was a crocodile because the water was brackish. But the snout was definitely an alligator's.

The waterway narrowed and grew dark as the canopy of trees overlapped the passage. Akoma watched for a place to bank his canoe. Ahead, he spotted a small swatch of oak and other trees that implied high ground.

When he reached the location, he dragged the bow of his canoe onto the bank. Akoma sat on the damp soil, watching the current, looking at the smears of thin white clouds through the maze of leaves and branches. He listened to the wind, the water, and the wildlife. Yes, this was a good place for a vision. The spirits must have led him here.

There were things he needed to do before darkness fell. It was possible he could be here for days. He would stay however long it took for the spirits to speak to him.

He cleared a small area high up on the dry ground beneath a large oak. The area looked perfect for a small temporary camp.

Akoma piled some rocks and deadfall as high as the top of his thigh. The area was rich with all kinds of trees and plants. He scoured the surroundings for just the right branch that would serve as the ridgepole for his shelter. He finally saw a bough that he liked, one about the size of his arm and longer than he was tall. He pulled on it until it cracked, and then cut it away with his knife. The wood was hard and the knife-cutting slow, but finally the branch came down. He stripped the leaves and stems and dragged it back to camp.

He secured one end of the pole in the top of the debris pile and set the opposite end on the ground. He gathered smaller fallen branches and leaned them close together at an angle along both sides of the pole. The shelter was just large enough for him to crawl into and sleep. He tested the construction, shaking the ridgepole. Nothing fell. Satisfied with his work, he filled in the empty spaces between the stick ribs with leafy branches and brush. Along the top he piled sticks, grasses, brush, debris, and airplants, creating an airy dome that would insulate and keep him dry if it rained.

Akoma also wanted to build a basket trap for fish. He figured if he put the trap in the water now, when it was time to end the fast, he would have a fresh supply of fish.

He cut some thin young saplings and vines and used them to construct his basket trap. He sat by the water as he worked the weave of the trap. The sun was still high. He was going to finish everything before dark. There was plenty of time to get a fire going.

Akoma finished the trap with an attached pivotal gate, so the fish could swim in, but the gate wouldn't pivot in the opposite direction. He looked over the completed trap. It was a good trap. He staked it in the water, the wide, gated end pointing upstream. He picked up some snails and caught a few crayfish, cut them up, and used them to bait the trap.

A great egret, as white as the clouds, suddenly swooped overhead, coming from behind him, around the bend of the winding water. Something or someone had startled it, Akoma thought. To be cautious, he pulled his canoe into the brush. He hunkered behind a thicket of tall sedge that kept him out of view, yet still allowed him to see the water.

In a moment, two canoes silently snaked up the small river. Ais! Their oiled skin shone in the light. They wore no paint. It was not a war party. One man stood out from the rest. He bore many tattoos and adorned himself with beads. Perhaps it was Chogatis himself. What did the Ais do in Jeaga territory? Where did they go? Of course, they traveled the smaller tributaries, where there was less chance of being spotted.

Akoma watched as they glided past. They must have come from the opposite direction or he would have detected them on the long stretch of straight river. They would have seen him also. So strange, he thought.

As the sun went down, Akoma sipped water from his water pouch. The water here was too salty to drink. He could have stayed on the main river all the way to the Big Water, but something inside him led him to this place. He stripped himself naked, making himself more vulnerable to the spirits. He gathered some dead wood, mostly small buttonwood branches, and propped them up in a cone over several handfuls of dry grass and bark. Then he collected fine tinder. The ground was too damp for this task, so he sliced some bark from a tree to give him a dry work space. Akoma placed the small nest of dry grass and cattail fluff on top of the bark, then laid his fireboard gently on top, with the v-shaped notch directly over the tinder. He checked over his bow drill and the handhold, the block of wood he would hold on the top of the spindle. The socket in the handhold needed greasing. From a small parfleche he took out a seagrape leaf that was rolled and tied shut with sinew. He untied the knot and rolled out the leaf. A lump of tallow rested inside. Akoma rubbed the tallow in the socket of the handhold. He placed the handhold over the spindle and tested to see if it rotated smoothly. Content that all was ready, Akoma knelt on his right knee and put his left foot on the fireboard, bracing the handhold against his shin. The tip of the spindle sat in the socket at the point of the open notch. He held the bow at the end, making slow and steady strokes, exerting a little downward pressure. He built speed until the socket in the fireboard smoked, and dark powder formed in the notch. Faster he worked the drill until a steady stream of smoke and burning dust poured into the notch and onto the tinder bundle. A tiny coal formed. Akoma carefully withdrew the spindle, then lifted the fireboard. With the tip of his knife, he encouraged the coal to drop through the notch. He nested the tinder around the coal, cradling it in his hands, and gently blew on it. When he could feel the heat, he deftly placed the bundle beneath the propped kindling wood. He blew softly, a slow whispering stream of air, until the bundle burst into flame. At last he had a fire.

Akoma rocked back on his heels. This was a good fire. It always amazed him how quickly the sun disappeared under the horizon once it began to set. Beneath the earth, the sun still made an effort, its pinks and golds shining on the clouds. Then darkness came.

The vision would probably not come tonight; his body was not completely pure with only a day's fast. Tomorrow, perhaps. He watched the fire for a while, then rolled out his sleeping hide and stretched out beneath the stars.

The next morning Akoma did feel the twinge of hunger in his belly. He gladly acknowledged it, knowing his body was going through a cleansing process. He took a drink of water. Water was good, flushing undesirable things from the body.

He spent the day meditating and making small sacrifices to the spirits. Near dusk, he fed the fire and chanted a spirit song. From the berries of the yaupon holly tree, he brewed the black drink, cassina. He drank it hot, feeling it glide down his throat to his empty belly. In a moment, the cassina did its work. He fought the nausea, keeping the tea down as long as he could. Finally, he backed away from the fire and vomited until his stomach was empty again. Everything had been purged from his body. He was ready.

At nightfall, Akoma drew his knife down the length of his forearms. Thin red rivulets formed. He held his arms over the fire and allowed a few drops of blood to fall on the flames. He thought of his father's arms, striped with thin, light lines where he had done the same, asking the spirits for guidance in leading the People.

The fire blazed and hissed. The flames lapped at the darkness. Akoma rocked to the side, suddenly swept with dizziness.

At last, the vision!

Before him sat a basket filled with juicy cocoplums, coontie bread, palmetto berries, and succulent grapes. He was hungry, hungrier than he had ever been in his life. This sensation caused him much distress, and he felt the compulsion to eat everything in the basket as quickly as he could. He reached for the food. Then he heard a spirit speak.

"Akoma, your discomfort is understandable, but do not eat from this basket."

Akoma drew his hand back. "But why?" he asked. "I have a great hunger."

"Then eat," another voice said. "If your belly is hungry, then fill it." This voice was lilting, persuasive, provocative . . . the voice of a woman.

Confusion stirred in his head. He was hungry, indeed. Why would he be directed not to eat?

"The food in this basket is not as it seems," the first voice said. "Be patient."

The wind came up, cool and brisk. Akoma's hair blew back from his face. A ghostly image of a woman appeared before him. Her voice sounded like the wind, whispering to him. She lifted the basket and held it before him. "Take, eat," she said softly.

Intrigued by the image of the woman, he stared at

her. He wanted to see her face, but her hair, blown by the wind, obscured it, and the firelight did not reflect off her face. He strained to see better, finally taking her free hand and encouraging her to come closer. He could smell her now, the breeze carrying the soft scent of flowers.

She leaned over, her hair brushing his bare shoulder. Still, he could not see her face.

"There is nothing to fear," she whispered, so close to his ear that he felt her breath. "You hunger." Her hand caressed his cheek, and then a single finger traced his lips. "Here," she said, putting a grape to his mouth. "Bite into this luscious fruit and you will taste the delicious juice as it flows into your mouth."

She knelt in front of him. "Yes," she whispered.

Akoma's lips parted.

"It is not as it seems," the first voice said again. "You are deceived."

The woman put the grape in Akoma's mouth and pulled his head to her breast.

She was so soft and warm, he thought. His teeth pierced the skin of the grape and the juice burst forth. It was the most delicious grape he had ever eaten. His hunger rose, peaking to near pain. The woman withdrew and offered him the basket. Akoma grabbed a handful of the grapes and shoved them into his mouth.

Suddenly, he realized something was wrong. There was movement in his mouth, coiling . . . squirming. Worms! The creatures slid down his throat, out his nose and eyes, leaving trails of slime.

Akoma sputtered, trying to spit out the foul things. As he breathed in, he realized he sucked some of the worms into his lungs and swallowed them into his belly. The creatures were everywhere inside him, creeping out his ears, his rectum, and every opening in his body. Even he was changing—narrowing, slimming, elongating. He was becoming one of them. They had taken his soul and now he belonged to these horrid creatures!

"No!" he screamed, choking on the clump of snarled writhing worms in his throat. He couldn't breathe, or see, or hear anymore!

Abruptly, the vision ended, and Akoma realized he still sat in front of his fire. There was no woman, no basket, and no worms.

He was exhausted from the experience. Every bit of the little energy he had vanished, washed from him by the intensity of the vision. He curled on his side inside his shelter.

"What does it mean?" he whispered before falling into a deep sleep.

The night passed quickly, Akoma sleeping soundly through it without interruption or even dreams.

At dawn he awakened. A smudge of pink highlighted the clouds low in the eastern sky. The vision remained a puzzle to him. Perhaps the spirits would reveal its meaning slowly over time. He did recall that the spirit had said to be patient.

He rolled up his sleeping hide, gathered his fire drill and materials, and put them inside the canoe. He added fuel to the fire to cook his first meal and end the fast.

His fish trap was full. Akoma roasted one of the fish and turned the others loose. The delicious meat flaked in his mouth. When he finished, he sat for a few moments by the fire, gazing into the flames, thinking about the vision. Then he pushed off in his canoe.

When he finally reached the village, it was near dusk. The sky was speckled with birds coming in to roost, and fanned with the golden rays of the sinking sun.

Yahga-ta called to him as he made his way across the village. "Come, we must talk."

Akoma nodded and followed Yahga-ta into his lodge.

"There is trouble," Yahga-ta said.

31

Yahga-ta sat and gestured for Akoma to do the same. "Ufala persuaded a few men to seek out the Ais and attack. He took advantage of your absence. I am not so sure they would have gone had you been here."

Akoma shot his hands in the air. "Stupid!" he said. "Ufala has no sense anymore. When did they leave?" he asked.

"Yesterday," Yahga-ta answered. "Not many. Perhaps five."

"Idiot," Akoma said. "Ufala will invite more trouble." He finally sat across from Yahga-ta. "The Ais are near. I saw them. Three canoes."

"Where?"

"A half day's trip from here. On a small branch of the river."

"A war party?"

"No," Akoma said. "They did not appear to be either a war or hunt party. I think one of them may have been Chogatis."

"I do not understand," Yahga-ta said. "It makes no sense to me." Yahga-ta leaned toward his son. "And did you have a vision?"

"Yes," Akoma said. "A bizarre vision that I do not understand yet. The spirits do not choose to reveal its meaning."

"There is nothing you can do about Ufala now, so concentrate on the meaning of the vision. Go to Putiwa. Ask his opinion."

Akoma stood. "Did you ever have difficulty interpreting visions?"

"Many times," Yahga-ta answered.

"Did you ever have a vision that you never did understand?"

Yahga-ta shook his head, slowly blinking his eyes. "Neither will you."

Akoma nodded his appreciation for the confidence his father had in him, then turned and headed straight to Putiwa.

Near the shaman's hearth he saw that Putiwa spoke with Sassa. Ufala treated his wife and children so cruelly, except for Nocatee, he thought. He felt sorry for Sassa. At least she had Kitchi. He was sure both Sassa and Nocatee missed Talli.

"How are you, Sassa?" he asked.

The young girl looked up at him with tears in her eyes. "My mother is not well. Putiwa says there is nothing that can be done for her. She will slowly get weaker and weaker."

"I am so sorry. It must be difficult."

"Mother will not tell my father. But he has to know. He must see that she is not well."

"Ufala has many things on his mind," Akoma said.

"I wish Talli were here. It would please our mother greatly if Talli came to visit."

"Then it will be," Akoma said. "I have business in the Panther village. I will bring her back."

An enormous smile spread across Sassa's face. "That would be wonderful! I am going to tell Nocatee and Mother right now." She paused a moment. "No, not Mother. I will let Talli surprise her." Sassa threw her arms around Akoma's neck, then pulled away quickly and ran off as if she thought she had acted inappropriately.

"How sick is Kitchi?" Akoma asked.

"It is a slow sickness, but eventually she will succumb to it," Putiwa said.

"Is there no treatment? No cure?"

"None. Near the end I can give her medicines to reduce the discomfort. That is the best I can do."

"This is very sad news. Ufala should be taking care of her."

"He should," Putiwa said. "But as we have discussed

before, Ufala's insides have turned rancid since the skirmish with the Ais. He does not think. Sassa came for me one day, dragging little Nocatee behind her. Both children were upset. Sassa said her father had struck Kitchi and bruised her face. Kitchi's teeth were tender and Sassa wanted some medicine for her mother. I told her I would go and see Kitchi, but Sassa did not want me to do that. She said she begged her mother to come to me, but Kitchi refused, saying she did not want anyone to know. But Sassa could not bear to see her mother suffering, so she wanted a medicine she could hide in Kitchi's tea. I gave her something and have not spoken to her since, until today."

"I will go for Talli in the morning," Akoma said.

"That will be good," Putiwa said. "Now, tell me what brings you to my hearth?"

"I have had a vision," Akoma said. "However, I do not understand its meaning. Perhaps you can help."

"Let us sit by the fire," Putiwa said. "Tell me from the beginning, what did you see, hear, feel?"

Akoma retold what he had experienced. When he was finished, Putiwa closed his eyes.

Akoma waited patiently to hear what the shaman thought.

In a few moments, Putiwa opened his eyes and looked at the cacique.

"It is a strange vision, indeed. But spirits keep their meanings disguised in visions so only the wise and worthy can interpret them. A man is supposed to be challenged, made to think. That is part of the vision. It makes a man search inside himself, perhaps look at things he does not want to, face his own inadequacies and fears in an effort to unravel the meaning."

"I have done that," Akoma said.

"Let them speak to you. Seek the truth inside again." Putiwa gave Akoma a few moments to ponder. "I can tell you what I see," Putiwa said. "But I am not the one to interpret the vision. The spirits gave it to you."

Akoma shifted, wondering if Putiwa understood the vision, but would not tell him everything.

"I see you have a great need for something in your

life," Putiwa said. "That is the hunger in your vision. You know what is good for you and what is not. The spirits tell you to be patient and this need will be satisfied, but you allow others to persuade you to do what is not good for you. The food in the basket is not what it seems. I see the food as something you think will end this overpowering need and will satisfy the woman in your vision. And so you partake of this food, to find that, indeed, it is not what it seems, and it does not satisfy the hunger at all."

"But what is the hunger, the need, the fruit, the woman? I am not sure what need you speak of."

"The answer is inside you. I do not dwell there and so I cannot answer." The corners of Putiwa's mouth turned up in a faint grin. "Listen to the voice inside yourself. Listen carefully so you can hear the spirits when they whisper. The answers may come slowly, a piece at a time, or at all once in a great revelation."

"I will think about it," Akoma said. "I will let your words steep in my head for a while."

"Trust yourself. You are chosen. You are the cacique, the leader of the Turtle Jeaga."

Akoma got to his feet.

"I think I will visit Kitchi and see how she is."

"Akoma," Putiwa called. "The worms represent pain. The hunger is not of the body, it is in the heart. Whichever you choose to do, go hungry or attempt to satisfy the hunger, there will be pain. Be ready for that."

As Akoma walked away, a wisp of understanding flickered in his head. But it wasn't enough to hold on to.

Talli held the baby to her breast and watched Ceboni flit about the fire.

"Joog, take the fish off the grate," Ceboni said. "It is ready to eat. Go for Tawute, he will enjoy this fish."

Joog ran off, leaving Talli and the baby alone with Ceboni. "He still limps a bit," Ceboni said.

"He is lucky. I thought the boy would die," Talli said.

"Do you think he will ever speak?"

"He has been through so much." She recalled the vivid image she had experienced through the affliction, the horror that he felt. "It was terrible." Talli sucked in a breath, realizing what she was saying.

Ceboni stopped stirring the tea she brewed. "What do you mean? What did he see? How do you know?"

"W—well," Talli stammered. She had to be more cautious or one day she would give away her secret. "I assume he must have seen what happened. Banabas said he was hiding when they came upon the bloody sight."

"Oh," Ceboni said. "I suppose you are right. The shock must have taken his tongue. Or maybe he never talked," Ceboni added. "Maybe he just does not want to."

"No, Ceboni," Talli said. "He would speak if he could. Maybe he will talk again someday. If we make him feel sheltered and safe, the return of his speech is a possibility, I think."

"I suppose." Ceboni went back to her task. Talli could tell she was thinking hard about something. Now and again Ceboni glanced at her and the baby.

"What is wrong?" Talli asked.

"Nothing is wrong," Ceboni said. "You know that I like Joog and certainly Tawute enjoys him. But do you ever wonder if he would turn on you? He is Ais." Ceboni held the stirring stick in the air as she spoke. "I should not have said that. I did not mean anything bad."

"He is just a child," Talli said. "Actually, I think he has come to love us. I cannot imagine he would ever do anything to harm us."

"But if you get him back to his people and he grows up and there is a skirmish with the Ais, or suppose he grows up here and never goes home, then one day an Ais raiding party comes to our village, what would Joog do?"

"That would be a long time away. He is still only a boy."

"Do you ever talk about those things with Banabas?"

"No," Talli said. "We do not consider him Ais anymore. Joog is part of our family."

"Speaking of your husband, I thought he would be back by now. I hope he and Ramo are all right."

"He said he might be gone for several days. He will return soon, I am sure."

"I hear the men speculate about where they went. Your husband and Ramo are secretive, and I think the other men find that annoying. They wonder why Ramo and Banabas cannot share where they go and what they do. Iquan speaks with the other men and tries to calm their irritation, but he has little success. I think this mystery breeds bad feeling and some distrust."

"Do you think so?"

"Maybe you might mention it to Banabas when he returns. Perhaps if Ramo and Banabas are aware, they can still any rumors or misgivings."

Tawute and Joog trekked up to Ceboni. "I am hungry," Tawute said. "We are ready to eat."

"Ceboni, will you watch Mikot while you and the boys eat? I want to go bathe."

Ceboni reached for the baby. A large smile broke out across her face.

"I will not be long," Talli said.

A woman still shedding the birthing blood could not bathe in the same area as others. She was considered unclean, and the blood would contaminate anything and everyone it touched. And so Talli gathered some things and walked down the bank of the river away from the village to where menstruants were allowed to bathe. The water ran fast there, sweeping all contaminated water away from the village.

When she reached the place, Talli removed her skirt and also the leather strap and its packing that captured the blood. The first thing she did was scan the banks and water for signs of alligators and snakes. Then she took a stick and slapped the water loudly, so if any creature was nearby, it would be alarmed by the noise and move away.

She stepped into the water. Thunder rolled in the distance. A storm was coming. She was glad the winter had passed with so few cold days. The water still had the reminder of the seasonal chill, but it was refreshing. Perhaps the warmer weather would at last bring enough rain to destroy thoughts of a drought.

Talli sank beneath the water, soaking her hair. She did not like being in the water alone. There was always the danger of an alligator or water moccasin she had not seen.

Talli rubbed the skin of her body, loosening dust and dirt. She leaned her head back again, letting the bulk of her hair trail in the water. The sky was darkening with the threat of rain. She shouldn't stay long.

Talli gathered her hair into a thick black ribbon and twisted it, squeezing out the water as she made her way onto shore. Once on dry ground she dressed herself and glanced down the river. To her surprise she saw a canoe. She backed into the trees. Talli filled the strap with the fresh packing she had brought with her, put it on, and then tied on her skirt. She wondered if Banabas and Ramo were in the approaching canoe.

Closer to the edge of the river, she hid behind a tree and peered around it.

There was only one man in the dugout. A moment of apprehension raced through her. Was only one of them returning? Who?

Talli continued to stare at the oncoming vessel. As it got closer, she couldn't believe what she saw.

32

In her disbelief she had forgotten to keep herself hidden. Akoma spotted her about the same time she realized who he was. He stood in the canoe.

Talli clung to the tree. She didn't know whether to step out and appear calm and composed, or if she should pretend she hadn't seen him at all. Akoma raised his hand in greeting.

Talli couldn't move. Her feet felt as if they had been staked to the ground, and her leg muscles were so weak, her knees wobbled.

Another clash of thunder rolled through the air. Akoma sat in the dugout and paddled the canoe to the shore. Talli grabbed the nose of the dugout and pulled it up onto the bank. So many things swam through her mind as she watched him climb from the canoe. She wanted to speak, but the right words just wouldn't come.

"How are you, Talli?" Akoma asked.

Talli kept her head down. "I am all right," she said. "And you?"

Akoma put his fingers beneath her chin and tilted her head up. "Why do you not look at me?" Talli didn't answer, though she knew why she did not look up. She feared her feelings would be obvious, and she would make a fool of herself. He would see how much she still loved him.

"I am glad to see you," he said.

Talli felt warmth rush throughout her body, and her face flush. His eyes were so dark and pure. His fingers left her chin and found her bare shoulder. She wanted to tell him everything. If he would just ask her to go away with him. She wished they could climb in the canoe and disappear. But that was not going to ever happen.

"I have come to see you."

"Me?" she asked.

"I need to tell you something about your mother."

A sense of dread and disappointment surged inside her. She feared what he had to say and felt disheartened that he had not come to see her because he loved her, but because of bad news. "Tell me," she said.

"Kitchi is not well. Putiwa says the sickness will get worse eventually. Your sister is concerned and says it would do your mother good if you visited."

"She is dying?" Talli asked.

"Yes," Akoma said. "But the sickness lingers. It will not be sudden. She has some time."

Talli's throat tightened. Her eyes stung as she fought back tears. "No," she whispered. The tears overcame her effort to suppress them.

Akoma put his arms around her. "I am sorry, Talli."

The feel of his embrace, the sensation of his skin touching hers, the despondency in her heart, made her weep.

Akoma stroked her back. He nuzzled in her hair. "It will be all right. I told Sassa I would bring you back to visit."

Talli rested her head on his chest, and Akoma stroked her hair. "Banabas is not here," she said. "I cannot leave."

"Tell someone to tell him where you went and why. Certainly he will understand."

Talli nodded. Akoma was right, Banabas would understand. She could leave Joog with Ceboni and take the baby with her. "I want to go tomorrow," she said.

"Then we will."

"I do not want my mother to die," she said, choking on her tears.

Akoma lifted her face and gently kissed her.

Oh, how she still loved this man with everything inside her. In her life she had experienced terrible things, felt others' pain, all because of the affliction. Now she ached to understand what Akoma felt inside. Did his heart still keep a small corner for her? But she could feel nothing. Surely it was a punishment. She could not command the affliction.

Talli pulled away. Banabas was a fine man and did not deserve her infidelity. No matter how she felt about Akoma, no matter how profound those feelings, she was Banabas's wife.

Akoma stared into her eyes. Suddenly his attention was drawn elsewhere.

Talli looked where Akoma gazed.

"Joog!" she cried.

The boy turned and ran back to the village.

"He saw us," Talli said. "He will misunderstand." She twirled a strand of hair in concern.

"Who is the boy?"

"It is too complicated to explain."

"You think he will say something to Banabas. Is that what upsets you?"

"He cannot speak."

"Then there is nothing to worry about."

"It was wrong," Talli said. "I have a husband and a son. Did you know that? I have a boy named Mikot. He is a beautiful boy. The shaman says his guide spirit is Climbing Bear. Mother will be so pleased. Father will, too."

"You are rambling, Talli."

Talli hung her head. "I need to go back to the village and speak to Joog. Then I can gather my things and prepare for the trip home."

"I will take you," he said.

"No, I should go by myself," she said, walking away.

"I will see you there," Akoma said.

Talli didn't turn around. How easy it had been for her to accept his mouth on hers. She had not objected; in fact, she enjoyed it, wanted it. Yes, she loved him, but what morals did she have? She was married to Banabas, not by her choice, but still it was the spirits' design. They would certainly be angry with her now.

Joog stood by the fire. Tawute and his little sister, Zowhi, sat next to Ceboni.

"Where have you been?" Ceboni asked. "I sent Joog

to look for you. I was concerned, especially when he came back without you."

"The water felt so good. I stayed in it a long time." She looked at Joog.

"That was a dangerous thing to do," Ceboni said.

"Yes, it was foolish of me." She looked at the fish Ceboni had prepared. "My mouth waters," she said. "Come, Joog. Have some."

Joog shook his head and sat by the lodge, away from the others.

"Are you sick?" Ceboni asked. "Come and eat."

"Come on, Joog," Tawute said.

Joog made his way next to his friend and glared at Talli.

"Joog looks sad," Zowhi said.

Ceboni put a white piece of fish into her mouth. "Mmm," she agreed. "Something is wrong with him."

Talli's palms began to sweat. The boy had witnessed . . . She needed to talk to him alone.

"Joog," Talli said. "Come, let us take a walk. Perhaps it will make you feel better."

"Maybe he should eat something first," Ceboni said.

Talli ignored her. "Joog," she said firmly, "come with me."

The boy slowly got to his feet and the two of them walked off. Talli put her hand on his shoulder. Joog shrugged as if to move her hand away, but Talli persisted.

Once away from the village, Talli stooped in front of him. "Do you still miss your mother?" Talli asked. "Of course you do," she said before Joog could respond. "I miss mine, too. Akoma brought me terrible news. I know you will understand how I feel. He told me that my mother is ill. She is dying. I am very upset. When he told me I cried. Akoma and I once loved each other. It was natural for him to console me. He cares about me. Do you understand?"

Joog refused to look at her.

"It did not mean anything, Joog. I was crying and Akoma felt sympathy for me. He has come all this way at my sister's bidding. She thinks I should visit my mother. I want to go. It may be the last time I see her."

Joog stared at the ground.

"If you had a chance to see your mother, you would go, would you not?"

Talli noticed a faint nod of Joog's head.

"Yes, I am sure you would. I want that for you some-day. For now, I need you to understand."

The boy finally looked up. Talli put her palms on Joog's cheeks and looked deep into his eyes. The eyes still showed signs of being troubled, but they had softened.

"I will leave in the morning. I am going to ask Ceboni to let you stay with her until Banabas returns. He should be back soon. She will tell my husband where I have gone and why."

The dark clouds that had rolled in from the east swelled with moisture. The belly of the thunderhead sank low in the sky, a slow swirl of billowing gray. With a brilliant flash of light and loud crack of thunder, the clouds opened, and a downpour washed onto the earth.

Talli swept her wet hair from her face. "Do you understand?" she asked. She experienced a swift insight into Joog's emotions. He was angry and confused.

He turned and ran back to the village.

Ceboni stood on the bank, Zowhi on her hip, Tawute and Joog by her side. She and her children waved good-bye. Joog did not. He stood with his arms at his sides and a blank expression on his face.

Talli sat in front of Akoma's canoe with Mikot in her arms. The air was humid and misty, but the rain had stopped.

Akoma pushed off. Coming behind Ceboni, Talli saw someone else. Liakka. The woman's arm danced in the air as she waved boldly.

"I am anxious for your return, beloved," she said. "Come back quickly!"

Talli's stomach knotted. She wanted to look behind her, to see Akoma and his reaction, but she didn't dare.

Instead, she clutched Mikot and fought the strangling in her throat.

For quite some time, after the Panther village was out of sight, Talli sat without speaking. Akoma paddled steadily.

When the sun was directly overhead, Akoma put down the paddle. "Are you hungry?" he asked.

"No," Talli answered.

Akoma moved up behind her. "You must be hungry by now. You have to keep up your nourishment for the child."

"I am fine," Talli said, shivering at the touch of his hand moving her hair away so he could touch her shoulder.

"Turn so I can see you, Talli. I want to talk to you."

Talli twisted and shifted her position so she faced the back of the canoe and Akoma.

"While I was in your village—"

"The Panther village is not my village," she interrupted. "I am Turtle."

"You live in the Panther village with your husband," Akoma said. He paused and stroked her cheek. "Do not be so defensive."

Talli leaned her cheek into his hand.

"While I was there," he continued, "I gave Liakka's father hides and antler for his daughter. The People are impatient with me. They want this seal between the Turtle and the Panther to take place soon."

"You will take Liakka as your wife?"

"The marriage is agreed upon. When Ramo returns and gives his consent, it will be finalized."

"That soon?" Talli's voice crimped with the effort she made to keep from crying.

He held her head in his hands and pulled her forehead to his chest. "How did all this come to be?" he asked. Akoma pressed his lips to the top of her head.

Talli thought of telling him about Mikot, but that would complicate things even more. There had been enough pain. There should be no more, not for her, not for Akoma, and not for Banabas.

She closed her eyes, feeling the body of her infant next to her and the warmth of Akoma.

"We said many things to each other, things we meant at the time," he said. "They were not lies, just promises and vows that were made in the passion of our love, promises we really could not keep."

Talli wanted to let the words gush from her, to tell him that she had kept her promise as best she could. Mikot was Akoma's son, and if she had lain with Banabas that single time, it was her sacrifice for everyone's protection.

"We were young and very much in love," he said. "It seems we have grown much older in a short time."

"Yes," Talli said. "So much older." She lifted her head. "I hope you will find happiness."

"Are you happy, Talli? Is Banabas a good husband to you?"

"He loves me and takes good care of me. I have learned to care for him." Talli started to speak again, opening her mouth, but then hesitated.

"What do you want to say?" he asked.

"Do you love her? Will the marriage to Liakka make you happy?"

"I am responsible for the People," he said. "When the Jeaga are safe and at ease, that will make me content. Having things I want, making myself happy, is not a privilege enjoyed by a cacique. The People come first."

Talli gently touched her palm to his face. She smoothed his brow with her thumb. One day, when she was very old and near death, she would summon him. She knew he would come, and she would tell him everything. Perhaps as she lay dying, he would stretch out along her length, cradle her head, and hold her while she crossed over. That was probably all she could possibly look forward to. She hoped that she would die first. Such a wish was selfish, she knew, but living on knowing he was no longer alive would be unbearable.

Talli sat and leaned over Kitchi, who was sleeping. "Mother," she said softly. "It is Talli."

Kitchi slowly opened her eyes. "Talli?"

"I have come to see you."

"Oh," she said, looking out the doorway at the afternoon light. "I fell asleep. I only wanted to rest." Kitchi pushed herself up on her elbows. "That is you, Talli," she said, sitting up. "Oh, my." Her eyes filled with tears and her arms reached out.

Talli hugged her mother. "Akoma said you were not feeling well."

"Nothing really," she said. "I am getting old. You know how the old ones get. They complain about all their little aches and pains. Now I find I am one of them."

"Look, Mother," Sassa said. Sassa held Mikot. "Talli has a son."

Kitchi's face contorted as if she were going to cry and smile at the same time. "Bring him closer."

Sassa handed Mikot to Talli. The baby whimpered.

"He is going to cry," Nocatee said.

Mikot stirred and fidgeted. "He is fitful sometimes," Talli said.

"Like his mother was," Kitchi said.

Mikot began to cry. "Shh," Talli said, rocking him. "I think he needs a grandmother's arms."

Kitchi's eyes, gray now instead of the dark brown they had been in her youth, lit up. Talli gave Mikot to her mother. Kitchi started a song, singing close to Mikot so he could hear her over his own screaming.

Undaunted by the child's crying, Kitchi kept up the song, still in the soft, peaceful tone. Mikot fussed a bit, then locked onto his grandmother's gaze, apparently entranced by the voice and the new face.

"Ocaab tells me his guide spirit is Climbing Bear."

The old woman's voice trembled. "Climbing Bear," she said.

Ufala's shadow fell over the light coming in the lodge. "So, our daughter comes to visit," he said, moving inside.

"Father," Talli said, acknowledging him.

"Look at your grandson," Kitchi said.

Ufala peered over Talli's shoulder. "So Banabas still has the fire," he said and chuckled.

"Ufala!" Kitchi said. "Talli is your daughter."

"Arrgh, you women are so difficult!" He turned on his heel and left.

Just outside his lodge, Akoma stopped him.

"Ufala, there are issues I wish to discuss with you."

"Well, I have nothing to discuss with you, Cacique. I have said everything I intend to."

"No, Ufala, the well-being of the Turtle is at stake. You will sit and listen, and answer my questions. Do I make myself clear?"

Ufala grumbled.

"Let us do this with respect. Come and we will sit by my hearth. We will air our differences with regard for one another."

Ufala followed Akoma. Akoma sat by the fire and motioned for Ufala to do the same. "I understand while in my absence you took it upon yourself to solicit a few others and go and seek the Ais. Is this true or am I misunderstanding?"

Ufala crossed his arms in a defiant gesture. "You have not been misinformed. I have spoken openly of my opinion of what we should do. Unfortunately, we did not come across any Ais. We did find evidence of a campfire. Could have been Jeaga . . . Panther."

"Just because you have spoken your opinion does not mean it has my sanction. You cannot act on your own. We do not provoke or invite the Ais. We are not in a position to do that. With the strain we suffer with Ramo, your actions were very unwise. I understand how you feel about the Ais, but even more reason not to give them the advantage."

"You have no—"

Akoma interrupted. "This has nothing to do with courage. We must depend as much on our judgment as we do on our muscle. And, since we are fewer in number and do not have the assurance of the Ais, we must be certain to evaluate and analyze our options and actions. Council will deal harshly with another act of dissension."

Ufala stretched, ready to get up. "Is that all?"

"No, I have something else to speak with you about."

"I think we are done," Ufala said, rising.

"Sit!"

Ufala halted his attempt to stand.

"Your wife is ill."

"Of what concern is that to you? Just because you are the cacique does not give you privy to a man's life with his wife."

Akoma kept his voice calm, though Ufala was irritating him. "When any Jeaga man strikes another man or woman, it becomes the concern of the cacique. We have an enemy; we do not need to turn on ourselves. That is intolerable."

"I have heard enough," Ufala said.

"No, you have not. You lose everyone's respect, Ufala. You are a big man, and your wife is small." Akoma watched Ufala twitch. The man was uncomfortable for certain. "She is also ill. Are you aware of that?"

"She has not been feeling as good as usual. We all have spells like that, especially at this age."

"It is not a spell. Putiwa says she is dying. Kitchi has a sickness that will slowly take her life."

Ufala got to his feet. "We are finished," he said.

"Keep in mind all that I have said," Akoma said. "You have the wisdom of the years, the common sense and sagacity that comes with experience. Do not disregard all that because of your injury. Rise above it, Ufala. Your gut sours with hatred, and it spills over onto those who care for you, your Turtle brothers and your wife."

Ufala stomped away. Near his lodge he heard Nocatee screaming.

33

Talli's body trembled, her eyes rolling in her head; her face blanched white as lime. Nocatee clung to her mother, her voice high and wailing in fright. Sassa braced Talli's shoulders.

"Get out!" Ufala's voice boomed. "Now!" he said, grabbing Talli by the hair. "You will ruin us all!"

Ufala yanked on the cord of her hair, jerking her head back.

Nocatee screeched even louder.

"Stop," Kitchi cried. "Leave her alone. She cannot help it!"

Ufala grabbed Talli's arm and wrenched her off her knees, throwing her facedown.

Sassa backed away in fear. "Father, no, no," she cried.

Ufala continued to drag Talli out of the lodge. She scrambled to her feet, the effects of the affliction quickly departing.

Ufala raised his arm up, his hand balled into a fist. Talli's eyes grew large in fear. She turned her head, expecting a blow to her face.

"Do not come back here," he yelled, ready to strike.

Suddenly someone grabbed his wrist and twisted his arm behind his back. He flinched at the feel of the sharp, beveled edge of a knife poised at his throat. "If you move I will slit your throat," Akoma said, jerking Ufala's arm up higher so it hurt. "Do I have your attention?" he asked.

Ufala didn't move.

"Good," Akoma said. "If you ever think about hurting her, I will kill you," he said. He slid his knife across the surface of Ufala's throat, leaving a shallow slice in the skin. "Never even think it," he said, "or you will be dead on the spot."

Akoma let go of Ufala's arm, then sheathed his knife. Talli huddled on the ground, shaking. Akoma stooped next to her. "Did he hurt you?"

"I am all right," she said, watching Ufala walk away.

"He is crazy," Akoma said. "Instead of healing, he grows worse."

Sassa poked her head out the doorway.

"She is unharmed," Akoma said, helping Talli to her feet.

Talli heard Mikot crying inside the lodge. Kitchi came to the doorway with the baby.

"He is hungry," Talli said.

"Are you certain you are all right?" Akoma asked.

"Yes," she answered.

"Do you or your mother need anything?"

Talli shook her head. "Thank you," she said.

Talli took Mikot and went inside the lodge. Sassa and Kitchi followed.

Talli put the baby to her breast. "I am going to stay here and take care of you," she said. "You are not well."

"No," Kitchi said. "Someone will find out about your secret. You cannot stop it from happening."

"But once I am used to the situation, the affliction does not usually continue to return over and over again."

"You cannot be sure. You do not know when it will happen again. Staying here, caring for me, is too dangerous for you. Sassa and Nocatee are here."

"Why do you not come with me?"

"It would be the same there. Someone would find out. You have to go home, Talli."

Talli hung her head. "In a few days," she said.

Ufala did not return to his shelter that night or the next. Talli slept next to her mother, the baby at her other side. She prepared the meals with Sassa's and Nocatee's help. She always had enough for Ufala, but he said he would not eat with his wife until Talli was gone.

Talli performed all the tasks that Kitchi usually did.

Kitchi tried to help, but Talli would not allow her. She told her mother to rest as long as she was here.

On the afternoon of the third day, Banabas arrived. He saw Talli from a distance. Akomá was tenderly stroking her hair. Talli put her hand in his. Akoma held her hand a moment, they spoke, and he left.

Banabas felt a cleft in his heart open up. He wondered if he could ever make her love him. She never responded to his touch the way she appeared to respond to Akoma's. He felt sick and even angry.

Banabas leaned against a tall, sweet bay tree, watching her. He wanted her so badly, wanted to join with her and have her enjoy his lovemaking. He wanted her to be his wife.

After a while he approached her.

"Ceboni told me where you were," he said.

"I am sorry I was not there when you returned. I worried about my mother. I wanted to see her, and I was not sure when you and Ramo were coming back. Is Joog all right?" Talli asked.

"I believe he misses you. His mood is melancholy."

"I miss him, also," she said. "I was going to go home soon."

"We will leave tomorrow," Banabas said. "Where is Ufala?"

"I am not sure," she said.

"Is something wrong? You sound odd."

"No, not really," she answered. "Ufala and I do not get along. You know that."

"I think I will look for him," Banabas said.

As Banabas crossed the village he came upon Akoma. "Cacique," he said in greeting, "thank you for bringing my wife to visit her mother. I would have done so."

"She was anxious to see Kitchi," Akoma said.

"I was gone longer than I expected. I understand you have set the marriage to Liakka."

"Yes," Akoma said. "Tell me, did you and Ramo see any Ais?"

Banabas appeared startled. "No. Why do you ask?"

"Not many days ago I sighted a party on the river."

"Really," Banabas said. "What kind of party?"

"They were traveling a small tributary, not the main river. They did not appear to be either a hunt or war party. I am curious as to their purpose. I am surprised you did not come upon them. You traveled quite a few days."

"It is a big river," Banabas said.

Akoma's curiosity showed in his expression. "Where were you and Ramo?"

"About the river, on an excursion."

"What was the purpose?"

"We had many things to see and check on." Banabas began to walk away. He took note of Akoma's curiosity and feared that Akoma harbored suspicions about Ramo being in collusion with Chogatis.

"You love your wife, do you not?" Akoma asked.

Banabas whipped around to face him squarely. "Of course I do."

"You would not want to see her hurt. She loves her mother and sisters. You would not do anything that would lead to their harm, would you?"

"Are you really asking me such a question? It is absurd to think I would do anything that would cause Talli unhappiness."

Both men stared at each other. The air about them thickened. A mosquito sucked the blood from Banabas's upper arm. He slapped it, leaving a spray of red on his skin. "Ah, there is Ufala," Banabas said. "I was looking for him."

"Perhaps you can talk to him and he will listen. He is not the man you knew as a friend. Kitchi has already suffered his fist, and he tried to strike Talli, but I intervened."

Banabas could not keep from staring at Talli most of the way home. He could not help wondering what she felt about Akoma. He fantasized, picturing her in Akoma's arms, then conjuring the image of what it would be like to join with her again, to have her beneath him.

When they arrived in the Panther village, Ramo greeted them.

"How are our Turtle brothers?" he asked. "Akoma,

Ufala, Yahga-ta? Oh, and your mother, Talli, how is she?"

"She is a strong woman," Talli said. "She was happy to see her grandson. I hope she will have other opportunities. I want to visit her again."

"I have given the consent for the marriage of Liakka to Akoma. Her family is very excited. Akoma is anxious, and who can blame him? Liakka is quite a woman." Ramo laughed and slapped Banabas on the back. "You know what I mean," he said. "A man does not need furs in the winter with her in his bed!"

Banabas watched Talli's face turn gray as the ash of her cook fire. "Talli is tired. This has been a trying time for her. I want to get her to rest. We need to talk, but I will speak with you later. There are important things we need to discuss."

"Good," Ramo said. "Come to my lodge."

Banabas escorted his wife and baby to their shelter.

"Where is Joog?" Talli asked. "I thought he would come running."

"Maybe he has not gotten the word that we have returned. He will be along."

Talli sat inside the lodge. "You are right, I am tired."

Mikot's eyes were closed in peaceful sleep. His small mouth pursed, as if nursing in his dreams.

Banabas stood in the doorway. "Here comes Joog with Ceboni and Tawute."

Ceboni brought a basket of food. "I thought you might not feel like preparing anything," she said.

"That is so kind of you," Talli said.

Joog hung back outside the lodge.

"Come in and see Talli and the baby," Banabas said.

Joog took a few steps inside the lodge.

"Have you had fun with Tawute?" Talli asked.

Joog nodded, but without enthusiasm.

"I have missed you," Talli said.

Joog did not offer any kind of response.

"Go and play," Talli said.

Joog nodded again and left.

"He sulks often," Ceboni said. "Something bothers

him. I thought he just missed you. I guess he has a lot of things he worries about."

"I thought he was doing well," Banabas said. "He did not seem so moody before I left. I will talk to him."

Talli grew more uncomfortable. She hoped Joog would not divulge what he had seen if Banabas questioned him. "Perhaps with the baby he thinks of his mother more often," Talli said. "He will adjust. I do not think we should keep after him to express to us what is wrong. That probably perpetuates his focus on his family and that he is really Ais, not Jeaga. He must have many mixed feelings."

For the next cycle of the moon, Banabas observed Joog. While with Tawute or Ceboni, the boy appeared fine. He even seemed to enjoy walks with Banabas. The only strange thing was that Joog tended to avoid Talli.

"Why do you think Joog withdraws from you?" Banabas asked Talli.

"Does he? I have not noticed that. I think he has moods. Sometimes he is sad. As I said before, the baby may remind him of his mother. He may even be jealous."

Banabas watched as Mikot suckled at Talli's breast. The village prepared for the celebration of Liakka's marriage to Akoma. Because she was becoming the wife of a cacique, there was planned a night of feasting and dancing. Liakka's father would take her to Akoma's village for the ceremony. More often a woman was married in her own village, but when the marriage was to a cacique, the cacique's village took precedence. Perhaps this marriage would end any pining Talli did for Akoma. Perhaps Talli would become a real wife.

The baby nuzzled and cooed at Talli's breast. The bleeding had stopped, yet she had not given Banabas any indication that he was welcome. Joining with her had been on his mind more and more. He often woke up in the middle of the night, ready for her, but he did not pursue his desire. Even when he watched the baby nurse, he sometimes became aroused. He was going to have to discuss the matter with her.

"I am going to catch fish for the feast," he said. "Perhaps some rabbit or deer."

Talli looked up and smiled.

Banabas gathered his fishing and hunting tools. Joog came alongside. He picked up his lance.

"Not this time," Banabas said. He wanted to be alone.

Deep in the forest Banabas put down his weapons. "Talli," he whispered. He leaned his back against a tree. He needed some kind of relief. He closed his eyes, and the image of Talli's supple body came into his head. She was naked and she danced for him, moving sinuously, rubbing against him.

Banabas reached inside his breechclout.

The night air reverberated with the sound of turtle-shell rattles, skin drums, and the strands of tinkling shells. The central hearth blazed into the night sky, lapping the night.

Ramo stood near the fire, the rest of the village circling him and the flames. He was dressed in full panoply. His hair was knotted and secured with polished bone pins carved with graceful designs. About his neck was a large, shell pendant and strings of pearls. A cape of cascading feathers hugged his shoulders.

Placards, slabs of wood carved with the images of deer, kingfishers, osprey, and turtle were put on top of posts about the village.

Liakka's father joined Ramo. He had provided an enormous amount of the food, though each man did contribute.

Talli stood just outside the circle, holding Mikot. She watched as Banabas assisted Ocaab. Ocaab's face was painted with red and white stripes. He took a staff, taller than himself, and planted it in the ground. Midway up the staff was the carved image of a panther. At the crest was the head of a deer with a moveable mouth. Ocaab sang out. Everyone hushed while the shaman summoned the spirits. When he was finished, several dancers appeared wearing carved wooden masks of turtles, pelicans, bears, and cormorants. They shook rattles and sang songs, stepping high, then planting their feet, toes first.

They spun and swayed, moving like the animals they portrayed. The bear's footsteps were heavy and exaggerated, landing with a thud on the ground. The cormorant's arms waved in the air, simulating flight.

As the dancers performed, Ocaab and Banabas mixed a large pot of tea. This was the tea of celebration, much like the black drink, but less of an emetic and more of an intoxicating drink. This was a double occasion. They celebrated the full moon and Liakka's noble marriage.

Ocaab dramatically sprinkled the final herbs into the pot, chanting and waving his arms. Banabas stirred, then ladled some out with a gourd dipper. He offered it to Ocaab, who tasted it, waited a moment then nodded with approval. Everyone cheered, and the feast officially began.

Gourd after gourd dipped into the tea, and the music and song grew louder and louder.

Banabas filled his gourd often. As he sipped, he looked over the dipper to find Talli. She had backed away and was half hidden in the shadows.

Talli watched the attention Liakka received from the women. They gathered about her with giggles and laughter, excited by the idea of what it might be like to be the wife of a cacique, and such a handsome one! Liakka appeared to revel in all the focus.

When Mikot was sleeping soundly, Talli put him in his sleeping skin inside the lodge, then walked outside to continue to watch the activities. She did not feel like taking part, but could not keep herself from looking on. She punished herself, she thought. She stood in the shadows of the trees, but knew she had to spend a little time in the crowd. Someone might wonder why if she did not participate.

She was just about ready to join Ceboni and congratulate Liakka when she felt a hand thrust up through her hair and another reach around and clutch her breast.

34

Talli snapped around. "Banabas! You frightened me."

Banabas bit into her neck and pulled her closer, his hands firm on her buttocks.

"What are you doing? Stop!"

"You are my wife," Banabas said.

He planted his mouth on hers. His mouth was wet and hot, and his breath smelled of the tea. He was sweaty, and he breathed rapidly.

"Do not do this," Talli said.

Banabas ignored her and forced her to the ground. "I have been patient," he said. "Do you dream of having Akoma inside you, his mouth on you, his hands stroking your body. Like this?" he asked, nipping her breast. "*I* am your husband," he said.

His hands ripped her skirt, shredding it, leaving only the thin leather cord that was tied around her waist.

Talli twisted and pushed on his shoulders, but he was much larger and stronger. She managed to flex one of her knees, bringing it up hard and fast between his legs. Banabas let out a throaty cry, doubled up, and rolled off her.

Talli sprang to her feet and ran to the lodge. Inside, she started to cry. She grabbed Mikot and held him, rocking back and forth. The baby stirred, and Talli realized she was waking him. She lay on her side and held her son in the crook of her arm.

Long after the village quieted and the feasting and dancing ended, she heard Banabas creep into the lodge. In a few moments he was snoring. The snoring woke Mikot. She didn't want Banabas to wake up, so she took the baby and walked outside. There was something peaceful and calming about the full moon. The village glistened with its silvery light. Talli strolled in the shadows, humming softly to the baby. Near Ramo's lodge she heard a noise. She did not want to be questioned about her wandering so she backed deeper into the trees. She kept an eye on Ramo's lodge. A faint shadow played in the entranceway, but she couldn't tell who it was. She continued to watch. As soon as it grew quiet again, she would go back home.

Mikot's nursing made a slurping noise. She adjusted the child and swayed back and forth in a gentle rocking motion.

The shadow stepped into the moonlight and Liakka emerged from Ramo's lodge.

Ramo also came into the open and gave a quick brush of his lips to Liakka's breast. Talli was astonished and puzzled. This was the woman who would become the wife of the cacique! What was she doing with Ramo?

Liakka scampered away, using the trees and brush for cover to keep herself out of the moonlight. Before Talli realized it, Liakka ran straight in her direction. Talli flattened against a tree, hoping Liakka would pass without noticing her. The full moon was not to her advantage. If there were no moonlight, she felt Liakka would surely miss her. She heard the brush swishing and Liakka's footfalls coming close.

Mikot whimpered. Liakka stopped and searched for the source of the sound. Her eyes settled on Talli. She stared, looked as if she might speak, but did not, then quickly moved on.

How bizarre, Talli thought. Why would Liakka want to become Akoma's wife is she loved Ramo? There was no advantage. Both were caciques. She knew of women like Liakka. She'd heard the stories. When caught, they were shamed and tortured, their hair cut off, and the flesh on their arms scored with shark's teeth.

How tragic for Akoma to take a wife like Liakka! Talli wanted to warn him, but knew there was no way. And a warning from her would itself appear strange.

She returned to her lodge and curled up next to the

baby. How perfect it would be if Akoma lay on the other side of Mikot. A family. Even Joog could be a part.

She looked over at Banabas, but could barely make him out. Talli felt sorry for him. He deserved a wife who was willing to satisfy all his needs. He was a good man. She had driven him to his behavior tonight.

Talli closed her eyes. Sleep was her only escape.

When the sun rose, Banabas got up. Mikot stretched and yawned. Talli offered him her breast, even before he fussed with hunger. When a baby cried, it was custom that the mother pinch him to teach the infant not to cry. If the group ever needed to be undetected by an enemy, a child's crying would give them away. In their first months, Jeaga babies learned not to cry.

Talli didn't like to pinch Mikot. It hurt him, but she knew she must, so usually she predicted his needs and prevented him from crying.

She picked up the baby and sat by the cold cook fire. Banabas returned in a few moments. He brought a coal from the central hearth and started their fire. He sat facing east. He folded his legs, placed his hands with palms up on his thighs, closed his eyes, and greeted the day.

When he completed his morning prayers, he turned to Talli. "I am ashamed," he said.

Talli stopped him. "Do not say anything. I have not been a good wife, Banabas. You have been more than patient with me." Talli hung her head.

"There is no excuse," Banabas said. "What kind of man am I?"

"You are a good man, a good husband and father. You are a good provider. Any woman would be lucky to be your wife."

Banabas fed the growing fire.

"I cannot be a good wife. Perhaps you should throw me out and look for someone more suitable."

Banabas lifted her chin. "Do not say such a thing."

"But Banabas, I will never enjoy—"

"Then I will not press the issue again. Not ever."

"Husband, I am unable to be a wife to you in that way. I just cannot."

"Then I must accept that," he said. "I wish you felt differently, but I cannot make you feel something you do not. I realize this marriage was not something you desired. I thought I could make you love me."

"I do," Talli answered. "Just not in that way. You are good, and kind, and gentle."

"We will not discuss this again. If you wish to leave, I will allow it."

"I am not going anywhere. Joog, Mikot, and I need you."

"Then seal your tongue on this matter."

Talli's tears trailed down her face. Banabas wiped them away with his hand. "No need for any tears."

It was not long before Joog joined them. Banabas and Talli sat quietly through the morning meal. When they finished, Talli asked Banabas for a favor.

"Will you watch Mikot for a little while? He is fed and will probably sleep. I want to spend some time alone with Joog."

Banabas agreed. Talli took Joog's hand and stood up. His hand was stiff, and he refused to clasp her hand back.

"Stand up, Joog. We are going for a walk by the river. It is a beautiful day."

The boy got to his feet.

"We will not be long," she said as they left.

Talli picked a sweet cocoplum and shared it with the boy. "Have you noticed there are two kinds?" she asked. "The ones on the beach at the Big Water are different from the ones that grow on the hammocks."

Joog nodded. "So, you have traveled a lot," she said. She took another bite out of the cocoplum. "You are growing up fast, Joog, and growing up is a difficult thing. I recall how often I was confused, angry, and sad. I wanted to be an adult, but did not want all the responsibilities. I wanted to be an adult, but wanted the simplicity of being a child. This passage from child to adult is cruel sometimes."

Talli wanted her words to penetrate, so she paused and they walked on in silence for a little while.

"I want you to understand what happened with Akoma," she said. "He is a friend, and I was so upset about my mother. That has not changed anything between Banabas and me. You, Banabas, Mikot, and I are a family. You are safe with us."

Talli put her hand behind the boy's head. Joog sniffed, and she knew he was fighting tears. She pulled his head to her so he could hide his face.

"I knew you would understand," she said. "I think you were afraid I was leaving for good when I went to the Turtle village. I would never leave you."

Joog's arms went around Talli's waist.

When they returned to Banabas, he was pacing with Mikot on his shoulder.

"He started to cry," Banabas said. "Walking makes him happy."

Talli grinned. "Yes, he likes me to walk and jiggle him."

Villagers passed them on their way to the central hearth. "Are you going to see Liakka off?" Banabas asked Talli. "Perhaps we should go now."

Talli did not want to go, but didn't want Banabas to suspect she was jealous. She was certain her distaste for the woman would show.

"Yes," she answered, knowing she would have to guard herself from showing her feelings. Liakka was a deceitful, wicked woman.

When everyone gathered, Ramo led the procession, followed by Liakka and her family. They advanced to the river.

Liakka's father helped her into the canoe. Then he shoved off and took up the paddle. Liakka waved to everyone. She was the image of a perfect bride.

Talli's eyes traveled to Ramo. He, too, was smiling. There was something very wrong, she thought.

Putiwa sat by the spitting fire. Akoma sat across from him. The shaman fed the flames fresh green pine. the fire crackled and hissed, orange sparks spread through the air like fireflies. From a pouch he withdrew a pinch of herbs he had ground into a fine powder. He sprinkled it on the fire. The color of the flames changed from the golden orange and yellow to blue, then green, then returned to normal.

Putiwa threaded a piece of sinew through the lash holes of a pot. He poured water from another container into the pot, then suspended it from a wood pole that crossed above the fire.

Akoma waited quietly as Putiwa continued his preparations. "The winged seed of a red maple, shredded bark of the graybeard tree," Putiwa said.

The shaman lined up small baskets in front of him. Each contained a different ingredient. He picked up the first one. "Raccoonberry leaves." He compressed a small amount of the pulverized particles between his thumb and index finger, then dropped it into the steaming water. Putiwa pointed to each pot and told Akoma what was in them. "A piece of manroot, traded for with the people who live north. Root bark and stems of wax myrtle, flowers of lobelia, gum of hazelwood, rhizomes of snakeroot."

After adding all the ingredients, Putiwa took a shell from another pouch. He had drilled a hole through it to allow him to lace it for a necklace. He dipped the shell in the boiling liquid. "This will bind you and your wife. It will keep her true to you as long as she wears it. A symbol of the lasting love you have for her and she for you. Give it to Liakka after the ceremony. It is a soul-blessing amulet."

Putiwa lifted the dripping amulet and held it up in the moonlight.

"It is beautiful," Akoma said.

"Take it and have a happy heart when you put this about your wife's neck."

Akoma took the amulet from Putiwa. He suspended it in front of him for a few moments, deep in thought.

"We will see," Akoma said. "Now, Putiwa, tell me what the spirits tell you about Ramo—about Chogatis and the Ais."

"I have seen nothing good, Cacique. There seems to

be only trouble with both. Ramo wants you to fall from power. He schemes, but I do not know how. Chogatis wants all the Jeaga. The two of them are a powerful force. Be watchful. The spirits say be vigilant and trust nothing and no one."

"Nothing and no one," he repeated.

Akoma dropped the amulet in a pouch and drew the string tight.

"So you think we should go on an excursion together?" Ramo said to Bunta, who had come to meet with the Panther cacique.

"Yes, at Akoma's request. He feels the Panther and Turtle should go and look for signs of encroaching Ais. It was not long ago he saw them for himself. They might still be in the area. Perhaps they even assemble in greater number, slowly forming a boundary around all of us."

Ramo laughed. "I think your cacique is overly suspicious."

"Prudent," Bunta corrected. "He does not seek confrontation, only observation."

"He sends you. Why does he not come himself?"

"Just as you send Banabas as messenger, Akoma sends me. I am the war chief."

"He has no plans on participating in this excursion?"

"There only need to be a few of us. Some Panther. Some Turtle."

"I will think about this proposal and give you an answer later."

Ramo got to his feet and left Bunta sitting by himself inside the lodge.

"Banabas," Ramo called as he approached. "We must speak."

"What do you think he wants?" Talli asked as Ramo got close.

"I have no idea. He met with Bunta alone."

Ramo did not sit until Banabas and Talli both stood in respect. Then he sat first, as was the custom.

"Akoma has sent his war chief to ask us about going on an excursion to look for signs of Ais. He does not want us to engage in any conflict, just see if they are near. I think, under the conditions, it would be wise for us to go along."

"I have no objections to joining him," Banabas said.

Ramo laughed. "Akoma does not go. I think Liakka keeps him in the hut all the time. Bunta says the cacique is exhausted. I hear rumors she already carries his child."

Talli realized she was staring and quickly went back to her handwork.

"We need to make certain there is no confrontation with the Ais if we go," Ramo said. "Such a mistake could cost us." He looked at Talli. "Go inside, woman," he said. "Your husband and I must talk."

Talli left her weaving and took Mikot with her inside the lodge. She stayed to one side near the doorway. She wanted to listen. She hoped she would hear something about Akoma. She had last seen him six moon cycles ago. She could not rid herself of those same questions that plagued her. Would she ever forget what he looked like. Would his image slowly fade with time? Would she forget the smell and taste of his skin?

"I do not want Akoma to ruin all our negotiations," Banabas said.

Ramo's expression lightened. "He will be taken care of soon enough if all goes as planned."

"Explain," Banabas said.

"In time. But about this excursion with the Turtle, I think you are the one to go."

"I will prepare," Banabas said.

Ramo twisted two strands of sedge. "I should not lose my trust in you because of your wife, should I?" He asked. "She is Turtle, and I know you love her. I think it was better before when you had no wife."

"You have no reason to withdraw your trust, Ramo. I do love my wife, but I am still Panther and your adviser. Have I given you reason to doubt me?"

"No. But you must admit, what I share with you is very confidential."

"I understand," Banabas said.

"Good. Then I will tell Bunta you and another will join his group in a few days."

"I will be ready."

Ramo stood. He kept his eyes hard on Banabas without talking. Banabas knew he was emphasizing the trust discussion. He did not look away, or Ramo might take that as a sign of guilt. Finally, the cacique turned and left.

Ramo did not go straight to Bunta, however. He sought another man, another adviser, younger than Banabas, Ceboni's husband, Iquan.

"I have something I want you to do," Ramo said.

Iquan listened and agreed to accompany Banabas and the Turtle party.

"Keep an eye on Banabas," Ramo said. "I am not sure if I can trust him anymore."

35

Liakka rolled over and stretched. "The sun is almost up," she said, seeing the spray of pink in the sky. There were also dark clouds, and the wind was blowing. "It is going to rain again," she said.

Akoma attempted to sit up, but Liakka pulled him back. "Do not leave our bed so quickly." She ran her fingers up and down his side. "I like the feel of your muscles beneath your skin."

Akoma cupped her breast. "You have an appetite," he said. "Do I not satisfy you?"

Liakka grinned. "Oh, but you do satisfy me. That is why I have such a hunger for you."

"But," he said, pulling up and getting to his feet, "I have many things to do this day. You will have to wait until later."

"What do you have to do?"

"I must speak with Bunta and Yahga-ta before they leave."

Liakka sat up. "Where are they going?" she asked. "I hear you discuss an excursion."

"That is right," he said. "Bunta and Yahga-ta will meet up with Banabas and Iquan. The four will go about the river and search for signs of Ais."

"Four will not have much of a chance if they do find a party of Ais."

"No, no," he said. "They will not engage them. I only want a report of what the Ais are doing, where they are, how many. Then Ramo and I must come to an agreement about what to do."

Liakka's finger combed her hair.

"Cacique!" a loud voice called.

Akoma stepped outside. "Good day, Ufala. What brings you so early?"

"I think I should go with Bunta instead of Yahga-ta."

"I disagree," Akoma said.

"Because of my arm? When will you see that I am a whole man? I hunt and fish."

"That is not the problem. You have done well, considering the injury you suffered."

"Then why do you deny me?"

"If you came upon Ais, I do not think you would resist the urge to attack. Such bitterness festers inside you."

"And why should we not destroy the Ais if the opportunity comes?"

"Ufala, we need a strategy, a plan to deal with the Ais. In order to do that, we must first identify what we are dealing with. We are smaller in number, so we must use our heads more. That is what will give us the advantage."

"I say slay any Ais, anytime."

"I know that is how you feel, and that is why I do not choose you to go. I do not want them alerted that we are aware of their proximity."

Liakka stood in the entryway.

"I cannot believe Ramo agrees with you," Ufala said. "He has courage."

"The discussion on this subject is ended," Akoma said. "Tell me, how is Kitchi?"

Ufala spat on the ground and walked away, his gait a visual display of his frustration.

"He is a dangerous one," Liakka said. "Ufala is his name, is that correct?"

"Yes," Akoma answered.

A crack of thunder and gust of wind issued in the rain. Akoma trotted quickly across the village to Bunta's hut. Bunta sat just inside. He got up and moved aside to give Akoma space to enter.

Akoma shook his wet hair, sending a fine spray of water into the air. He wiped his face with a piece of hide Bunta handed him.

"Now comes too much rain," Bunta said. "First the

earth cooks, then we have trouble keeping ourselves out of the water."

"You are right," Akoma said. "I wish the rains mellowed the Ais. Even though it appears the drought comes to an end, I do not see the problem with them going away. Ramo complicates matters." Akoma paused in thought, then spoke again. "Bunta, be careful with the Panther. Do not trust them."

The two men sat watching the rain. The thatch rattled and streams of rain flowed off the fronds. Where the ground was bare and low, the water pooled.

"Bunta, keep what I am about to tell you to yourself," Akoma said. "I share this only with you and Yahga-ta. There is no reason to alarm everyone."

The rain reduced to drizzle. Bunta and Yahga-ta made good time. They reached the island in the river just after Banabas and Iquan arrived.

The four men greeted each other.

"We should make camp, then get a start in the morning," Banabas said.

"I agree," Yahga-ta said.

When dusk came, Bunta started a fire. Banabas returned with two rabbits and Yahga-ta and Iquan had fish. They all sat about the fire, cooking their evening meal. The mood was more formal than usual when the Panther and Turtle were together.

"So, Banabas, I hear you have become a father," Yahga-ta said.

"I am a fortunate man," Banabas said.

"Talk to me about Ramo and his outlook," Yahga-ta said. "I am curious. He sees things differently sometimes."

Banabas turned the skewer that held the rabbits above the fire. "He is young and has new ideas. Age and experience will temper him."

Iquan tweezed a piece of flaky white fish between his fingers and put it in his mouth.

"What do you think, Iquan?" Yahga-ta asked.

Ceboni's husband removed a small bone from his mouth. "I agree with Banabas. Ramo has a lot of zeal."

Yahga-ta's eyes set on Banabas. "Has he ever met Chogatis?"

"Chogatis is the enemy."

Bunta removed the skewer from the forked supports and offered rabbit to Iquan and Banabas. "The Jeaga do not negotiate with the Ais."

Banabas shifted nervously, and Yahga-ta and Bunta watched him closely.

At the end of the meal, Yahga-ta said, "Extinguish the fire." Often the men on a journey kept the fire going all night. A fire kept animals away. But fire burning through the night also gave away location. Better to deal with a creature in the night than a party of Ais.

When all the coals were extinguished the men took out their sleeping skins and lay down on them.

In the morning, they snacked on the leftovers, then boarded their dugouts.

Bunta and Yahga-ta led the way.

"Akoma told me he suspects that Ramo has been meeting with Chogatis," Bunta said as they paddled. "He said he spoke to you about this, also."

"Yes," Yahga-ta said. "At the time he saw the Ais, Banabas and Ramo were gone on an expedition, the purpose of which is very vague. It is possible that they met secretly with Chogatis."

Bunta stroked the water with his paddle. "Akoma does not want to upset everyone by divulging his suspicions. I think he is right. We will watch Banabas and Iquan for any indication that Akoma's suspicions are correct."

"It is a frightening thing if his suspicions are fact," Yahga-ta said.

They stopped several times, going on shore to search for signs of campfires or any other thing that might indicate the presence of Ais in their territory.

Along the bank of a small creek that branched from the river, Bunta spotted what could be a camp. "Put in over there," he called to Banabas.

"I do not see anything interesting," Banabas said. "Let us go back to the river."

"I want to see this," Yahga-ta said. "If there is nothing, we will turn around."

Banabas did not bank his canoe, hanging back while Yahga-ta and Bunta went ashore.

"Someone has been here," Yahga-ta said. "The brush is trampled and some of it cleared away." He motioned for Banabas and Iquan to come ashore.

"Could this be where Akoma camped when he saw the Ais?" Iquan asked, getting out of the dugout.

"I do not think so," Bunta said. "This is too large an area for one man. There were several camped here."

Yahga-ta poked his hand into the ash of what had been a fire. "More than one day," he said. "There is a lot of ash. I would say three or four days. Could be more." He rummaged through the ash, picking out food bones. "More food than for one man," he said.

"What about you and Ramo?" Bunta asked Banabas. "Could this be your camp?"

"We were not here," he said.

"Let us look around," Bunta said.

The men split up in different directions. Banabas got on his hands and knees, scouring the area. This was the spot he and Ramo had met Chogatis and his party of Ais. Ramo wanted to negotiate with Chogatis. Banabas had listened, sometimes disagreeing with Ramo, but not saying so in front of Chogatis. The Ais cacique not only wanted space on the river, he hated the Turtle. Ramo actually incited some of Chogatis's rage, remarking about the death of Chogatis's son at the hands of Turtle men. Ramo had even taken Chogatis aside, without Banabas or other Ais, and spoken to him. Ramo had not shared the discussion with Banabas. Banabas hoped Ramo would continue to listen to his advice as he had in the past. If he openly disagreed with his cacique, there was the risk that Ramo would not confide in him anymore, and that would mean he would have no opportunity to influence Ramo.

Banabas crawled about, inspecting the ground for evidence that the Ais and Panther Jeaga had been together. His stomach soured with the thought that he was a traitor. But what else was he to do? Staying close to Ramo was the best way to serve the Jeaga.

His eyes were not as good as they had been when he was younger. Now things too far away or too close blurred. In one spot he ran his hand along the ground under some brush, thinking he saw something.

He caught his hand on a thorny vine. He drew back with the sharp pain. The thorns left puncture marks and tore narrow gashes along his palm. What he thought might have been fletching from an arrow had only been a single mockingbird feather. Banabas squeezed blood from the cuts, hoping to wash as much of the black dirt from them as possible.

"Bah!" he said, getting to his feet and going to the river. He doused his hand in the water. It stung. How stupid to have been so careless, he thought. He knew those vines. Usually it was the ankles that suffered from the plant.

"What have you done?" Bunta asked, coming from behind.

"I cut myself on thorns," he said.

Bunta looked closely. "Nasty," he said. "It is not good when they puncture like that."

"It was Ais," Yahga-ta said, coming out of the brush. "If neither the Panther or Turtle have been here, then it must have been Ais."

"They come so close. I wonder why?" Bunta said. "What did they do?"

Yahga-ta ran his fingers over the top of his head. "We can spend a few more days, see if we find more evidence. Maybe we will see a pattern." He glanced at Banabas. "How did you do that?"

Banabas explained about the thorns, making light of it and admonishing himself for his carelessness. He suggested they get back on the river. He was thankful they had found nothing to implicate an Ais and Jeaga rendezvous.

They traveled the river for two more days, but found nothing and decided to return home.

Banabas gripped the paddle awkwardly. His hand was sore, and redness surrounded two of the punctures.

"Show me your hand," Iquan said.

"It is sore, that is all."

"Show it to me."

Banabas opened his hand and held it palm up. "Just some scratches."

"I do not think so," Iquan said, taking a close look. "Bad spirits are inside. We need to get home and have Ocaab and your wife look at it."

Banabas knew his hand was not doing well, but did not want to complain. Not only was the flesh red, but his hand swelled and throbbed. He did not feel well in general and was glad when they reached the Panther village.

Ramo was anxious to talk as soon as Banabas got out of the dugout. He waited until Iquan had gathered his things and left. "So what did you find?" Ramo asked.

Banabas checked to see if anyone was near. He spoke softly. "Bunta found our camp where we met Chogatis."

"What assumptions were made?"

"Only that the Ais had been there. But I think Akoma is suspicious. Bunta and Yahga-ta asked questions. They wanted to know if you had met Chogatis."

"Did you deny—"

"I did not have to. There is no evidence. You must be careful, Ramo, not to alienate our brothers. You have bold new ideas, but you must go with what the People want. You cannot become an ally of the Ais at the expense of other Jeaga."

Banabas stumbled. His head felt light. Ramo stared at him. "You do not look so well."

"I am all right," Banabas said.

"Go home and rest," Ramo said.

Banabas still felt unbalanced. The day was warm, but he was chilled and clammy. He looked at his hand. He was afraid Iquan was right. It appeared that bad spirits did indeed get into his wounds.

Talli and Joog greeted Banabas. "Husband, I am glad you return."

Banabas's legs felt weak. He wanted nothing more than to fall onto his sleeping skin and sleep for days.

Talli hiked Mikot on her hip and took Banabas's arm. "You are ill," she said.

"A little tired."

Inside the lodge, he held out his hand. "Do you have a medicine for this?" he asked.

Talli took his wrist and pulled his hand closer. "Banabas, what has happened?"

Joog tugged at Talli's arm. He wanted to see Banabas's hand, too.

"I got my hand caught in some thorns," Banabas said.

She handed Mikot to Joog. "Let me go heat some water and medicine for a poultice."

Banabas reclined, his head heavy, his limbs nearly numb with weakness. If the journey had taken any more time he was certain he would have collapsed. A jolt of fear ricocheted through his body. How bad was this going to get? He felt so terrible!

Talli put a pot to boil over the fire. She searched the pouches and parfleches for the proper medicinal herbs. She located some of the dried plant parts, but was not satisfied. Banabas's hand was in awful shape. If something was not done immediately, things could worsen quickly.

She found seagrapes, wormseed leaves, rattleweed roots, prickly elder bark, and roots. Talli put the collection in the pot of water. After it boiled a few moments, she removed the pot and took it inside the lodge.

In the decoction she soaked a small piece of deer hide that had the hair removed on both sides. She tweezed it out of the pots with two sticks and wrung out the excess liquid.

"Give me your hand," she told Banabas.

He outstretched his arm. Talli grimaced as she lifted his hand. "You should have treated this with something right away. You know how serious even small cuts can be."

She wrapped his hand in the medicine-saturated hide.

Banabas flinched when the hot hide touched his skin.

"I know it is hot, but that will help drive out the evil spirits. I am going for Ocaab," she said.

While she was gone, Banabas let his eyes close. He

could not recall ever being so tired. His whole body felt weighted and sluggish. The light bothered his eyes, and he was cold. When Talli got back, he would ask her for a blanket.

In a few moments, Ocaab squatted beside Banabas and removed the dressing. "Ugly hand," he said. The shaman traced one of the red lines that traveled up Banabas's arm from his hand. He felt the hard knots along the line under the skin. "How did you do this?"

"Thorns," Banabas answered.

Ocaab touched Banabas's chest, then his head. "As I thought," he said. "Your body is heating up. Chew these," he said, offering Banabas a mixture of blue verbena and sweetbay leaves. Then he took pokeberry leaves and tied them to the soles of Banabas's feet and another bunch to the palm of his good hand. "These medicines will help. It can be dangerous if your body gets too hot."

"I am cold," Banabas said.

Talli retrieved a blanket and put it over her husband.

Ocaab sat, legs crossed. He unrolled a narrow but long, soft hide, exposing a collection of plant parts. He drew a line with his finger in the dirt floor surrounding Banabas. Then, as he sang, he sprinkled on the line a white powdery substance made from dried, pulverized plants.

Ocaab circled Banabas four times, then bowed to the east, then the south, then west, and lastly to the north. He selected several leaves, and then stood again. He tossed the leaves in the air as he chanted.

"Bring me an ember from the central hearth," he said.

Joog nodded quickly, indicating he wanted to go get it.

"Go, Joog," Talli said.

The boy ran out.

Ocaab scooped out a shallow depression in the dirt, then placed some dry leaves in the middle and tented several small twigs over them. When Joog returned, he would place the coal on the leaf bed beneath the twigs.

Talli moved toward Banabas.

"No," Ocaab said. "Do not step inside the circle."

Joog returned. Ocaab took the coal from him with

two sticks and gingerly placed one on the leaves. He blew softly and fed the small ember cattail fluff and shredded pine bark. In a moment, he had a small but hearty blaze.

Ocaab tossed a pinch of the white powder on the flames. The fire crackled, grew very bright for an instant, then returned to its normal state. The shaman closed his eyes and sang in the old language.

Talli wondered what the words meant, or even if they really did mean something. The shamen passed the song on from generation to generation. The actual meaning of each word might have been lost by now.

Ocaab took up a handful of green pine needles and slowly dropped them on the fire. They drifted down, a few at a time, causing a lot of sizzling and smoke.

The shaman leaned over the fire with a hollow reed in his mouth. He sucked in a mouthful of the smoke and then blew it out in Banabas's face. He repeated this three times.

Joog coughed as the hut filled with more and more smoke. Talli rubbed her eyes, then backed out the door with Mikot.

Ocaab's chanting increased in volume. He took Banabas's hand and lifted it. With one last howl he drove a stingray spine into each of the festering wounds, bit down on the hand and sucked. He spat.

Joog's nose wrinkled, and his mouth twisted with disgust.

Ocaab sang again, then closed his eyes and shuddered. When he opened his eyes again, he took in a deep breath. "I have drawn out some of the bad spirits, the poison in your hand," he said. "I have purified you and your lodge with pine smoke. Now, you must communicate with the spirits. Tell them how indebted you are."

Ocaab stopped to speak to Talli when he left. "Redress the wound. Change the poultice often."

By nightfall, Banabas's condition worsened. He refused his evening meal and groaned with discomfort. The blanket did not seem to keep him warm enough, and he shivered.

In the middle of the night, Banabas whispered to Talli,

"I am going to die." His legs shook and his teeth chattered.

"No, you are not," Talli said. "We need you, Banabas. Fight back."

He mumbled something Talli did not understand. She moved close to him and lay against him. His body radiated a tremendous amount of heat.

Suddenly, Talli felt dizzy. Her eyelids fluttered. She attempted to move away from Banabas, but it was too late. The affliction!

Talli's body trembled from the cold she felt. Her hand throbbed with pain, but the rest of her body felt numb and heavy. Her head ached, her stomach churned.

"Talli!" Banabas said. "What is wrong? What is happening?"

Mikot began crying, waking Joog.

The boy crawled over to Mikot, Talli, and Banabas.

"Something is wrong with her," Banabas said. His voice sounded weak and gravelly.

Joog put his hands on Talli's shoulders and shook her.

White spittle collected in the corners of her mouth, and her eyes rolled back in her head.

"Talli!" Joog cried out.

36

Talli suddenly stopped shaking. Her body was stiff and slow to respond. Her eyes opened to narrow slits. The haze faded, and she gradually relaxed and realized what had happened. Both Joog and Banabas had seen her when the affliction took over.

"Talli, Talli, Talli," Joog cried, his hands still rocking her shoulders.

"Joog, you speak," she said, her body and voice weak. "Oh, Joog, you can talk."

"I was afraid," he whispered.

Talli sat up and held him close to her. "I am so sorry," she said. "I need to tell you both something . . . something terrible about me." She turned toward Mikot, who still wailed. "Get the baby," she told Joog.

"I am sorry, husband," she said, sweeping the hair back from his forehead. "You have taken a woman that you did not know is disfavored by the spirits. I have caused you nothing but pain from the start," she said. "When you hear the truth, you will no longer want me."

Banabas shook his head in disagreement.

"I must tell you about myself," Talli said. "Can you hear me? Will you listen?"

"When I am well."

"You are right," she said. "I burden you while you are ill. See how selfish I am?"

Banabas shivered. Talli pulled the blanket to his neck. "Oh, Banabas, please heal. You are suffering so," she said. She ran out of the lodge and fed the fire. When the flames were strong enough, she suspended the pot of medicine over it and soaked a new dressing for her husband's hand.

What would Banabas decide to do with her? She had
to tell him, now. And Joog! The sight of her must have
been so terrible. Well, she thought, if the affliction had
ever done any good for anyone, at least it had prompted
the return of Joog's speech.

Talli took the hot poultice to Banabas and put it on
his hand. She noticed how Joog stared at her.

"I will explain to you, also," she said. "I will tell you
both at the same time."

Joog handed her Mikot and went back to his sleeping
skin. Banabas was soon sleeping, too, but Talli sat and
watched them all until morning.

Early golden and rose light blushed the village.
Feather down, dust, and gossamer fibers floated in the
air. Tiny swarms of white insects whirled just outside
the lodge.

Mikot gurgled and cooed as he played with his toes.
Such small things intrigued babies, she thought. Talli put
him to her breast. She touched Banabas's forehead. He
remained warm, but she thought perhaps not as hot as
during the night.

Maybe he would sip a little tea, she thought as she
crept quietly out of the hut. A few embers still glowed,
so she added kindling. She would not blame Banabas if
he banished her. But what would she do with Mikot?
Would she be able to care for him on her own? Who
would teach him to hunt, and fish, and the men's ways?
She could not bear the thought of leaving her son behind.

If Banabas banished her, she realized that whether she
took Mikot with her or not would not be her choice.
Ramo might even have her tortured before sending
her away.

"Banabas is awake," Joog said, coming out of the
lodge. "He asks for you."

Talli touched the boy's cheek with her fingers, then
went in to see her husband.

"Do you need something?" she asked.

"Water," he said. "I have a great thirst."

"I will bring you some," she said. "I also brew you
some tea."

Talli turned to leave.

"Wait," Banabas said.

Talli looked back.

"I do not know what happened last night," he said. "You do not have to tell me anything. We will forget about it. Joog will forget."

Talli didn't say anything. Her eyes burned with the threat of tears. She lifted Mikot and rested her cheek against the top of his head.

"Fetch some fresh water from the river," she told Joog. "Banabas is thirsty."

She watched the boy sprint away. Ceboni came toward her. The woman yawned and rubbed her eyes.

"Good day," Talli said.

"Iquan told me that Banabas is ill, that bad spirits and poison have gotten into a hand wound."

"He is very sick," Talli said.

"Can I do something to help?"

"Ceboni," she said, "if something happened to me . . . if I had to leave, or if I died, would you help Banabas look after Mikot and Joog?"

"Of course, but what would make you think of such a thing?"

"Mikot is so small, he needs a woman. And Joog . . . who would raise an Ais child?"

"Oh," Ceboni said. "I do not think Iquan would permit me to take him in, but he is old enough to stay with Banabas. Why are you asking me these questions?"

"Everyone should have a plan if something happened to them. What if you got sick? Would not Iquan need help in caring for Tawute and Zowhi?"

"I suppose," she said.

"Promise me you would look after Mikot."

Ceboni cocked her head inquisitively. "You are not going to tell me everything, are you?"

"I cannot," Talli said.

"I would watch over your son," Ceboni said.

Over the next ten days Banabas continued to improve. The time had come for her to tell both Banabas and Joog about the curse she carried.

As the three of them sat at their hearth one afternoon, Talli said, "I want to explain now. You are well, Banabas, and my conscience is heavy."

"I do not ask for an explanation."

"I know that," Talli said, "but I will feel better."

"Then we will listen," Banabas said.

Talli told them how her ancestor had been a traitor and how the spirits had punished her bloodline. Only when the debt is paid would the affliction end.

"If you choose to banish me, I understand. I am prepared to accept the consequences. I know if others find out, you will be dishonored and so will our son. I do not want that."

"You are my wife. I would not send you away. Joog and I will keep your secret and guard you from situations that are dangerous for you."

"I will not tell," Joog said.

Talli put her hands over her face and cried.

Ufala limped out into the morning light. He could feel Kitchi's eyes on his back. He hated this stiffness in his knees and back. "Old man," he grumbled to himself. He shook each leg, raised his arms and stretched. It seemed everything was sore and slow. He scrunched his shoulders forward and bent his chin to his chest. A low groan escaped his throat.

He was hungry. Lately, Kitchi had been lazy. She neglected him, turned him away from her bed, did not rise early or prepare his morning meal. What kind of woman treated her husband this way? Was this what he got in return for being a good provider?

He stooped to take a coal from the central hearth. "This fire should be alive and blazing," he said aloud. "Fire Keeper!" he called out. The Jeaga were declining, he thought. No one had courage. No one did his or her tasks with pride anymore. "Bah," he said, shoveling up an ember with a large clam shell.

A sultry voice came from behind him. "Ufala," Liakka said.

He turned and faced her.

"Does your wife appreciate you? You are up so early, taking care of her fire."

Ufala was astounded.

She moved extremely close to him and put a hand behind her head. Her way of stretching was thrusting her chest forward and leaning her head back.

Ufala could not keep his gaze from wandering her body. She definitely had smooth curves. Her throat seemed so long and delicate. Akoma was a fool. If she were his, he would adorn her neck with jewelry, not let it go bare. He would want everyone to notice her beauty.

"You are about quite early, too," he finally managed to say. He spied the leaves she held in her hand.

"I gather ingredients for my morning tea," she said, closing her fist around the leaves, putting them out of sight, but not before Ufala got a glimpse of them.

"You add bitter button and rue to your tea?" he asked.

"It is a special tea . . . for women," she said.

"Hmm," he said, perplexed by her choice. He was not familiar with those plants for use in tea. He knew rue was used sometimes as a medicine for upset stomach, and bitter button in a soak for aching feet. Perhaps this tea was unique to Panther women.

"I did not realize what a big man you are until now as I stand next to you. No flab," she said, touching his belly with her fingertip. She palmed his good arm above the elbow. "So much muscle." Liakka flashed a coy smile.

"I work hard," he said.

"You know what I like the most?" she asked.

Ufala didn't have a chance to even think of an answer. The flattery deadened his head.

"This," she said, stroking his maimed arm. "This tells me how brave you are, that you do not cower in the face of the enemy. It shows me you would give your life for the Jeaga."

"I would!" he said quickly. "I was just thinking a moment ago that so many men do not feel the allegiance and loyalty they used to."

"Especially the younger men," she said. "That is why I find older men so attractive."

Ufala's eyes gleamed.

"Well," she said, "I am glad we have had an opportunity to talk. But now I best return to my husband."

"Maybe we can talk again," Ufala called.

As he returned to his hearth, Ufala did not feel as old as he had a moment ago. He flexed the muscles of his good arm. Liakka could see that he was a strong in both muscle and determination.

He liked her attitude about his injured arm. He should take a lesson from her, he thought.

"Kitchi," he called as he got his fire going. "I am hungry."

"Shh," Sassa said. "Let her sleep. She does not feel well."

Nocatee wandered out behind Sassa. She rubbed her eyes and then squinted.

"Your mother sleeps all the time," Ufala said. "She grows lazy in her old age."

"She is sick," Sassa said.

Ufala tapped his bad arm. "Did I stop providing for you because of this?" he asked.

"That is different," Sassa said.

Kitchi struggled through the opening. Her ashen skin clung to the bones of her face. Her hair hung in oily strings close to her skull, and her eyes appeared deeply recessed behind dark circles.

"There," he said. "Your mother has decided to be a wife this morning. She is lucky I do not throw her out."

Kitchi squatted by the fire, wrapping her sleeping skin around her bony shoulders.

"Can you hear my stomach grumble?" he asked.

"I will brew some fresh tea for you to sip while I prepare your meal."

"Have you ever heard of using rue and bitter button in tea?" he asked.

Kitchi swirled the berries in the pot of water. "For medicines," she answered. "Is that what you wish me to brew? I would think it would not taste good."

"No," he said, watching her fix the tea. "Why would they be used specifically for a woman's tea?"

Kitchi looked up as if she had a sudden thought. She recalled hearing women talk about those plants. Supposedly, the use of a tea brewed from those two plants caused abortions. "To encourage an unborn child to leave its mother's womb . . . early," she said. "Who prepares such a tea?"

"Interesting," Ufala said. "I spoke with Akoma's wife just a moment ago. She gathered rue and bitter button this morning to put in her tea. A woman's tea."

"I have heard women whisper about such a tea. No one talks openly about it."

"I suppose she did not think I would know anything about it, especially since I am a man," Ufala said.

"Do you think she is trying to rid herself of Akoma's child?" Kitchi asked.

"Why would she do that?"

"She is a vain one," Kitchi said. "Maybe she does not want her figure altered."

"Akoma would not allow her to do that."

"If Liakka prepares a tea to abort his child, I doubt he is aware." Kitchi suddenly swayed to the side. She lost her balance and dropped to the ground. She held her forehead in one hand and propped herself up with the other hand.

"Mother!" Sassa said.

Nocatee ran to her father and held on to him. Her hands clutched his arm tightly.

"She is fine," Ufala said. "She needs to eat something. She has not been eating like she should. She will be better after she eats."

Sassa stooped in front of Kitchi. "Can you get up?" she asked. "Let me help you back to your bed."

Kitchi faintly nodded. Sassa took her arm and helped her mother slowly to her feet.

"Can you walk?" Sassa asked.

"I think so."

Kitchi's feet barely moved in a shuffle. "Thank you, Sassa," she whispered.

Ufala scooted up to the fire. "I suppose I will have to

finish what she started." He peered into the pot over the fire.

"I can help," Nocatee said.

Ufala looked to his youngest and his face expressed more delight than it had over the last few days. "My little mud turtle," he said.

"Father!" Sassa called from inside the lodge. "Hurry. Go for Putiwa!"

37

"Come on," Joog said to Tawute. He carried a bundle beneath his arm and ran away from the village.

"Where are we going?"

"You will see," he said. "Follow me."

Joog ran as fast as he could, with Tawute right behind. Out of the village and through the trees he continued to run, leaping over deadfalls and stumps. The scrub whipped and scratched his brown body as he passed. He ran and ran, farther and farther from the village.

Deep in the forest Joog finally stopped, collapsing on a fallen tree trunk. He lay back, laughing and heaving for air. "How far could we run?" he asked breathlessly. "How far can a person run? How long?"

Tawute fell in a heap next to Joog.

"Did you ever wonder?" Joog asked. "Ais who do not live on water must run great distances. Messengers run to other villages."

"I do not think I would want to be a messenger," Tawute said, panting. "Why have you brought us way out here?"

"Banabas showed me something on one of our journeys," Joog answered, still puffing. "Come here," he said, getting to his feet. He walked about, head down.

"What are you looking for?"

"A trail," he said. Joog got down on all fours. "Look here," he said, motioning for Tawute to come. "A rabbit run."

The boys peered through a tubelike trail made from bent grasses.

"We will follow it and see where it leads. I say we put a snare at the end of the run," Joog said.

"A trap?"

"Sure. I have everything we need."

Tawute and Joog followed the rabbit run. It ended in a small soft grass prairie.

"Shh," Joog said. "Do not make any noise."

They crept up on the prairie, hoping to catch a rabbit feeding.

"I do not see any," Tawute said.

"Me either. So we will set a snare." Joog unrolled his large bundle, then looked about. "Here," he said, pulling up a long, satin leaf sapling. "Drive it into the ground beside the run."

Joog fiddled with the two hooked sticks and cordage he had brought. He tied a knotted loop in one end of the cordage, slipped the other end through and made a noose.

Tawute spun the sapling, drilling it into the ground. "Good thing the earth is soft here," he said. He let go, and the sapling stood on its own.

Joog bent the flexible sapling nearly to the ground and tied the snare to it. He used a hooked stake for a trigger and secured the snare in place with other small sticks.

"There," he said. "I like it. We will have a rabbit soon."

"What else do you have?" Tawute asked, seeing several drawstring sacks on the rolled-out hide.

"Bolas."

Joog loosened the drawstring on one sack and withdrew a bola, dangling it for Tawute to see. "I could not find good rocks," he said. "So I made these rawhide pouches, filled them with sand, wet the rawhide and let it dry. Feel them," he said. "They are as hard as rocks."

Tawute touched one of the three rawhide rocks that dangled from long strands of sinew. "Have you used it before?"

"Banabas let me use his. But I made these bolas," he said, handing Tawute the other sack.

"For me?" Tawute asked.

"We will bring home ducks," he said.

"I do not know how to throw it," Tawute said.

"Let us go by the river," Joog said. "Find us some waterfowl."

They trotted away from the snare, this time not running full out as they had done before.

In a low marshy area by the river they spotted all kinds of birds. There were ibises, storks, gallinules, coots, moorhens, herons, egrets, cormorants, and ducks. The storks waded with their beaks in the water, swinging their heads from side to side.

"Be still," Tawute said, "or we will frighten them."

The boys crept closer, keeping low in the cane and grass.

"Like this," Joog whispered, holding the bola's loop handle. "Use it sidearm in the open." Joog stood, squared his shoulders and swung his arm back and then forward in a flowing motion. With a snap of his wrist, he released the bola. It twirled through the air.

Suddenly, the birds became a flurry of motion. They winged into the air, squawking and fluttering.

Joog grunted his disappointment as the bola fell into the shallow water. "You can twirl it over your head, too," Joog said as they ran to retrieve the bola. "I need to practice."

"Look!" Tawute said, glaring over the marsh and down the river.

The boys hunkered down in the grass, hiding from the approaching canoe.

"Do you think they are Ais?" Tawute asked.

Joog looked at his friend and wondered what he would do if they were.

Tawute crept closer to the edge of the water for a better look. "No, there is only one man. Jeaga! Turtle!" Tawute sprung up. "We will announce him!" he said. "Hurry!"

Joog sat for a moment, not sure how he felt. He was Ais, yet experienced a sense of relief that the man in the dugout was Jeaga.

"Are you coming?" Tawute called. "Do you not want to announce him?"

Joog got to his feet, and both boys ran into the village.

Tawute whooped and Joog yelled, "A Turtle man comes."

Already men who had heard the announcement made their way to the river to see who the visitor could be.

Talli stayed back and watched for them to escort the Turtle man into the village. She wondered if it was Akoma. Did he have Liakka with him?

The crowd soon came into sight. Her stomach knotted with apprehension.

At first she could not make out who the visitor was, but quite quickly she could tell it was not Akoma. Her heart sank a little.

The group thinned out as they reached the center of the village, the greetings finished. Finally there were just two coming her way, Banabas and Bunta.

They headed toward Banabas's hearth. She feared she already knew why, though she hoped the purpose of Bunta's visit was business with Banabas.

"Good day," Talli said, getting to her feet.

"And a good day to you," Bunta replied.

Talli held on to her hope. "I will leave the two of you so you may get on with your business."

Bunta shot a look at Banabas, then fixed on Talli. "I am here to see you, Talli, not your husband. I am afraid I bring bad news."

"My mother," Talli said, slumping to sit on the ground.

"Yes," he answered. "It is near her time. Akoma and Putiwa thought that if you wish to see her again, you should come right away."

"Banabas?" Talli said, asking for permission.

"I will take you," he said.

In sight of the Turtle village Banabas said, "Are you prepared for the worst?"

"I do not know," Talli answered. "I realize she is dying." Mikot sat in her lap and played with her shell-beaded necklace. "I did not like leaving Joog again," Talli said.

Banabas lifted the paddle from the water and rested it over his knees. "We could not bring him. He is Ais.

There would be too many questions. It is dangerous as it is that he has freedom to wander about our village. One day someone from the Turtle village will visit and ask questions."

"Why not just tell everyone the truth?"

"I had to convince Ramo to save the boy. If people knew about Joog, it could become too perilous for him."

Banabas picked up the paddle again.

Liakka was the first woman Talli saw when she entered the Turtle village.

"Welcome," Liakka said. "It is unfortunate about your mother."

Liakka sounded *too* kind and sincere. "As the wife of the cacique, I want to offer you anything you might need."

Banabas put his hand on Talli's shoulder. "We will be fine, Liakka."

Liakka flipped her hair back from one shoulder with a flick of her hand. "Good. Then I will hurry back to my husband. He does not like me to be away from him." Liakka smiled and walked off.

"I do not like her," Talli said.

"Do not let her bother you," Banabas said.

Talli whipped around to face her husband. "I saw her with Ramo the night before she came here to wed Akoma."

"But now she is Akoma's woman. The past does not matter."

"She is deceitful, Banabas."

"Remember, she and Ramo had a kind of understanding. If they were together, it was to say good-bye. Ramo was pleased with the marriage of Liakka and Akoma."

Talli still did not understand what went on between Liakka and Akoma, nor did she understand Banabas's reasoning. Surely he could see how inappropriate—

"Talli," Banabas said. "You should forget about that. If you mention to anyone what you saw between Liakka and Ramo, it will only cause trouble. There need not be any more strain between the Turtle and Panther. Do you understand?"

"Yes," Talli said. Banabas was right about that. There

seemed to be so many secrets between the two Jeaga caciques. The Turtle and Panther should trust each other. They were all Jeaga.

Nocatee flew across the village, calling Talli's name.

"Sister," Talli said, handing Mikot to Banabas. She stooped down and hugged Nocatee. Talli let go, but Nocatee held on longer.

Sassa also came up. "I am glad you are here," she said.

Talli stood, her hand stroking Nocatee's hair. "I am not too late, am I?"

"No," Sassa said. "Mother was still attempting all her chores until a few days ago. She should have rested more, but would not. Father expected so much of her. He did not understand how sick she was."

"And now?" Talli asked.

"He sees it now, but is not apologetic."

"I want to see her," Talli said.

"Wait," Sassa said. "Nocatee, take Mikot and play with him. Go on."

When Nocatee was out of hearing range, Sassa said, "I need to prepare you. Mother looks very bad because of the illness, but there is more. She has some bruises. As I said, Father did not understand she was ill."

Talli turned her head into Banabas's shoulder.

Sassa ushered Talli and Banabas inside the lodge. Kitchi lay on a sleeping skin with a rabbit-fur blanket over her. Talli knelt by her side.

Kitchi's face was all bone with thin skin stretched over it. She had fist-sized blisters filled with fluids on several places on her body. Beneath one eye there was a fading yellowish bruise.

Her hair was gray and thinning. Talli recalled the rich dark hair her mother had once had. Talli stared, stroking the hair back from her mother's forehead.

"Mother," she whispered. "It is Talli. I am here. Can you hear me?"

Sassa spoke up. "Speak louder, Talli. Sometimes she opens her eyes and sometimes she mumbles."

Talli pulled the blanket away and took her mother's

hand. Kitchi's skin felt dry and her hand cold. Also fading were finger marks on her upper arm.

Talli looked up at Sassa.

"He was angry," Sassa said.

"Mother," Talli said, much louder this time. "Can you hear me? It is Talli."

Kitchi's fingers quivered lightly in Talli's hand. Then her lips moved, shaking at first, then forming a word. "Talli," she whispered.

Talli started to shake. The room grew hazy and dark. She heard a sound like rushing air, and then she was with her mother, feeling what Kitchi felt.

She could barely move, her body was so weak. There was no pain, except when she moved or when the blisters broke. She labored to breathe. Her throat was dry. She was ready to die, even looked forward to crossing over to be with those who had come before. Kitchi was anxious for this to end, but worried about Sassa. Ufala would take care of his "Mud Turtle," but Sassa would be on her own. Kitchi could hear and was able to think clearly, but found it difficult to expend the energy to speak. Talli felt her mother's sensation of crying, but no tears formed. Kitchi was disturbed. She wanted Talli to go home.

Banabas grabbed Talli and pulled her back when he realized what was happening. He held her against him, her head pressed to his chest. Sassa knelt beside them.

"You know about my sister?" she asked, looking at Banabas.

"Yes," he answered.

Sassa searched Banabas's eyes. "And you do not throw her out?"

"She is my wife," he said. "I love your sister."

Talli's eyes opened. She lifted her head. "I am sorry," she said.

Banabas rubbed her shoulder with his hand.

"Talli," Kitchi whispered.

"I am all right, Mother," she said, moving back to Kitchi's side. "You do not have to worry. My husband understands."

Kitchi appeared to relax and fall into a sleep. Nocatee entered the lodge with Mikot.

"There are times she is a little more lucid," Sassa said. "But not for very long or very often."

Mikot toddled to his mother. He held Nocatee's hand for balance. Talli smiled at her son.

"He walks early," Sassa said.

"He is very bright," Banabas said.

Talli stayed at her mother's side for three days. Kitchi ate nothing and had difficulty swallowing the small amounts of water Talli fed her. She moaned occasionally, but did not speak. On the third day, her mother opened her eyes. "I want to tell you something," Kitchi said.

"Banabas," Talli cried. "Look, she is awake. Yes, Mother, what is it?"

"Alone," she whispered.

Banabas stepped outside, leaving Kitchi and Talli by themselves.

"I am sorry," Kitchi said.

"For what?" Talli asked.

"Akoma. I should have fought for you. We have made your life unhappy."

"No," Talli said. "Everything is the design of the spirits."

"Liakka . . . she is wicked. I think she takes medicine to rid herself of Akoma's child, or maybe to prevent becoming pregnant."

"Does Akoma appear happy?" Talli asked.

"He will always love you."

Talli strangled back tears. "We cannot change things."

Kitchi closed her eyes and sank back into sleep.

Ufala appeared in the entrance of the lodge.

"Where have you been?" Talli asked.

"None of your concern," Ufala answered. "When you are here, I am not."

Talli stood up. "How could you abandon her now? You are not here to care for her, see if she eats or drinks. She would never—"

"You and your sisters are here. Kitchi does not need me."

"She has always needed you! When Climbing Bear died, you cast her out of your heart. You have been cruel to her ever since. His death was not her fault, it was yours!"

"Get out!"

Banabas came up behind Ufala. "Be calm, Ufala. Come outside with me."

"She is a witch," Ufala said. "How do you put up with her tongue? How dare she speak to her father in such a manner?"

Banabas led Ufala out. "You both have experienced many troubles."

"Take her home," Ufala said. "She is a witch like her great-grandmother. Have you not figured out there is something wrong with her?"

"I know about the affliction."

"So, you see she is evil . . . punished by the spirits. Her whole bloodline is evil!"

"I do not see it that way, Ufala."

Talli emerged from the lodge, tears streaming down her face. "It is over," she said.

Putiwa strolled to the outskirts of the village. Deep in the brush, shrouded by trees and bushes, he came upon the Bone Cleaner's small hut.

"Bone Cleaner," he called.

In a few moments a thin, gray-haired figure appeared in the entrance of the hut. Designs drawn in red and yellow ochre garnished his light-brown skin. His eyes appeared to be set deep in his head.

A chill ran down Putiwa's spine.

The Bone Cleaner was thought of as a sorcerer and was feared, but was still esteemed. Every man donated a part of his kill to the Bone Cleaner. Putiwa delivered his supplies without conversation. The Bone Cleaner stayed to himself, keeping out of sight, except when collecting the bodies of the deceased or when placing the cleaned, bundled bones atop the charnel platform.

"A woman . . . Kitchi," Putiwa said.

The Bone Cleaner acknowledged Putiwa with a subtle nod. He followed the shaman back to the village, staying about six long strides behind.

Talli stepped aside when he reached the lodge. Quietly, with total lack of expression, the Bone Cleaner picked up Kitchi's body. On his way out, Talli gave him a basket of articles to be placed with her mother's bones. Inside the basket was a small decorated pot, several shells, and a string of beads. The Bone Cleaner would "kill" the pot, smash it, at the time of putting her bones on the charnel platform. This would set free the pot's spirit so it could join Kitchi.

Talli followed him with her eyes. Banabas embraced her. She buried her head beneath his neck and cried.

"Look," Sassa said, "Ramo comes!"

Banabas wheeled around. "What does he do here?"

Ramo walked up to Banabas and Talli. "Talli," he said in greeting.

Talli bowed her head in respect.

"Banabas," Ramo said, "it is time we tell Akoma that we have met with Chogatis."

38

Akoma sat first. Ramo and Banabas sat on the bench in front of the Turtle cacique. They remained silent a few moments. Finally Akoma initiated the conversation.

"What brings Ramo to the Turtle village?"

Ramo's wry smile sat smoothly for a moment before he spoke. "I have just come from a meeting with Chogatis. I found him reasonable. I believe we can negotiate with him."

"What would you negotiate? That implies the Jeaga would have to give up something."

"All that is to be worked out. I told him I could not speak for the Jeaga on my own. He would also need to speak to you. Chogatis wishes an audience with you."

"Then let him know he can come to this village and I will meet with him."

Ramo rocked back, gave a brief glance to Banabas, then focused on Akoma. "Chogatis is a cautious man. He prefers to see you alone. He has suggested a place on the river to meet you at the time of the new moon."

"That is not acceptable," Akoma said. "I agree to meet with him. I think, however, we should meet at Fork Camp on the river. Tell him to proceed there, and I shall come within ten days, but I will not tell him exactly when. That would not be judicious of me."

"I am not certain that will be to his liking."

"Then there will be no conference."

"I will relay the message," Ramo said.

Akoma arched a curious brow. "It sounds as if you have frequent communications."

"No, not in the past. I must communicate with him

now if I am to give him your message. How else will he know?"

"Tell him what I have offered. Sometime near the new moon I will go to Fork Camp. If he is not there, I will assume he has no interest in pursuing peace."

Akoma raised his hand signaling the end of the conversation.

Banabas held his fishing spear in the air. He watched the water for fish. He had already gathered freshwater mussels.

A sound down the bank made him look that way. Something rustled the brush. It could be an alligator. Maybe a bobcat or a panther, though they usually moved with greater stealth.

Banabas put his spear on the ground and listened again. He was sure something stirred not too far away. He flexed his knees to make himself smaller, more hidden by the brush. Cautiously, he stole toward the noise.

He paused behind the trunk of an oak. He had to be close. Now he heard something else . . . a voice. Banabas stepped from behind the tree. He scanned the area. Movement in the grass attracted his attention. He moved toward it.

Suddenly he saw what had made the noise. Banabas realized he had come upon his cacique at a very bad time. He turned to leave and as he did, he heard a woman's voice.

"Ramo!" Liakka said, sounding startled.

In an instant Ramo called out to him, "Banabas wait. We must talk."

Banabas turned around. Ramo fumbled with his breechclout as he got to his feet. Liakka was propped up on one elbow.

"I must explain to you," Ramo said. He turned to the woman on the ground. "Go back to the village," he said.

"I await your explanation with eagerness," Banabas said.

Ramo put his hand on Banabas's shoulder. "We have spoken before about the unification of the Jeaga. Akoma obstructs us from achieving that goal. He must be eliminated."

Banabas squinted one eye. "What are you saying, Ramo? What does this have to do with being with his wife?"

"The Turtle and Panther must merge to become any kind of powerful force. As we are now, we are too splintered. Akoma will never consent."

"He does not object to more unification. He just does not want the Turtle to be swallowed by the Panther. He knows you want to destroy him and become the leader of both the Turtle and the Panther. He argues for the Turtle to retain their independence."

Ramo pushed slightly on Banabas's shoulder for emphasis. "That cannot be. Akoma must be eliminated."

"You plan to kill him?"

"Banabas, how simple you make it sound. Think. The Jeaga would never unite if anyone believed brother raised hand against brother. We will leave that to the Ais. If Akoma dies at the hand of an Ais, there will be even more of a cry for unification."

"I do not understand this," Banabas said. "How can you plot such a terrible thing? And what does Liakka have to do with this?"

"She will get word to me when Akoma plans to make his journey to see Chogatis. I will let Chogatis know. Akoma will be ambushed. Very simple."

Banabas paced. "Why would Chogatis agree?"

"I have promised him part of the Turtle territory once Akoma is gone. When the Turtle are without their cacique, I will be in a position to join the Panther and Turtle. Think about it, Banabas. In the long run, I will bring peace to us all. We will live in harmony with the Ais for the first time."

"And Liakka? What makes her cooperate."

"This was all planned. Liakka became Akoma's wife so she can keep me informed of his doings. I am sending Iquan to the coontie grounds near the Turtle village. The women frequent the area to dig the roots, so if Liakka goes there, she will not come under suspicion. She will inform Iquan when Akoma plans to leave to meet with Chogatis, and he will then tell me. I will get word to Chogatis. When Akoma is out of the way, I will take her as my woman and share the wealth with her.''

Ramo hiked one corner of his mouth in a corrupt smile. "You are a good man, but really, would you not benefit from having Akoma out of the way? We both know your wife still pines for him. Akoma's riddance will be in your personal interest, too.''

"I cannot think that way. How could I condone a man's death for my personal advantage?''

"You know in your heart that you wish him dead. Now it will be done. Feel no guilt. His blood is not spilled for you. Now, go back to your pretty wife and forget all about this. Let it settle, then sift through it. I am sure you will agree when the surprise wears off.''

The men gathered about the Turtle central hearth. Ramo and Banabas were invited to join them. The sun had not set, and the women huddled about cook fires preparing meals.

Ramo bragged about his last bear kill, how superior he had been to the creature. The men listened, most of them intrigued and entertained, especially Ufala. Only a few grew bored with his boasting.

Banabas considered the Panther cacique. He possessed many skills. He was handsome and virile with an aptitude for exciting others. Ramo was a good story-teller. He delivered his narrations with a flair, choosing powerful, image-provoking words and phrases. He added melodrama and gestures that brought the story to life. Men easily became enthralled with him and admired him. With little effort he could gather a great following. The thought sent the hair on the back of Banabas's neck straight up.

Across the way Banabas saw his wife. Mikot sat on her hip as she chatted with Mora, Akoma's mother, and Mora's sister, Raina. Mora appeared to be doing most of the talking. He watched Talli. How delicately beautiful she was. As he watched, he noticed she glanced toward the men often. He followed her line of sight. As he feared, her mindfulness was on Akoma. She appeared to be trying to catch a glimpse of him at every opportunity, as if obsessively fascinated.

She still did pine for him, just as Ramo said, Banabas thought. He had made the effort not to think of what he suspected she felt about Akoma because it stung too badly, but deep in his heart he knew.

He continued to watch her. She swayed, rocking Mikot, shifting her weight from one foot to the other. When Mora and Raina walked away, she moved on, but not before turning back for a quick last look at Akoma.

All night the thoughts of her wanting Akoma stayed on Banabas's mind, keeping him from restful sleep. He was glad they were leaving in the morning.

The night passed slowly for Banabas. Whenever he did drift off, his dreams were nightmares, and he awoke from them in a sweat. At the first hint of dawn, he rose from his sleeping skin and wandered about the Turtle village. For a long while he stood where he could look at Akoma's lodge. It was not as elaborate as Ramo's, yet still obviously the cacique's. Talli would always have her heart with the man that lay sleeping inside that lodge . . . a young and handsome cacique.

Deciding he tortured himself by dwelling on such thoughts, Banabas went to the river to see if he could catch fresh fish. After the morning meal, he would take his wife and son and return home.

The slice of sunlight coming through Akoma's lodge entrance fell on his eyes and awakened him. He looked at the woman next to him. She did not curl against him, nor did he curl against her. Her back was to him, and a distance of an arm's length separated them. She showed a great deal of affection most of the time and certainly had a sexual appetite. When they slept, after the moment of passion was over, she pulled away. Actually, he thought, he preferred it that way, yet he also knew there was something missing. When you loved someone, you wanted to be close all the time, wanted to touch them when you stirred in your sleep, wanted to feel the warmth of their body when the night air was chilled.

Akoma rolled onto his back. He had known this marriage would never be complete for him. Had Liakka felt the same?

He turned his head to see his wife. Physically, she was satisfying. She certainly knew the ways to please a man in the sleeping skins. But he had not taken her as his wife because he loved her or because she had so many *other* talents. Their marriage was arranged because it encouraged the peace between Panther and Turtle.

Akoma quietly got up and went out into the emerging daylight. His life and marriage were not terrible or intolerable, but he would never be really happy. He was the Turtle cacique and the People came first.

He saw Talli by her cook fire and decided to bid her a good morning.

Across the hearth from her he said, "The day comes with glory." Akoma looked toward the brilliant gold and pink of the eastern horizon. Every cloud appeared illuminated with sun fire.

Talli looked at the flares of color in the sky. "A beautiful day," she agreed.

Akoma admired the fine lines of her face, the thick black lashes over her eyes, the gentle curve of her arm as she held Mikot. He studied the boy. In his soot-black eyes he recognized Talli's reflection. The small ears were hers. The child's other features captured his attention. There was nothing of Banabas in him, but what was it that he saw? There were hints of someone.

Akoma glared at the boy. Mikot bounced on his mother's hip and tugged at her hair. The little one's hands were a familiar attribute. Akoma's mouth slipped open. Mikot's hands were like Yahga-ta's . . . like his! He looked at his own hands, then back at Mikot's. And the nose was definitely not Talli's, not Banabas's . . . his nose.

Akoma's eyes shot to Talli's. Mikot was not Banabas's child. Mikot was his!

A sudden tightening in his throat surprised him. His arms tingled all the way to his fingertips. He had been wrong about Talli. Perhaps she really had kept her promise to him. Did Banabas know? he wondered.

"Talli," he was finally able to say.

"Yes," she said, turning to him.

Akoma touched the boy's head, then pressed his finger in Mikot's palm for the child to grip. "May I hold him?"

Talli did not respond quickly. Akoma waited for an answer. Could she see what was in his head?

Talli lifted Mikot under the arms and gave him to Akoma.

"My son," he whispered.

Talli reeled. "Will you tell Banabas?"

39

Akoma forced himself to leave Talli. He wandered about the village, the revelation that Mikot was his son rushing through every fiber of his body. By accident he came upon Ufala pitching stones.

"You think this foolish of me," Ufala asked. "I suspect most men could not conceive of the steps I have had to take to be a *man* again. I am certain to you this seems a ridiculous task."

Ufala picked up another stone. "Come with me," he said, holding it out to Akoma. Akoma followed him a distance. "See that shelf fungus on this fallen log?" Ufala said.

"Yes," Akoma answered.

"From where we stood, do you think you could hit it in one throw, clean it from the log?"

"Maybe," Akoma said. "But I am not accustomed to throwing stones. Perhaps with my lance."

"No, with this small stone. How accurate can you be?"

"I will try," Akoma said as they returned to the spot where Ufala had picked up the stone. Akoma planted his feet and lined up with the target. "That is quite a distance to hurl a rock."

"Go ahead. Throw it."

Akoma gently tossed the stone in his hand several times, getting the feel of the stone in his palm. He took three deep breaths, and then in a burst of energy he pitched the rock.

When the stone thumped the ground several hand lengths from the log, Ufala roared.

Akoma shrugged.

"Now try it with the hand you do not use."

Akoma chuckled. "If I could not hit it with my strong arm, it is stupid to think I could be successful with my other arm."

"Exactly," Ufala said. "The Ais took away the use of my best arm." He extended the maimed arm as best he could and tapped it for emphasis. "I hate them for that." He picked up a stone. "This was not my strong arm," he said. "Imagine suddenly being forced to perform every task with your weak arm."

"I am sure it has been difficult."

"I am a strong man. I suffered a lot, not just pain but humility. I have survived." Ufala whipped around. "But who appreciated that? Anyone? They do not know how," he said with a sneer.

Ufala heaved air in and out of his lungs, swelling and shrinking his chest. He stared at the target, concentrating, and then with an explosive but smooth flow of his arm, he threw the stone. He grinned as it destroyed the target, knocking the fungus from the log. "Discipline," he said. "Practice and more practice, never giving up."

"That is remarkable," Akoma said. "Tell me, do you share your feelings with your family? Have you allowed them to be a part of your recovery?"

"What do you mean? I am the one who suffered the injury. Why should I make them suffer the daily frustrations I have felt? I am the man, not the woman in the family."

Akoma shook his head. "I think you have closed them out by sparing them. You have a wonderful family that loves you. Invite them to be a part of their father's life before it is too late."

Ufala grumbled and tossed another stone at a closer target. "Women are women and men are men. They do not understand each other. Kitchi did not understand me. We had a son, did you know that?"

"Of course," Akoma said. "A tragedy."

The big man's eyes watered, and he turned away. "It is already too late," he said. "Kitchi is dead, and all feelings are dead between me and my daughters, except Nocatee, of course."

Akoma threw his head back and chuckled. "I thought

you were the man who just told me he did not give up. Are you not the man who threw the stone over and over and over until you finally hit your target? Why would such a man give up so easily on those he loves?"

Ufala and Akoma then walked back to the village.

"Talli and Banabas leave this morning," Akoma said. "Give her a moment of your time."

"She has her own life," Ufala said. "It is better that way."

"How can that be? She is your daughter. She has just lost her mother and you lost your wife. You should find strength and solace in each other."

Ufala cleared his throat. "You do not understand, Akoma. There are things you do not know about Talli . . . things no one should know. I have done right by her."

"Do one more thing, then. Share this morning's meal with your daughter. Heal some wounds."

As they approached Banabas and Talli, Akoma said, "You have not even held your grandson. Think of the things you could teach him, as you would have taught Climbing Bear. This is your opportunity. Give him lessons in discipline and determination. Tell him about the old ways. Who better than you?"

Banabas rose to his feet when Akoma and Ufala arrived. "I must thank you," Banabas said. "Turtle hospitality has been wonderful."

"You are always welcome," Akoma said. "Your morning meal smells delicious. Talli, do you have enough to share with your father?"

Talli donned an astonished expression.

"Are you hungry, Ufala?" Akoma asked.

"I could eat a small portion," he answered.

"Well, ask if your daughter has enough to share with you."

"We have plenty," Talli said. "And you, Akoma? We have enough for both of you."

"Not this morning," he said. "Maybe another time."

Talli watched Ramo's canoe ahead of them. Banabas also appeared fixed on the cacique. He had not spoken much except to say he was glad Ufala had consented to share the morning meal. He briefly told her how he and Ufala had been friends and that there did exist good in him. Talli said she understood.

"What is wrong?" she asked. His eyes were set beneath furrowed brows. Something troubled her husband.

Banabas plunged the paddle deep and swept a mound of water behind them. He shook his head, but didn't look at her.

"Something disturbs you," she insisted.

Finally, Banabas let his eyes make contact with hers. "I would never do anything to hurt you. You know that, do you not?"

"Of course," she said. Perplexed, she tilted her head to the side. "What makes you ask?"

"Nothing," he said. "I just want to make sure you know I love you and would never do anything to hurt you."

"Banabas, I know our marriage is not ideal. I know that in some ways I am not the wife you deserve, but I have no doubts of your love for me. And, I do love you. You are my good friend. I know you would never hurt me."

Banabas focused in the distance.

Talli shifted Mikot to her other knee.

It was a beautiful day to be on the river. Twinkling stars of blinding sunlight sparkled on the water. Wading birds stood like sentinels along the banks, sometimes bursting into the air in a flurry of outstretched wings that beat the air. Turtles, like humps of brown earth, basked on every downed limb and trunk that jutted out over the water.

Talli let her hand trail in the river, leaving a small wake. She watched her husband paddle while she softly hummed a song to Mikot. Banabas was a decent man. Sometimes she felt so guilty. She wondered what troubled him. For some reason he did not want to share it with her.

Very near the Panther village, Joog ran down the bank. He waved and shouted happy greetings at their return. He followed them, sprinting along the edge of the river, leaping over deadfalls and debris, hopping across low spots, and rocks.

"Be careful!" Talli yelled.

Suddenly, Joog tripped. He soared through the air, then landed sprawled on the ground.

Talli clutched Mikot and stood up, rocking the canoe.

Joog rolled over and lifted his head, laughing.

Talli sighed in relief and sat again.

"In your concern for the boy you nearly tipped us," Banabas said.

He was smiling so she knew he wasn't angry. "I know," she said. "I am sorry. I thought he was hurt."

"Ahh, he's tough. Do you not know that by now?"

"You are right," she said.

Joog helped Banabas bank the canoe, then skipped alongside them on the walk to the village.

"Tawute and I are going to check our snare," Joog said. "If we have a rabbit, will you cook it?" he asked Talli.

"Are you going to skin it?"

"Yes," Joog said. "I will save the pelt for a blanket for Mikot."

"I am hungry," Banabas said. "Where is this rabbit?"

"I will be back," the boy said.

Joog ran for his friend. He paused when he saw Ramo at Iquan's hearth. He approached quietly. He didn't like Ramo. If not for Banabas, Ramo would have slit his throat. He shivered and flashing images of that day crashed through his head. Joog grabbed his head with his hands. He didn't want to think about it.

"Joog!" Tawute said, coming up behind him.

Ramo turned from Iquan and stared at the boys.

"Come on," Tawute said.

The boys ran into the woods. They didn't stop until they reached the place they had set their snare.

"We have one!" Tawute yelled, seeing the fur dangling from the snare.

Joog released the rabbit, and the boys sat to inspect their catch.

"He is a fat one," Joog said.

"We are men!" Tawute said. "Well, almost," he corrected himself. "We have to go through the trials, of course," he said.

Joog looked away.

"Oh," Tawute said, "I forgot. But maybe things will change and you will go through the Jeaga rites and become a man."

"I do not think so. When the snake bit me, Ocaab could not even treat me." Joog's face dropped.

"What is it like to be Ais?" Tawute asked. "Everyone is so afraid of them, but I am not afraid of you."

"Jeaga and Ais are the same," Joog said. "There are little differences, but not so much." He stopped and stared in the distance. "I do not feel Ais or Jeaga. I cannot tell anymore."

"Do you want to go back?"

"I miss my mother and my friends, but if I go back, then I will miss Talli, Banabas, and you."

Tawute picked up the rabbit by its hind legs and examined him. "What do Ais boys do to become men?" he asked.

"Our mothers' brothers teach us hunting and fishing, toolmaking, those kinds of things. Our fathers and grandfathers teach us also, but most of the time if your mother has a brother, then he is responsible. My father liked to teach me."

Tawute shrugged his shoulder. "Iquan does not spend much time with me. My mother's brother teaches me some things. I learn a lot from you and Banabas."

"When we are of age, we must fast for a day in front of the village, then go out into the forest and wait for our first vision," Joog said. "The shaman says that is when your guide spirit appears to you, usually in the form of an animal. All the time you cannot eat."

Tawute's face brightened. "It is the same for us," he said. "We are not allowed to take weapons or food with us. We are supposed to sit close to a fire and force sweat from our bodies, the whole time praying to the spirits to find us worthy enough to receive a guide from them."

"Do you build a pit?" Joog asked.

Tawute shook his head. "I have not heard of that."

"When we are deep in the forest and await our guide

spirit, we also build a fire, but next to it we build a pit.
We heat stones in the fire, then transfer them to the pit.
We are supposed to pour water over the hot stones and
lean into the steam. They say that in the summer it is
very torturous. Only the bravest do it in the summer. I
would do it in the summer."

Tawute grinned. "I would, too. And then when we
came back all skinny, dirty, and weak, our mothers
would say, 'Oh, oh, my son has come back. Oh, thank
the spirits.'" Tawute mimicked a woman's voice and
antics. Then he deepened his voice and stiffened. "And
our fathers say, 'My son has returned a man!'"

Both boys started laughing. Joog puffed out his chest.
"I can see Banabas now, all proud and . . ." His voice
trailed off as he realized what he was saying.

Tawute understood. "You are Jeaga, even if not born
to the People. Banabas is your father."

Joog stood up. "My father is dead."

Talli stooped by Joog, who rubbed the staked rabbit
pelt. "It will make a fine blanket," she said. "I will make
the blanket of nothing other than what you bring me. It
will be Joog's gift to Mikot. I am very proud," she said.

Ceboni, carrying Zowhi, followed Tawute to see Talli
and Joog. "Perhaps you two boys will catch us our dinner," she said. "I would like something fresh."

"Where is Iquan?" Talli asked. "I have not seen
him about."

"He left just after you returned from the Turtle
village."

"That has been days. Where did he go?"

Ceboni swept her hand in the air. "Secrets. He and
Ramo whisper and carry on. Then he tells me he will
be gone, but does not know how long. I ask him where,
and he tells me to be still. The first few days were not so
bad, I actually enjoyed being alone, but I tire of it now."

Talli pressed a plaited mat into the damp clay pot she
was making. She pulled it away and looked at the nice
impression the mat made. "Do you ever tire of your
husband?" she asked.

Ceboni plopped down on the ground and turned

Zowhi loose. "Go play with your sister," she said to Tawute. "Teach her a game."

Tawute grumbled. "How are we to hunt if—"

Ceboni shut him off. "Play with her for a while, then you and Joog can go hunting. Your mother needs a rest."

"Were you crazy in love with Iquan when you married him?" Talli asked.

"Oh, yes." Ceboni's face glowed with a smile. "We could not wait. We were fortunate, of course. My father promised his father when I was a baby."

"You were promised to Iquan?"

"My father owed Iquan's father a favor. Luckily, Iquan and I loved each other since we were children. We never thought of anyone else."

Talli stared at the pot, running her fingers over the rim to smooth it. "What about joining? Do you like to do that with Iquan?"

Ceboni giggled. "Old women talk about having to put up with husbands' privileges. You know how they mutter and complain. Their men should take a lesson from Iquan." Ceboni burst into an embarrassed twitter again. "I think I like it more than Iquan," she whispered. "These kinds of nights especially," she said. "With the new moon, the nights are so dark."

40

Akoma stretched out on his stomach. Liakka massaged his back. "I love the way I can feel your muscles beneath your skin," she said. Her hands dug in deep, her fingertips working out kinks and knots. "Does that feel good?" she asked.

"Wonderful," he said. "You are relaxing me."

"I am glad," she said. "You work so hard every day. You should have time to enjoy the pleasures of the body and let the mind stop thinking."

Liakka spread her body over his, lying on his back. "Mmm," she said. "I do not like to go to sleep by myself. I am lonesome when you are not here with me."

Akoma's eyes closed.

"Are you sleeping?" she asked.

"Ummm," he answered.

"Tell me you will not have to go on any journeys for a long, long time," she said.

"Caciques always have ventures that take them on journeys."

"No," she mewled.

Akoma slid from under her and turned over. "You need to get used to being the cacique's wife."

Liakka sidled against him, resting her head on his shoulder. "I do not have to get used to anything," she said.

"Sooner than you think," Akoma said.

Liakka blinked. "Why do you say that? I think you like to tease me."

"You are fun to tease," he said.

Liakka turned onto her side and propped herself up. She drew phantom designs on his chest with her finger.

"Are you planning on leaving me soon? Are you going away?"

"Men have things they must do."

"Akoma," Liakka huffed, "you are not answering me."

"In two days," he said. "I have to make a quick journey two days from now."

"Ohh," she whined. "I knew you were going away." She lay back down and drifted away from him. "I will miss you," she said, then closed her eyes.

In the morning Liakka prepared the morning meal. She shuffled through baskets.

"What are you looking for?" Akoma asked.

"I thought we had plenty stored," she said.

"What?"

"Coontie root. I guess I was wrong. I will go and get some this morning."

"Who is going with you?" Akoma asked. "You do not want to go alone."

"It is not that far," she said. "I do not mind the walk."

"That is not my concern," he said. "If something happened, there would be no way to get help. You know you should travel with someone else."

"But I will be back by the time the sun is straight above. You make too much of this."

Akoma grasped her hand to get her attention as she stirred the pot. "This is not a safe time for a woman to wander alone. I do not like the idea."

"All right," she said. "I will ask Sassa to go."

"Good," he said.

Akoma thought about the journey that he was about to take. He had decided that in two days he would meet Chogatis. He doubted they would come to agreeable terms, but he would make the effort. He would not give away anything that was Jeaga. If Ramo had such an idea, then let Ramo give up Panther holdings, though he would discourage it.

Later in the morning, he spoke with Yahga-ta.

"Ramo still concerns me," Yahga-ta said. "He is so

hungry for power. That makes him hard to predict. I am curious as to what he has already promised Chogatis."

"I will find out soon," Akoma said. "I leave two days from now to meet with him."

"Do not go alone."

"Those are the conditions," Akoma said. "I will be careful."

"I will follow, stay behind, but close in case of trouble."

"I am a man of my word," Akoma said.

Yahga-ta nodded. "How do Sassa and Nocatee fare?"

"Better. Ufala is such a troubled man. I think he is afraid to love anyone. He does not want to suffer a loss like Climbing Bear's again. And, of course, the injury made him bitter. There has been a bit of a turn since Kitchi's death. He softens."

"We all deal with pain in different manners. His way has been harsh, but perhaps he has learned."

Akoma bid his father good day and left. He decided to stop and check on Ufala and his daughters.

Ufala was filtering rendered animal fat through a grass strainer. When it cooled, he would mix it with the strips of dried meat he had hanging on horizontal poles that were lashed to a tripod. He would also add crushed berries. When all was mixed thoroughly, Ufala would pack the mixture in a casing made of cleaned animal intestine. The result would be a nutritious food that would last a long time.

Akoma took one thin strip of meat from the pole. He bent it. The meat snapped. "Perfect," he said.

Ufala sat the pot of tallow to the side. "Hand me that basket of berries," he said.

Akoma handed the basket to him. Ufala scooped a handful of berries and put them in the mortar and began to grind them.

Nocatee sat next to her father, attempting to weave a small simple basket. She lined up four splints then placed four more atop, but in the opposite direction.

"All of you are busy today," Akoma said.

"Most of us," Ufala said. "Sassa socializes. She has her eye on some boy, and they have gone for a stroll. She should be here helping."

"I thought Sassa went with Liakka to dig coontie."

Ufala looked up. "Sassa is not interested in working if she can spend time flirting with that boy."

"Did not Liakka ask her to go with her?"

"We have not seen your wife today."

Tawute and Joog each carried a duck in his hand. Their bolas, which felled the ducks, hung from the waist-bands of their breechclouts.

"I told you we could do it if we practiced," Joog said. "We are nearly men and now we prove it with our hunting skills."

"Do you want me to cook them for you?" Talli asked.

"I want Banabas to see them first," Joog said.

"He is not here. As soon as Tawute's father returned, Ramo summoned him. The three of them are in conference."

"My father has returned?" Tawute asked.

"While you boys were gone."

Tawute's face lit up. "Then he will see what a good hunter I am!"

"I am certain you will please him," Talli said.

Tawute took his duck and hurried home.

Talli ruffled Joog's hair. "We will surprise Banabas with succulent duck for his dinner."

Talli rotated the spit, turning the duck. "I think it is done," she said. "You serve it," she said to Joog. "This is your kill. Is that not right, Banabas?"

Banabas stared in the distance. "Banabas?" she said.

"What?" he said. "Did you say something?"

"You are far away this evening. What occupies your mind?"

Banabas stood up. "I am not hungry," he said.

Talli looked up at him. "Joog is proud that he has provided for us."

"Yes," Banabas said. He looked at Joog. "I am proud, also."

"Are you not going to eat any?" the boy asked.

"You will have a little, will you not?" Talli asked.

"Of course," Banabas said, sitting again. "I have not

much appetite, but how can I turn down such a fine
duck?"

Joog grinned and served Banabas.

For the rest of the meal, Banabas said nothing. He
continued to appear distant and preoccupied. Now and
again Talli noticed that he stared at her.

When both Joog and Mikot were sleeping, Banabas
sat by the dying fire. Talli came next to him and massaged his shoulders. "Something troubles you. Do not
bother to deny it."

Banabas leaned his head to the side, stretching his
neck and the shoulder she rubbed.

"Are you going to tell me?" she asked.

Banabas twisted around to look at her. He stared
without speaking.

Talli knelt down. "What is it? What is wrong? Tell
me. Have I done something that displeases you?"

Banabas closed his eyes and rested his head against
her. "No," he said.

Talli pushed him away so she could see his face. "I
cannot live this way," she said. "I do not like being kept
in the dark when something causes you such anguish."

Banabas let out a deep sigh. He got up and went inside the lodge, leaving Talli alone by the fire. When she
finally decided to rest, she found he was already
asleep . . . or was pretending to be asleep.

In the morning when she awoke, Banabas was not on
his sleeping skin. She went outside and found him sitting
beside the central hearth. He was doing more than greeting the day. She stood back and watched. Banabas
prayed to the spirits. She could not make out the words,
but the tone told her he experienced deep torment.

In a few moments he finished and began to walk back
to his hearth. Talli intercepted him. "You estrange me,"
she said. "I do not like it. If you cannot let me carry
some of the load, then I do not feel like you are my
husband. I feel as if you want me to leave and do not
know how to tell me."

They walked the rest of the way in silence. When they

reached the lodge, Talli said, "I will prepare to leave," she said.

Banabas grabbed her shoulder. "No," he said. "Talli, sit down."

Talli kept looking at her husband's face as she lowered herself to the ground. Banabas paced, rubbing his jaw.

"Ramo has set a trap for Akoma," he said.

41

"Stop him!" Talli cried.

"Ramo has already sent word to Chogatis that Akoma is on his way. The ambush is set. It is too late."

"Then you must intercept Akoma, and warn him! Banabas, you cannot allow this!"

"I am not the cacique. I do not make the decisions. I already argued with Ramo, but to no avail."

"Please," Talli said. She was crying now, sobbing, her hands clutching her husband. "Please!"

"You ask me to save the man who keeps your heart from me," he said.

Talli stared into Banabas's hurt eyes. Tears streamed down her cheeks and into the corners of her mouth.

Banabas pulled her to him. "All right, Talli. All right." His heart ached to see how deeply she still cared for Akoma. "Let me gather some things and I will go."

He looked at her again. He knew that if he interfered with Ramo's plans, he would be considered a traitor and put to death upon his return. But if she loved Akoma and not him, he might as well be dead.

Banabas poled his canoe through the shallow creek that snaked off the main river. This was a more dangerous passage, but a shorter route. He hoped he would be in the right position to cut off Akoma before Chogatis's party found him.

Banabas plunged the pole into the water again and shoved. He worked his way through the winding creek until, finally, it gradually opened into a wide channel in the river. Banabas pulled his dugout onto the bank. He sat scanning the river, hoping he was not too late.

The breeze rustled the leaves of the trees and the sky clouded, turning the day into a claylike gray. He flinched at the cracking of a twig.

Ais! Two Ais scouts came at him, dashing through the brush. As soon as they knew Banabas had detected them, they cried war whoops. One held a lance shoulder-high, the other, a celt lashed to a stick in one hand, and a knife in the other.

Banabas held his knife in front of him. He spread his feet, planting them firmly. He squared himself to the attackers.

As the warrior with the celt and knife came at him, Banabas tucked his head and rammed him, shoving his knife into the warrior's chest. Banabas heard a rib crack and felt the warmth of Ais blood on his hand.

Quickly, he pulled out the knife. The other warrior hurled his lance. Banabas used the knifed man as a shield. The lance penetrated the wounded man's shoulder, going all the way through and into Banabas's chest. Banabas reeled backward, the burning pain blazing in his chest.

He pushed the wounded man away which pulled the lance out of his chest. He charged the other Ais. Every breath felt as though fire spread through his lungs. With a burst of energy, Banabas threw himself on the weaponless Ais, knocking him to the ground. He yanked the man's head back by the hair and sliced his knife through the warrior's throat. The Ais's eyes widened as his blood pumped in spurts out of his neck.

Banabas looked over at the other Ais. He was dead.

For several moments Banabas sat astride the warrior, catching his breath. He pressed his hand to his chest, mixing his own blood with that of the Ais. There was so much pain. It hurt to breathe, so he kept his breaths shallow.

Slowly, he struggled to his feet and stumbled to his dugout. It took him several attempts to shove the canoe into the water. He flopped inside, his head propped on the rim of the canoe.

The river current carried the dugout. The heat of the sun as it emerged through the clouds felt good. Banabas was cold. A chill made him shudder.

His body was covered in blood. His chest wound

oozed a small but steady stream of red. He pressed the heel of his hand over the wound in an effort to stop the bleeding. He was tired, cold, and wanted to sleep. The gentle rocking of the canoe brought back early childhood memories of his mother rocking him and singing. For a moment he thought he heard her soft voice.

Banabas shook his head. He was hallucinating. Then in the distance, he saw another canoe heading in his direction. Banabas's eyelids fluttered. He had to stay awake.

He heard a noise and wondered what it was. He kept his eyes on the approaching dugout. In a moment, he realized what the noise was. It was a subtle wet rattling that came from his chest each time he inhaled. His eyes closed. He saw Talli and Mikot smiling at him. Then an image of Joog flashed, followed by flickers of other images. Some faces came from deep in his past. His first wife appeared with her back to him. She slowly turned around and smiled, holding out her hand for him to take.

Akoma grabbed the cordage attached to Banabas's canoe and towed it to the bank of the river. When the dugouts were grounded, he dragged Banabas out.

"Banabas," he said, pressing on the chest wound.

Banabas heard Akoma's voice, and the image of his wife faded. Slowly he opened his eyes.

"What has happened?" Akoma asked.

"Ais. Liakka and Ramo plot against you. They told Chogatis you were on the river. They planned an ambush."

"Ramo and Liakka arranged this?" he asked.

"Ramo promised Turtle territory to Chogatis once you were killed. Liakka will share in the wealth."

Banabas coughed, and a trickle of blood dribbled from his mouth. "I came to warn you," he whispered.

The pain in his chest had diminished to a dull annoyance. The cold bothered him more than the wound. Again, the image of his deceased wife appeared to him. She reached for him. "Come," she said.

Banabas took her hand.

Talli wondered what the commotion in the village was all about. She picked up Mikot and wandered to where the crowd gathered. As she approached, she noticed people turned and looked at her, even stepped aside so she could pass.

She moved through the crowd with trepidation. Finally, she saw why everyone had gathered. Akoma stood over Banabas's body. His jaw muscles tightened as he stared at Ramo. Talli sucked in a breath and stooped next to her blood-soaked husband. She looked up at Akoma and Ramo.

"He is dead?" she asked, even though she already knew that he was.

Ceboni took Mikot from Talli's arms and backed away. Suddenly, Joog pushed his way through the group. Tawute followed his friend.

"No!" Joog screamed and threw himself over Banabas. His small body heaved as he sobbed. Tawute put his hand on his friend's back for comfort.

Talli tugged at Joog until he finally got to his knees. He wiped his tears away with a dirty hand, leaving smears on his face. His nose ran, and he sniffed. "What happened?" he asked, choking on his words.

Akoma glared at Ramo. "Explain," he said. "Everyone wants to know how this has happened. Tell them."

"Tawute, take Joog to your mother," Talli said.

Ramo's shoulders moved with an exaggerated shrug. "How should I know?"

Akoma waited until the boys were gone. "He came to warn me," Akoma said. "All of you should hear how this man lost his life . . . for you . . . for the good of the Jeaga."

"Akoma, you are too dramatic. It was foolish for Banabas to be alone on the river. We all know the Ais are lurking about."

"Banabas came to warn me about your plan." Akoma studied the crowd. "Hear what I am about to say. Your cacique plotted with Chogatis to have me killed. Chogatis had no intention of negotiating with me. I was heading into an ambush. Ramo believed the Turtle would be so outraged at my death at the hands of the Ais that they would gladly rally around him and his plan to take over both the Panther and the Turtle. He promised Chogatis Turtle territory if Ais killed me. Ramo has betrayed the Jeaga for greed."

Ramo roared with laughter. "What a ridiculous idea! How long did it take you to make up such a tale?"

"It is true," Talli said. She put her fingertips on her husband's cheek. "Banabas confessed Ramo's plot to me. He was very troubled by it. I begged him to arrest the plan by intercepting and warning Akoma."

"As Banabas waited for me, an Ais scout party attacked him," Akoma said. "I found him dying. He told me of Ramo's betrayal."

A rumbling started among the men. A communal call for Ramo's execution resounded across the village.

"Let him have a choice," Akoma said. "Choose, Cacique. Die at the hands of your own people or salvage some dignity and lead them alongside the Turtle in an attack against the Ais."

Akoma sent for the Turtle warriors. Together, side by side, the Turtle and Panther would rise against the Ais.

When the sun was straight overhead, they pulled the dugouts high on the shore and covered them with brush and debris to conceal them. From this point on they traveled on foot. Ramo said he did not have knowledge of the exact location where the Ais lay in wait. But, because of the attack on Banabas, Akoma had a suspicion of where the Ais were waiting. Now the Jeaga would have the advantage.

"Ramo will walk in front of us," Akoma said. "His will be the first face the Ais see."

They trudged through tall grass and cane, through oak and cypress heads, hungry for the taste of Ais blood.

Ufala forged ahead, just behind Ramo.

"Do not be careless with your life," Akoma said to him. "I understand how anxious you are, but remember your daughters."

The day grew hot, and the thick foliage obstructed the breeze. Ufala wiped sweat from his brow. "Show yourselves," he said. "Ais have no courage!"

He parted from the chain of men. "I will go deeper," he said, indicating he would tread farther inland.

Akoma nodded his approval.

By midafternoon, the group grew hungry and thirsty. They stopped to refresh themselves with food and water.

Ramo sat alone, away from the others.

Ufala returned and made his way into the temporary camp. "I bring bad news," he said to Akoma. "There," he said, pointing to the north, "deep in the forest. I thought I saw something, but could not make it out. As I got closer, I realized what I saw was a man impaled on a stick. It was Iquan. He had driven a stake into the ground, then apparently flung himself upon it."

"He was the messenger," Akoma said. "He took Ramo's message to Chogatis." Akoma bowed his head. Iquan must have had such guilt in his heart that he could not permit himself to live. He followed his cacique's orders, even though he hated the deed.

"Ramo, you have cleaved such a gorge in the hearts of the Jeaga," Yahga-ta said, "it will take generations to heal. I do not envy your punishment by the spirits when you cross over. The Ais do not despise you as much as your own."

"It is true," Ufala said.

"Chogatis will kill me on sight," Ramo said. "He will think I deceived and tricked him."

The forest was dense, choked with thickets of saw palmetto and thorny vines that ripped the skin. Keeping low in the brush, Akoma ordered the men to halt. "The Ais should not be far from here," he said. "Do you agree, Ramo?"

The Panther cacique gave no answer.

Akoma looked at all the Jeaga, both Turtle and Panther. If the treasonous plan had succeeded, the Ais would have eliminated him. Then while the Turtle were vulnerable and disorganized, they would have attacked.

Akoma called three young men to his side. Their black eyes flashed with the thrill and anticipation of battle. Their brown skin rippled with the tensed muscles below, their bellies hard, their thighs bulging with the want to charge in attack. The older men listened and watched, remembering what it was like to be enthralled with the notion of going to war. Now their graying eyes peered beneath a copse of troubled brows. Their guts tightened with the thought that not everyone would be coming back. They surveyed each other, wondering who would live and who would die.

Akoma spoke to the three he had chosen as scouts. "You will go ahead and find the Ais, then report back. Tell me where, how many, what weapons. We will take every advantage."

The young men agreed, eager to find the Ais. Their bodies strained, resisting the urge to burst into the forest.

Putiwa stepped forward and raised his hand in front of the scouts. "Be swift as the deer and cunning as the panther. May your bodies be as strong as the bear's, your eyes keen as the eagle's. Go with the spirits' blessing."

He touched his thumb to their foreheads, leaving a sooty oval print. Then with a sharp point of a thorn, he pricked the skin of their chests, creating a design of dots and dashes. Putiwa rubbed dark ash into the nicks. The black soot sank into each shallow wound. In time, after the wounds healed, a permanent tattoo would remain.

An old man, the bony prominence of his face almost wearing through his skin, glanced down at his chest. His tattoo still endured and reminded him of the time he was a scout for a war party so many seasons ago.

When Putiwa completed the tattooing, Akoma gave a hand signal, and the scouts sprinted off into the forest.

While they waited for the scouts to return, the men aided each other in painting their faces and bodies with war symbols. Red and yellow ochre along with charcoal provided the colors.

Akoma looked at Ramo's face. The lines of the Panther leader's face angled and jutted. He presented a most fearsome countenance. What a waste of leadership, Akoma thought. He could have been an extremely powerful cacique, but instead he would be remembered with disrespect.

The men discussed strategies of the battle to come. Though there was vigor in their talk about attacking the

Ais, the older men's faces exposed their depth of understanding of what battle really meant.

Ufala rubbed his maimed arm, his mouth twisting with the thoughts in his head. The time was nearly at hand. How he had dreamed of this! He sniffed the air, his nostrils flaring, sure he could smell the filthy Ais. He yearned to taste the salty blood of the enemy, to feel the deep red fluid slick on his hands. He had no fear. If he died, so be it. He would die nobly, tearing the heart from an Ais—like a man—a Jeaga warrior!

Turtle and Panther huddled together, sitting in a tight circle awaiting the return of the scouts.

"Listen," Bunta said. "I hear something."

Silence rolled over the group. Brush rattled. Akoma waved to the men to take cover. They hunkered low, listening, waiting, their palms cold and sweaty.

To their relief a scout burst through the trees. "The others are coming," he said. "We found the Ais. There is a small group, perhaps the ambush party, and farther to the north there is a large band—more than the Turtle and Panther together."

"Numbers do not matter," Akoma said. "We have the advantage of surprise. And," Akoma added, "we will attack in the dark."

"Dark?" Ufala said.

"We do not need the light of the sun. They will not expect us in the dark. We know everything about our targets, where they are and how many. The Ais will be off guard."

Ufala nodded, liking the creative element to this attack. There had never been a battle in the dark before that he knew of. Most attacks occurred at daybreak. The Ais would never suspect such a thing. This battle grew better and better, he thought. His skin tingled, and the hair on the back of his neck prickled. He had not felt like this since he was a very young man. Heat pumped through his veins, rushing through his chest and down his limbs, even surging through his groin as if he were sexually aroused. His hand slid down his breechclout in curiosity. Indeed!

Akoma separated the men into two groups. "You will

be responsible for attacking the Ais ambush party," he
said to the smaller group. "While you attend to them,
the rest of us will circle the other Ais. We will wait until
you join us. Then when I sound the war whistle, we
will attack."

"Cacique," Ufala said, "you did not assign me to the
ambush party. I wish to go with them. It is my desire to
take on as many Ais as I can."

Akoma nodded consent.

"And I will watch Ramo," Ufala said. "If he so much
as twitches in a way that displeases me, I will slit his
throat."

Akoma addressed the Panther cacique. "You will lead
the ambush group. You will inform me when your group
is in place. After the sun goes down, we will take the
Ais." Akoma glared at Ramo. "Chogatis is yours. Do
you understand?"

Ramo nodded.

"Redeem yourself. Lead the Jeaga well. I expect no
losses in your group."

Ramo sneered. "There will be no losses."

The two groups split up. Ramo held up his lance and
waved to his men to follow him. In a moment the trees
swallowed them. They crept through the brush, following
the directions of one of the scouts. The men kept low,
staying in the shadows, careful where and how they
stepped.

Ufala came up behind Ramo. He spoke low on the
wind. "If the Ais do not finish you by morning, then
I will."

Ramo glared at him. "We will see who greets the
sun."

Soon they were close to where the ambush party
awaited Akoma. Ramo signaled the men to spread out.
Ufala kept near Ramo.

"Spread out," Ramo said to him.

Ufala slowly shook his head. He was not going to
leave any distance between himself and Ramo. If the
Panther cacique had a notion to flee, Ufala wanted to
be near enough to stop such an attempt.

All eyes sought Ramo. He skulked through the brush, waving the men forward.

In a moment, Ufala spotted movement ahead. He whistled a soft birdcall. Everyone came to a stop and peered through the trees. A grand smile came across Ufala's face. The ambush party was very small, perhaps only five. This would be swift. He looked over to Ramo and saw the cacique's chin thrust forward as he swallowed. His mouth must be dry, Ufala thought. The great Ramo did feel fear. He grinned at the Panther leader.

Ramo looked away. His chest inflated with a large breath. Then suddenly he leapt to his feet and cried out, beginning the charge.

The war cry rang through the small camp. Ais men scrambled to their feet. Their focus had been on the river, in wait for Akoma. Confused, they scurried about, unsure from where the enemy came.

In an instant, the Jeaga burst into sight. Ufala struck one man's head with his war club, a strombus shell bound to a wood shaft. He heard the Ais's skull crack and saw the blood quickly spill from his scalp. Ufala jumped over the man's slumped body. He threw down his club and pulled his knife from its sheath.

A heavy weight thrust against his back. He felt the slick, oiled skin of the warrior. Ufala blocked his own throat with his maimed arm as he swung his knife behind him and into the side of the Ais. The Ais knife aimed at Ufala's throat lost its target. The pain in his arm was not great as the knife slit open the skin. He felt no fear, as there was nothing else anyone could do to destroy that arm. He used it as a shield. It was a gift from the Ais.

The warrior grunted and fell away as Ufala drove his knife deeper.

Ramo screeched a victory cry. Ufala stepped away from the dying Ais and looked about. The Jeaga party whooped and thrust their weapons in the air in celebration.

Ufala dipped his fingers in the pool of blood by the Ais's body. When he stood again he drew his fingers down his face from forehead to throat.

*   *   *

Darkness began to creep into the edges of the sky. Ramo and the others had returned and found their places.

At the sight of the first star, Akoma's belly drew taut. He was anxious, but had to remain patient. He shimmied up a tree and perched between the notch of two branches. The Ais prepared for the night. Instead of numerous fires, only one small fire glowed. The enemy had not grown complacent. A single fire could quickly be extinguished.

Akoma could hear the Ais men talking, though he could not make out the words. The one he presumed to be Chogatis sat near the fire. He laughed with a few others. Curious thing, Akoma thought. Noise carried farther in the darkness than in the daylight.

He watched until he saw some of the Ais bed down for the night. A company of guards took their posts. Akoma slipped down from the tree. He cupped his hands about his mouth and made the sound of an owl. When each point person returned his call with selected sounds, Akoma knew his men were ready.

The Jeaga slithered even closer, tightening their circle. On the very perimeter of the Ais camp, Akoma took one last survey of the enemy. Satisfied that the time was right, he put a blade of grass to his lips and sounded the whistle.

Bunta, Putiwa, Ufala, and Akoma moved into the camp, hiding in shadows and taking advantage of the trees. The other Jeaga lay in wait until the sentinels were eliminated.

Ufala's heart pounded against his chest as he crept behind the guard he was to take care of. He clamped his bad arm around the Ais's neck and squeezed, shutting off the air so the man couldn't call out. He leaned his head around so the Ais warrior could just see him out of the corner of his eye. "See my face when you die," he whispered. Ufala allowed his mouth to turn up in a depraved smile. He took the heel of his good hand and put it against the tip of the guard's nose. Then, with a powerful shove, he drove the Ais's nose bone up into his skull and into his brain. The man went limp, and Ufala released him. He glanced about. The camp remained still and quiet. With the guards taken out, it was time for the rest of the Jeaga to move in.

Akoma blew on the blade of grass again. With the stealth of cats, the Jeaga warriors moved into the camp.

Chogatis shot up, grabbing his weapon.

By the light of the dying fire, Akoma witnessed the surprise on Chogatis's face. When the Ais cacique spotted Ramo, it was evident he immediately realized he had been betrayed. Chogatis lifted his lance.

An Ais lunged at Ufala. Akoma came from behind, grabbed the Ais by the hair and drew his knife across his throat. Akoma felt the tendons snap against the knife blade and felt the crunch of the voice box. He pushed the man to the ground.

"Akoma!" Bunta's voice rang out. Akoma spun around just in time to block an attack, but not before the Ais knife caught his side. Akoma grabbed the enemy's wrist and kept the knife from going deeper. With his other hand, he maneuvered his knife between them and sliced open the Ais's belly, then twisted the blade inside the gut. The warrior reeled back and Akoma withdrew his knife. A belly wound was sure death, not immediate always, but ultimately fatal. Akoma had seen a man die the slow death of a belly wound. It was better to die instantly.

The Ais clutched his wound, blood and entrails spilling between his fingers. Akoma bent over him and cut his throat.

Suddenly he heard the retreating call of the Ais. The camp grew strangely quiet.

Akoma stood up. The silence broke with Ufala's cheers of triumph as he came into the light of the small fire. "They are finished!" he said.

Akoma stared at the big man. High in the air Ufala held something in his hand that dripped blood.

"The heart of an Ais!" Ufala cried.

42

Akoma entered the Turtle village. He held his palm against his bandaged side. The wound was not deep, and for that he was grateful. If bad spirits did not get inside, he would be fine in a matter of days. There were a few men not so fortunate.

Sassa ran up to him, a frightened look on her face. Nocatee was at her heels.

"Where is Ufala?" Sassa asked.

"Your father is all right," Akoma said. "He is coming down the river. He has a slight wound on his bad arm, but he will recover. If anything good can come of this, Ufala feels he has proved he is a whole man again."

Sassa looked behind him to see the others coming into the village. The men were rowdy, their victory filling them with pride and exhilaration.

"Where is Liakka?" Akoma asked.

"She is gone," Sassa answered. "She knew council would have her executed."

"Banishment is as good as death. She will not survive on her own—the Jeaga spirits will make certain of that."

Sassa dipped her head in respect, then ran to the river with Nocatee to look for her father.

Inside his lodge, Akoma rummaged through his belongings until he came upon the small pouch he looked for. This he would take with him to the Panther village. He had never given the soul-blessing amulet to Liakka. It had never really been hers to wear.

Every day Tawute and Joog kept watch on the river. This morning, fog settled over the water.

"Look!" Joog said, pointing at a canoe slipping through the fog.

"They return!" Tawute shouted.

Joog and Tawute ran back to the village, heralding the news.

Talli and Ceboni stood, waiting to see who would emerge from the trees. Ceboni hoped that Iquan had joined them. Her face fell when she realized neither Ramo nor Iquan were among the returning men.

Ocaab came up to them. "Talli," he said, "gather the children and occupy them. I need to speak to Ceboni."

The Panther celebrated their victory with a great feast. They sang and danced and ate until late into the night. When it grew quiet, Talli lay on her sleeping skin with her eyes open.

"Are you sleeping?" Joog asked.

"No," Talli said.

The boy sat up. "I do not know how I should feel," he said. "My blood is Ais, but I live with the Jeaga. What am I, Talli?"

"You can never deny your heritage, but to me it does not matter."

"How will I grow up? I cannot become a man amongst the Jeaga. And what if, when I am a warrior, I shed Ais blood?"

Talli patted the ground next to her. "Come over here," she said.

Joog crawled next to Talli. She kissed the top of his head. "This has been so difficult for you . . . so cruel. I know what I must do."

Joog and Talli then drifted off to sleep.

At first light, Joog quietly got up and went for Tawute.

"Let us check the snare," he said.

Tawute rubbed his eyes.

"Your eyes are swollen," Joog said. "Did you cry all night?"

"They are not swollen. I am almost a man. Men do not cry."

"But your father is dead. That is good reason for you to cry."

"I do not want to talk about it," Tawute said.

The two boys meandered into the forest.

"A sly one," Joog said, seeing the snare had been sprung, but it held nothing.

"Maybe the rabbits have gotten wise and they do not use this run anymore," Tawute said.

"This way," Joog said. "We will go back a different way. Maybe we will see something interesting."

The boys bent beneath limbs, pushing branches and vines to the side. Tawute picked up a stick and swabbed spiderwebs.

"You have so many in your hair you look like an old man," Tawute said.

Finally the brush thinned. When they entered the village, Talli called to them.

"Where have you been? I was worried."

"I did not want to wake you or Mikot," Joog said. "Tawute and I checked our snare, but there was nothing."

Tawute looked around. Smoke curled in the air from the cook fires, and the aroma of coontie bread and berry teas saturated the village. "Everyone seems awake early."

"Council meets this morning," Talli said.

Ocaab stood and welcomed Akoma into council. "We have had much discussion today," he said. "As you know, we lost Banabas. He often offered wise advice. Though we have many voices, we all say the same thing."

"What is that?" Akoma asked.

"As we have discussed before, there is greater strength in unity, yet still the Panther and Turtle wish to keep their identity. We would like you to lead us until we choose a cacique. That may be a while. We were not prepared."

"I will serve the People in whatever manner they wish."

The men talked among themselves. As Akoma spoke

to one man, he looked past him to see Talli, their son in her arms.

He touched the man on the shoulder and moved around him. "I must speak to Talli," he said, walking away.

When close to her, he stopped and waited for her to look at him.

"You are hurt," she said. She stepped back, afraid to be too close.

Akoma palmed his side. "It is nothing. I am sorry about Banabas. He was a good man."

"Yes, he was," she answered. "His death is a loss for many, not just me."

"I am certain," Akoma said. "Are you all right?" he asked, reaching out.

Talli took another step back, looked at his eyes and nodded faintly.

"What is wrong?" he asked. "You act as though you are afraid of me."

"No, no. It is not that." She stumbled over her words, then paused before she spoke again. "I know you suffer sadness and disappointment," she said. "I am sorry about Liakka."

"Talli," he said, "I have things to explain. Things I need to tell you." He moved closer.

"What?" she asked, backing away. Mikot squirmed in her arms.

"About Liakka. The People expected me to take a Panther wife. I did what was good for them. I did not love her. And as we know now, she was only one of Ramo's ploys to destroy me."

Talli searched his face. "But I see pain in your eyes."

"Because it is you who has always been in my heart, Talli. You see the pain of having to be without you, of having to see you with another, of knowing we have a son and not being able to be his father. I want all that to change. I want to make you my woman, as I have wanted for so long."

Talli hung her head. "When I was younger, I was foolish. I did not want to accept my heritage. I thought if I ignored and denied it, then it would not matter. But I was wrong. There is something you need to know about me. I am not suitable to be the wife of a cacique."

"Do not speak that way."

"It is true. I am cursed."

Talli told him about the affliction and how she came to have it. As she spoke, she studied him for signs that he thought she was unbefitting. She was afraid she would see revulsion in his eyes, but she had to tell him everything.

When she finished, Akoma held her face in his hands. "Do you not see?" he asked. "You say your ancestor was the wife of a cacique. You come from a noble line. You are very suitable to be the wife of a cacique."

"But the affliction," she said. "If anyone knew, I would be banished, and you would be shamed. Akoma, I am the descendant of a traitor. The Jeaga spirits have not forgiven the pain my ancestor brought upon the People. Only when they consider the debt paid will this curse end. Until then, the women born in my bloodline will randomly find themselves with the affliction."

Akoma's face brightened in a broad smile. "Do you hear yourself? You have sacrificed your whole life to ensure peace for the Jeaga. And you saved my life by sending Banabas to warn me. The spirits find grace in you, not offense." Akoma touched his son's hand. "And one day he will be the cacique."

Talli shifted. "No, Akoma. We will never be together as husband and wife. We are tools of the spirits and have no room for our own wants and desires. You know that."

"Do you still not see?" he asked. "The spirits have brought us together . . . gave us a son. We have served them well, and now they reward us. Believe in yourself. Believe the spirits find grace in you for all you have done for the Jeaga. Find the peace in your heart, and it will be. You need not suffer any longer."

Akoma cradled the back of her head with his hand and drew her near. "Permit the spirits do their work. You shut them out. Trust in the good. See that they favor you."

Talli stood rooted, waiting for her body to give way

to the curse. At any moment she would feel the pain in Akoma's side. Her eyelids would flutter, and her body would shake.

Akoma took her hand and placed it on top of his bandaged wound. "What do you feel, Talli? What is this terrible thing that happens to you?"

She trembled, waiting to be overcome. He would see how horrid such a curse was.

Akoma stroked her hair. "It is over, Talli. Whatever your ancestor did, the debt is paid through all your sacrifices. Do you not see that now?"

Talli pulled back. Was he right? Was the curse finally ended?

Akoma touched his lips to her forehead. "You have nothing to fear, now."

Talli's throat nearly closed, and her eyes stung with tears. She held Mikot snugly against her and cried. Akoma embraced them both. She was forgiven. The feeling of liberation and deliverance overwhelmed her. At last she was free of the dark secret! The terrible shadow that loomed in her heart was finally gone. She felt whole and unashamed for the first time in her life. The thought made her think of Joog and how incomplete he had to feel to know he would never be allowed to pass through the rites to become a man as long as he remained with the Jeaga. He needed his people.

Talli spoke softly. "The boy, Joog, is Ais. Ramo and Banabas came upon him. The party he was with were all killed. He is Chogatis's grandson. Ramo wanted him dead, but Banabas persuaded Ramo to let the child live. He has lived with Banabas and me as our own."

"He is a fortunate boy."

"He needs to belong. He is so confused. Joog will never be Jeaga and is denied all the rites. I will miss him terribly, but I have promised to get him home. Will you help me?"

Talli stared ahead. She had never been this far away from the river.

"The Ais village is close," Akoma said. "Joog, are you ready?"

The boy nodded.

"They will see we mean no harm. They will see we bring Joog home," Talli said.

"That is the chance we must take."

"I will tell them," Joog said. "I will walk in front."

"We will walk together," Akoma said.

As they entered the village, everyone stopped what they were doing, startled at the presence of Jeaga in an Ais village. A shocked hush fell over them. Even the breeze seemed to stop, and the bird sounds disappeared.

Chogatis sat by the central hearth. The sudden silence made him turn. Upon sighting them, Chogatis stood.

Joog held Talli's hand as Chogatis made his way toward them.

A petite woman suddenly cried out and opened her arms. It was Joog's mother.

The boy looked up at Talli, turned and hugged her. Talli closed her eyes. "Go," she whispered.

Joog hugged her hard one last time, then let go and ran to his mother.

Chogatis and Akoma stared at one another. There was still not a sound in the entire village. Each cacique stood tall, the sun warm on his body. Chogatis finally nodded an acknowledgment of appreciation. Akoma returned the gesture.

Kneeling, Joog's mother held the boy, her eyes cast on the woman who brought her son home. It was a mother's stare, a mother's deep gratitude that shined in her dark eyes. Talli understood, thinking how she would feel if it were Mikot.

Akoma grasped Talli's hand. They turned and walked away.

Talli could feel the amazed eyes of the villagers on her. She turned back to catch another glimpse of Joog. He waved.

"Wait," she said to Akoma. She turned around and waved back at the boy. "Do not forget me," she called. She looked at Akoma.

"Are you ready?" he asked.

"Yes," she answered.

Talli and Akoma walked away from the Ais village. She wondered if she would ever see the boy again.

In the dugout, Talli said, "We did the right thing. This is where Joog belongs. I will miss him so much."

"He is a bridge between the two peoples, the promise of lasting peace and understanding between Ais and Jeaga," Akoma said.

"Where are we going?" Talli asked when Akoma banked the canoe short of the Turtle village.

"You know," he said.

"No," Talli said, a sparkle of curiosity in her eyes.

"Close your eyes."

Talli grinned, but kept her eyes open.

"We go no farther until you shut your eyes. I am the cacique and I demand you close your eyes."

Talli blinked, then peeked. Akoma scolded her with a look. "Oh, all right," she said.

"Be careful," Akoma said. "I will lead you slowly. Step with care."

He guided her through the forest. As they walked, he recalled the vision he had had, and at last he understood. The great need he suffered was the need for love. That was what he hungered for . . . Talli's love. The spirits told him to be patient, even when presented with a basket of fruit. Liakka was the deceiving fruit, the worms.

Talli smelled green grass and ferns as they crushed under her feet. The air hinted of jessamine and moonvine. Without seeing, she knew this was a special place.

Finally he stopped. "Open them," he said.

Talli looked around, then realizing where they were, she put her head on Akoma's chest. She knew this place well. This was *their* place. This was the quiet, beautiful spot in the woods where they had often secretly met and held each other when it was forbidden. This was where Mikot was conceived.

"I have something for you," he said. "It was meant for no other, and this is the place it should be given."

Akoma untied the drawstring pouch that hung at his side. "Take it," he said.

Talli took the pouch and teased it open. "What is it?" she asked.

"Take it out."

She pulled the amulet from the pocket and dangled it in front of her. "It is beautiful."

"It is a soul-blessing amulet," Akoma said. "This is a promise of my love for you." He lifted the necklace from Talli's fingers and put it over her head. "Nothing will ever keep us apart again."